Angelina

Angelina

Janet Woods

ROBERT HALE · LONDON

© Janet Woods 2002
First published in Great Britain 2002

ISBN 0 7090 6979 0

Robert Hale Limited
Clerkenwell House
Clerkenwell Green
London EC1R 0HT

2 4 6 8 10 9 7 5 3 1

Typeset by
Derek Doyle & Associates in Liverpool.
Printed in Great Britain by
St Edmundsbury Press, Bury St Edmunds, Suffolk.
Bound by Woolnough Bookbinding Limited

For my daughter Alison, with love.
Last, but definitely not least.

PROLOGUE

Extract from the journal of Thomas Wrey, Earl of Winterbourne
15 July 1760

Today, Elizabeth went into premature labour and we were obliged to break our journey and find refuge in the women's charity hospital founded by Lady Alexandra Chadwick.

The infant is not expected to survive, and as she is destined for the angels, I have taken it upon myself to have her baptized by the hospital chaplain.

Elizabeth will be inconsolable in her grief. She has long wished for a child and after the pain and loss of blood she suffered, I fear for her life should she bear another.

For myself, the loss of the infant will not be so hard to bear. I have James to inherit the title, and although my youngest son displays his mother's vagaries of nature, William has a quick and clever mind. I have high hopes for his future.

Earlier, the hospital's founder came to me with a proposal, which I discounted at once. Now, when I look upon the beloved face of my wife and contemplate the grief she must surely wake to, I pity her, and am sorely tempted.

Would it be so wrong to give her what she desires most? Only three people would be aware of the substitution and only one would need inducement to keep the secret . . . the wet nurse. Mary Mellor.

CHAPTER ONE

1778

In London, James Wrey – Viscount Kirkley and heir to The Earl of Winterbourne – held up his port and watched the firelight dance through it.

'The damnedest thing, Rafe. Why should old Lady Chadwick want to see me?'

'Perhaps she intends to leave you her fortune.'

James grinned at Rafe Daventry's words. 'Hardly likely. On the last occasion we met I formed a distinct impression she disapproved of me.'

'I'm not surprised. You almost killed her dog.'

'It was the other way round. Her dog dashed under my mount and almost unseated me. When she screeched, the animal took off with its tail between its legs.'

'And you followed in a likewise manner.'

'More or less.' James laughed. 'A girl came from the house to persuade the old lady to go inside. Her niece I should imagine. She was a pretty little thing, not much older than sixteen.'

Rafe contemplated him over the rim of his glass for a moment. 'It may not have occurred to you, James, but the old lady might be seeking a match for her.'

A sudden jerk, and a splotch of red appeared on the pristine whiteness of his stock. No, it certainly hadn't occurred to him! He scrubbed ineffectually at the stain with the end of his finger and succeeded only in spreading it. 'It's rumoured Lady Alexandra didn't have a younger sister, that the girl is an orphan she took a liking to. A man would be a fool to commit himself to such a match without a thorough investigation of her background, besides—'

9

'I know, I know. You've resolved to wed only for love. Some of us cannot afford to indulge in such romantic notions. Perhaps you'll oblige me by putting a good word in for me with Lady Alexandra when you visit.'

James grinned. 'There is no need. You could have Caroline Pallister if you would but say the word.'

'I doubt if she could incite in me the necessary incentive to provide an heir.'

'And you think the Chadwick girl might?'

Rafe's eyes were alight with laughter. 'Invite her to Rosabelle's coming out ball. It might be amusing to look her over. There cannot be two heiresses lacking both intellect and beauty. If I cannot have both I'll settle for intellect.'

'Will your sister be attending the ball?' James asked. It had been a long time since he'd seen Celine.

'Would that she could.' Rafe gave rueful sigh. 'You forget the state of our finances. Our mutual father has drank and gambled away our inheritance and will not give either of us a penny piece. I doubt if Celine has a gown left unpatched, let alone a gown fashionable enough to wear to a ball.'

'Then you'll buy her one.' James laughed when Rafe frowned. 'A mutual neighbour of ours wants his library catalogued, and has asked me to recommend someone trustworthy to undertake the task whilst he's abroad. He's leaving shortly. The house is only twenty minutes' ride from Ravenswood and the undertaking supports a remuneration. Both you and Celine will be able to reside there for the duration. What do you think?'

'I'm beholden to you, James.' Rafe rose to his feet and stretched his tall frame. His smile broadened. 'I shall take my leave of the Pallisters as soon as possible. They've been good hosts, but common decency prevents me taking advantage of their generosity indefinitely.'

Accompanying the earl into the hall, James watched his friend shrug into his top coat. Rafe was looking a little threadbare, he reflected, and determined to slip an advance to his tailor, enough to purchase a new suit of clothes without causing him embarrassment.

'I hope your meeting with Lady Alexandra goes well,' Rafe said on parting. 'I've heard she's a creature of intellect, a female inclined towards reasoning. If the niece takes after her she will make an admirable wife for an attorney such as yourself.'

'Or you, Rafe,' he called out, as Rafe strode off into the mist.

*

Lady Alexandra Chadwick reclined in a large four-poster, her face the colour of parchment. Her eyes were fiercely alive, like those of a bird of prey. Her voice was strong.

'I'm dying, young man.'

'My commiserations,' James stammered, disconcerted by her forthright manner.

Her glance impaled him. 'There's no need to commiserate when I mean nothing to you.' A wave of a claw-like hand sent a maid scurrying from the room. 'I suppose you want to know why I've sent for you?'

'I await your indulgence.'

Lady Alexandra shifted slightly on the pillows. 'My niece is the purpose of this consultation. It's her eighteenth birthday soon.'

James gazed at her with some nervousness. 'Before you continue, I must inform you I've resolved not to marry for convenience.'

Lady Alexandra's cackle was reminiscent of a hen. 'Marriage between you is out of the question: Angelina is your sister.'

The woman was stark staring mad! James rose to his feet. 'Perhaps I should ask your maid to call your physician. You seem a trifle overwrought.'

'You don't have to humour me, young man,' she snapped. 'I'm neither insane nor overwrought.' She pointed at a bureau. 'There's a package in the drawer addressed to you. Kindly fetch it.'

When he attempted to hand it to her she pushed it back at him. The effort of seeing him seemed to have exhausted her. Her eyes were half closed, her hands shaking. Her voice dropped to a whisper.

'You have a reputation for being a fair and honest man, Viscount Kirkley. Promise you'll read the contents. Judge them fairly, then come again when you're sent for.' Her fingers plucked at his sleeve. '*You must promise*!'

The desperation in her voice intrigued James, despite his conviction she was mad. 'My word of honour.'

She seemed satisfied, for she smiled and relaxed against her pillows.

A light rain was falling when James left the house, but he didn't notice as he mounted his bay gelding and guided it through the throng. Angelina Chadwick his sister? It was preposterous! What was Lady Alexandra inferring, that his father had indulged in an affair with her sister and a child had been a result of the union?

James frowned. Was it so impossible? The earl had fathered the son of

a woman who'd been wet nurse to his sister Rosabelle. His father still saw
Mary Mellor, and supported her financially. He didn't disapprove of the
liaison, but he *did* disapprove of the woman living in close proximity to
Wrey House.

He liked his stepmother, Elizabeth, and knew her to be deeply embarrassed about the whole affair. If she discovered another past infidelity. . . ?
He shook his head. It didn't bear thinking about.

It took James but ten minutes to reach his residence in Chiswick. He
turned the package over a few times. As a man he was reluctant to open it;
as a lawyer, curious to know what it contained. Taking a deep breath he
slid his thumb under the Chadwick seal, extracted a wad of papers and
began to read.

Fifteen minutes later he crossed to the sideboard. Hands trembling, he
poured himself a large brandy and sank into his favourite chair in front of
the fire.

'*God's truth*!' he muttered, staring at the dancing flames. 'This could
cause no end of a fine scandal if it's not handled properly.'

CHAPTER TWO

Unaware of the changes about to take place, Angelina Chadwick finished embroidering a border of yellow roses on the hem of her chemise. Her sharp white teeth bit through the silk and she smiled as she held it up to her maid.

'There, Bessie, doesn't that look pretty?'

Taking the chemise from her charge, Bessie carefully smoothed the creases from it before placing it on a shelf in the *armoire*. 'Pretty it might be, my love, but if Lady Alexandra sees it she'll make you unravel every stitch for your vanity.'

'I doubt if my aunt will lift up my skirt and inspect my under-garments,' Angelina said practically. Amusement set the serene green eyes sparkling for a moment. Rising gracefully from her seat, she crossed to the window and stared out at the garden. It was one of those mornings when the sun chased after showers, and the whole garden sparkled with glittering raindrops. As a rainbow arched beyond one of the spreading elms, her smile became blissful.

'The sun through the raindrops is brighter than a hand covered in sparkling gemstones. Come and see how pretty it looks, Bessie.'

Bessie slipped an arm around her waist. 'And how would you know that, missy? When did you last see a hand covered in gemstones? Not on Lady Alexandra, I'll be bound.'

'The cloth-merchant's wife wears a diamond ring to church on Sunday. It sparkles so in the candle glow.'

Bessie snorted. 'Glass, most like. Those who can afford diamonds ain't fool enough to flaunt 'em like that there uppity madam. They keeps 'em locked away so some plaguey highway robber don't thieve them.'

'Since when have there been highwaymen here?' Pressing her nose against a cool diamond of glass Angelina gazed in the direction of the road and laughed. 'No self-respecting highwayman would brave Aunt Alexandra's wrath by setting foot on her land. Her tongue is sharper, and certainly more lethal than any weapon he might care to brandish.'

'Don't be impudent, young lady,' Bessie said sternly. 'Your aunt's been good to you. If it weren't for 'er ladyship you'd be dead right now. Poor wee scrap you were when she brought you 'ere. As pale as death, and as small as a skinned rabbit. " 'Er name is Angelina, Bessie", she says. "She's my own dead sister's child. Give her comfort until the good Lord takes her soul".'

Angelina kissed Bessie's cheek. 'Cook told me you set me on the window seat in the sunshine and fed me milk sweetened with honey. Cook said that's how my hair got its funny colour. From too much sunshine and honey.'

'Funny colour, indeed.' Bessie sent a dark look in the direction of the kitchen and stroked the shining amber braid that hung to Angelina's waist. 'Angel's hair is what you've got. The angels 'ad already picked you for their own when God decided to spare your life.'

'Would that God had given me wings as well. Wouldn't it be wonderful to fly amongst the clouds with the birds?'

'Well I never.' Bessie gazed at Angelina with wondering eyes. 'You 'ave the most peculiar ideas. Tis all them books Lady Alexandra makes you read. Being ejercated ain't natural for a woman, and no good will come of it. No man wants a clever woman for a wife.'

Angelina smiled. 'I have no intention of becoming a wife. My aunt has promised I may help out at the hospital when I turn eighteen. She said it will not harm me to learn a midwife's skills. I've been studying the books in the library to such end.'

'Could be your aunt will change her mind, my bonny. She ain't getting any younger. Perhaps she'll find a nice young man for you to marry instead. Someone who can protect you, and run the estate after she's gone.'

'Mr Cottrill runs the estate for Aunt Alexandra, and I run the household. I see no reason why the arrangement cannot continue.'

'You'll have every fortune-hunter in the land after you.' Bessie shuddered. 'Some of them men can do terrible things to a maid when the scent of money is in their nostrils. Why, just the other day I 'eard of a young woman abducted from her bed in the dead of night by some rake. By the time she was found by her relatives it was too late. The poor child 'ad killed herself from the shame of it.'

Angelina's eyes rounded. 'What did the rake do to her, Bessie?'

'Best you not know, my love.' Enfolding Angelina in her arms Bessie rocked her charge back and forth. 'Lady Alexandra is a good woman, little one. No 'arm will come to you if you respect and obey her wishes. Promise old Bessie you will.'

'I cannot promise.' Wriggling from her maid's arms Angelina pulled off her apron and threw it on to the stool she'd recently vacated. Her eyes held the stubborn expression Bessie knew so well. 'Aunt Alexandra has already said she will not make me wed against my will; I'll expect her to honour her words.'

'You was only young then, my love. You're of marriageable age now, and it ain't natural you should stay a spinster.'

'Nevertheless, I shall wait until I meet a man I wish to wed.' Tiring of the conversation, Angelina headed towards the door. 'I'm going to the stream to see if the otters are at play.'

'Not without me, you ain't. I'll sit on the bank and let the sun warm my bones.'

Angelina didn't protest, Bessie wouldn't walk as far as the stream, she never did. There was a feeling in the air, like when the season changed from summer to autumn. It unsettled her. She was happy at Chevonleigh and didn't want anything to change.

'Don't you think it odd that my aunt doesn't have a likeness of her sister?' she murmured. 'I wonder which of my parents I resemble.'

'Your aunt said 'er sister married beneath 'er and was cast out by the family.' Bessie lowered her voice, 'Lady Alexandra has forbidden either of them to be mentioned. She gave you 'er name to save you embarrassment.'

'What was I called when I was born?'

'I can't say I ever knew.' Bessie pushed a stray wisp of grey hair up under her bonnet. 'And don't ever ask your aunt that question. 'er ladyship ain't likely to look kindly on it. She might think you're ungrateful.'

'Never.' She gave a slightly sad smile. 'Aunt Alexandra will always have my gratitude.' But she would never have her love, for it was something never given or encouraged all these years.

Please, God, she prayed as they strolled across the garden. *If I must become a wife, give me a man I can respect and love.*

James had never felt quite so nervous in his life. Carefully, he checked that his buff-coloured breeches were immaculate, his high-buttoned waistcoat free of stains, and his brown leather boots polished to perfection. Holding out his arms he allowed his servant to assist him into his coat. It was mid-brown, almost sober, but excellently tailored and the newest in his wardrobe.

'Your hat and cane, My Lord.'

James took them with a smile. 'My horse is ready?'

'These last five minutes, sir.' His servant brushed an imaginary piece of lint from his coat. 'If I may be so bold, good luck with your young sister, My Lord. I hope the meeting goes well.'

James had taken it upon himself to inform his servants of his sister's existence, saving unnecessary speculation regarding their relationship. 'Thank you, Dawson.'

He cut a fine figure as he left the inn behind and made his way along the lanes leading to Chevonleigh. He was glad of the shade the trees offered as their branches intertwined above his head, for the day had turned out to be warm and slightly humid after the wet start.

The air was perfumed with the headiness of summer. The drone of bees lent an air of timelessness to the countryside. James stopped at the top of a rise. He gazed around him with interest whilst he savoured the delight of it after the unhealthy aroma of the London streets.

Ignoring the profusion of gaudily hued wildflowers seeking to distract him, he observed through the eyes of a businessman. Chevonleigh land had already converted from the old strip system of farming, the fields and livestock looked well managed. The estate steward was obviously efficient, James thought.

From where he paused, James could see the roof and part of a house nestled in a clearing. The portion visible was of Tudor design, the upper part half-timbered, the brickwork decorative, the windows tall and narrow. The diamond-shaped panes reflected back gleams of sunlight. Through the trees surrounding the house, James could see a ripple of water on what seemed to be a sizeable lake. A series of walled gardens provided sheltered beds for vegetables and herbs, and situated off to the left was an orchard laden with summer fruit.

His mind strayed to Angelina. She was unaware of the changes about to take place in her life, unaware she was now wealthy young woman with a family of relations she'd never known. James's heart went out to her.

'Help me carry out my responsibilities to this child with wisdom and humility, Lord,' he prayed out loud, then added as an afterthought before spurring his horse forward, 'Also, I'd be eternally grateful if you could persuade Angelina to like me a little.'

*

James came across Bessie asleep against a large stone standing sentinel at the top of the rise. This had to be the maid the steward had mentioned.

'Are you Bessie Higgins?'

The old woman jerked awake, rose painfully to her feet and bobbed a curtsy. 'That I am, sir.'

'Where is your mistress?'

'Gone to the stream to see if the otters are abroad, sir.'

'You let her go to the stream unaccompanied?'

Her fists went to her hips. 'If only you knew how fleet of foot Mistress Angelina is.' She placed a hand over her heart for effect. 'I just stopped to catch my breath a minute.'

James gave her an amused glance. 'Where is this stream with the otters?'

'Through the copse and over the next hill. But . . . sir . . . wait a minute,' she cried, as he kicked his horse into motion. 'She has no chaperon.'

'She doesn't need one,' he shouted back at her. 'I'm Viscount Kirkley, Lady Angelina's brother.'

'Angelina doesn't have no brother,' the woman yelled out. 'And if you harm one hair on her head I'll. . . .' He was out of range when the threat was uttered, but hoped the woman wouldn't be too hard on him. When he looked back she was hobbling after him as fast as her legs could carry her.

He smiled when he emerged from the copse. A pair of white kid slippers and some neatly darned hose were placed side by side on a log. Just at the top of the rise he caught a glimpse of his prey as she disappeared over the top.

Tying his horse to a branch at the edge of the copse he continued on foot. When he reached the top of the rise he saw his sister halfway down the sloping meadow. Running in circles amongst the wind-teased summer grass, her arms were outstretched in childlike exuberance. Around her, scarlet poppies and white daisies danced in lively confusion with brilliant golden dandelions.

Angelina was plainly dressed, her blue gown similar to those worn by the servants at the house. As James followed after her, she snatched a ribbon-bedecked straw bonnet from her head and threw it high in the air. She laughed as the wind caught her hair and sent it whipping in strands around her face, then raced after the hat as it sailed towards the stream.

She giggled when it fell into the water, picked up her skirts and waded into the shallows. The hat spun out of her reach when she bent to retrieve it. James laughed; he couldn't help himself.

'Oh! Who are you?' Angelina didn't think to leave the stream before she dropped her skirts. Consternation uppermost in her expression, she gazed at the sopping hem before bringing her eyes back to him. 'Look what you've made me do, sir. My maid will most surely scold me.'

'Allow me to help you.' James retrieved her hat with his cane, then held out his hand to assist her from the stream.

She took a step backwards. 'You're on Chadwick land, sir. Would you state your name and business?'

Any lingering doubt about this girl being his sister was instantly dispelled. Her features and colouring were those of his stepmother, Elizabeth. She displayed the same high cheekbones and creamy textured skin, the same arresting green eyes. Her hair was a tawny shade rather than chestnut, and hung to her waist in a severe braid.

'I'm James Wrey, Viscount Kirkley, and heir to the Earl of Winterbourne.'

The green eyes remained a blank. It was as Lady Alexandra had informed him: Angelina had been kept in total ignorance of her background. 'Your business, My Lord?' Her eyes narrowed slightly and her voice became fierce when he didn't answer straight away. 'You can tell me now, or wait until my three brothers arrive with their dogs. They are not far behind.'

If only she knew how close to the truth she'd come. James tried to banish the amusement from his eyes. The girl was quick-witted in the face of danger, her spirit admirable. He couldn't resist the opportunity to tease a little and settled himself comfortably on the grass. 'My business is with a young lady named Angelina. If you are she, perhaps it would be as well to wait for your three brothers to arrive. My news is of the utmost importance, and confidential.'

'Is it bad news or good?' Her lovely eyes were intrigued, but her body had the stance of a skittish colt. She'd shy away at the least sign of danger.

'Both,' James replied, enjoying the encounter and wanting it to last. 'Understandably, you are nervous of me; we will wait for your brothers to arrive.'

'You do not look like a man who'd harm a woman.' She slanted her head to one side, curiosity written in her eyes.

'I'd never harm a woman. You have my word of honour upon that.'

'I'm Angelina Chadwick,' she admitted. 'What did you want to see me about, My Lord?'

'If you'll emerge from the stream I'll tell you.' James's encouraging smile was met by an uncertain frown. 'Your maid tells me you came to see the otters.'

Angelina glanced with a certain amount of anxiety towards the ridge. 'Bessie will be here in a moment.'

'She is on her way. I wished to speak to you alone, first.' The time had come to stop trying to gain her confidence and tell her the news. He stood up and offered her his hand again. 'Take it, Angelina. I'm sorry to be the bearer of bad news, but Lady Alexandra is dead and I've been appointed your guardian.'

She gave a small, distressed cry, her eyes rounded in shock. In an instant she placed her small hand in his and came to stand in front of him on the grassy bank.

'Aunt Alexandra is dead?' She did not cry, but a haunted expression came into her eyes. 'I hope she did not suffer.'

How disconsolate she sounded. James ached to take her in his arms and told a small lie to comfort her. 'Lady Alexandra died suddenly. She was buried two days ago at St Martin's cemetery next to her husband.'

'I see.' She withdrew her hand. Although her face had paled and tears blurred her eyes, she did not seem unduly distressed by the news. For that James was thankful.

Slanting her head to one side in that altogether charming manner of hers, she gazed at him with curiosity. 'Why were you appointed my guardian, Viscount Kirkley? Have you been appointed by the court?' Her eyes narrowed as she gazed at him once more. 'Your face seems familiar. Have we met before?'

'Briefly, about two years ago. Your dog ran under my horse and—'

'Poor Muffin got such a fright he ran away and was lost,' she accused. 'And you didn't even apologize.'

'Apologize?' He raised an eyebrow. 'The dog nearly unseated me.'

'Perhaps it's I who should apologize then.' She gave a soft laugh. 'I remember thinking how well you got your horse back under control at the time.' Her eyes glinted greenly. 'My aunt thought you a most disagreeable young man. She said the language you used was unfit for my ears. I cannot imagine why she should appoint you my guardian.'

Her words had a strangely provocative quality. James found himself on the brink of apologizing when he glimpsed the mischief in her eyes.

'Perhaps you'd consider your three brothers more suitable guardians?'

She gave a delicate shrug. 'If I admit to not having any brothers, will you say how my wardship became your business?'

'Most certainly.' He took both her hands in his and gazed at her. 'Perhaps things will become clearer if I correct your mistake: you *do* have brothers, and I am one of them. You also have a sister, a mother and a father. You're Lady Angelina Wrey, my dear, and far from being alone, you have a family waiting to welcome you home.'

'How?' she murmured.

'Lady Alexandra stole you from your mother. All these years your mother thought you were dead.'

The sun still shone, the breeze still sent the flowers and grasses dancing, the bees still droned amongst the flowers. To Angelina, the world appeared to have as much substance as shifting shadows upon the water.

She gazed into eyes as dark and soft as midnight, and they were full of concern. *Her brother? This tall man with his kind face, her brother?* Her mind was in turmoil. There were others, he'd said. 'How many?'

The merest hesitation. 'One. His name is William.'

'My sister?'

Another hesitation. 'Rosabelle.'

'How old is she?'

'The same age . . . twins . . . no, you're not alike . . . she's dark. Your mother? Her name's Elizabeth. You are very much like her. Rosabelle takes after her father.'

Angelina thought she could grow to like this man. Her brother? Dear God! Tears pricked her eyes. She had a family. No more loneliness. She'd have someone to talk to, a mother to advise her. But what if. . . ? Terror raced down her spine as she asked quietly. 'I will be a stranger to them. What if they do not like me?'

She appreciated the fact James didn't deny the possibility. 'You'll have me. I do not take my responsibilities lightly.'

'Is that what I am to you? A responsibility?' Of course she was. How could she expect this man to have feelings towards a sister he'd never known? At least he was honest with her. They had only just met, yet she felt she could trust him.

'I will not deny that you are.' His smile was teasing. 'Legally, I'm your guardian until you reach the age of twenty-five, or a suitable husband is found to take you off my hands. That should not be too difficult. You're Lady Alexandra's heir, and you come with a large dowry.'

Dismay sliced like a knife into her heart. She stared at him with dread in her eyes. 'You don't intend to marry me off to a stranger, do you?' Her voice heated as her temper took over. 'Aunt Alexandra may have stolen me, sir, but her trust was misplaced if she thought you a proper guardian for me. She'd never have forced me into marriage against my will.' The ground under her suddenly seemed as delicate and slippery as the first ice on the lake in winter.

She snatched up her hat and was about to walk away when a thought occurred to her. She rounded on him. 'How do I know the tale you've told me is not a pack of lies? How do I know you are not here to compromise me, thus to claim my aunt's fortune for yourself? I've been educated about the wicked ways of men.'

His eyes widened in astonished denial, but she didn't give him a chance to speak. She wanted to escape back to the house, to the safety of her room and the possessions familiar to her. She wanted to bury herself in Bessie's comforting lap like she used to as a child, pretend things were just the same.

Bessie had arrived at the top of the hill. Placing a hand to his chest Angelina shoved James backwards. He stumbled, lost his footing and toppled backwards into the stream. She took off as fast as she could when he uttered an oath.

'Quick, Bessie,' she said when she reached the top of the hill. 'We'll take his horse before he catches us.'

'Go on, my love,' Bessie gasped. She was out of breath and puce-faced with effort. 'I can't run another step.' She picked up a stout branch, holding it in a threatening manner in front of her. 'I'll brain him before he gets to yer.'

'Wait!'

Angelina heard the man shout as she reached the spot where his horse was tethered. Her fear increased when he decreased the distance between them with long strides. There was no sign of Bessie. Angelina took a panicky breath. The man had killed her maid, now he'd kill her.

The horse was a giant, or so it seemed to her startled eyes. Her sudden appearance sent it snickering and dancing nervously. Riding was a skill she'd never been taught seriously, usually contenting herself by walking, or using a gentle old hack that had been put out to grass.

She scrambled on to the low branch and took a handful of its mane. But this horse was not the plodding old Dobbin. This horse was a bunch of muscled power waiting for release. It sensed her panic when she tried to scramble on to its back and crabbed sideways. She fell on to her hands and knees. Suddenly, it jerked its reins free from the branch it was tied to and reared high above her. She cried out in fright as its hooves slashed downwards.

She was thrown sideways with such force it robbed her of breath. Pressed into the earth by a damp, warm body, she heard James grunt, then the horse go crashing off through the undergrowth.

'Thank God you're unhurt.'

She clung to him for comfort when he brought them both upright, and her heart leaped in her chest like a demented frog.

'I should have handled this better,' he said, rocking her back and forth. 'I wouldn't have you harmed for the world, my dearest sister.'

As her breathing gradually slowed to normal Angelina knew she'd been stupid. Had he meant to harm her he'd have done so at the stream when they were alone. He'd had ample time. Shyly, she raised her eyes to his.

'There's nothing to forgive, My Lord. I acted stupidly and with undue haste.' She returned his smile. 'I'm sorry I pushed you into the stream.'

'So am I.' His rueful chuckle brought a giggle to Angelina's lips. 'My dignity will never recover, and my manservant will never forgive you. He fussed about me like an old hen this morning, determined I'd make a good impression on you.'

'I can only reassure him that you did, My Lord,' she said, as they scrambled to their feet.

'You must call me James,' he said gently. 'As your brother and guardian, I insist.'

'James.' She said it slowly, almost caressingly, then gave an approving smile. 'The name suits you well, despite your drenching in the stream.'

He grinned. 'It's an event I will long remember.'

'Aunt Alexandra says my imagination is too vivid for my own good at times. I'm truly sorry I doubted you.'

'Then you'll not object to your brother kissing you. I deserve something for the uncivil treatment I've received at your hands.'

He was still holding her, and Angelina found herself lifting her cheek towards his lips. He was tall and had to stoop. His mouth had just brushed her cheek when she caught a glimpse of Bessie sneaking up behind him with the branch raised threateningly over her head.

'No!' she yelled in a horrified voice, but too late. With a sickening thud the makeshift weapon made contact, and James dropped like a stone at her feet.

CHAPTER THREE

'Rosabelle, my dear, stop fidgeting.'

Elizabeth was subjected to a rebellious glance. 'Yellow makes me look hideous. No one will ask me to dance.'

'Nonsense.' Elizabeth exchanged a glance with the dressmaker. 'The neckline is too low. Trim it with the same lace and ribbon you're using on the petticoat.'

'Mama!' Rosabelle wailed. 'It's my eighteenth birthday ball in six weeks. Stop treating me like a child.'

'Stop behaving like one,' Elizabeth snapped. 'You're trying my patience to the limit.' As usual, she thought, wishing she could feel closer to this only child of hers.

Rosabelle giggled when her brother, William, stuck his head around the door and made a face at her before continuing on his way. 'Will said Rafe will be coming down from London for the ball.'

Elizabeth gave her a searching look. 'The earl has accepted the invitation. I believe he'll be accompanying the Marquess of Pallister's party. He's their house guest at the moment.'

'Rafe cannot possibly be interested in Caroline Pallister,' Rosabelle scorned. 'She's almost an old maid, and has a bad complexion.'

'Caroline will inherit to her father's fortune, and Rafe needs money if he's to restore Ravenswood.' She gave a cold smile when alarm touched Rosabelle's eyes. 'Caroline might not be a beauty, but she comes with a large dowry, is accomplished, and conducts herself well in public. She'd make a fitting wife for the earl.'

'If Rafe had intended to offer for her it would be announced by now.'

'No doubt he will do what he considers best for his future,' she mused, for Rosabelle was right. 'And what's best for Ravenswood, of course. He's sworn never to step foot in the family home and has vowed to restore the house of his maternal grandparents and live there.'

'That old pile of stones,' Rosabelle muttered.

A scruple of guilt attacked Elizabeth Wrey when Rosabelle reluctantly paraded in the gown. The delicate shade of yellow she'd chosen was all wrong for Rosabelle. Dark-eyed and olive-skinned, there was a bold earthiness about her that invited the attention of men. Rosabelle's responses made it plain the attention was welcome. It was high time the girl was married.

But the elegant and impoverished Rafe Daventry, a man who set female hearts fluttering wherever he went, was not the man for Rosabelle, whatever her inclinations.

Rosabelle needed a firm hand, and her godfather, George Northbridge, was twenty years her senior. The marquis was extremely wealthy, and although his first wife had been fertile, she'd miscarried regularly before she'd died.

George had always been fond of Rosabelle. In hindsight, Elizabeth realized his regard for Rosabelle was more than mere fondness. He was unable to tear his eyes away from the breasts which had transformed her daughter from a pert, pretty child into a voluptuous young woman almost overnight.

Secretly, Elizabeth thought George the most disgusting of men. She hated the way he stood with his legs spread wide, as if his breeches could not contain that with which God had given him to procreate.

Picking up her fan, Elizabeth vigorously applied a cooling stream of air to her face. Such thoughts should be kept for the privacy of the boudoir, and even there should not be encouraged, for the shameful reminder it lent to her own celibate state.

Thomas had not sought her bed since Rosabelle's birth. It was common knowledge that his mistress and the son she'd borne him, were cosily settled in a large secluded cottage on the edge of the village.

Despite the traumatic birth of Rosabelle and the warning she could not bear another infant without endangering her life, the chance to have another child had been denied her by the presence of her husband's mistress. Elizabeth frowned. No wonder Rosabelle was so forward. The girl had suckled from the whore for the first two years of her life.

Rosabelle had turned to Mary Mellor when she'd needed comfort. The first word she'd uttered had been the woman's name. The second word had been Frey. Elizabeth's eyes narrowed in cat-like concentration. The second nursery maid had been evasive on being questioned, but Elizabeth had soon got the truth from her.

Furious at the deception, her rage was absolute when she learned that Rosabelle's wet-nurse had birthed a bastard son under her own roof. Worse, was the knowledge that her own husband was the boy's father.

She'd intended to flay the skin from Mary Mellor's back with a riding crop when she returned, but someone had warned the estate steward who intercepted the woman on the road and got her to a place of safety.

Elizabeth waited all day, the crop firmly grasped in her hand The maid did her best to placate the squalling infant, whose shock at being denied the warm bounty of Mary Mellor's breast would not be placated by a horn of sweet goat's milk.

Rosabelle's cries for Mary grew louder and louder. Just when Elizabeth thought she might use the crop on the screaming toddler instead, Thomas appeared to confront her.

'We're waiting dinner for you, madam,' he said coldly.

Thwarted by the loss of her prey, Elizabeth lashed out at him instead, striking him ferociously about the shoulders as hard as she was able, and for as long as her strength allowed.

Her husband stood there without flinching, his eyes understanding her rage, her need to punish someone for her hurt. When she'd all but exhausted her strength, she slumped against him. Gently, he picked her up in his arms and carried her to her chamber, leaving her in the care of her maid.

They'd never spoken of the incident, but Elizabeth knew she'd never forget the anguished sound of her daughter screaming Mary's name over and over again.

She poked Rosabelle between the shoulder blades, reminding the girl her posture needed correction. She would marry the marquis. She could forget dreams of love and a union with Rafe Daventry.

'Lengthen the hemline,' she snapped at the dressmaker.

'Mama! It barely exposes my shoe.'

Elizabeth dismissed her complaint as one of many. 'I don't have the time to argue with you. Be in the study in half an hour. Your father has something to say to us.' Thomas had worn a troubled expression on his face of late, and she prayed he wasn't going to subject them to one of his tedious lectures about economizing on household expenses.

The wounded look in Rosabelle's eyes gave Elizabeth a moment of remorse. More than anything, she wished she could love the girl. Troubled, she turned and left the room.

'What cruel jest is this, Thomas?' Elizabeth's usually soft voice cut like a sliver of ice through the room. 'Do you imagine I'd have forgotten if twin daughters had been born to me?'

Her husband's dark eyes shifted away from her direct gaze, as well they might.

Rosabelle stared at her father with shocked eyes. For once, she had nothing to say for herself. A tiny shudder crept down Elizabeth's spine at the thought of a second Rosabelle.

'You were out of your mind with pain and fever, Elizabeth.' Thomas picked up a cut crystal decanter and poured a generous amount of brandy into a glass. Automatically he inhaled, appreciating its fruity aroma. It was a fine blend, one of a brace of bottles William had given him for his birthday.

Will was watching her through dark, narrowed eyes. A tiny smile played around his mouth. He was a darker, stockier version of James, but lacked the grace and the strength of character his older brother possessed.

Will was too obviously enjoying Elizabeth's discomfort. They didn't really get on, though he was hardly ever disrespectful towards her. He saved that for his father.

'I couldn't bear to see you suffer, my dear.' Thomas crossed to where she stood and took her hands in his. Despite the warmth of the day they were cold. He lowered his gaze from the accusatory light in hers. 'Lady Alexandra convinced me the infant wouldn't survive.' Giving an insincere smile he said, 'Angelina was beautiful, such a tiny little thing. Her hair was a wisp of red, and you wound it around your finger. I'd never seen a woman gaze with such love at a child, nor a child who looked so much like her mother.'

Elizabeth closed her eyes as forgotten memories pressed in on her. The child had been like an exquisite doll, her hair the colour of spun gold. The feeling of contentment had been indescribable, and surfaced now as a deep grieving ache in her heart.

She'd gone to sleep feeling such divine love for her baby daughter, then when she awoke. . . ? She shook her head. They'd given her laudanum to ease the pain. Had it confused her, had she forgotten she'd birthed two daughters? It was possible. The infant she remembered, the one she'd lost, had been nothing like the one she'd brought home to Wrey House.

Her tongue clove to the roof of her mouth, then her heart fluttered in hope when she understood the ramifications of what Thomas was saying to her. Her fingers curled around those of her husband as she gazed anxiously into his eyes. 'My dear little Rosabelle is truly alive?'

Eyes rife with anger, Rosabelle sauntered across the room with her hands on her hips to confront her mother. 'That is my name. I believe my *sister's* name is Angelina.'

'You'll be gratified to know I had the child christened thus so she'd be assured a place in Heaven.'

'Very laudable, Thomas.' The dry comment brought a flood of colour to his cheeks.

Her eyes swept over both William and Rosabelle, then she rose from the stool and swept towards the door, saying softly as she half-turned 'God obviously didn't appreciate the sacrifice you made on His behalf, for He allowed her to live. How could you do it, Thomas? How could you abandon your own daughter while she still breathed, cheat me of her love, then live a lie for all these years? What sort of man are you?'

Thomas could have shrivelled from the wounded expression in her eyes.

When the door closed behind her, relief rushed through him. He'd done it, fooled Elizabeth into thinking the two girls were twins? But there was no satisfaction in the victory. Needing a stiff drink, he turned once more towards the decanter.

He encountered the eyes of William, and bristled at the sight of the cruelly amused expression they contained.

His younger son sauntered towards him, his voice softly mocking. 'Are there any more of your offspring we should congratulate you on, Father? First it was your bastard, Frey. Now we're being introduced to a long lost sister.'

'Hold your tongue, Will,' Thomas growled. 'I'll have your respect.'

'Haven't you always told us respect has to be earned?'

'Don't, Will.' Rosabelle placed a restraining hand on his arm. 'If anyone should be out of countenance, it should be me. Papa did what he thought was best at the time. We must try and accept this outsider as our sister.'

Linking her arm through Will's, she drew the three of them together. 'How can I bear to share the love of my two favourite men with another?'

Sliding an arm around Rosabelle's waist, William kissed her cheek. 'Twenty sisters could not mean as much to me as one of the hairs on your head.'

'And you, Papa?' Her dark eyes shone with unshed tears, a catch trembled in her voice. 'Will you grow to love Angelina more than you love me?'

'No other daughter can steal the place you hold in my heart.' Neither she or Elizabeth must ever discover Rosabelle was a nameless orphan. Avoiding her eyes, he drew the hand to his lips and kissed it before taking a box from his waistcoat pocket. 'See what I bought you whilst I was in town.' His smile was indulgent when she opened what was little more than a conscience gift.

'It's beautiful, Papa.' She let go of his hand and turned the brooch towards the light. It was the colour of blood. 'A ruby,' she whispered, her eyes shining.

'It's a garnet.' Will's voice was dry as he took the brooch from her fingers and pinned it to her bodice. His devaluation of the gift enraged Thomas. Will was a schemer and manipulator. He and Rosabelle were two of a kind, Thomas admitted to himself.

Will turned with a mocking inclination of his head. 'I beg your leave, sir. No doubt you have important matters to attend to.'

Perspiration beaded Thomas's forehead as he strained to be civil.

'You may go, William.' Thomas turned his back on his second born, his hand reaching for the brandy decanter as the door closed on him.

'Let me pour that for you, Papa,' Rosabelle said. 'I wanted to talk to you about my ball gown. Mama insists on yellow—'

But Thomas was in no mood to listen to Rosabelle's prattle. He was expecting George Northbridge any moment. They were to discuss the terms of Rosabelle's dowry. She should be grateful she had a dowry, and suddenly he couldn't wait for her to marry.

'You will take your mother's advice on this, Rosabelle. Leave me, I have more important business to discuss.' She flounced off in a rustle of taffeta and slammed the door behind her.

Lady Celine Daventry nodded with satisfaction as she finished embroidering a bluebell on the small apron she held in her hands. All that remained was to attach the apron to her bodice, then the most recent patch on her blue petticoat would not be noticed. Tomorrow, she thought, wearily, gazing out at the neglected grounds of Monkscroft Estate. I'll do it tomorrow. The light is almost gone and my eyes are tiring.

From the window of her chamber, Celine could see the spire of the distant church, and the adjacent roof of the manse. Her face puckered in a frown as the portly Reverend Locke came to mind – his wig slightly askew, his face red and perspiring as he preached the duties of a wife to her husband the previous Sunday.

It had been a public declaration, as the congregation had been aware. Every pair of eyes in the church had turned her way.

After the service, the reverend had insisted on accompanying her back to Monkscroft, there to press his suit with her father. The marquis had later informed her she'd become the wife of the reverend, who although without title, was a wealthy man and willing to take her off his hands without dowry.

The good reverend had eight children to three wives. The oldest son was exactly like him in manner and profession, the younger ones were well-mannered and never smiled, the spirit having been beaten, or was still in the process of being beaten, out of them, as the welts and bruises on them testified.

'I will not marry him,' Celine muttered, the blue eyes she'd inherited from her mother clouding with fear as she fingered her own bruises. 'Whatever Father does to me I'll never marry that man.'

Crossing to the door, she rattled the knob, wondering if her father had forgotten he'd locked her in her room two days before. She was thirsty and hungry, yet hesitated to bring attention to her plight by calling out. Her father's beatings were not an event she wished to experience too often, and at this time of day he'd be well into his cups.

Moving back to the window, she stared speculatively at the branch of the oak stretching towards her window. So near and yet so far. When she'd been small, Rafe had helped her climb from her window to hide amongst the leafy branches. There they'd hidden from the harsh realities of their world. If she stared into the shadowy depths of the foliage she could almost see his laughing face peering out at her, hear his soft whisper calling her to join him.

'Celine?'

She smiled to herself. If she was hearing voices she must be faint from lack of food. Her pulse quickened in hope as her glance searched through the deepening gloom. Perhaps Rafe had come for her. She knew he'd written to her. The letter had been intercepted by her father so she was unaware of what news it contained.

'Celine.' Rafe's husky whisper clearly reached her now. 'I'm below. Come down the back way.'

She resisted giving a small thankful cry when she saw her brother's tall figure concealed amongst the ivy clinging to the grey stones. He stood to one side of a pair of French doors leading into the room where their father spent most of his time. The doors were directly under her window, and ajar.

'Thank God you've come,' she whispered. 'I cannot come down, I'm locked in. Be careful, your note was intercepted. Father will be expecting you.'

Rafe glanced up at the tree, then darted across the terrace and began to scale its lower branches. A frenzied barking came from the room behind the doors and a pair of emaciated hounds bounded out and leapt with ferocious howls at the base of the tree.

'Quiet, you mangey curs!' A bottle skittered out through the door and smashed into shards upon the weed-infested flagstones of the terrace.

Rafe took advantage of the dogs' temporary fright to scale the tree, edge along a sturdy limb and scramble over her window sill. He barely had time to conceal himself behind a curtain before the marquis weaved drunkenly from the room waving a pistol in the air. A shot whistled up through the leaves of the oak, and the dogs took off towards the stables with their tails between their legs.

Tipping a bottle to his mouth, the marquis glared up at the window. 'Don't think I've forgotten you, missy,' he roared. 'You'll stay in there until you wed Matthew Locke, and if your ungrateful brother comes skulking around here I'll set the dogs on him.'

'I'll never agree to marry Matthew Locke,' she cried out.

A string of curses left his mouth. 'Agree or not, you'll wed him anyway. I've arranged a private ceremony at the church on the morrow, with Matthew's son presiding and myself as witness.'

Tipping up the bottle again, the marquis took a swallow, then began to cough as a drop of the liquid invaded his wind-pipe. He lost his balance, staggered backwards and sprawled amongst the broken glass. His red-rimmed eyes stared up angrily at the darkening sky whilst his chest heaved in a spasm of coughing. When the coughing ceased, his eyes drifted shut and he started to snore.

Sickened, Rafe pulled his sister against his chest and kissed the top of her head. 'Gather together what you need. I'm taking you away from this house, and you'll never return.'

'I'm locked in.' Sobs racked her thin body. 'I'll have to obey. I have no choice.'

Rafe shook with rage when he noticed her bruises. 'You'll not be locked in for long.' Grim-faced, he picked up a heavy iron poker and splintered the lock. 'And you'll not have to obey him. I refuse to let you marry that pious old hog, Matthew Locke. Somehow, I'll find the means to care for you, Celine. If Father comes looking for you I'll call him out and kill him.' Striding to the window he gazed down at the recumbent form with disgust. 'I'm in half a mind to skewer him whilst he lies there.'

His sister managed a watery smile as she threw her meagre belongings into a sheet and knotted the corners. 'You're too honourable a man to commit murder, however justified you consider it to be. I cannot wait to escape from Monkscroft, but how will we live? I've nothing of value to sell.'

'I'll think of something to keep the wolf from the door.' But what? Rafe wondered. The library job wouldn't last forever, and although he'd agreed to Celine becoming companion to James's ward, the position would only last until Angelina was restored to her family.

An ironic little smile quirked the corner of his mouth. He shrugged as he shouldered Celine's burden.

As they crept out of the house Rafe had sworn never to enter again, he gave a mirthless grin. If matters became really desperate, he could always propose marriage to Caroline Pallister.

CHAPTER FOUR

'Where the devil am I?' Still befuddled, James's glance wandered from the gold brocade bed hangings to the disapproving countenance of a bulbous-nosed gentleman captured for posterity in a frame over the fireplace.

'I think he's finally coming around.'

The deep voice came from James's left. He turned towards it, groaning as pain shafted through his head and shoulder. A lighter, sweeter voice.

'Pray do not attempt to move, James.' Something cool was placed against his throbbing head. 'You received a blow from a branch, which rendered you unconscious. But do not worry, you've been brought back to the house and a physician is in attendance.'

A face swam into his vision – anxious green eyes, a halo of tawny hair. 'Elizabeth?' he croaked. 'What are you doing here?'

'It is I – Angelina.' The eyes became all the more anxious. 'Have you forgotten who I am, James?'

'How could I forget?' Lights exploded in his head when he tried to smile. 'I beg your pardon, Angelina. I seem to be addle-brained at the moment.'

'And no wonder, My Lord. If your shoulder hadn't taken the brunt of the blow your skull would have cracked like an egg.' The owner of the deeper voice moved into his vision. Fingers were raised, eyes examined. 'Good . . . good . . . no lasting damage done.' He tasted laudanum when a glass was raised to his lips. 'You must rest, now, My Lord. I'll return on the morrow.'

Worry laced Angelina's voice. 'Will my brother return to full health?'

'He'll suffer from a headache for a day or two, and may feel an urge to vomit when he wakes. Have a servant on hand in case he needs assistance.'

'I'll stay myself. The accident was my fault, after all.'

Her fault? James had no intention of letting Angelina suffer remorse over the incident. 'Nonsense,' he managed to say, his words slurring a little as the laudanum started to take effect. 'You cannot be blamed for a tree branch falling on my head. My man is at the Royal Hart Inn. Send a servant to explain, and bid him attend me immediately.'

'But, James . . .' Angelina began, only to be interrupted by the physician's firm voice.

'Later, my dear.' The voice became a slow sonorous echo coming from the depths of a well. 'The sedative's taking effect. Explanations will only serve to confuse him.' The physician leaned over him, addressing him as if he were profoundly deaf. Which was just as well, thought James, for his ears were buzzing like a hive full of honey bees. 'Do not worry about anything, My Lord. I'm passing by the Royal Hart and will inform your servant myself.'

The physician's face blurred as it floated off into the distance. James had never encountered such a soft bed Sucked into its feathery folds, he panicked, momentarily struggling to hold on to conscious thought. For one lucid moment he stared directly into the eyes of the man in the portrait. Then the disapproving countenance began to revolve, faster and faster, until it spun off into the darkness and disappeared into nowhere.

The eulogy seemed to be taking forever. Angelina slanted a glance at James, wondering if he was as bored as she. His face was grave, and he seemed to be paying close attention to the words Reverend White spouted abut Lady Alexandra.

Except for the remains of a bruised swelling concealed amongst his hair, James seemed to have recovered quickly from his ordeal at the hands of Bessie. To her everlasting relief he'd reacted with amusement when she'd told him the true story of his injury.

Affection for him stole into her heart. She'd grown to like and respect her brother over the past two days, especially when he'd had the sensitivity to summon the remorseful Bessie into his presence and commend her for being a loyal servant to her mistress.

Angelina sighed as the reverend's voice droned on, and she tried not to wriggle. The black dress she'd found in Lady Alexandra's wardrobe was hot and itchy. The church was packed for the memorial service and smelled ripely of massed humanity. How could her brother sit there with such an engrossed expression on his face?

Then she saw he was watching a spider crawl up the pulpit. Her glance went from the spider to the parson's wife. The woman's eyes were intent upon the creature, too, her nose quivered like that of an eager blood-hound.

Armed with previous knowledge, Angelina spread her fan across her lips and whispered, 'I wager the spider will not reach the top before the testimonial is over and I'm obliged to leave the church.'

James's lips twitched. 'How much?'

'A guinea in the poor box.'

'You have a guinea on you?'

The eyes she turned his way danced with mischief. 'No doubt you can provide me with one should I need it.'

His eyebrow lifted a fraction. 'Then I'm the loser either way.'

'The money will go to a good cause, James.' She tried not to laugh when he took her hand, gently squeezing it in assent.

The tribute to Alexandra Chadwick finished just as the spider reached the top of the pulpit. One of its legs delicately tested the air before moving over the edge. She held her breath, releasing it with an audible sigh when the spider slipped back a little.

The Reverend White beamed genially at the congregation as the spider made up lost ground again. Stepping from the pulpit he made his obeisance to the altar, then turned towards the aisle. The spider managed to get a second leg over the edge. She held her breath again.

The reverend nodded to her as he walked towards the door. Time she joined him outside the church to receive the condolences. Reluctant to abandon the wager, she squeezed James's hand when the parson's wife rose to her feet. Propriety would keep the congregation in the pews until she left.

The Bible slapped against the pulpit, the loud explosion enough to make people jump in the quiet church. She cast a triumphant glance at James, who was gazing at the woman in disbelief. A wry grimace on his face, the bemused James dropped a guinea in the poor box on the way through the door.

Fifteen minutes into the condolences and the congregation had thinned. 'Thank you, Mrs Pendergast ... Mr Pendergast. My late aunt would be most gratified.'

'Lady Alexandra was a good woman.' A kiss brushed against her cheek, another set of curious eyes lit upon James.

'My brother and guardian, Viscount Kirkley.'

No one had the ill grace to question the sudden appearance of a brother, though the curiosity displayed in the glances aimed at James was undisguised.

She repeated the same response time and time again until, finally, an ageing gentleman supporting himself on his stick appeared in front of them.

'May I present the Marquis of Flaverley, James. My aunt's good friend and adviser.' She curtsied. 'Viscount Kirkley, My Lord. My brother and guardian.'

'Your servant,' James murmured, and found himself being thoroughly examined by hooded grey eyes.

Lord Flaverley's rank afforded certain privileges, and his loud interrogation brought ears and eyes turning in their direction.

'You must be heir to Thomas Wrey. I haven't seen the earl in London for some time. How is he? Well, I hope?'

'My father's in robust health, My Lord.'

'Good, good.' The marquis lifted his wig to scratched his head, exposing a glimpse of gleaming bald pate before setting it back upon his head. Hearing Angelina catch in her breath, James prayed she wouldn't laugh.

'Rum business eh?' the marquis said. 'I didn't know Lady Alexandra was related to the Wrey family. Peculiar arrangement, what, having her bring up the girl here?'

He pinched Angelina's cheek familiarly between a finger and thumb. 'Doesn't do to pry too much into family, eh? Too many skeletons? Count on my complete discretion, my dear child . . . ahem. Condolences, what? G'day to you, sir. Lady Angelina? Give my regards to your father when next you meet. He won't know you after all these years.'

'Thank you, My Lord.' Angelina curtsied to the marchioness, who hovered behind her husband like a pale-grey wraith.

'Dearest, child.' The marchioness gave her a vague smile, then kissed the air by Angelina's ear as she drifted away in a cloud of lavender water.

How good Angelina is at this, James thought. Her countenance and demeanour were grave, and though her manner was warm in appreciation of the condolences, it was distant enough to discourage maudlin familiarity.

During the service he'd had occasion to catch her eye. In their depths he'd encountered a soft desperation, as if she'd rather be running amongst the flowers in the meadow instead of performing such a sad duty.

Admiration for her grew in him. She was little more than a child in her ways, possessing no worldliness. Alexandra Chadwick had made sure she'd been well trained in her duties. Life was unkind to those unprepared, he mused, but Angelina, although seemingly delicate, had an in-built toughness that surprised him.

As he observed her old-fashioned mourning gown, James realized it would be unfair of him to introduce her to his family just yet. He'd never seen a woman of rank so badly outfitted. She'd make a bad impression on those who did not know her, and be disadvantaged wherever she went.

His forehead furrowed in thought. Elizabeth was elegant, her taste impeccable in both dress and manners. She had a serene and gentle way with her on the whole, and was well liked in the district. He admired her lively wit on occasion, but when roused to anger she could be unexpectedly cutting, and sometimes cruel, especially towards Rosabelle, who was as selfish as she was vain.

How would she treat this beautiful innocent daughter of hers, the child she'd never been given the chance to love? His frown deepened as he began to realize his guardianship of Angelina was more than just a duty. The girl's appearance needed to be improved considerably before she was presented to her mother.

It would be of advantage to Angelina if he took her to London. With Celine and a new maid to advise her, she could be outfitted with the fashionable fripperies that gave a woman confidence. She also needed to learn the latest dances in time for the ball. *Then* he'd present her to the family.

His frown disappeared when she glanced at him and smiled.

'It's time we left, James.'

He'd have to make sure she was protected, made aware of the deceit practised by men as a means to an end. A lump came into his throat as he watched her eyes sparkle when he smiled back at her. He resolved to do everything in his power to make her happy.

It was then he glanced up. Catching sight of Rafe leaning nonchalantly against the trunk of a tree in the lane outside the church his face lit up. Rafe was travel-stained and dusty, his horse weary. He straightened up when James caught his eye, made an attempt to brush the dust from his coat with his hat.

Rafe's dark hair was roughly fashioned into a plait. Unable to afford a personal servant, he refused to wear a wig unless absolutely necessary. If James hadn't known his friend to be scrupulously honest, he'd have judged his appearance to be disreputable. Unfortunately, that was exactly the impression he had on Angelina.

'What took you so long in getting here, Rafe? You didn't encounter trouble on the road, I hope.'

'My horse was lamed, and we were obliged to take up lodgings for a while whilst the poor fellow recovered. I've left my sister at Chevonleigh to rest.' Lazily, his glance went to Angelina. His eyes widened. 'Exquisite,' was the word that involuntarily left him. 'The girl is a beauty, James.'

'And you are impertinent, sir.'

'An enchantingly unsophisticated child goddess,' Rafe went on, apparently intrigued by her. His smile widened. 'Introduce us, James,' he drawled. 'I'd prefer to be an impertinent friend than an impertinent stranger.'

Angelina gazed frostily at The Earl of Lynnbury when she was introduced. Tall, powerfully built and dark-haired, the man had a direct and penetrating gaze which was disconcerting. She'd never seen eyes of such a deep green, and although she found their gold-flecked darkness beautiful, contrariness wouldn't allow her to concede they were anything more than peculiar.

Only a woman should have such dark and sweeping lashes, she thought a little scornfully, and his smile? His slow, beautiful smile became wearily enigmatic when she didn't respond to it.

'I seem to be losing my touch.'

Surprisingly, the earl took her hand and bore it to his lips, whispering in a sardonic tone, 'Lady Angelina Wrey. You are fairer than the angels.'

Discomforted, she blushed and jerked her hand away.

'Behave yourself, Rafe.' Her arm was drawn protectively through her brother's. 'Angelina has never been introduced into society, and is not used to such attention.'

She was subjected to another uncomfortable scrutiny from the deckled green eyes. This time the earl's smile was a little less practised. One dark eyebrow lifted a fraction. 'Of course she hasn't. Angelina is a mere child.'

'I most certainly am not!' She glared at this insulting stranger. 'I'm almost eighteen.'

The man had the effrontery to wink at James. 'Heaven protect me from her wrath. The infant is nearly an old maid.'

'I would be obliged if you kept a civil head in your tongue, My Lord.' Having learned from Lady Alexandra that rudeness must be firmly stamped upon, Angelina took a determined step forward. 'You will apologize for being so . . . so forward, Sir. And from now on you will treat me with respect.'

'Rafe is teasing,' James said, trying not to laugh when an expression of incredulity flitted across his friend's face. He'd never seen Rafe so completely routed before. 'He is an old friend who considers the taking of liberties his right. His sister Celine has been kind enough to agree to act as a chaperon and companion to you.'

'That does not give Lord Lynnbury the right to be overfamiliar.' Indignant green eyes met his.

'Come, come,' James chided, aiming an apologetic glance at Rafe. 'You mustn't presume to teach the earl manners.'

Reminded of her place, Angelina's eyes widened with shock.

'And you mustn't chastise Angelina for what is my fault, James.' The deckled eyes became slightly less teasing. 'I most humbly beg your pardon, Lady Angelina. I ask you to forgive my impertinence.'

Angelina's blush started at her toes and worked its way up her body. She'd *never* forgive him for making her blush. Already incredibly hot in the black dress, a trickle of perspiration edged its way between her shoulder blades and set up an itch. She nodded, uncomfortable with the encounter, then turned her suspiciously glowing face towards James and pleaded, 'Can we return to the house, James? I'm weary, and would like to rest before meeting Lord Lynnbury's sister.'

Though the walk to the house was not far, it seemed interminable to Angelina. Lord Lynnbury's sophisticated worldliness made her aware of her inadequacies and pin-pointed her lack of feminine attributes. She, who'd often been chided for her chattering, suddenly found herself tongue-tied.

As soon as they reached the house she made her excuses, fleeing upstairs to the safety of her room. There, she pressed her over-heated face against the cool glass and stared out over the grounds of her inheritance.

Angelina knew she'd been rude in not staying to be introduced to the earl's sister. Aunt Alexandra would have been furious at her lack of manners. But being taught manners was one thing, and putting them into practice when the recipient didn't react in the way he was supposed to, was something different all together.

Aunt Alexandra had not taught her to deal with that. It was something learned from interacting in a social sense, and that she'd not been encouraged to do. It was a skill she'd have to learn if she were to be mistress of her own estate. Aunt Alexandra was dead and her life would never be the same again. Apprehension shivered along her spine. What would become of her?

You will face up to that which life brings you with honesty and courage and count your blessings. The words came into her mind as loudly as if Aunt Alexandra was standing at the foot of her bed saying them to her. *I will not have you snivelling every time something goes wrong. Do you understand girl?*

'Yes, Aunt.' Rising from the bed she changed into her best blue gown, the one with the lace collar. She pinned a spray of forget-me-nots she'd picked from the garden that morning to the bodice, took a deep breath and left the room.

Angelina discovered her guests on the terrace. Facing away from her, they were discussing the grounds.

'The trout lake is in good condition,' the earl was saying. 'It must be fed naturally, but I can't see where the water comes from.'

'The lake is artificial,' Angelina said quietly, not quite knowing if it was correct for a woman to admit to such knowledge. She gazed hesitatingly at James, moving to his side when she received a smile of encouragement. 'Lord Chadwick discovered a lake of water in a cave and devised a series of sluices. The water is filtered through the chalk of the hills which cleans impurity from it. When the sluice is open the water flows into the lake.'

'Apart from natural evaporation, how does the lake drain?' Lord Lynnbury's question displayed no patronizing humour, just interest.

'In the same way. There is a sluice, the water drains underground until it joins the stream again. The system is very ingenious.' Head to one side, she regarded her tall guest. 'I do not pretend to understand it all, but Lord Chadwick's plans and calculations are in the library if you are interested in studying them.'

'You have studied them yourself, I see.' His mocking smile appeared, bringing an instant blush to her face. 'An educated woman is a rarity, Lady Angelina.'

'That's because men will not allow them to be educated,' she rejoined. Noting his eyes widen in astonishment, she hastened to place the uttered wisdom back where it came from. 'At least, that's what Lady Alexandra used to say. Personally, I'm not schooled in what men *do*, or *do not* allow women to be, as I have known neither father, brother nor husband. My maid thinks book learning gives me peculiar ideas.'

'She could be right,' he murmured, his eyes dripping with amusement.

'Stop teasing her, Rafe.' A shabbily dressed woman with blue eyes and a weary smile stepped forward. 'Forgive my brother's bad manners in not introducing us. I'm Celine Daventry. James said you'd overtired yourself. I trust you're rested now?'

Angelina took an instant liking to Celine, but the woman seemed in need of more sustenance and rest than herself by the look of her. She thought it best to get the niceties dispensed with as directly as possible, and said with her usual candour, 'I owe both you and your brother an apology.' Her eyes flickered from James to Lord Lynnbury, then back to Celine. 'It was unforgivable of me to neglect you because of a touch of the vapours. Please forgive me.'

Celine's face suddenly lost all colour and she swayed. Anxiously, Angelina placed a hand on her arm. 'You're feeling unwell. James? Lord Lynnbury?'

It was James who caught Celine before she fell, Rafe who conveyed her to the chamber Angelina had prepared for her. He laid his burden gently on the bed. 'My sister has not eaten properly for several days. She was locked in her room by my father. I should have made sure she had more sustenance on the journey here.'

Poor Celine! The small amount of information told Angelina exactly what she suffered from. Although she wanted to know the reason why, the tone of her guest's voice hadn't invited the question.

'It was not your fault, Rafe,' James murmured.

Her fists clenched and she rounded on the two men. 'Do not make excuses for Lord Lynnbury's behaviour. It's reprehensible of him to allow Celine to collapse from exhaustion and lack of food. He's already admitted he was wrong, so why seek to exonerate him when the evidence is in front of your eyes?'

Angrily, she jerked on a bell pull to summon a maid. That she sounded just like Lady Alexandra didn't occur to Angelina. 'Fetch some chicken broth and wafers of bread please,' she said to Agnes. Her glance was tender as she gazed down at Celine, her fingers smoothed across her brow in comfort when she showed signs of recovery. 'Send Bessie up to help me get Lady Celine into bed She needs food and rest.'

Angelina was right to put Celine's welfare first, James mused, but she had reached the wrong conclusion. Besides the fact that his friend might not have had the price of a meal on him, she shouldn't have disagreed with his own comment on the matter. It was not a woman's prerogative to take a man to task, especially when the man was a guest in her home.

He applauded Rafe's forbearance on this occasion. Rafe could be proud to the point of arrogance sometimes and his laconic manner concealed a man of great passion. He had managed to avoid matrimony in the past, despite a surplus of suitable candidates and the need to restore Ravenswood. Women usually found Rafe attractive. His absolute discretion in matters of love ensured he was never without female companionship when the need arose.

And that, thought James, gazing at his sister's delicate face, was the reason he couldn't understand Angelina's reaction to him. Nor for that matter, Rafe's reaction to her. Angelina seemed almost scornful of Rafe, and Rafe, far from retreating behind a barrier of hauteur, seemed to find her flashes of temper and lack of sophistication entertaining.

James heard Rafe's stomach growl when a tray of steaming broth was carried in. The sound must have reached Angelina's ears, for her general demeanour softened when she glanced at them again.

'James, perhaps you'd send a maid to fetch some sustenance for Lord Lynnbury whilst Bessie and I administer to Celine's needs. I doubt if he's eaten either. Two invalids in one week are enough, and your friend does not look as though he'd make an agreeable patient.'

'I'd be content enough with you caring for me,' Rafe murmured. 'Were I your patient, you might unbend enough to call me Rafe.'

'It's more likely I should not.' Angelina's voice was tart despite the faint rush of colour that came to her cheeks. 'I hardly know you, sir.'

'But your brother and guardian does.' Rafe was gently teasing, extracting from Angelina a confusion of shyness and determination that was altogether charming. 'Is that not recommendation enough?'

'I hardly know James, either,' she reminded him, sending a glance both apologetic and appealing his way. 'You will not think too badly of me for saying that, James? It doesn't mean—'

A groan from the bed brought Rafe in two strides to his sister's side. 'What is it, Celine, are you in pain?'

James laughed when Celine said in a weak, but determined voice, 'If you do not stop baiting our host I'll disown you, Rafe. You're a rogue, and I'm ashamed of you. Leave us this instant, and do not return until you're sent for.'

'As you say, my dear.' Rafe planted a kiss on Celine's cheek, at the same time managing to slide a smile in Angelina's direction. 'I leave you in capable hands I think. Lady Angelina seems to be a paragon of feminine virtue.'

If Rafe's grin was designed to disarm, it failed miserably. Angelina's eyes became a tumult of provocation, her face flamed red, and her mouth opened as if she'd been about to answer. Then she thought better of it and turned away to busy herself at the bedside.

Rafe's expression was self-satisfied, and James gave him a steady glance. The shrug Rafe gave was almost imperceptible. James knew it was the only acknowledgement Rafe would give that his behaviour had left much to be desired.

Over the next two days Celine regained her strength, and the two girls became good friends and confidantes. Much to Angelina's relief, once Lord Lynnbury was convinced his sister was safe, he announced his intention of departing.

Angelina had hoped to avoid Rafe's departure by escaping from the house early that particular morning. Luck furnished her with the duty of visiting the wife of one of the estate workers who'd been delivered of a son the day before.

There was a fine mist rising from the ground when she slipped out of a side entrance with Bessie. By the time they reached the tiny hamlet of workers' cottages, spider webs laced into the hedgerows were hung with milky pearls of dew and fields sparkled with diamonds of light as the sun absorbed the moisture.

Angelina's gifts of a soft woven blanket for the child's cradle, a pot of mutton broth, bread, and a crock of honey for the table, were appreciated.

'*Do not give the estate workers gifts that are not useful, and do not embarrass them by prolonging the visit.*'

Angelina, heeding the late Lady Alexandra's often repeated advice, admired the red-faced infant, then thankfully made her escape from the stuffy abode and darkly curious stares of two grubby children who played on the hard-packed dirt floor beside their mother's bed.

She took a deep breath, enjoying the sun on her face, the soft breeze soughing through the branches above her head and the sounds of the birds singing in the trees. Despite Lady Alexandra's demise, life had been good to her of late.

'James is a wonderful brother,' she said, giving Bessie a radiant smile and no time at all to comment. 'And am I not lucky to have a good friend like Celine?'

'You are that, my bonny,' Bessie got in.

'It's a pity her brother is so disagreeable.' She frowned. 'He doesn't appear to be rude, but he has an uncomfortable way with him . . . oh!'

Rafe appeared suddenly, as if he'd materialized from inside the tree his mount was tethered to. Heart pounding, she placed a hand against her chest. 'I thought I had missed your departure.'

'I didn't want to disappoint you by leaving without saying goodbye.' A flicker of an eyebrow gave a nuance of irony to his words. 'It's bad form for a guest to depart without presenting his hostess with a small token.'

His smile was beautifully timed, coming at a moment when she realized it was equally bad form for a hostess to allow her guest to leave without a farewell. There was nothing she could do but appear gracious.

'James probably informed you my financial state is not one to encourage the bestowing of expensive gifts, so I hope you'll accept this small token of my regard, along with thanks for your hospitality.' His eyes held as much mischief as his smile when he plucked a posy of wildflowers from his saddle to present to her with a flourish. 'Your servant, Lady Angelina.'

'Thank you.' With a sense of shame Angelina realized she'd been impossibly rude to him. She didn't deserved his thanks, let alone a posy as reward. He didn't seem the least bit annoyed though. A ghost of smile curved her lips. 'I'll admit I have not been the most gracious of hostesses.'

'Like good wine, you will improve with age.'

She spread her fan across her blush, wishing his smile didn't have such an effect on her. 'You'll forgive me, I hope?'

'No doubt I deserved every unkind word you uttered.'

How despicable of him to point it out. Prickles of anger raced up her spine and she snapped her fan shut. 'I do not recall being *that* unkind, Rafe.'

'You were perfection. I'm the most arrogant of men sometimes, and need to be made aware of it.' Taking her hand he bore it to his lips, kissing each finger in turn. Etched on the classic lines of his face was the gently sardonic expression she hated. He chuckled when he plucked an embroidered handkerchief from her sleeve and slipped it inside his waistcoat. 'A memento of the first time you called me Rafe,' he whispered. '*Adieu*, Angel. Don't think too unkindly of me.'

'I doubt if I shall think of you at all, Lord Lynnbury,' she snapped, completely flustered.

'Then you'll break my heart.' Bestowing another of his mocking smiles upon her he spurred his horse into motion and cantered off without so much as a backward glance.

'I despise that man,' she said furiously, as he disappeared from sight. Her glance went to the posy. There were satiny yellow buttercups, deep red poppies, tiny blue forget-me-nots, orange marigolds and a sprig or two of lavender. Still sprinkled with dewdrops, they were freshly picked, the stems bound in an initialled handkerchief. Hotly, she dashed the bouquet to the ground, then changed her mind and picked it up again.

'It's a pity to let them die so soon,' she explained to Bessie.

'Yes, my bonny.' Bessie smiled. 'His Lordship is a fine-looking man, and has quite a way with him when he wants. He'll be popular with the ladies no doubt.'

Feeling a curl of dismay in the region of her heart, she gave Bessie an irate glare and flounced ahead faster than her maid could go. She held the posy to her nostrils breathing in its scent. It was the first time a man had given her a gift, and the fact that he'd taken the trouble to pick them himself made them all the more precious.

No, she thought firmly, her finger tracing the gold embroidered initials on the fabric. It was not a romantic gesture. Rafe couldn't afford food for his sister, let alone a gift. It was a token of his appreciation, nothing more, nothing less. Besides, as Bessie had said, Rafe would be popular with the ladies, and must be well practised in the art of flirtation.

Slowly she came to a halt, waiting for Bessie to catch her up. She slipped her arm through Bessie's and laid her head against her broad shoulder. 'What am I going to do in London without you?'

'You'll manage. I'm not getting any younger, and your brother is right when he says you must have a maid who knows how to do the latest hair-styles and such. If you're to take your rightful place in society it stands to reason.'

'I'll miss you.'

Bessie smiled. 'I've got it into my head to retire to my brother's place in Dorset if that's all right with you. He's a widower, and I've got grown-up nieces and nephews I ain't never seen. Imagine that?'

'Oh, Bessie.' Tears filled Angelina's eyes. 'I've been selfish all these years. Of course you may go. I'll instruct Hugh Cotterill to book you a seat on the coach, and I'll arrange with my brother that you receive a generous pension. That way you'll not have to rely on anyone's charity should you not wish to.'

'I cannot take such a gift,' Bessie protested.

'You can, and you will.' Fiercely she hugged Bessie to her. 'You've been almost a mother to me.' The tears spilled over on to her cheeks. 'My life is about to change and my childhood must be put aside. I couldn't bear to send you off and imagine you wanting in any way. If your brother is cruel you must let me know and I'll come and get you. Swear you will do this.'

'I swear it.'

Wrapped tight against Bessie's chest, Angelina sobbed away the last sorrowful tears of her childhood. After a while, Bessie joined in.

CHAPTER FIVE

'A little to your right.'

Rosabelle held the pistol at arm's length, aiming it directly at the mounted figure of the Marquis of Northbridge.

'Fire,' William said.

Her finger tightened on the trigger and the hammer clicked. She laughed. 'Straight through the heart.'

William plucked the pistol from her fingers. 'Kill him *after* you're married, Rosie, and preferably when you've given him an heir. If you don't give him a son his distant cousin will inherit.'

She shuddered. 'I'll never marry the old goat willingly. Having him touch me would make me sick.'

'Consider, Rosie? George is not only stupid, he's disgustingly wealthy. He'll give you everything you desire if you play your cards right.' He aimed the pistol at the centre of her breast. 'Come here,' he said, and circling her waist with his arm, pulled her against him. 'You enjoy the desire in his eyes, Rosie. When the time comes, he will not leave you wanting.'

Her eyes hooded with pleasure when she pressed against him. If she wasn't his sister, he'd take advantage of her wildness. George would exploit it if he had any sense, give her no choice.

Her breast brushed soft against his chest. *Damn her!* She tormented him, as if she suspected he ached with a shameful lust for her. He sucked in a swift breath when she laughed, and pushed her away.

When George entered the room, Will was examining his pistol and Rosabelle gazing out of the window.

She looks flushed, he thought, his gaze going to the swell of her breasts, barely hidden by the lace of her fichu. He'd been given permission to court her, even though he'd expected opposition from her mother.

If he succeeded, the betrothal would be announced at the ball. If he didn't. . . ? George grinned to himself. He wanted her enough to abduct her if the need arose. Once compromised, she would have no choice.

She turned, staring at him through hostile eyes. 'My Lord?' She accepted his gift of a posy with a barely concealed sneer, dropping it on the window sill to wilt when she left the room. She pushed past him with her haughty nose raised.

Her behaviour didn't put him off. George knew women, and Rosabelle Wrey was ripe for the plucking. He could smell the woman of her as she brushed against him on the way out. She was aware of herself, teasing him with swaying hips and thrusting breasts, she couldn't help herself.

You'll not be so hostile when we're wed, he thought, his grin wolf-like. I'm master of my own house. If you do not come to me willingly, I'll flay the skin from your buttocks until you scream for mercy. His body reacted at the thought of her humbled before him, sharing his bed. The girl had strong, wide hips and would bear him many children.

His glance flitted to Will. His mocking grin made George feel uncomfortable. The earl's younger son had never been less than friendly towards him, but Will's sly cleverness seemed to be one step ahead of his own thinking.

'Rosie is out of countenance,' Will said. 'Her mama will not allow her to have the ball-gown she desires. She's worried our sister will outshine her at the ball.' He smiled. 'If you really wanted to impress her. . . .' To George's disappointment Will shook his head. 'No, it would be too simple.'

George sighed. Will did nothing without recompense. 'If I like your suggestion it might be worth something.'

'Five guineas, say.'

The money safely in his pocket, Will said, 'There's a French dressmaker of your acquaintance in attendance at the Marley residence. She's much in demand, I believe.'

How the hell had Will known about the Frenchie?

'Rosabelle's curious as to what other women will be wearing to her ball, so I'm taking her to call on the Marley sisters tomorrow. What if she discovered a secret admirer had commissioned the Frenchwoman to design her the most beautiful gown at the ball?'

'That would do the trick, eh?'

William sighted down the barrel of his pistol. 'It would if the gown was accompanied by a small trinket. Rosabelle is uncommonly fond of rubies.'

'She is, eh? What would you suggest?'

'What do I know about women's trinkets?' He loaded the pistol and shoved it into a pocket under his coat. 'If I recall, she admired a pendant in Winchester not long ago. I'm on my way there now. If you like I could point it out to you.'

It crossed George's mind that William might have arranged a commission with the jeweller, but he couldn't see how. He nodded.

Rosabelle came back into the room. Crossing to the window seat she picked up the posy, holding it to her nose in a pretty gesture. 'I forgot these, My Lord.'

When she dropped a curtsy her fichu gaped, just enough to draw his eyes to her wares. Her eyes shone with a mixture of excitement and avarice. The minx had been eavesdropping. There was not a suggestion of a blush when she allowed him to brush a kiss across the back of her hand.

You're a born harlot, Rosie, he thought dispassionately. You'll soon learn to earn my attention.

Mary Mellor pushed the brick back in the chimney piece and turned to her son. 'If anything happens to me there's enough gold to pay for lodgings in London for a while.'

'Nothing's going to happen to you,' Frey muttered, and frowning in concentration, added a flourish to his signature to the letter. He put the quill to one side and stoppered his precious supply of ink. 'If I get this position I'll stick it for a year or so. London isn't cheap and I should be able to save enough to give us a good start.'

'I daresay the earl would drop a word in the right ear, if I asked him.'

An obstinate expression surfaced in Frey's dark eyes. 'My father can keep his fine words. I pay my own way from now on.'

Mary knew better than to argue with Frey. His resemblance to Thomas Wrey was more than surface. It struck her as funny that, of the earl's three sons, his bastard should be the one to resemble him most. There was no hiding the fact who Frey's father was.

He'd been about ten when he'd first realized that the man who visited them on occasion was his father. It didn't take long for his childish bragging to reach the ears of William.

At fifteen, William hadn't been far off manhood, his adolescent blood surging hot and turbulent. The thrashing he'd given Frey had been merciless. Even the earl had paled at the sight of Frey's bruised and broken body.

When he'd recovered, the earl had pointed out to her son that his position depended on acceptance of his circumstances. Frey had lost his innocence that day. From then on he'd applied himself to his education with a humble acceptance that such a privilege should be afforded him. He'd never given William reason to thrash him again, however much he was goaded. But neither had he forgiven him.

As Frey rose to his feet, he automatically bowed his head to avoid the low beam as he made his way to the door.

'You're going out?'

'I want to slip this letter under Cruickshank's door so he'll get it first thing in the morning. After that, I'm off to see the rector for an hour or so. He has some Latin text he wants me to look at.'

'I was hoping you'd stay home. Rosabelle might visit this afternoon. She'll be disappointed if you're not here.'

'Only because she enjoys queening it over me.' Frey dropped a kiss on her head and opened the cottage door. 'You shouldn't encourage her. If she gets caught there will be hell to pay.'

His mother's eyes began to shine. 'The Marquis of Northbridge has asked for her hand. Imagine that, my little Rosabelle, a marchioness.'

Frey gazed at her for long seconds. 'Lady Rosabelle isn't yours, she's the daughter of the countess.'

Unconcerned, Mary snorted, 'She's never been a real mother to her.'

Frey warned. 'I wouldn't want to be in your shoes if she decides she's had enough. This latest indignity—'

'And what's she going to do about it?' His mother's words were over-confident for one in her position. 'It's not my fault her daughter didn't die like she was supposed to. The earl should have waited until the runt was dead before he—'

Frey's eyes were sharp on her face. 'Before he what?'

'Nothing,' she mumbled. 'What happened ain't none of my business, nor yours.'

Two strides brought him back to her side. 'Like hell it isn't! You were there at the hospital.' His hands clamped around her arms to stop her turning away. 'I'm not so stupid that I don`t know the earl's been giving you regular payments all these years. Everyone knows I'm his bastard, so it isn't that. He's paying you to keep your mouth shut about something, isn't he?' He sneered as he gazed down at her, he couldn't help himself. 'You can't tell me he pays you money for the odd tumble. He could buy something younger for less.'

She bridled at the sting of his insult. 'You watch your lip, Frey Mellor,' she snapped. 'I'm not so old I've forgotten how to make a man happy.' Her eyes lit up when the sound of a horse snickering came from the back meadow. 'There's my Rosabelle,' she cried out, trying to struggle free from his grip.

Frey jerked her back to face him. 'So that's it,' he breathed. 'I've always suspected Rosabelle was *your* child. She was substituted at birth for the other one.' His mother looked shocked. 'That's it, isn't it, Ma? That's what keeps the earl paying up.' He dropped her arms and turned towards the door.

Desperately, she ran after him, and grabbing his sleeve held on tight when he tried to shake her free. 'She's not mine, I swear. I hadn't even met the earl when she was born. She was an orphan. He wanted the infant for his wife 'cause hers was set to die.'

'Why didn't he give her one in the normal way?' he said harshly.

'The countess nearly died when she delivered that child. He couldn't bear the thought of losing her to childbirth, so he left her alone and turned to me.'

Frey believed her. 'You took advantage of him.'

'It wasn't like that.' Tears came into her eyes. 'Oh, it was at first. Then, when you was born he was good to us and I grew fond of him. He's not a generous man, but he's honourable. He's looked after us and given you an education. I'm grateful to him for that.'

'And what about the countess? Did you give any thought to what she might be suffering?'

'You're not going to tell her, Frey.'

'Tell her?' He gave a bitter laugh. 'She can't even bring herself to look at me.'

His mother lowered her voice to a whisper when the back door creaked open. 'Everyone thinks the girls is twins now, including the countess. If you tell anyone different, the earl will kick us out of the county.' She gazed at him in mute appeal. 'Think what it would do to Rosabelle.'

'Ah yes . . . Lady Rosabelle.' Frey gave an ironic grin when the girl he'd always thought of as his half-sister came into the cottage. She was flushed from her ride; her dark eyes shone with excitement as she gazed at his mother.

'Walk my horse while I talk to your mother,' she said imperiously. 'I rode her too hard and she's lathered.'

'Walk her yourself,' he said quietly. 'I've got business of my own to attend to.'

An astonished expression crossed her face. Frey smiled when her mouth opened slightly. She was the same as him, a lowborn bastard. No, she was less. A surge of triumph flooded through him. At least he knew who *his parents were*.

Taking the hat from his head he swept it across his body, giving a parody of a bow before sauntering from the cottage and firmly closing the door.

It was almost midnight. A horse picked its way through the leaf litter on the forest floor. Black coated, its glossy hide was unrelieved by markings. The rider, clad in a black voluminous coat despite the warmth of the evening, was in no hurry.

Now and again, the narrow gap between the low brimmed hat and the black cloth covering the lower part of the rider's face revealed a glimpse of dark eyes. Those eyes watched the track off to the right, where another horse and rider ambled aimlessly along. The object of the felon's attention was singing lewd verses at the top of his voice.

Presently, the highwayman turned the horse to the left, spurring it into a canter. Swiftly, the black covered the ground until the junction branching towards the stables of the Marquis of Northbridge was reached. There, where the track curved, the highwayman took up position in the middle of the track.

'Whoa, nag.' George peered owlishly at the figure barring his way. 'Stand aside fellow, or I'll shoot you.' He fumbled for his pistol, then realizing he wasn't wearing one roared with false bravados: 'Damn and blast you for a knave. I am unarmed.'

'I'm relieved, sir,' the highwayman said, voice muffled by a scarf. 'I have no wish to kill you.'

'You don't, eh? If it's money you're after I have none. A man must pay for his pleasures and I've just enjoyed the company of a couple of Winchester harlots.'

'And won a small fortune at the gaming house afterwards if your reputation does you justice.' The highwayman indicated with the pistol. 'Throw me your purse, My Lord.'

Reluctantly, George did as he was asked. Shocked into sobriety, he was embarrassed by being caught without a weapon to see this rogue off. He scowled as he watched his winnings disappear inside the thief's coat.

'Empty your pockets.'

His hands tightened on the reins. 'Out of my way . . . *God's truth!*'

The pistol jerked, a ball cut through his reins and he tumbled over his mount's rear to sprawl in the dust. Spooked by the shot, his horse bucked a few times then trotted off up the track. It stopped at a patch of succulent grass and started to graze.

The highwayman expertly brought his horse under control as George scrambled to his feet. A second weapon appeared in his hand. 'Your pockets, sir. Empty them into your handkerchief then hand it all to me.'

George scrambled to obey.

The highwayman sifted through the contents, removing a silver snuff box and jewellery case before tossing the remainder to the ground. He whistled as he dangled a ruby pendant from a black gloved finger. 'A handsome bauble.'

George bristled. 'That's a gift for a lady. Take my horse instead.'

The highwayman chuckled. 'A noble beast, but doubtless he knows his way home. I'd not have him long. Tell me about this lady. Your mistress?'

'*No, damn it*! She's a maid of barely eighteen years, and I intend to wed her.'

'Her name?'

'Lady Rosabelle Wrey.'

The highwayman gave a high-pitched laugh and threw the pendant back. 'Perhaps this bauble will buy you a kiss.'

'I'll thank you not to speak of her thus,' George growled.

The felon wheeled his horse around. 'Take my word for it, she will be hard to catch. I believe she's set her sights on the Earl of Lynnbury.'

'For all his fine manners, the earl hasn't a penny to his name,' the marquis sneered.

The highwayman's eyes glittered. 'I've heard he's sought after in the bedchamber.'

'I'm not without expertise myself,' the marquis muttered. 'And her dowry will not be enough to catch the earl, for many have tried and failed.'

'It's said he is not immune to the Wrey girl's charms.'

'The devil take him!' George said. 'That snippet of information is worth the loss of my purse. I'm indebted to you.'

'Glad to be of service, My Lord.' The highwayman gave a mocking half-bow before touching heels to his mount and melting into the darkness of the undergrowth.

'Rum fellow,' George muttered to himself, and his brow furrowed in thought. He'd been well spoken, and young from the pitch of his voice. He knew the forest well, *and* the local gossip.

His nerve ends twitched when an owl hooted. A mist rose from the ground, darkness pressed in on him. Picking his goods up from the dirt, he set off after his horse at as brisk a pace as he could muster.

CHAPTER SIX

'James, you must come and help us decide.' Angelina started when Rafe uncoiled from the chair nearest to her. She cursed the colour that suddenly bloomed in her cheeks. 'I didn't realize you had company; please forgive the intrusion, My Lord.'

Rafe's sardonic good looks pushed everything else to the shadows. She'd forgotten how large he was, how dark, how powerful of body and feature. Most of all she'd forgotten his grace, until he covered the space between them in two lithe strides.

He bore her hand to mouth, lightly brushing his lips across her fingers. 'I thought we agreed you would call me Rafe the last time we met. You're looking well, little Angelina. Having James for a brother obviously suits you.'

'James is kindness itself.' The pressure of Rafe's fingers stopped her from sliding her hand away. She darted James a glance. He was smiling, not at all bothered by the small impropriety. She gave him a loving smile. 'He spoils me.'

'Beautiful women are meant to be spoiled.' With a show of reluctance, Rafe allowed her to slide her hand away. 'What would men do without ladies to spoil?'

'I hope you do not expect me to seriously apply myself to that question?'

Rafe's grin had a mischievous edge to it. 'I'd be curious to hear your opinion.'

Sensing an ulterior motive she gazed at him, wary. 'Why?'

'In all seriousness?' His eyebrows quirked. 'Disregarding the fact that men are naturally superior, and therefore more assertive, any information a lady could impart with regards to his shortcomings would only serve to improve him.'

Did he think she was a fool? She ignored the glint of amusement in his eyes. 'If we are to disregard the fact of a man's supposed superiority, why did you see fit to mention it, Rafe? A man cannot regard himself as superior and admit to needing improvement in the same breath. You are being illogical to goad me into debate, thus to amuse yourself at my expense.'

Rafe didn't look at all put out by her charge. 'You are wrong, Angel. I find your reasoning a refreshing change from the conversation of most women. It amuses me, yes, but it does not bore me. So, dear heart, pray tell. What can a man do to keep himself out of mischief?'

'Now let me see,' she pondered, her voice as mocking as his. 'Perhaps you could be employed dreaming up further tea taxes to impose on England's other unfortunate colonies. Surely we need the revenue, the country is in so much debt, Parliament is beginning to disintegrate with Lord North at the helm.'

'No doubt the Rockingham Whigs will reorganize it once they are in power,' Rafe murmured.

'They must reorganize Ireland too. Men, women and children are being persecuted because of religious differences there. Your Whigs can feel at their most superior whilst they bury our starving Irish cousins, Rafe.'

Rafe's smile was gently goading. 'An emotional basis for the politics of Parliament. Lady Alexandra was well-known for her outspokenness on such matters. Redoubtable as she was, you must not let her opinions dissuade you from forming your own.'

'I cannot be less than emotional when I see the effects of poverty all around me. Everywhere I go there are crippled beggars in the streets, and women forced to . . . to . . . assume degrading employment to enable them to feed their children.' The heat of her argument left no room for caution. 'Children die in abject poverty and the workhouses are overflowing.'

'Enough, Angelina.' James took her elbow and gently turned her to face him. 'Although your concerns are pertinent, it's an unseemly topic for a young lady to pursue.'

She would have fled if James had not restrained her. Mortified, she stammered, 'I beg your pardon if I have crossed the bounds of propriety, Lord Lynnbury.'

Rafe laid a hand on James's arm. 'You must not chastise her for what was my fault. It was unforgivable of me to invoke such passion in her.'

'I know, and as soon as Angelina has left the room I intend to call you out for such disgraceful behaviour.'

Alarm raced through her. 'You must not! Rafe is your friend. I would never forgive myself if you. . . .' She gazed from one man to the other in uncertainty. Both had difficulty in hiding their smiles. '*Oh, you!*' she choked out. 'I cannot turn a moment of censure into one of brevity at a whim.'

In an instant James's arm came round her. 'All was spoken in jest, Angelina. Come, let me see you smile.'

A tentative smile edged across her mouth. 'I doubt if I shall speak to either of you ever again.'

'Then you're not going to say why you needed me so urgently?'

'Celine!' She pressed her hand against her mouth. 'I had almost forgotten. We are having an argument over whether she should wear a cap with her new blue gown, or a hat trimmed with feathers and ribbons. You've been appointed adjudicator.'

He darted Rafe a look of long suffering. 'Let it be the hat.'

She sensed an opportunity to get a little of her own back. 'But you've not seen either,' she coaxed. 'Please indulge us by coming to inspect them. Celine intends to wear the gown when we attend Lady Snelling's assembly this afternoon. We understand she's the most sought after hostess. Although you've declined her invitation, we are determined to go and make an impression.'

'There's no need to be intimidated by Constance,' Rafe drawled. 'She learned her superior manners in the theatre.'

'She was an actress!' Angelina's eyes flew open in shocked excitement.

'A good actress, and a woman of great wit and beauty. She married old Snelling when he was practically on his death-bed. He doted on her.'

'She married him for his money?'

'And the title. A common enough occurrence.' Rafe's expression became bland. 'In return, Constance produced an heir for the estate before her husband died. That son came of age recently. Lady Constance is selecting candidates for a wife for him at these assemblies.'

'She intends to choose a wife for her son?' Angelina gave a delicate shudder. 'How dreadful. I refuse to be used for such a purpose and shall cancel the visit.'

'What a prissy miss you are,' Rafe said with a smile. 'Did I detect a nuance of snobbishness in your manner?'

'If you did your imagination must be severely strained.' *Was society full of irritating men such as Rafe?* 'It was not snobbishness, it was revulsion. I'd prefer to have been invited because my hostess wished to spend time in my company, not because she views me as a likely daughter-in-law.'

'You are young, Angelina, and wealthy.' He gave a weary smile. 'You must expect to be regarded as prey by the enterprising mamas of this world.'

She felt a little nauseated at the thought. 'Is this true, James? Am I to be regarded as a commodity?'

His smile reassured her. 'That's not exactly how I'd describe the marriage market, Angelina.'

'Good, because I will never marry a man I have no regard for,' she said with determination, and stepped away from him. 'If you have ideas to the contrary I beg you to change them now.'

'Forcing you into marriage against your will is the last thing I'd do. But how do you expect to meet suitable men if you do not accept social invitations?'

Her heart sank. Why did things have to change? It seemed like only yesterday she'd been a child, with all the freedom of a child. She hated London with its dirty streets and its beggars, and didn't know how to handle worldly wise men like Rafe. Alexandra Chadwick had kept her ignorant of society ways, and now she was being forced into it without knowing how to cope.

'I'm scared of meeting men,' she admitted. 'How will I know which are suitable and which are not?' Her voice rose. 'To attend Lady Constance Snelling's assembly and be looked over as though I was some thoroughbred mare she might buy for her son is distasteful. I do not want to be bought, and most of all' her eyes sparkled with imagined affront 'I do not wish to suffer the indignity of being told I'm not a suitable wife if she decides she does not like me.'

Rafe roared with laughter. 'No fear of that, my vain little angel. Any enterprising mama will covet a prize such as you for her son. The young lordling will do exactly as his mama says, and will, no doubt, carry you off to the altar with as little delay as possible.'

She met his laughter with scornful toss of her head. 'I am *not* vain.'

'Enough of this,' James said. 'If it worries you so much, I shall escort you and Celine to the assembly myself.'

'You'll find such duty tedious in the extreme.'

'No doubt,' he said wryly. 'But if the price of your peace of mind is the loss of mine, I'll gladly pay it.'

'Put thus, you make me feel horribly indebted to you.' Strolling to the door she turned, bestowing on her brother a cherubic smile. 'It has just occurred to me, that perhaps I should select suitable candidates to be a wife to you.'

'Then the thought should be discarded, immediately.' James glanced at the grinning Rafe. 'Tell Celine that Rafe and I will inspect her by the by, and we shall all attend the assembly together. The carriage will be brought round, allowing Rafe the chance to show off his driving skills. The young lordling shall be inspected by us all and it will be us who shall decide whether or not he's a good enough suitor for Lady Angelina Wrey.'

'You may inspect, James, and as always, I will listen to your counsel.' Her chin lifted slightly as she warned: 'Ultimately, I will decide for myself.' Giving him the warmest of smiles she hurried away to pass on the message to Celine.

'Angelina displays an unexpected independence of spirit,' Rafe drawled when the door was safely closed behind her.

'Yes,' he admitted with a slight frown. 'I believe she has lacked both guidance and self-discipline in her upbringing, yet I am loath to censure her too often.'

'I was in no way criticizing her.' Rafe's mouth crinkled into a grin. 'She is vulnerable, James. You must guard her heart carefully, for once it's lost she'll never give it to another.'

There speaks a man just as vulnerable, James mused, rising to his feet. 'We had better not keep the ladies waiting. I am much in demand as a fashion expert of late. Let's go and inspect Celine's hat.'

The resignation in his voice brought a hoot of laughter from Rafe. 'I was expecting to go to the horse sales this afternoon.'

'Since I've no need for a new horse, and you cannot afford one, I see no point. Besides,' he gave Rafe a keen glance – 'Angelina, as you have recently experienced, is unschooled in the ways of society, and Celine is unattached. Do either of us really want to risk being related to Nicholas Snelling?'

It did not take Rafe long to ponder the question. 'You have a point. Despite getting a place at Cambridge, Nicholas is the biggest fool in all of London. He takes after his father in that respect.'

'And his mother in looks.'

'Yes,' Rafe said softly. 'Nicholas is certainly pretty, don't you think?'

'You have heard something?'

'Whispers.' Rafe shrugged. 'An acquaintance of mine is a tutor at Cambridge.'

'Does Constance suspect?'

'Possibly. She is a woman of the world and seems overly anxious to settle a match on her son. Perhaps she thinks marriage will make a man of him.'

James frowned. 'Thank you for the warning; I'm indebted to you.'

'Surely you were not considering Nicholas Snelling.' Astonished, Rafe gazed at him. 'Good God, James, I don't believe it. You of all people should not encourage such a match. Even if Nicholas was worthy of her, Angelina is too intelligent to be wasted on such as him. She would shrivel up and die of boredom in such a union.'

Rafe's voice was touched by tenderness. 'Angelina is like a wildflower. Her beauty is unspoilt, and will blossom whilst her roots are firmly planted in the soil. But put her amongst the hot-house flowers. . . .' He suddenly shrugged. 'Why am I telling you this, when it is you who is her guardian? Surely you can see how unique a creature she is.'

James gave a glimmer of a smile when Rafe's voice trailed off on an ironic note. So that's how the wind blows, he thought and wondered if Rafe realized how revealing his words had been.

Drily, he said, 'Angelina would cause havoc amongst the hot-house flowers. I'm thankful Celine is here to guide her.'

Rafe frowned slightly. 'Angelina mentioned a new gown for Celine.'

James placed his hand on his arm. 'I'm going to be frank with you, and to hell with your pride. Angelina threatened to go abroad in the clothes Lady Alexandra provided if Celine did not accept a complete wardrobe. That would cause me no end of embarrassment.'

'Surely a young woman of vanity wouldn't go to such lengths to get her own way,' Rafe spluttered.

'Angelina would. As one of us is to be put in the position of losing face, I've determined it will be you on this occasion. If Celine can accept the gift with pleasure and grace, would you spoil it for her?' His face softened when Rafe relaxed. 'Your pride will not hurt so much when you see how well your sister looks. Come, I shall let you have the honour of choosing her hat.'

Rafe was bored, but didn't allow it to show as he stood behind the chairs occupied by Celine and an ageing dowager. The slightly remote smile he wore was assumed for such occasions, donned like a pair of stockings, or a hat. His manners, learned through familiarity with society, were a set ritual of grace and blandness. He commanded respect despite his poverty, for his powerful size when combined with his enigmatic approach was attractive to both men and women alike.

The salon was hot and stuffy, redolent of the jasmine perfume Constance wore. The perfume was as familiar to Rafe as the layout of her bed-chamber, for he'd indulged in a brief, but passionate affair with the woman two years previously. Beneath the petticoat flounces, perfume and learned graces was a woman of coarse nature, well versed in the darker pleasures of love-making. His disenchantment had soon turned to disgust.

His glance touched on Nicholas and he was hard put to stop his lip curling. The youth's cut-away jacket was fashioned from striped lilac satin, his buttons were mother-of-pearl and his purple stock matched a pair of bows adorning his shoes. Even his stockings were striped, with posies of flowers embroidered at the ankle.

Nicholas was talking to Angelina, his dark soulful eyes intent on her face, his rouged lips parting every now and again in a smile. A stab of annoyance shot through him when she laughed for the second time in as many minutes. What did she find so amusing about the fellow?

She glanced at Celine, who was deep in conversation with a dowager. The appeal in them turned to desperation. For a second her eyes caught his. They widened a fraction, then moved on to James, who was trapped on a sofa between two determined looking mamas.

Unhurriedly, Rafe worked his way through the crush towards his prey. Angelina was elegant in a gown the colour of toasted almonds, with a flounced hem and striped overskirt. Her hair was fashioned into tiny curls, and ringlets bounced against her shoulder every time she moved her head. He preferred her hair as he'd first seen it, hanging in shining ripples of liquid amber down her back.

She resembled a delicate figurine. But inside. . . . He grinned to himself when she edged away from Nicholas. Inside her, he suspected, there lurked the disposition of a tiger, if someone were to push her hard enough.

'James is neglecting you, Angel,' he drawled with easy familiarity. 'Take a turn around the garden with me.'

'I was just about to recite a love poem I composed.' Nicholas looked petulant for a moment, then his eyes turned up to Rafe's and his dark eyelashes fluttered. 'Perhaps you'd care to hear it too, Lord Lynnbury?'

'Some other time.' When Angelina's hand touched lightly on his offered arm Rafe steered her through the open windows on to the terrace. The deep breath she took was faintly audible, her eyes took on the green of summer leaves as they turned his way.

'Thank you, Rafe. I didn't know how to escape from him without being rude.'

'You manage it with me,' he said with a chuckle. 'Though I must admit you've not yet learned the knack of graceful withdrawal from a skirmish.'

A faint blush tinted her cheeks and she giggled. 'You're different from anyone else I've met, Rafe.'

He led her down the steps towards the rose garden. 'Should I be flattered or offended by that remark? Pray, elaborate.'

'You will not tease or laugh?' How trusting her eyes looked. That same second resignation crept into them. 'Of course you will laugh. You're of the opinion I'm an ignoramus who deserves to be teased.'

'Do not presume to know my opinion of you,' he said lightly. 'I tease you because I like the reaction I get. Sometimes you're angry, sometimes you blush and sometimes you're confused. Always, your reaction delights me.'

'I'm pleased I'm able to provide you with such amusement.' A scornful toss of her head contradicted the words.

'You're not pleased at all.' He placed his hand over hers so she could not flee. 'There's a difference between amusement and pleasure. It's pleasure your reaction gives me.' He picked a white daisy from the garden bed, holding it out to her. 'If my pleasure is gained at your expense I'll cease the practice of teasing you instantly.'

'Then I should have nothing to chastise you for.' She accepted the daisy, briefly inhaling its fragrance before threading it into the ribbon tied around her throat. 'I've noticed the banter we engage in is very fashionable in society, so I must confess to being grateful for the practice you afford me.'

'Then you do not wish me to stop?' He chuckled when she pursed her lips in annoyance. 'You said yourself I would be perfect if I did. To my mind there's nothing worse than being considered perfect, except, of course, being aware of one's perfection and acquainting others with the fact.'

Tipping her head to one side she regarded him with mock seriousness. 'Those were not exactly the words I used, nor the sentiment expressed.' The smile she gave was unguarded, almost intimate. 'Your perceptions are correct though. Nicholas Snelling is convinced he is perfect. To be honest,

I've never met anyone quite so tedious.'

He lifted her gloved hand to his lips and placed a kiss in the palm. 'You'll cross him from your list of prospective husbands then. Undoubtedly, you can do much better for yourself.'

'I haven't got a list. If I did have, the beautiful Nicholas would be at the very bottom.' Her voice dropped to a whisper. 'He is gynandrous, I think.'

Shock rippled through him. Where had she learned such a word, and did she know its meaning? His eyes hooded in contemplation of her. 'Some subjects are considered unseemly for young ladies to have even heard of, Angelina, let alone discuss. James would not find such comments amusing.'

'I apologize,' she murmured, her eyes lifting to his in horrified awareness. 'I spent too much time in the library when I was growing up. Lord Chadwick was a physician by profession, and many of the books in his library were medical in content.' Her hands covered her heated cheeks. 'I studied them merely to learn midwifery skills. I hoped to work with Lady Alexandra in the charity hospital amongst the poor.'

'A worthy aspiration, but I would not have you witness the bitterness and misery of the poor as yet. The experience will rob you of much of your joy and innocence. Promise me you'll abandon that pursuit for the present.'

'If that's your wish,' she murmured, 'I'll make you that promise.'

Removing her hands from her face, Rafe gazed into her limpid green eyes and forgave her indiscretion. He hoped James would not be in too much of a hurry to see her settled. He had strangely ambivalent feelings towards this girl.

Constance had been watching Angelina Wrey. The girl seemed to have the earl wrapped around her little finger. She smiled at the thought, finding it oddly satisfying that this pert little snip could capture the interest of an elusive and charming rogue like Rafe.

Rafe wasn't a man to be trifled with. He'd been the best of lovers, until she'd wanted to play games. He'd declined; she'd insisted, sure of her power to win him round. On finding another man in attendance one night, he had simply walked away. This was the first time he'd entered her house since. He was not a man to be bought despite his circumstances, and to see him so obviously enamoured by this girl amused her.

Angelina's wealth would not sit easy with him, and his arrogant pride would get in the way of a match.

And as for Angelina Wrey? Her eyes swept over her again. The girl's air of independence was vexing, as though the objectionable Lady Alexandra had set her in the same mould as herself. She did not look biddable.

Yet Nicholas had shown considerable interest in her, which led her to believe he was not as she'd suspected, and his affectation was just that. She would prefer his future wife to be less intelligent than the Wrey girl. Without thinking, she shook her head and said out loud, 'If it wasn't for her fortune, Angelina Wrey would not do for Nicholas.'

When Angelina gazed at her with an offended expression, she wasn't given a chance to redress her insult with a lie or a pretty witticism. Cold green eyes narrowed almost cruelly on her when Constance smiled disarmingly to cover her *faux pas*. Angry rags of colour skimmed the young woman's cheeks. Her voice was soft, but pitched to carry. Ears were always canted to catch the latest tidbit of gossip.

'Your son informs me you were once an actress, Lady Constance.'

Anger threatened to choke her. *Damn Nicholas!* Why didn't he keep his stupid mouth shut about family matters? She managed a noncommittal smile. 'One does what one must to survive. My family came from French nobility.'

'How odd' Her smile was all sugar. 'Nicholas told me they ran a tavern in Bristol.'

Constance gasped at her impudence.

The battle lines were drawn, and this slip of a girl with her pale complexion and flaming crown of hair was not going to retreat an inch.

Celine Daventry plucked at her wrist, pleading, 'Come Angelina, we must join our brothers.'

But their respective brothers were right behind them, and had overheard every word. The stuffy James Wrey was tight-lipped with anger. He bowed stiffly, then curtly bid her goodbye. It sounded final.

Rafe's eyes were as cold as winter. He ignored her completely, looking through her as if she'd never existed for him.

Her cheeks ached from the brilliant smile she kept on her face, knowing from the whispers and looks that word was going around. One by one, her guests began to drift towards the door and she wondered if she'd be welcomed in society again.

Nicholas flounced past her, looking thunderous. 'I hope you're satisfied now, Mama,' he hissed. 'I found Angelina Wrey to be admirable in the extreme, and if I don't receive an invitation to her ball, I'll never speak to you again.'

CHAPTER SEVEN

It was early morning. The rising sun warmed the stone façade of Wrey House as Elizabeth was assisted into her coach by her maid. The driver cracked his whip over the backs of the matched greys and the coach set off down the carriageway.

Rosabelle glowered as she watched from her window, her mind seething with the unfairness of it all. Her mother was going to meet Angelina, and it hadn't even occurred to her that she might have wanted to meet her, too.

Not that she did. With Mama safely out of the way she could have the dressmaker attend her for the fittings of her ball-gown. She'd chosen the colour and style herself, a deep rose satin with a flounced petticoat and ruched overskirt. The dressmaker had assured her the style was quite the thing in Paris. Her eyes began to sparkle.

It *must* be Rafe who had ordered the surprise. She didn't believe the earl was as impoverished as everyone said. How could he be when his father was a marquis and Monkscroft Hall was one of the largest estates in Sussex?

It was reputed to be a pleasant county. She might be mistress of Monkscroft Hall one day. *If Rafe ever offered for her!* She scowled when she compared him with George. George was a lecher.

Crossing to the mirror, she cupped her hands under her breasts. She'd noticed the way his eyes kept lingering on them. Her eyes became slumberous and she smiled. imagining they were Rafe's hands . . . or Will's.

There was power in knowing Will desired her in a way that was sinful. She wished she could entice him to give in to his urges, but other than a stolen kiss or two, he'd back off, leaving her feeling strange, empty and reckless.

Her nipples thrust against the thin fabric of her chemise. Perhaps she'd tease George a little when he took her riding this morning, she mused, allow him to touch her accidentally. She knew the effect it would have on him. Men were not like women. Will had told her they suffered if they were aroused and did not find release. That was why her father visited Mary.

'Men,' she whispered scornfully. 'There are only two I'd be willing to surrender my maidenhood to, and neither of them are willing to take it.'

Hearing hoofbeats, she rushed to the window. George, already? She wasn't even dressed. Pretending she hadn't seen him she took a deep breath to outline her breasts against her flimsy chemise then flicked her dark hair back from her shoulders with her hands. She slanted her eyes down to him, widening them in feigned surprise. 'Oh!' For a few seconds she allowed him to gaze his fill, then darted back from the window.

Will's chuckle brought her spinning round. 'You have the makings of a harlot, Rosie. If you ever decide to go into business, let me know.'

'Will you be my first client?'

Although tempted, William didn't answer. His dark gaze lingered on the ripe perfection of her body. 'Why aren't you dressed?'

'My maid must have overslept.'

'I promise you she didn't.' His smile was smugly calculating. 'I kicked her out of my bed just over an hour ago.'

Anger surged into her eyes. 'I hate you, sometimes.'

He jerked her against him and stared down at her. 'Never say that again to me, Rosabelle. Have you seen Elizabeth? Father's looking for her.'

'She left early this morning for London. She thought it about time she met Angelina.'

Will grinned. 'Has she, by God? Father will have his nose put out of countenance when he learns.'

'Perhaps he'll beat her when she returns, and serve her right.'

'Stop being a jealous cat, Rosie.'

'I can't help it.' She grinned and moved against him. 'Do you love me, Will?'

He kissed her a mere inch from her luscious mouth. 'I've always loved you, Rosie, but I'm your brother, I can't enjoy you in the same way I enjoy other women. You'll forget what you feel for me once you're safely married.'

'I hate George, I'd prefer to marry Rafe, he pays such pretty compliments.' She gazed at him, all smiles. 'I think he's paying for my ball-gown.'

Can I count on your support with him, Will?'

He tried not to grin at her foolishness. 'Rafe has sworn not to marry until he can restore Ravenswood.' Will doubted she'd have the will-power to wait that long before satisfying the hot blood surging in her.

Her eyes slanted slyly at him. 'He doesn't look the type of man to keep a woman he desires waiting, and I can make him want me. You might do well to remember that, Will.'

'*You* remember it, Rosie. Rafe wouldn't think too highly of a girl who lusts after her own brother.'

'You wouldn't dare—' She sprang away from him when her maid sauntered into the room. Sharp-voiced, she accused, 'You're late.'

The maid sent him a sly look and a faint grin.

Grabbing up a hairbrush Rosabelle threw it at her. 'Be careful, slut,' she warned her. 'I might have you dismissed.'

Encouraged by his presence, and no doubt the mistaken notion that a night spent in his bed was of some significance, the maid met his sister's warning with a bold stare.

Rosabelle slapped her soundly across the face. 'If you dare look at me like that again, I'll take a horsewhip to you. Go and prepare my bath.'

He laughed, amused by her display of temper. Whoever she married, Rosabelle would be a handful. 'I'd better go and occupy George whilst you dress. Father can ferment in his own ignorance.' Whistling, he strode from the room.

When Elizabeth entered the carriageway of James's house, her heart was in her mouth. The decision to see her daughter for herself had been made on impulse, fired by curiosity and a pressing need to display her independent streak to her husband.

She had not been prepared to submit to his will on this matter, so had simply allowed him no opportunity to voice a negative answer.

Her thoughts had been in turmoil since she'd learned of Angelina's existence. She'd decided to be charitable, accepting her husband's words as truth to what had happened eighteen years previously. But, try as she might, Elizabeth could not recall giving birth to twin daughters.

James's most recent letter had been the catalyst which had brought her in such haste to London. He'd described the girl as being so much like her in looks and colouring that anyone would think they were sisters.

He had written: *Angelina is deprived of social skills after being kept in seclusion in the country. She is, however, an accomplished musician, and can sing very sweetly. She is also clever and eager to learn. I'm taking her to London for a while where she may acquire some polish, and also a new wardrobe. Lady Celine Daventry has agreed to act as her chaperon and companion. I assure you, dearest Elizabeth, you will most heartily approve of Rafe's sister. She is a most modest, good and gentle person, and will be a beneficial influence on Angelina. I think. . . .*

James had devoted a great deal of space to praising the virtues of Celine Daventry. Elizabeth allowed her thoughts to drift back to Angelina's birth. Strange to think the child had inherited her looks and colouring. Her stolen infant daughter had been so tiny, sweet, and vulnerable.

She stared at the façade of James's house, knowing that infant was within its walls, now a woman grown. Uncertainty beset her. Before her courage deserted her entirely she gathered up her skirts, descended from the carriage and made her way to the entrance.

'Tell Lord Kirkley that Lady Elizabeth has arrived and will be waiting in the morning-room for him,' she said to the footman who appeared. 'And please ask the housekeeper to bring me some refreshment.'

The morning-room was being used as a sewing-room. The place was littered with materials in various colours and designs, patterns, pins and cottons. Two nearly completed gowns hung from a rack. One was of blue taffeta with a striped overskirt and lacing at the bodice. It was very pretty, but it was the other which caught Elizabeth's interest.

The gown was a froth of lace-covered silk, and changed from the merest blush of pink to pale yellow as she moved its folds. The bodice and sleeves were embroidered with delicate golden flowers. Straight away she knew this gown was being made for her daughter. Her heart-beat accelerated when she heard the sound of voices and laughter outside the door.

'You must be on your best behaviour today, Angelina. If you fidget I'll instruct the dressmaker to stick a pin in you.'

A quiet giggle raised the hairs on the nape of Elizabeth's neck.

The same voice as before said softly, 'I've forgotten my embroidery. Will you come back upstairs with me, or wait here?'

'I shall wait inside. I'm eager to see my ball-gown again. It's the most beautiful gown I have ever seen.'

Elizabeth smiled at the soft cadence of Angelina's voice.

'You say that about every gown. James thinks you are the most easily pleased woman he's ever known.'

'James spoils me.'

'He's a wonderful brother to you, and a kind and good friend to me.'

'I think he is much taken with you, Celine.' There was a teasing quality to the voice now. 'He smiles when you are mentioned, and his eyes dream when they're upon you.' There was a short pause, then when no reply was forthcoming, a sweetly toned enquiry, 'You admire him, do you not, Celine?'

'We are both lucky to have such agreeable brothers.'

'You have put your prim voice on, Celine. Come, you can tell me,' she coaxed. 'Do you do not think him the sweetest man alive?'

'Shush, Angelina. He might hear you.'

'Then whisper the answer in my ear.'

There was a short, whispered exchange, followed by a soft laughter, then Angelina said, 'You must not tell Rafe I paid him a compliment in return. He will tease me and make me cross.'

'I'll not say a word. We've agreed confidences between us will not be revealed.'

Elizabeth was still smiling as the voice faded away, already prepared to like Celine Daventry. She held her breath when the door swung open.

'Oh!'

The eyes gazing into hers could have been her own, and the surprise in them mirrored the shock she felt at being face to face with someone almost the image of herself. The girl knew straightaway who she was. A smile of incredulity came and went on her face, her eyes narrowed and her head slanted to one side.

Elizabeth began to tremble. She made a steeple with her hands, supporting her chin to steady herself whilst the inspection took place.

'Mama?' The lilting voice quivered, the eyes became enormous, moist and luminously vulnerable. 'Can it be? Why didn't James tell me you were arriving?'

'*My dear, dear child*!' Elizabeth couldn't trust her emotions. Tears welled in her eyes as she recaptured the heady rush of love that had lodged in her heart so many years ago. 'I didn't inform James because I could wait no longer to see you.'

'Mama?'

It was almost a plaintive sigh, but how sweet the word from her daughter's lips. Unable to move, Elizabeth stared at her through her tears, drinking in the sight of her sweet face.

Angelina was crying too, tears trickling unheeded down her cheeks. She was lovely, Elizabeth thought with pleasure. Elegant and dainty, the difference between her and Rosabelle marked. In fact, they were nothing alike.

Somehow, she willed her legs to carry her across the space between them. Her eyes swept across the strange, but familiar face. 'You are everything James said you are.'

'And you, Mama.'

Her daughter gave a shuddering sob when Elizabeth gently drew her into her arms. 'Don't cry, dearest one. We're together now.' She experienced relief, as if she'd been waiting all her life for this moment to happen.

Glancing up, she saw James staring at them with an oddly tender grin on his face. Elizabeth could have sworn there were tears in his eyes also, but then, he'd always been soft-hearted, and for that she was eternally grateful.

'My dear James,' she said, hugging her daughter tight, and determining to get one thing straight right from the beginning. 'Alexandra Chadwick may have thought she was doing the right thing by making you Angelina's guardian, and I agree you are the best person to handle her fortune, but let me make one thing absolutely clear: Angelina is *my* daughter, and as such, the woman had no right to dictate terms regarding her guardianship. I *insist* she be given into my care at once. Do you understand?'

James sprawled in his chair watching the minutes tick by. Now Elizabeth had taken charge of Angelina the relief was almost palpable.

Half an hour of blissful silence had been broken only by the clip-clop of horses on the road beyond his boundary wall.

Elizabeth had taken Angelina and Celine shopping again. Beginning to think he'd need to hire a coach to convey the women's trunks and boxes to Wrey House, he gave a wry smile. He'd thought the clothes he'd already ordered were adequate, but no, Elizabeth had declared there were inadequacies. Now, the morning-room was piled high, parcels still arrived by the day and he was exhausted by it all.

Relieved he hadn't been born female, he glanced once again at the clock. Only a minute had passed since he'd last checked it. He frowned, wondering if the timepiece was still working properly. He checked it against his pocket watch then nodded to himself.

How quiet it was. He'd got used to the women's chatter and laughter, the whisper of footsteps and the rustle of their skirts. He rose and, hands in pockets, crossed to the window to stare into the garden. The day was humid and cloudy, the air still. He wouldn't be at all surprised if night didn't bring a thunderstorm.

About to turn away, a flash of blue caught his eye. On the seat under the shady branches of the elm tree, Celine rested. She had a book in her lap, but was gazing at the doves fluttering at her feet with a dreamy expression and a faint smile.

What was she dreaming about? he wondered. The calm and quiet demeanour she'd had in childhood hadn't left her, but of late he'd discovered other qualities. A sense of humour, joy, and above all a sympathetic and sensible nature that struck a corresponding chord from him. He'd grown very fond of her and his heart lifted at the thought of being able to converse with her alone.

She gave him a warm smile when she saw him coming across the lawn. She was still too slender, he thought, but the sad expression had gone from her eyes. He hoped he'd contributed to the change in some small measure.

'I understood you'd gone out with Elizabeth and Angelina.'

'I had a headache this morning.' She bade him sit beside her, smiling at his concerned expression. 'It's quite gone now, but it offered Angelina and her mama the opportunity to spend time alone together.'

'And me the opportunity to enjoy your exclusive company.'

He knew he was regarded by his friends as slightly stuffy, and by women as dull. He wasn't the adventurous type, and pretty speeches didn't trip easily from his tongue. He'd never considered himself the type of man to make female hearts beat faster, so Celine's blush surprised him. 'I expect you regard me as a dull fellow, Celine.'

'Not at all.' She glanced shyly at him. 'We have much in common, I think, James. Your quiet nature encourages others to take you for granted. You must not think badly of yourself for a quality so endearing to others.' She gazed down at the book in her lap and a smile flitted across her lips. It was a romantic novel, James saw, before her hands spread across the title, as if to hide it from him. 'I think you are a very kind man, James.'

'I try to be.' A light perfume surrounded her, like spring flowers. James breathed in her scent, experiencing an empathy with her he'd never felt with anyone else. How very nice it would be to be married to Celine, he thought. He gazed at her in bewildered surprise as warmth spread through him. How odd. He'd fallen in love without even realizing it.

'What is it, James?' she said. 'You look as though something has astounded you.'

'I was thinking how very fond I've become of you,' he stammered, wondering how she'd managed to become the object of his affection after such a short acquaintance.

He experienced a dizzying happiness when she answered quietly, 'And I you.'

He thought his heart might burst. Taking her hand he lifted it to his lips. 'My dearest, Celine.' Experiencing a moment of panic he gave her a shocked look. 'I had no intention of declaring myself when I sought you out. My brain is acting quite illogically at the moment.'

'Then I'll forget you spoke.' She rose from the seat, eyes averted, her face pink with embarrassment. 'I trust you are gentleman enough to forget the answer my heart gave you.'

Feeling unusually agitated he watched her hurry away, then buried his head in his hands. What had come over him? Not only had he humiliated the sister of his best friend, he'd made a fool of himself into the bargain. Only an oaf would have acted as he just had. Celine was of gentle birth and needed to be courted. First, he must convey his intentions to Rafe and seek approval from her father.

'I must consult with Rafe this instant,' he declared, the sound of his own voice consolidating the thought.

Rafe was run to ground at the fencing academy. Dressed in breeches and a shirt, he and his opponent were warily circling each other. Using French foils with blunted tips, both wore padding and mesh masks. Rafe seemed to have the right of way. His thrust was easily parried however, and his opponent scored the next point. Five minutes of point scoring and the match was over.

He waited whilst Rafe washed the perspiration from his torso and dressed. Rafe took as much care with his shabby suit as if it were new, and James was in a fever of impatience when they finally strolled towards their horses.

Rafe gave him an easy smile. 'Your business must be urgent if you were motivated to seek me out. Had you forgotten I intended to pay my respects to Lady Elizabeth later this afternoon?'

'It's about Celine I wish to see you,' James blurted out.

'She's been taken ill?' Anguish flared in Rafe's eyes as he sprang into the saddle and urged his mount forward.

James scrambled hastily on his horse, his superior mount quickly drawing level with Rafe. 'Your sister is not ill,' he shouted. 'It is myself.'

Slowing to a walk, Rafe gazed at him. 'You do appear flushed. What ails you?'

'Nothing of a physical nature. I enjoy robust health, and as you know, drink only in moderation. I trust you regard me as a solid citizen, a man of honour and good sense. Not usually a person given to irrational impulse.'

'That's so.' Amusement filled Rafe's eyes. 'I hold your friendship in high esteem.'

'Then I cannot understand why I risked your good opinion by declaring myself. I've given a lady cause to misunderstand my intentions, and stand to lose your much valued friendship.'

Rafe's eyebrows rose. 'With your permission I'll put the lady straight about your intentions.'

'Thank you, Rafe.' Relief flooded him. 'You'll tell her my intentions are honourable, my feelings towards her profound. I did not seek to trifle with her affections.'

Rafe gazed at him, puzzled. Surely James didn't intend to wed the widow he had the occasional dalliance with? 'Your family would never countenance such a poor creature as your wife.'

'It matters not if Celine comes without dowry.' His friend's eyes absorbed a faraway expression. 'The fact that I'm in love with her came as a revelation, and I spoke too hastily. Forgive my presumption, Rafe. I should have sought your advice on the matter first.'

'Celine?' he spluttered. 'I thought—' He collected his scattered wits and regarded James with a sudden, relieved acuity. 'Are you saying it's my sister you intend to offer for?'

'Of course, haven't I made that perfectly clear?'

A faint grin played around Rafe's lips. He'd been stupidly obtuse. Of course James wouldn't wed the widow. What had he been thinking of?

'May one ask if Celine reciprocates these feelings of yours?'

'I'm led to believe she may.' Anxiety drained his face of colour. 'I think I confounded the whole issue, causing her to withdraw her words.'

Rafe grinned at the desperation in James's eyes. Usually a man of logic, for once he seemed unable to form coherent thought. Rafe had despaired of his sister ever being offered the chance for happiness. Fate had brought together the two people he loved most.

'I hope you don't intend to ask permission of my father? He will not countenance it.'

'I see no reason why he should dismiss my petition as unsuitable.'

'He's in debt for a fortune to the Reverend Matthew Locke. The man is a distant relative, is heir after me, and holds the deeds to the estate. He covets both the title and the estate.

'Matthew is wealthy, and he keeps my father well supplied with liquor whilst he fuels his fire of hate towards me.' His grin held no warmth. 'My father will punish her by disinheriting me if she defies him. He's promised her to Matthew Locke in exchange for the cancellation of his debt and the return of Monkscroft's deeds. He'll be ruined without this match. He'll not give you permission to wed Celine.'

James's heart sank like a stone. 'If that be the case I'll not press my suit. Monkscroft estate is your birthright.'

'A birthright I cannot afford the upkeep of. As far as I'm concerned, Matthew can keep the deeds. I have Ravenswood, and Celine's happiness is far more important to me than Monkscroft.' Rafe smiled gently. 'Believe it or not, so is yours. If Celine will accept you it's with *my* blessing. You must wed privately and quickly, before my father gets word of it. I've heard Matthew Locke is making enquiries as to her whereabouts.'

'You're encouraging me to ask her to elope?' James was shocked. 'You think she'll agree to such a marriage?'

'The adventure of it might appeal to her. The heroines in the books she reads seem to enjoy being swept off their feet.'

James grinned sheepishly at the thought of sweeping any woman off her feet. 'I'll expect you to act as witness if Celine agrees to this foolishness.'

'That will bend Angelina's nose firmly out of countenance.' Rafe was chuckling at the thought as they turned into James's carriageway. His smile faded at the sight of a vehicle drawn up outside the house. 'Talk of the devil,' he muttered. 'If I'm not very much mistaken, that's the carriage of Matthew Locke.'

Entering the house, they handed their hats to a footman. James instructed the man to stay within earshot and the pair hurried into the drawing-room.

'James, my dear, and Lord Lynnbury.' Elizabeth's smile was unruffled, Rafe thought, as she rose gracefully from the couch and glided towards him, both hands outstretched. 'I'm so glad you're here.' Her hands trembled slightly when Rafe lightly kissed them. Close up, her eyes teemed with indignation.

'Your arrival is fortuitous.' Smile fading, she looked as uncertain as Angelina did on the occasions he teased her. 'I'm led to believe this gentleman is of your acquaintance.'

'I've never set eyes on the fellow in my life,' Rafe growled.

Elizabeth frowned. 'How odd.' Her hand waved in a dismissive motion towards the figure of a stocky curate who stood with his back to the window. 'The maid informed me he used your name as reference to gain admittance to the house. He says he's Samuel Locke, and *insists* he's the son of Lady Celine's affianced. He bears a letter, which he says is from her father, *demanding* she be returned to Monkscroft at once.'

Elizabeth turned, cutting the man in half with one glance before turning to James with a hint of what had gone before. 'I've advised him Lady Celine is ill and cannot be moved. In return, he offered me insult, insisting on examining her himself to determine if I'm telling him the truth.'

'That's not exactly what I said,' the curate protested.

'The sentiment behind your sermonizing was unmistakable, sir. You threatened me with the Lord's wrath.' Her green eyes spat scorn at the man. 'Take care, sir. The Lord may not regard you in such high esteem as you imagine. His wrath may fall upon your own head in the form of these two men here.'

The friends exchanged a grin.

'My words were not designed to caused you offence.'

'You'll excuse us, Stepmother.' James kissed Elizabeth's cheek and watched her go. He waited until the door closed before turning to Samuel Locke and engaging his eyes. 'Explain your outrageous behaviour at once, sir.'

'I'm curate to Reverend Matthew Locke, who is my father, and who is betrothed to Lady Celine Daventry.' Samuel Locke's voice was cold as he held out a paper waxed with the Gillingborn seal. 'The Marquis of Gillingborn has entrusted me with this missive, ordering Lady Celine to be placed in my care.'

'The missive has no jurisdiction in my home.' James's voice was deceptively mild and Rafe prepared to enjoy the encounter. He'd watched James at the law courts on occasion, and admired the way he was able to draw out a witness with his mild manner, then turn the prosecution on its head.

'You've been informed Lady Celine is indisposed, so I suggest you leave forthwith.'

'I'd sooner determine that for myself.' Samuel Locke's truculent expression matched his bullying tone of voice. 'If Lady Celine is too ill to be moved, I'll question her to acquaint myself with the nature of her sickness.'

'You are impudent, sir. I shall not allow you to submit my guest to such an indelicate interrogation.'

Rafe relaxed against the mantelpiece when James tugged at a bell-rope. To the manservant who appeared, James instructed, 'If this person does not remove himself from my house within the next few seconds you'll hasten to fetch a Runner. Tell them Samuel Locke is to be conveyed to the watch-house, where he's to be charged with obtaining entry by false pretences, trespass, and failing to obey an order lawfully given by a peer of the realm.'

Rafe chuckled when the curate's face paled. His lips thinned as he hastily snatched up his hat and headed for the door.

'Shall I relay your wishes for a speedy recovery to my sister?' Rafe asked, unable to resist a parting shot.

'You've not heard the last of this, Cousin,' he sneered. 'I'll be back with a warrant issued by the Archbishop of London himself. Lacking any means of support, you placed your sister in moral danger when you removed her from her father's loving care. By the time this is over she'll be grateful for the respectability my father's name offers, for no other man of standing will honour her with such.'

'Do not call me Cousin again, you parsimonious snipe.' Samuel Locke backed through the door when Rafe straightened, his fist smacking lightly against the palm of his other hand. 'Inform my father Celine is of an age to choose whom she'll wed. And as for moral danger, my sister is well chaperoned and her morals have never been safer.' As he stared into the mean little eyes of the parson's son, he shuddered. God help Celine if she's forced to wed into this family, he thought.

Rafe turned his back on the man in dismissal, not trusting himself to turn again until the door banged shut. He smiled ruefully when James poured them both a brandy.

'That man will never know how close he got to having his blood spilled all over your carpet. Can the charges be made to stick?'

'I'm unaware if such charges even exist.' James's eyes were troubled. 'We've not heard the last of Samuel Locke. If he petitions the archbishop on morals grounds—'

'I'll counter petition on the grounds that my father drove my mother to suicide, cast Celine's mother from the home without support and is not fit to have her in his care. When I rescued Celine, she'd been locked in her room without food for two days.'

'That has nothing to do with the corruption of her morals. She is subject to your father's will until she weds. A scandal of this type will ruin her prospects forever. She'll be ostracized.'

'Then so be it.' Neither of them had heard her enter the room. 'I'd sooner be dead than marry Matthew Locke.' Tears gathered in her eyes as she convinced herself of the fact by tasting the words again. 'Yes, I'd much rather be dead.'

'Rafe and I have a plan,' James mumbled. 'Actually, I think it was I who thought of it' He fell on one knee before her. 'If you'll have me, we shall elope this very night.'

Unable to stop himself, Rafe laughed. 'What an awkward oaf you are, James. If I was Celine I'd refuse you right away.'

'But you're not me, Rafe, and didn't I just hear you say I'm of an age to choose whom I shall wed?'

Celine was blushing quite prettily, Rafe noticed. Her eyes were shining as she gazed at James with something akin to worship. His friend's feelings were all too apparent. He gazed back at Celine with a hungry happiness Rafe envied. A look like that from a woman would be worth the wait, he mused, feeling decidedly superfluous as he edged towards the door, and a man should be afforded the luxury of proposing marriage in private.

'Do not keep me in misery,' James was saying as Rafe swiftly slid backwards through the door.

The next minute he sprawled flat on his back as he tripped over Angelina's foot. He gave a muffled curse and scrambled to his feet, his dignity in tatters. 'You were eavesdropping,' he accused, when she laughed.

'Such language is not fit for a lady's ears, Rafe Daventry. You'll apologize, I trust.'

'Most humbly, if that's your desire.' Inhaling the piquant perfume she wore he began to grin. 'Damn me, if that perfume isn't different from the one you usually wear.'

'It's French. Mama thought it was time I graduated from rose water, and took me to a perfumers. Being a woman is quite a business.' Drawing him away from the door, she said, with a lilt of laughter in her voice. 'I've discovered that perfume is the very essence of a woman.'

'And here was I thinking you were flesh and blood.'

'We're of one mind on that.' Her voice assumed a slight shyness. 'The perfumer told me, a scent, when properly chosen, absorbs the spirit of the wearer, changing to reflect her personality and mood.'

'You are the mistress of provocation then,' he accused, taking her hand to sniff the pulse where young ladies usually fragranced themselves. His second sniff increased in volume. 'Definitely provocative. It's well chosen.'

Her low, husky laugh sent a shiver up his spine. 'If there's a master of provocation it's you, not I.'

'Angelina, my dear, I thought I sent you to fetch my embroidery from the morning-room.' Elizabeth gazed from one to the other when Angelina snatched her hand away from his.

He took a step backwards, creating distance between them.

'I hope that unpleasant business is cleared up,' Elizabeth said, crossing to Angelina's side and giving her a penetrating glance. A faint blush surfaced on Angelina's face. Elizabeth turned the same glance his way, making him prickle uncomfortably. 'Lord Lynnbury, you should know better than encourage Angelina to linger in dim hallways.'

Chastised, he bowed slightly. 'You're right, Lady Elizabeth.'

'But it's not his fault—'

Elizabeth kept her voice gentle. 'Hush, child, Lord Lynnbury is well aware of the impropriety of the situation. He's accepted the rebuke and that's the end of it. Is that not so, Rafe?'

'It is.'

Angelina appeared most indignant for the second or two it took to realize the rebuke had been for her rather than for him. Her face became downcast. 'I'm sorry, Mama,' she murmured. Her contrite words brought a smile of forgiveness to Elizabeth's face and a glint of amusement to his own.

Rafe exchanged a small understanding smile with Elizabeth when she turned back towards him. 'You may think me indelicate, Rafe, but I wish to make my feelings known, even though it is not my business. I consider that cleric's family completely unsuitable for a gentle girl like Celine to marry into. As she's unburdened her heart to me, I intend to offer her the protection of Wrey House. My patronage of her will attract no gossip to damage her reputation or status.'

Angelina's eyes began to dance with excitement. Before Rafe could stop her she whispered, 'Do not worry about Celine. Something wonderful has happened. James is on his knees proposing marriage to her. They're going to elope this very night.'

A flash of lightning followed by a crack of thunder echoed in the hall. Angelina paled, gave a small whimper of fright and sidled closer to her mother. A protective arm was placed around her waist, drawing her close.

Elizabeth took the news in her stride, but Rafe saw delight sparkle in her eyes. 'James always knows how to do exactly the right thing at the right time,' she remarked, allowing a small, affectionate smile to illuminate her features. 'I'm glad he's found his heart's desire in Celine. In the short time we've been acquainted I've grown very fond of her. However' – her elegant shrug said it all – 'they will not be going anywhere tonight in this storm.'

She looked as if she had another plan up her sleeve. 'What else would you suggest?' he murmured.

'My suggestion is we discuss the marriage arrangements together over dinner. Your sister should not be obliged to wed without attendants, or in such a clandestine manner, and I'm surprised James suggested it.' Her smile became impish. 'A cousin of mine happens to be both minister of a small parish, and godson to the archbishop.'

'Really, Angelina!' She appeared indignant when Angelina gave an excited squeal and hugged her. She grinned at him over her daughter's shoulder, for a moment looking just like a young girl. 'This behaviour is not seemly for a young lady to indulge in,' she said, and placing her hands each side of Angelina's face she tenderly kissed her forehead. 'But on this occasion, I intend to allow you to get away with it.'

Three days later, James and Celine exchanged vows in a small church just outside London. Angelina, Elizabeth, and Rafe were all in attendance, as were several invited guests, carefully selected for their respectability and discretion.

The archbishop himself officiated at the ceremony. The guests included a relative of King George, a man for whom James had once provided a service. Elizabeth's meticulous planning had turned the wedding into a celebration, and given it the necessary stamp of approval.

That same day, Elizabeth and Angelina, accompanied by a baggage coach and Rafe on horseback serving as outrider, set out for Wrey House, leaving the newlyweds to begin their married life alone together.

CHAPTER EIGHT

It was almost dusk. Boredom had become the highwayman's companion. Traffic had been light over the past hour, the pickings lean. The excitement had gone out of the game.

One carriage only had fallen into the felon's clutches. The driver, a pale, perspiring merchant of wide girth, had been lightened by the removal of his bulging purse. His daughter had been relieved of a cameo brooch. Afraid she'd be ravished, she'd begged her father to save her. Had she but known it, she had nothing to fear. Any maid expecting a kiss to giggle over in like-minded company, would be sadly disappointed.

About to kick the stallion into a canter and abandon the evening's sport, the outlaw's ears picked up the faint sound of an oncoming carriage. Backing into the bushes, horse and rider melded with the shadows of the forest.

'We'll be home in just a little while.' Elizabeth took one of Angelina's hands between her own. 'You must be tired.'

'No more than you, Mama.' Angelina's eyes were sparkling with excitement. 'I'm so looking forward to meeting my sister and the rest of my family. If they are all as good to me as you and James, I cannot help but love them.' She raised her mother's hand to her face, her voice choked with emotion. 'You cannot imagine how happy I feel.'

Elizabeth's mind gave rise to misgivings. She couldn't imagine Rosabelle welcoming her sister with open arms. Had Angelina been plain, she might have tolerated her presence. But the girl was delicately beautiful, and Rosabelle vain.

Thomas would welcome her once he got over his initial awkwardness. Though obdurate at times, he was not a stupid man. She respected his judgement, appreciating the fact that he solicited her opinion on matters concerning the estate.

Sometimes she surprised a softness in his expression, as if he still felt towards her as he had in the early days of their marriage. The day before she'd left for London he'd come across her in the garden. Quite gently, he'd touched her cheek, then cleared his throat and hurried about his business.

Will's reaction to his new sister was harder to judge. He was complex, often displaying an ambiguity of nature. As a child he'd had a tendency to sulk when he couldn't get his own way. Sometimes he was utterly charming, other times, unbearably insolent or cruel.

Thomas had offered to buy his second born a commission in the army, a fitting career. Will had refused, coercing him into leasing a tumbledown village, instead. Situated on land bordered by hills and a small sheltered cove, there he successfully bred and schooled horses. Once used for smuggling, the village was rumoured to be haunted by ghosts of villagers who were slaughtered by the drunken crew of a pirate ship who'd put ashore for water.

Elizabeth sighed, wishing her relationship with Will was a little warmer. Only Rosabelle was close to him. From the time she'd brought her home, Will had doted on her. As she'd grown he'd taught her to ride almost as well as himself. Rosabelle was not clever, and adored her manipulative brother.

A tremor of apprehension ran through her. Angelina was as different from Rosabelle as fire was to ice. If Will and Rosabelle joined forces against her, Angelina would suffer.

'You mustn't expect too much,' she cautioned. 'As I explained, your sister is very different from you in looks and temperament.'

'Both James and Rafe have told me Rosabelle is very beautiful.'

Elizabeth's eyes sharpened. 'Rafe said that?'

She relaxed again when Angelina said artlessly, 'He agreed with James, which is much the same thing.'

Angelina glanced at the shadows of the forest, shivering when she thought she caught a glimpse of a horse and rider keeping pace with them between the trees. She chided herself for having such an active imagination. 'I wish we'd waited for the other carriage,' she said apprehensively.

They were travelling through a thicker part of the New Forest. The baggage coach had mired whilst fording a stream. Her mother, eager to reach the safety of home had elected to continue the journey on to Wrey House in the lighter, hired vehicle before it got too dark.

'Rafe will not be far behind us,' Elizabeth said lightly. 'The coachman will be stopping to light the lanterns soon. We should arrive home just after dusk.'

As soon as the words left her mouth the carriage slowed to a halt. But it was not to light the lamps. When her mother opened the door at the sound of voices they were confronted by a rider dressed from head to toe in black. A pistol in his hand was pointed at the coachman, whose arms were firmly held aloft.

Elizabeth blanched. 'What's the meaning of this? Only a coward would attack and rob two defenceless women.'

The highwayman turned and stared at her for long moments. His gun hand wavered slightly whilst the other tightened on the reins. There was a feverish glitter in the rogue's eyes, as if he was struggling to hold back laughter. When he spoke his voice was strangely muffled by the scarf around his lower face.

'Hand over your coin.'

Angelina pulled the door shut, glaring at the man with all the ferocity she could muster. 'We will do no such thing. If you take one step towards my mother and myself you'll be extremely sorry.'

'Angelina,' her mother implored, seeming almost near to fainting. 'Do not inflame him with harsh words, I beg of you.'

'You'd be wise to listen to your mama.' The outlaw's dark eyes swept over her face and she nearly recoiled from the animosity in them. Her heart began to pound, her hand curled about her mother's cane as the horse sidestepped towards them.

'Be gone,' she hissed, surprised she could speak at all considering her fear. 'We have no valuables with us and my mother is alarmed almost to fainting.' She smiled as the sound of the second carriage came to her ears. 'In a few moments our escort will be here, then you'll be routed, sir. We have a company of soldiers with us.'

The robber gave a wavering laugh. He stared in the direction they'd come from, muttering, 'There is but the sound of one carriage and a horse.'

Raising the cane above her head, Angelina brought it down upon the flank of his mount. The horse reared and the highwayman's pistol discharged, effectively disarming him.

'*Lucifer's oath!*' he cursed, in a high-pitched squeak as he fought to regain control. Leaning into the coach he snatched the cane from her and raised it.

Moonlight touched on a glint of gold at the exposed wrist between gauntlet and sleeve as it descended, two hearts entwined. Giving a moan, her mother threw herself forward. The cane glanced off her shoulder, causing her to cry out in anguish.

'You blackguard!' Angelina sprang at the man, raking at his face with her nails. The cloth fell away, giving a glimpse of a smooth, youthful countenance before the disguise was snatched back over his face.

'You'll pay for that,' the highwayman warned, and wheeled his horse about. Within seconds he'd been swallowed by the forest, the sound of his departure fading within seconds.

Rafe arrived to find the coachman frozen with fear, his arms still raised on high. Elizabeth had collapsed in Angelina's arms.

'A highwayman,' she explained briefly when he sprang from his horse. 'Do not bother to go after the man, Rafe. It's almost dark and we need the comfort of your presence here. My mother has been injured.'

She gazed at the coachman, saying with a certain amount of asperity, 'You may lower your arms and go about the business of lighting the lanterns, Biggins. The black-hearted coward has gone.'

Rafe marvelled at her strength. She was no shrinking violet when faced with adversity. A sharply astringent scent reached him when she held a silver-topped vial under Elizabeth's nose. She murmured with satisfaction when Elizabeth recovered enough to recline against the cushions. Returning the vial to her pocket, she gently fanned her mother's face.

'You were struck on the shoulder, Mama. Can you tell me if you are badly injured?'

'Just bruised,' Elizabeth whispered, beginning to cry.

'Hush, Mama,' she soothed. 'Rafe's here, so we're quite safe now.' She took the monogrammed silver flask he offered. 'Sip a little of this brandy. When you feel stronger we shall resume our journey.' Presently, the colour returned to Elizabeth's face. Angelina turned to him, her eyes stormy in the lantern light. Her hair had been loosened in the fracas and was shot through with a coppery glow.

Struck by the vibrant beauty of her mood, he smiled at her. 'You have a great deal of courage, Angelina.'

'Damn me, if she didn't strike the horse with a cane,' the coachman suddenly babbled, his eyes nearly bulging from their sockets with fright. 'She soon showed him she wasn't some shrinking miss. I've never seen the likes of it before, a young scrap of a thing like 'er takin' on a highwayman with a pistol cocked and ready to go—'

'That's quite enough, Mr Biggins.' The firmness of her voice stilled the flood of words. 'Because of the ordeal we've suffered I'll overlook your impertinence this time.' She rolled her eyes and sent him a smile. 'Lord Lynnbury, perhaps a small nip from your flask will soothe his nerves long enough to enable him to do what he does most admirably, and that is to drive this carriage safely on to Wrey House.'

'And what of you,' Rafe murmured, wondering at her presence of mind, 'have you not taken fright?'

'I was terrified out of my wits,' she admitted. 'But when angry, I'm often endowed with false courage.' She shot an astutely calculating glance at her mother. 'Lady Alexandra told me it was an unfortunate trait, which I should strive to curtail.'

Elizabeth's spine straightened as if she'd been drawn up on a string. 'So is stealing another woman's child. I would prefer that woman's name not to be mentioned again, Angelina.'

'Yes, Mama.' Although the glance she turned his way was innocent, a grin flirted at the corner of her mouth.

Cunning little minx, he thought, trying not to grin himself. She has an instinct for saying the right thing to suit the circumstances.

Just then the second coach came up behind them and all was pandemonium again. Rafe took charge, bidding them light the lanterns and arming the second coach driver with one of his pistols as a precaution. He issued instructions that they must stay together for the rest of the journey.

Half an hour later, they turned into the elaborate wrought-iron gates of Wrey House. Noticing the nervousness in Angelina's face, Rafe's heart went out to her. Keep your courage high, little Angel, he thought. You'll undoubtedly need it over the next few days.

Although the splendour of Wrey House was unexpected, Angelina did not allow her surprise to show. James had told her the house had been remodelled by his grandfather in the Palladian style, but he'd given no hint of its grandeur.

The hallway was of chequered green and white marble with the family crest set in the circle in the middle. Over it, hung a huge chandelier of glittering crystal. Doors were set in alcoves, and flanked by columns. There was bronze statuary of men engaged in heroic action. A stairway stretched upwards from either side to a gallery above, which was lined with portraits.

Angelina was disappointed she couldn't see the charming inner courtyard James had described. He'd told her it contained a fountain, and was surrounded on three sides by the older part of the house.

Elizabeth led her straight to the chamber prepared for her, one not far from her own. It faced west to take advantage of the afternoon sun. Candles blazed in wall sconces.

The room had wall panels of watered grey silk, and delicate blue bed hangings embroidered all over with peacocks. Matching curtains hung at the windows, and a soft Aubusson carpet stretched across the floor. The furniture was painted eggshell blue and gilded with gold. Joined by a dressing-room large enough to accommodate her gowns and accessories twice over, was her maid's quarters.

Clara, the plain, sensible maid hired by James, earned a word of praise from Elizabeth when she immediately set about unpacking her mistress's things. Despite her ungraceful appearance, Clara was clever with her hands and had a good eye for style. Angelina was more than pleased with her, though she missed Bessie.

After refreshing themselves, Elizabeth, still pale from her ordeal and carrying her bruised shoulder a trifle stiffly, sent a servant to inform her husband they would present themselves in his study in a little while.

Angelina received a brief embrace and a word of warning before they left. 'My husband ... your father, is not a demonstrative man. If his welcome is a little restrained, I'd ask you to bear that in mind.'

'I will, Mama.' She gave her mother a tremulous smile and strove to control the catch in her voice. 'It must have distressed the earl when he discovered I still lived. I'm thankful you did not reject me. My existence must have been a complete shock to you.'

'I clearly remember holding you in my arms for a brief moment. It's Rosabelle I cannot. . . .' Her voice trailed off, the faraway look in her eyes replaced by a determined brightness. 'Let's not get too maudlin, my dear. The earl becomes rather brusque when presented with sentimentality.'

'You make him sound like an ogre,' she murmured, shivering a little as she remembered the treatment Celine received from the hands of her own father. 'Is he a man to be feared?'

Elizabeth linked an arm through hers and led her from the room. 'He's a good man at heart, desiring only to be obeyed and respected. He does not seek fault where there is none, and although reluctant to admit to being in the wrong, he does not lay blame on others unjustly. I'm sure Thomas will grow to love you as I do, in time.'

Angelina wasn't so sure the earl wanted to get to know her. He gazed at her curiously when she sank before him in a curtsy, saying in a gruff voice, 'You're like your mother, child.'

The earl resembled James a little, she thought. He was darker, the hook in his nose more pronounced. Tall and upright, his skin was tanned and creased from the outdoors. His greying, dark hair was thick and wavy. There was nothing welcoming about his dark, unwavering eyes, but neither were they unwelcoming. He ignored her tentative smile, and her voice shook with nerves when she requested, 'I ask for your blessing, My Lord.'

'You have it, Daughter.' She took the strong, calloused hand he offered and stood trembling before him. 'I welcome you to the home you've never seen, to the family you've never known. I hope you'll be happy amongst us.'

'Thank you.' She gave her mother an uncertain look, then encouraged by her smile went to stand demurely by her side.

'Rafe told me you were waylaid by a highwayman,' the earl said, his glance softening as it went to her mother. 'I trust you were not badly hurt.'

'It's just a bruise.'

'Good, good.' When his eyes flicked suddenly back to her, Angelina held her breath. 'My wife's injury was due to a certain recklessness on your part, I believe.'

'I . . . I do not understand what you mean, sir,' she stammered, spots of colour staining her cheeks. 'If anything I did contributed to Mama's injury it was unintentional, and I most deeply regret it.'

'You did nothing, my dear.' Elizabeth's voice was decidedly frosty. 'Had it not been for her courage I'm sure the rogue would have killed us both . . . or worse.' She gave a delicate shudder. 'If Rafe's account of the incident gives substance to such accusation, I'd be interested to hear it, Thomas.'

'Perhaps I misunderstood.' The earl shrugged and managed a smile. 'You must think ill of a father who welcomes you home one minute and chastises you the next.'

'Indeed, I'm glad to discover I *have* a father. I'll do my utmost to conduct myself in a manner of which you'll be proud.'

He gazed reflectively at her. 'That's well said, child.' Stooping, he brushed her forehead with his lips. 'Let us be done with formality. As I'm your father it's fitting you should address me thus.'

'Thank you . . . Father.' How sweet the word tasted on her lips. *Her father, at long last. All the time she was growing up, how she'd longed for a family.* Without thinking she crossed to where he stood and laid her head against his shoulder. 'Dearest, Father, how I've longed for this moment.'

A hand awkwardly patted her shoulder.

'*How touching, Papa!*' The earl stiffened and moved away when a flurry of rose-coloured taffeta pushed between them. Luminous dark eyes swiftly assessed her. 'Strange, we look nothing alike.' Her sister's eyes narrowed as she took possession of the earl's arm. Her exotic beauty was flawed by the hostility in her eyes when she drawled, 'I am Rosabelle.'

'I'm Angelina.' The instant surge of dislike she felt for Rosabelle dismayed her. They were as unalike as two people could get, and she sensed it had very little to do with looks.

Her mother took her hand, squeezing it in comfort. Not by word or gesture did Angelina betray her feelings. Her smile remained serene. 'I'm happy to meet you at last, Rosabelle.'

They stared at each other, she and her sister, with nothing else to say. The silence deepened, yet neither broke it. Rosabelle clung to the earl's arm. There was a closeness between the two Angelina would never enjoy. It was a closeness of familiarity, of the love a father bears for a daughter.

I'm your daughter, too, her heart cried out. *It was not my fault your love was denied me.*

The silence was broken by the door clicking open. Footsteps advanced, and with the sound came tension. A man moved into her vision, a deep voice said quietly, 'I'm sorry I was not here to greet you, Angelina.'

Prickles crept slowly up her spine, as if an unseen menace existed in the room. The man was big and strong-looking, his hair and eyes dark, his appearance handsome. His smile didn't reach his eyes, which were disconcertingly direct and never wavered from her face. She wondered if this direct gaze was characteristic of the Wrey family.

'You must be William.' She couldn't understand why she whispered, except her throat had become unaccountably dry.

'That's so.' His eyes searched every inch of her face as if to imprint it on his memory. A small intake of breath hissed annoyance between his teeth. 'You are very much like your mama. I expected some resemblance to Rosabelle.'

Angelina wanted to step back when William embraced her, but was prevented by the pressure of his fingers on her arms. She managed to keep her voice light. 'Both you and James resemble the earl, but in different ways.'

'If you think that you haven't met Frey.' William's glance flicked to the earl; his mouth twitched. 'Frey is the image of the earl.'

'Frey?' She was so tense she staggered, off-balance, when William released her. Her mother's hand touched against her elbow to steady her.

'That's enough, Will.' Her father was having trouble keeping his temper under control. Rosabelle gave a soft giggle when Will threw him an insolent glance.

'Angelina has to know sooner or later, Father. After all, your bastard is her half-brother too.'

'Your behaviour is unfit for a gentleman, and inappropriate for this occasion.' The earl bowed stiffly to his wife, his eyes unable to conceal the humiliated rage he felt. 'I'm sorry, Elizabeth. Perhaps you'll take our daughters upstairs where they may become better acquainted. I wish to speak to William alone.'

It was a silent trio who left. Halfway up the stairs they heard voices raised in anger, then the sound of a blow.

Rosabelle turned on her mother, her face contorted with rage. 'See what you've done by bringing this creature into the house? If Will is hurt, I'll never forgive you.'

'Control yourself. Will should not have spoken to his father so.'

'You've never understood him. *Never!*' Gathering her skirts together, Rosabelle fled up the stairs. She turned at the top, accusing 'And you've never loved me.'

'That's not true,' Elizabeth protested. 'Without knowing it I was grieving all this time for Angelina.'

'Well, now you have her back,' Rosabelle spat out. 'But don't think anyone will like you any better for it. You're cold-hearted, Mama. Even your husband seeks his pleasure in another woman's bed.'

Elizabeth's gasp was anguished. Angelina gave Rosabelle a shocked glance when she swaggered back down the stairs, smiling at her mother's ashen face. 'Mary knows how to make your husband happy in bed. The earl cannot bring himself to enjoy you like he does his mistress, not even from duty.'

After the highwayman, this was the last straw. The sound of the slap was so loud it shocked them all. Anger burning in her, Angelina knew it had been she who'd dealt the blow. Rosabelle stared at her, cheek reddening, tears of shock gathering her eyes.

She'd deserved it, Angelina thought, feeling not one iota of guilt as she hissed, 'Your lack of delicacy is so disgusting it shames and dishonours the name you bear.'

The enormity of her behaviour suddenly dawned in Rosabelle's eyes. She began to sob, though more from fear than remorse, Angelina suspected. Her father would surely be furious if he found out. 'I'm sorry, Mama, I didn't mean any of it.'

'Go to your bed-chamber, Rosabelle,' Elizabeth said faintly. 'Wait there until I send for you.'

As Rosabelle fled, Elizabeth clutched at the balustrade. 'I feel unwell, my dear. Help me to my chamber.'

'Perhaps I can be of assistance.'

Rafe came up the stairs behind them, scooping Elizabeth up in his arms just as she collapsed. Following her to her mother's bed-chamber, Rafe gently laid her on the bed. He turned to her, his eyes understanding and absorbing her distress. 'Is there anything else I can do?'

'Thank you, Rafe, but no. It's only a faint, the maid and I will take care of her.' As he made his way to the door she said in a tremulous voice, 'Did you observe what took place?'

She could have blessed him when he answered, 'I had only just come from the library. If I overheard anything. . . .' He shrugged. 'Rest assured, I'm the soul of discretion.'

'Thank you, Rafe.'

'If I do not see you tomorrow before I leave, sleep well, Angel.' Two strides brought him back to where she stood. His lips touched her nose, then he tipped up her chin and brushed her lips with his mouth. His kiss was soft, like the touch of butterfly wings. It robbed her of her breath and her voice.

She knew she should have protested and darted a swift glance at her mother, relieved to find she'd not come round from her faint.

Rafe chuckled when she blushed. Giving her a small bow, he turned and strode off towards the stairs, leaving her open-mouthed with astonishment.

CHAPTER NINE

Thomas Wrey's eyes brooded on Mary Mellor.

How different she was from Elizabeth, he thought, experiencing a mixture of guilt and revulsion. He loved his wife, every minute spent in her company was an agony of desire and he longed to recapture the earlier days of their loving. He just couldn't risk it, not while she was still young enough to conceive a child.

Conscience churning, he pulled on his breeches and jacket, then fumbled in his pocket for some coins.

Mary frowned when he threw them on the bed. 'Frey has applied for a clerk's position on the Marquis of Northbridge's estate, My Lord. He'll be needing a new suit of clothes if he's taken on.'

'If Frey wants anything, he only has to ask.'

'And you knows he won't ask you for nothing.' Fisting her hands to her hips Mary's voice rose. 'Why can't I have an allowance for him?'

Thomas looked askance at her. 'Frey has had more than most in his position. He has a decent roof over his head, an education, and food in his belly. He's reached manhood and has to make his own way in life now.' He turned away in dismissal. 'I'll put in a good word for him with the marquis.'

'And the clothes?' she demanded.

'No doubt Will's servant can find something he has outgrown. You can collect them from the gate-house.'

'Charity,' Mary mumbled. 'He won't thank you for it.'

'Frey has too much pride.' He turned, fixing her with a hard stare. He should terminate this relationship, the woman was getting above herself.

'He takes after you in that. You give more to the daughter of a harlot than your own blood. What would Lady Elizabeth do if someone told her about Rosabelle?'

Two strides took him back to her; his fingers gripped her arms. 'Never mention My Lady's name with your foul breath again! Be careful, woman; if your tongue loosens, it may be necessary to detach it from your mouth.'

Face turning to ashes, she struggled to get free of him. 'You wouldn't.'

Of course he wouldn't, but it wouldn't hurt to frighten her a little. 'Be warned, my dear.' He shoved her on to the bed and his cane descended with a carefully aimed thwack just an inch from her head. She gave a frightened squeal.

The whole house shuddered when the earl slammed the door shut after him.

Mary was still trembling. He'd never threatened her with violence before. She should have just taken his money and kept her mouth shut, the way she always did.

Why had she brought his wife into the conversation? She should have remembered he whispered her name in the heat of his passion.

Mary convinced herself that her threat was empty chatter. She'd do nothing to harm Rosabelle. Hadn't she cared for the girl as if she were her own? Rosabelle had never forgotten her old nurse, but the earl and his fine lady would have a fit if they knew about the visits.

Pulling on a patched gown, she rebraided her hair. She smiled as she tied a strip of rag around the end. She'd not lost her looks, and if she'd gained a bit of flesh . . . well, a man liked a bit of padding in the right place. No wonder the earl preferred her to that thin wife of his. The countess was insipid with her milk-white skin, pale hair and narrow hips. She was probably frigid.

'And who would want eyes that horrible green colour?' Mary muttered. 'They're downright peculiar if you ask me.'

Strange how the sickly child had turned up, and without a breath of scandal. Who'd have thought it of that old sour-puss, Alexandra Chadwick? She grinned, imagining the expression on the earl's face when he'd been informed.

Voices in the garden drew her attention. She moved to the open window. Frey had arrived back from town just in time to meet his father. The pair stared at each other, mirror images, both as prickly as a pair of fighting cocks.

She wanted to laugh when Frey stated firmly, 'I'd prefer to gain employment by my own merit, sir.'

'At least let me buy you a suit of clothes, Frey. Damn it, my boy, blood is thicker than water after all.'

'No thank you, sir.' Frey's aggravated politeness bordered on inso-
lence.

Stubborn young fool, she thought.

The earl, his face a picture of haughty affront, mounted his grey. 'I
could find you a position on the Wrey estate.'

'The position would be untenable, sir.'

'Perhaps you're right.' He leaned down to pat Frey on the shoulder,
frowning when Frey took a step backward. He cleared his throat. 'The
rector informs me you applied yourself diligently to your lessons.'

'The rector is a learned man, and as he pointed out to me' – a bitter
smile curved Frey's lips – 'opportunities for education seldom occur for
the likes of me.' He stared straight into his father's eyes. 'I hope the
expense of my education was justified. I'd prefer you didn't feel cheated
in any way.'

'Quite so.' The earl's face turned a mottled shade of red when he
glanced up and saw her watching from the window.

'You'll have to excuse me, My Lord, I need to complete some Latin
translation before the daylight goes.'

The earl took a purse from his pocket, weighing it in his hand as Frey
strode, stiff-backed, towards the house. Deftly, she caught the purse when
he threw it up to her.

The grey gave a shrill, startled whinny when the earl dug his heels into
its side. She watched him retreat from her sight, then feverishly tipped the
contents of the purse on to the rumpled bed. She smiled triumphantly
when she saw gold gleaming amongst the silver.

Thomas regretted his over-generous gesture as he rode away from the
cottage. Frey and Mary were becoming a problem, he realized, nodding at
a couple of villagers who doffed their hats. The village women resented
her. She was not from these parts, and because of their relationship she'd
never earned either their trust or respect. Frey was in the unenviable position of being of neither class, and was scorned by both.

Frey had exceeded all his expectations with regards to his education.
He experienced a flare of pride. Like James, he'd taken Latin in his stride,
could pen a good hand and had an aptitude for figures.

Priding himself on the fact that the boy had inherited more of his traits
than just looks, Thomas, as always, decided to bury the problem for the
time being. The purse he'd given Mary would effectively silence her, even
if his threat had not.

As for Frey? Once he'd matured a little he'd realize how well off he was. He had a birthday soon. He'd noticed that the nag the boy rode was almost on its knees. The gift of a sound horse would soon bring him round.

Pushing Frey to the back of his mind he gave thought to Rosabelle's birthday and a suitable gift. He'd considered buying her the ruby pendant she so desired, but there was the expense of the ball and the dowry. He frowned. Rosabelle fared badly when placed against Angelina. He'd spoiled the girl over the years. However, she was eighteen, and would soon be wed and off his hands. Something of value would be appropriate for the occasion, something from the family jewel collection? Perhaps he wouldn't go that far, he thought.

Rosabelle has no Wrey blood, a voice in his head reminded him. *Angelina is your true daughter*.

He experienced a grudging respect towards Alexandra Chadwick, who'd raised her well, then salved her conscience by making the girl her heir. There would be no trouble finding Angelina a husband, and with James as her legal guardian, it wouldn't cost him a penny piece.

It never occurred to him that he could challenge James's rights to her guardianship: he was as happy to leave her future to another, as he had her past.

Rafe's worn riding boots had been burnished to a high polish. He tapped his crop against them, pleasing the servant who'd accomplished the miracle with a word of praise.

He was about to visit Ravenswood. Seeing it in its dilapidated state was a depressing prospect, but the memories it held for him were dear, giving him a sense of happiness and peace. He owed the caretaker couple several months' wages, and the fact that he now had funds to pay them, pleased him.

Rafe had taken up residence in Tewsbury Manor a week previously, and welcomed the solitude. For too long he'd been a guest in someone else's home, socially obligated to be on his best behaviour and at the beck and call of the host family. Except when in the company of James, Rafe couldn't remember when he'd felt so relaxed.

The owner of the estate was a minor peer. Sir Edward Truscott possessed a vague and retiring nature, and had been pathetically eager to have Rafe take charge of his home in his long absence.

'You'll be doing me a great service,' Sir Edward had said, immediately making Rafe feel *he* was the one doing the favour. 'Since my steward left

I've been forced to run the estate myself with a clerk to assist. I've had a devilish time trying to find a steward who's competent. Unfortunately, the clerk has stated his intention to leave at the end of the month. If I could prevail upon you to find suitable staff in my absence. . . .'

Rafe was pondering where he could find a decent clerk at short notice when the sound of a carriage came to his ears. Shortly afterwards, Elizabeth Wrey and her daughters were announced

Elizabeth kissed him lightly on both cheeks. 'We thought we'd call and make sure you're settled in. You're looking quite rested. The country air suits you.'

Rosabelle's appearance took Rafe's breath away. He remembered a precocious, pretty child with bold eyes who'd flirted foolishly with him. She had become a woman of exotic beauty. Clad in a gown of burgundy stripes over pink, a gauze scarf was draped modestly around the neckline and secured with a bunch of violets. It emphasized, rather than hid, the full swell of her bosom.

Her eyes sought his as he automatically bore her hand to his lips to be kissed. They were still bold, seductive almost, and filled with a cupidity that made Rafe wonder if she was still intact. He dismissed the errant thought as being unworthy of him. She would be well chaperoned by her family, the opportunity to confer her favours on anyone, unlikely. Deciding to steer clear of the girl he turned to Angelina, immediately feeling comfortable.

She was a breath of spring in a white dress embroidered with garlands of green flowers. Her tawny hair was piled high and topped with a frivolous straw bonnet tied under her chin with green ribbons. A mass of white daisies decorated the brim. She grinned widely, as if overjoyed to see him. Damn it if he hadn't missed her.

'Hello, Angel.'

'My Lord.' Mischief in her eyes, she dropped him a deep curtsy. 'Your invitation to visit has been noticeable by its absence, so I persuaded Mama to call on you. I intend to take you to task.'

Rafe chuckled as he took her hands in his, bringing her upright. If Elizabeth hadn't been present he'd have hugged her. He contented himself with kissing her silk-gloved hands. 'Hasn't your mama told you it's unseemly for a young woman to take a man to task?'

'I've not noticed any reluctance in Mama to do exactly the same when needed.' Her eyes sparkled when she sent Elizabeth a smile. 'Besides, you're not *any* man, Rafe. Now you're related to me by marriage, you must consider yourself almost a brother.'

'I didn't notice you taking James to task,' Rafe observed, his glance flicking to Rosabelle in a vain attempt to discover a shred of familial likeness between the two girls.

Rosabelle's full lips were parted slightly, there was an unmistakable invitation contained in her smile. Her dark, limpid eyes rested seductively upon his face, sucking him in like a velvet whirlpool. A tiny prickle of unease chased through his body. Tearing his eyes away from her disconcerting ripeness, he concentrated on what Angelina was saying.

'James doesn't need taking to task. Indeed, the only time he teases me is when he's in your company.'

'Then I plead guilty only to being a bad influence on him.' He chuckled, peering at her creamy-complexioned face with mock seriousness. 'I do believe you've gathered a country freckle or two.'

She looked crushed and placed her hands against her cheeks. He wished he'd never mentioned it when Rosabelle gave a malicious laugh. 'It must be tedious to be covered in unattractive brown blotches.'

'I didn't say they were blotches, nor did I indicate they were unattractive.' He managed to keep his voice even, though Rosabelle's catty remark annoyed him enough to offer up a reproof. 'One or two freckles add charm.' He bowed in Elizabeth's direction. 'I've always thought ladies of Angelina's complexion to be exceedingly attractive.'

The complexion under discussion turned a delicate shade of pink. Rosabelle's reddened with annoyance.

Having extricated himself as best as possible from an awkward situation, Rafe changed to a safer topic. 'Will you stay and take some refreshment?'

'We do not wish to detain you,' Elizabeth said firmly. 'You're dressed for riding and must have more pressing business to attend to.'

'I was going to Ravenswood. There are some minor domestic details I must attend to.' An idea came into Rafe's head and he moved towards the bell-pull. 'A man would be a fool to part company with the three most beautiful ladies in the district. The day is fair and I have use of Sir Edward's carriage. If you'd agree to accompany me I'll instruct the staff to pack us a basket of refreshments and we can picnic by the stream.'

Angelina clapped her hands in delight. 'Please say yes, Mama. I've heard much from Rafe about Ravenswood and am eager to see it for myself.'

'I have a headache,' Rosabelle said sullenly, obviously set to spoil Angelina's enjoyment. She pressed her fingers against her forehead, making small sounds of distress.

Elizabeth saw right through her subterfuge. 'I'll instruct the coachman to drive you home, Rosabelle. I'm most interested see Ravenswood, myself. There's plenty of time for the carriage to come back for us.'

Rosabelle withdrew her hand from the site of her pain. 'I don't want to spoil the outing. No doubt my headache will improve.'

'I won't hear of it, dear.' Elizabeth grasped her arm and encouraged her to her feet. 'You must go home and rest, otherwise you'll be disagreeable company.'

Before Rosabelle had time to protest she was ushered gently, but firmly from the house and into the carriage.

'Ingratiating upstart,' Rosabelle snarled, when the carriage turned towards home. 'If you think Rafe will fall in love with a skinny little lap dog like you, you've got a surprise coming.' She forgot her ire when she remembered the way Rafe humoured Angelina, as if she was a child.

Rafe was a man with a man's appetites. Her mouth parted in excitement at the desire she'd seen in his eyes. He'd tried to disguise it, but it had flared up every time he'd glanced her way. It thrilled her. He would be able to satisfy the urges that plagued her.

Rosabelle couldn't put Rafe from her mind, and by the time Wrey House hove into view her blood was in turmoil. Changing into her riding outfit she sent for her horse. Once mounted, she turned its nose towards the sea, heading for the village where William kept his stud. She rode the horse hard, her lips parted in a smile as she recklessly pitted it against obstacles in her path.

William was her confidant and friend; he'd like to be her lover. He would help her with Rafe. If her father knew of Will's unhealthy desires, he'd throw him out without a penny. He might even kill him.

Her eyes widened with the thrill of finding a weapon to use against her brother, and she wondered why she hadn't thought of it before. Oh yes, William would help her trap Rafe Daventry into marriage. She'd give him no choice.

'Ravenswood is a beautiful house. How can you bear to live anywhere else?'

With Angelina perched beside him, Rafe had drawn the carriage to a halt at the top of a rise and was gazing down at his home, a rueful half-smile on his lips.

From this distance the decay was not apparent. The house nestled between gently swelling hills, and looked beautiful indeed. Between them and the house was a stone bridge, beneath which a stream sparkled in the sunlight.

'The stream joins the Lymington River which flows through the New Forest,' Rafe told her.

Elizabeth pointed. 'What are those figures on the gables? I cannot quite make them out.'

'They're mythical gods. The one on the left corner is Pan. The pipes he holds are hollow and have a legend attached to them. It's said if Pan's pipes rouse a maid from her slumber, she'll fall in love with the Master of Ravenswood.'

'Is the legend true?' Angelina asked in breathless anticipation.

'I've not put it to the test.' Seeing the delight in her eyes he teased her with a smile. 'My grandmother vouched for the legend's authenticity. She swore she heard a refrain played on the pipes, and immediately fell in love with my grandfather. They were very happy together.'

A wistful smile touched her lips. 'A home must be a happy place when the occupants love each other.'

Remembering she'd had been deprived of her mother's love, Rafe told her as he set the carriage in motion, 'Ravenswood certainly holds happy memories for me, but do not expect too much. Much of it dates back to the sixteenth century. The hall is medieval, and quite beautiful. The rest of the house has been added over the years and is full of narrow passages and steps. For me, its unpredictability adds to the charm. Dry rot has rendered some of the upstairs chambers unsafe, and until I can afford to restore them they must remain locked.'

As they drew closer, Angelina could plainly see the neglect. The honey-coloured sandstone walls were discoloured, ivy had taken a hold and had made inroads into the mortar. Dislodged by a storm, slates lay upon the ground, or haphazardly on the slope of the roof. The windows were mullioned, the upper lights painted in heraldic designs.

The arched gateway through which they passed revealed sagging, rusted gates. The gate-house was deserted. Weeds were everywhere. Amongst the neglect was a rose garden, heavy with blooms. The plants were choked with alien growth and old wood, gnarled from lack of pruning.

Yet the garden was alive with colour, fragrant with perfume and humming with marauding bees. It was a garden of hedged-in places and surprises. Here was a lime tree walk leading into an archway of climbing roses. The other side revealed a fountain and pond enclosed in a walled arbour, with stone seats and ivy climbing up walls. One secret place led into another, and she was enchanted by the image of what it had once been.

When Rafe helped her down from the carriage, a couple of red-coated hounds bounded through the open front door and barked with frenzied delight as they nearly bowled Rafe over. She was the subject of a variety of sniffs, then whipped by furiously wagging tails before Rafe managed to subdue the animals and send them packing.

He was trying not to laugh when she straightened her skirts. 'I should have warned you they were ill-mannered brutes.' He offered his hand to Elizabeth. 'You may alight with complete safety now.'

'Thank you, Rafe.' Her mother came to stand beside her as an elderly man, still buttoning his coat, made his way towards them. He was out of breath and ill-at-ease at being caught unprepared. 'I'm sorry, My Lord. If I'd known you were coming, I'd have been properly dressed.'

'It's quite all right, Mr Eastman. Were not staying long. How is your good wife?'

'Well, My Lord.' Eastman gave him a dignified smile. 'She'll be pleased to see you, sir, very pleased.'

'Tell her I'll be along to see her presently.' Rafe escorted them both to the drawing-room then excused himself, explaining that Mrs Eastman had once been his nurse and would surely box his ears if he neglected to pay his respects at once.

Angelina gazed around her with curiosity. The room had a shabby comfort. The furniture was old and heavy but polished to a high patina, the upholstery was threadbare. Though the floor lacked rugs the bare boards were cleanly swept.

A huge fireplace dominated one wall, the mantel was free of ornaments except for a French clock in the shape of a lyre and a bowl of freshly cut roses. Over the fireplace was a paler shape on the panelling where once a picture had hung.

She crossed to a harpsichord, which was beautifully painted with scenes of dancers in various poses. The scale she played rang true. 'How odd,' she murmured. 'The harpsichord is still in tune.'

Rafe said from the doorway, 'Mr Eastman used to teach music when he was younger.' He took a sheet of music from a drawer and handed it to her. 'Do you know this piece? It was my grandmother's favourite.'

'By heart. Johann Sebastian Bach was also a favourite composer of my. . . ?' She gave a swift glance in her mother's direction, and noted her frown. 'Of mine.' She began to play the sonata, her touch light and sure.

When the piece ended there was silence. She gazed nervously around her, wondering if her lack of practice had been apparent. Eyes closed, her mother rested her chin on one gloved hand. Rafe was staring at her, his countenance of such serious expression her heart grew apprehensive wings.

'What's wrong?' she whispered.

Rafe crossed to her side, his eyes moist. 'I had not realized you were quite so accomplished. For a moment I imagined it was my grandmother playing.'

Elizabeth came to enfold her in a hug. 'Even though that woman deprived me of your love, I'm thankful she educated you in the proper manner.'

'She did indeed, Mama.' Angelina frowned in disgust. 'Lady Alexandra was disagreeably obdurate when it came to my education. As for depriving you of my love, I prefer to think the pleasure was postponed, because my eyes touched upon your face and I experienced a love I'd never known.'

'Dearest, child.' Elizabeth's voice trembled with emotion as she gently touched her daughter's cheek. She gazed at Rafe with tearful eyes. 'Ravenswood must be enchanted. See how maudlin we've become.'

'Your happiness touches my heart.' Rafe turned towards the decanter, allowing Elizabeth time to control herself. 'Will you take a glass of Madeira before I show you the rest of my humble home? Near the river is a sheltered glade. At this time of day its shaded from the sun, and perfect for a picnic.'

'I've no head for Madeira. Let's inspect Ravenswood then proceed to your glade before the sun encroaches upon it.' Her mother sounded determinedly gay. 'The difficulties of handling a parasol whilst trying to eat are almost insurmountable, do you not think so, Angelina?'

'Undoubtedly.' She wondered if her face reflected the happiness she felt here. 'And I promise you, Rafe, I'm so hungry I shall probably eat an entire pie all by myself.'

Rafe chuckled as he ushered them from the room. 'Be careful, Angel. The pie is as big as a carriage wheel. You may be forced to don a larger gown to accommodate it if I hold you to that promise.'

The day passed pleasantly, but too quickly. Angelina found Ravenswood's gentle shabbiness charming. There was a sense of quiet hope about the place, of longing. It breathed with a magic all of its own and touched her spirit, drawing her into the unmistakable warmth of its welcoming aura.

When she and her mother returned to the more formal, and much larger, Wrey House, Angelina realized it would never feel like home to her.

CHAPTER TEN

'You're giving her Moonlight?' Rosabelle gazed stormily at her brother. 'I thought you disliked Angelina.'

'I can't recall saying I disliked her.' William drew a brush through the mare's silky mane, making no reaction when Rosabelle stamped her foot.

'She's a pretty horse, why didn't you offer her to me?'

'You already have a horse, besides, your temperaments wouldn't suit.' Her tantrum was beginning to bore him. 'She's shy of the whip, when you lose patience you're heavy-handed.'

'And you think that whey-faced little cat will be able to manage her, when by her own account, she cannot stay upright on a rocking horse.'

'I'll teach her to ride,' he murmured, slipping a saddle on the horse.

'That's a new saddle. Where did you get the money?'

He shrugged. 'Father bought a horse for Frey.'

She laughed. 'I wager you sold him a broken-down old hack.'

William ignored her assumption, pride wouldn't allow him to sell an inferior beast, not even for Frey. Casually, he changed the subject. 'Have you wondered where Angelina's fortune would go if some mishap befell her?'

Rosabelle's face lost a little of its colour. 'What are you suggesting, that you'd kill her to get at it?'

He gave her an amused glance as he adjusted Moonlight's leading rein and mounted his gelding. 'Don't be so melodramatic. I just thought it might pay you to swallow your pride and be nicer to her. With all that money at her disposal, she might prove to be generous to those she likes.'

Moonlight was a pretty creature, Angelina thought, admiring the cascading tail held high above her silver patterned rump and her high-stepping gait. Even so, she couldn't quite conceal her panic. 'She's a most wonderful gift. Alas, I've never learnt to ride.'

Thomas, who'd come to witness this surprising gesture by his second son, smiled his encouragement. 'Will intends to teach you. Go and change into your riding habit, my dear.'

'I do not possess one.' She bit her lip when her father sighed in exasperation. 'I've never needed one before.'

Rosabelle shrugged. 'I'll give you one. There's a tear in the skirt, but I daresay it will do until you get one of your own.'

'Thank you, Rosabelle.' Suspicious of her sister's change of attitude, Angelina's eyes narrowed. 'Perhaps morning will be a better time for my first lesson.'

'I didn't realized you were scared of riding.' Will seemed a little distant now.

Worried he might think she was dismissing his generous gift, she shrugged, admitting, 'I wanted to prepare myself. I've only ridden on a plough horse before and I'm nervous.'

He relaxed enough to smile. 'There's no need to be nervous. Come, make her acquaintance, then when you've changed I'll give you your first lesson. I promise you'll be quite safe on her back.'

Moonlight snickered softly when she stroked her velvety muzzle. Her soft eyes were ringed with dark lashes, her mane and tail flowed like spun silver in the breeze. Angelina fell instantly in love.

In a short space of time, she was perched on Moonlight's back. The red velvet habit Rosabelle had given her was worn, and stained with perspiration under the arms. Her nose wrinkled at its musty odour. The colour ill-suited her and she resolved to purchase a new outfit as soon as possible. The boots were too large, the leather stiff and cracked with age. They chafed her calves unmercifully.

Ignoring the discomfort, she concentrated on remembering William's instructions as he walked them up and down the carriage-way. He was surprisingly patient, showing her how to hold the reins, how to set the horse in motion and rein her in. Eventually he detached the leading rein and gave her control. Her sweet little horse was well schooled, and responsive to her instructions.

Satisfied she'd mastered the rudiments, Will said, 'Do you feel confident enough to go for a short ride to the edge of the forest and back?'

Angelina had thoroughly enjoyed her riding lesson. She nodded, her eyes shining. 'This has been a wonderful day; thank you for making it so.'

William sucked in a breath, trying to ignore the pleasure her words gave him. She was easily pleased. He stored the thought in his memory.

He slowed to a walk when they reached the forest so he could observe her progress. She hadn't done badly for a first lesson, but she'd never be really comfortable on a horse, like Rosabelle.

When she disappeared from his view he was annoyed. She was on one of the main tracks so he saw no reason to worry. He knew the forest well, if she became lost he'd find her easily. It might teach her to heed him, and give her reason to be grateful.

When Angelina reached a clearing where several tracks met, she slowed Moonlight to a halt. She turned in the fading light, expecting William to be behind her.

A bird flew out of a bush, making her jump. 'William!' She inhaled a deep steadying breath whilst she waited for him to answer. The forest was quiet, the sunlight, which had previously dappled the forest floor in dusty shades of gold, had gone. She shivered as she turned Moonlight's head around. She was lost.

She took a grip on herself. All she need do was retrace her path. She'd soon find her brother. Ten minutes later, the path narrowed and curved downward to the left. She frowned. Surely she should be out of the forest by now.

'William?' she whispered dejectedly. 'It's getting dark and I'm scared. Please find me.'

An owl hooted. She shuddered as stories of goblins and evil witches flitted through her mind. The forest was a mass of gloomy, shifting shadows pressing in on her. A horse snickered, causing her to sigh with relief.

'William, I'm over here.' Goose-bumps prickled her skin when she received no answer. 'Will?' In the shifting shadows she made out a shape coming towards her. It was not William, but the dark visage had a familiarity about it.

The highwayman? Her blood ran cold when she remembered his cold eyes and his threat. Her tongue stuck to the roof of her mouth as, without thought, she flicked the reins, sending Moonlight plunging wildly down the nearest bank.

'Stop!' A hand grasped her reins and slowed her mount to a halt. 'A few more strides and you'd have ended up in the bog.'

'Do not kill me,' she begged, cringing away from him. 'My brother, the Viscount Kirkley, will willingly pay ransom to get me back.'

'Why should I want to kill or ransom you?' There was a hint of laughter in the man's voice.

'You're not a highwayman?'

'Do I look like one?'

She gave the man a quick glance. He was about her own age. She gave him a longer, more reflective look. 'Indeed not,' she blurted out. 'You look exactly like my father.'

'Aye. There are those who say I resemble him.'

Remembering her first meeting with William, and the disagreement he'd had with the earl, she smiled. 'You must be Frey. I'm Angelina Wrey, and I'm glad to make your acquaintance.'

In the deepening gloom she saw a bitter smile etch Frey's lips. 'Tell me that if we meet under different circumstances, and I might believe it.' He turned her horse about, starting to lead her back to the path. 'What are you doing in the forest alone at this time?'

'William was teaching me to ride. I became lost.' Her muscles were beginning to ache from the unaccustomed exercise. 'He'll be angry with me for going on ahead.'

'If William let you go on ahead he'd have had a motive. He knows the forest almost as well as I do, and if nothing else, he's a superb rider.' Frey suddenly grinned. 'I'd best guide you out of here before it gets dark.'

They took a twisted route through the forest. Before too long, Angelina found herself on a sloping meadow behind the stables.

'You can go the rest of the way alone. If I run into William I'll tell him you're safely home.'

She placed a hand over his to restrain him a moment. 'Thank you, Frey. I hope we'll meet again.'

'I daresay we will.' He looked down at her hand, gave a wry smile and squeezed it. 'Take care of yourself, Angelina Wrey. It would be best if you didn't tell your family we met. They'll not like it.'

Her chin lifted a fraction. 'I was brought up by a woman who believed people were equal in the eyes of the Lord. I'll not allow *anyone* to tell me how to think, nor lower my estimation of you.' She smiled when their eyes met in an instant of rapport. 'Not even you, my reluctant brother, Frey.'

He inclined his head, giving a hint of a smile before turning his mount back towards the forest. She watched him go, but he didn't turn. When she could see him no longer, she headed downhill towards the stables.

William was in a foul temper after spending over an hour searching the forest. Frantic with worry, he'd ridden a good horse almost to the point of exhaustion to return home and organize a search party.

He discovered Moonlight safely stabled for the night, Angelina with the rest of the family in the drawing-room, where a lively game of cards was in progress. It took every shred of willpower he possessed to return her smile when she rose from her seat and came towards him.

'I'm so sorry I caused you inconvenience,' she apologized straight-away. 'It was silly of me to get lost. I hope you'll forgive me.'

'No harm done,' he grunted, inclined to place his hands around her slim, white throat and choke the life from her when his father took advantage of the situation.

'Angelina insisted this incident was her fault, so I'll not censure you.' The earl's eyes said otherwise. 'Nevertheless, Will, you must take more care with your sisters. Bear in mind, a highwayman is still at large. From now on I do not wish the Wrey women to be abroad at dusk.'

'Yes, sir.' Rosabelle's amused glance was met with a cautious frown before he excused himself for the evening. He and his sister were often abroad at night, sometimes frequenting the local playhouse or the gaming-rooms, where Rosabelle went masked. Life would be dull without their forays into town, and he doubted if anything would change.

He encountered Rosabelle's maid on his way to his chambers. He smiled when she gave him a flirtatious look. Taking her by the shoulders he propelled her ahead of him, watching her hips sway in invitation. The aroma of Rosabelle's perfume surrounded her.

When they reached his chamber, he closed his eyes and reached out for her.

Used to her own company, the presence of another proved tiresome to Angelina, especially someone as restless as her sister.

Rosabelle distracted her from her embroidery today as she paced up and down, prattling incessantly about the coming ball.

'I'll spurn all suitors except for Rafe,' she declared, stopping to preen herself in front of the looking glass. Sucking in her waist, she pulled herself straight and thrust out her bosom. 'When he sets eyes on me in my ball-gown he'll find me irresistible.'

Angelina sighed, hoping Rafe would have more sense. 'I thought you didn't care for your ball-gown.'

Rosabelle's smile was secretive as her glance shifted to the window. 'I've decided I like it after all. What's your gown like?'

'It's pink and yellow—'

'What can you be thinking of,' she said, giving a theatrical shudder. 'You have all that money to spend and you choose pink. It will clash horribly with your colouring.' Striding to the dressing-room she threw open the door, demanding imperiously, 'Show it to me.'

Angelina was about to tell her the gown was packed to prevent accidental soilage, when Rosabelle threw the dust cover from her rack of gowns and began to rifle through them.

'Please do not crease them,' she cried out. 'Clara has just finished hanging them up.'

'That's what maids are paid for.' Dragging a delicate yellow gown from the rack Rosabelle gazed at its flounced petticoat with critical eyes. The bodice was laced, and decorated with pink rosebuds to match those at the hem. It was one of her favourites.

As Rosabelle held it against her and whirled around, her heel caught in the flounce. She appeared not to hear the ripping sound as she untangled her foot. She smiled gaily and hung it back on the rack. 'You should wear another, something less insipid. Green perhaps.'

Angelina frowned, almost sure the damage to her gown had been deliberate. 'I'm quite capable of deciding for myself.'

'Well, don't blame me if no one asks you to dance.'

'As I've already been promised dances by James, William, my father and Rafe, that's hardly likely to happen.' Asperity filled her voice when Rosabelle wandered to her dressing-table and removed the stopper from the perfume her mother had bought her. 'Can't you find something useful to occupy your time, Rosabelle?'

'You sound like Mama.' She choked out a mocking laugh. 'Poor Mama. She does not attract affection from those around her.'

'I find her a most warm and loving person.'

Rosabelle didn't answer. She'd wandered to the window, her attention now focused on a figure on horseback coming along the carriageway.

'It's Rafe.' Her eyes shone with excitement when she turned. 'God, how handsome he looks. Let's go down and greet him.'

Angelina joined her sister at the window. 'If the purpose of his visit is our company, we will be sent for.'

Rosabelle made a face at her. 'If we're accidentally in the hall when he enters, he cannot fail to notice, and will be obliged to pass the time of day.'

'You must do as you think fit.' Longing to see Rafe again herself, and seething inside that Rosabelle should make herself so obvious, she returned to her seat and applied herself to her embroidery. She expelled a deep, frustrated breath when Rosabelle left in a flurry of skirts, and abandoning her needlework hastened to the window again.

Rafe chose that moment to glance up. Her heart began to race as he reined in his horse and gave her his slow, beautiful smile.

'Greetings, Angel.'

'My Lord.' He wore an elegant new suit of sober black with a stand-up collar. She couldn't resist giving him a mischievous grin when she spotted the glimpse of a striped grey waistcoat, and the touch of lace at his cuffs and throat. His dark hair had been drawn back and neatly fashioned into a black bow. 'You are looking quite the dandy this morning.'

'A well-brought-up girl should not comment on a gentleman's attire.' He laughed when she made a face at him. 'If you were not safely out of my reach I would—' His voice faltered and his glance went beyond her. 'Is that you, Lady Elizabeth, or is it Angelina's image in a looking-glass?'

She whirled round when her mother gave a soft laugh. 'Fine words, My Lord, but I'm more interested in what you were about to say to Angelina.'

'He was about to threaten me with violence, I believe.' Gaily, she kissed her mother's cheek. 'He cannot scale the walls, so I'm quite safe.'

'But you're not safe from me, young lady.' She pulled her from the window and gave her a severe look. 'I'll not countenance you hanging out of the window like some tavern wench, and Rafe should know better than encourage such familiarity.'

Angelina gasped with mortification when she heard Rafe move off. He could not have failed to overhear the chastisement. Her face began to burn. To be likened to a tavern wench was condemnation indeed. 'I'm sorry, Mama, I had no intention of being forward.'

'It's a pity you were not introduced into society earlier, you have so much to learn.' Elizabeth sighed. 'Come, do not look so crestfallen. We must be thankful it was Rafe. He's a man of good sense and discretion. From now on you must think of your reputation before you engage a man in conversation.'

Angelina considered her remark unfair. 'Rafe isn't just *any* man.'

'Oh?' Elizabeth's eyebrow rose a trifle. 'Pray explain.'

'He's more like a brother.'

'Since you lack the experience of growing up with brothers you cannot possibly know that.'

Turned towards the light, her face still crestfallen from her scolding, Angelina kept her chin tilted at a stubborn angle. 'I did not grow up with a mother either, yet when I was alone and needed a mother's guidance, I sensed her presence and imagined she watched over me with love. She would not have used cruel words.'

Elizabeth's eyes softened. 'Were you very lonely?'

'At times.' Her eyes centred somewhere in the past, it all seemed so very long ago. 'Aunt Alexandra did not believe in idle hands. Every moment of my day was accounted for. Besides my book lessons, music, and embroidery, I was taught to run the household. I was also expected to visit the sick families of the estate workers.'

'She encouraged you to expose yourself to disease?' Her mother sounded horrified.

Angelina gave her a level look. 'No, Mama, Lady Alexandra would never have allowed me to do that. Those suspected of carrying infection were kept in isolation. I was merely encouraged to show compassion to those less fortunate than myself.'

Elizabeth realized she'd heard the woman's name mentioned without flinching. That she'd not encouraged Angelina to talk of her childhood had been wrong. If she was to know and understand her daughter, she had to put her anger and jealousy aside. What did it matter now? Lady Alexandra was dead, she posed no threat.

'Tell me, child,' she hesitated, not really knowing whether she wanted to hear the truth, 'were you happy living with Lady Alexandra?'

'I seldom saw her.' Her daughter looked troubled. 'When I did she was not affectionate, yet. . . .'

'Yet what?' she encouraged.

There was an uncertain expression in Angelina's eyes. 'Although I worked hard to earn her approval I could never capture her affection, nor could I find love in myself for her. That made me unhappy.'

Immense satisfaction flowed into Elizabeth's body. She drew her daughter close, tenderly stroking a tendril of hair back from her face. 'Love must be nurtured to make it grow, yet lack of it can make you vulnerable. That's why I do not encourage your familiarity with Rafe. He's a handsome and charming man who has a way with women. I do not want you to be hurt.'

'Rafe has no interest in me as a woman.' She smiled wistfully. 'Besides, he might decide to offer for Rosabelle.'

Elizabeth's breath hissed in her throat as she took a step back. 'He told you that?'

'No, of course not. Rafe would not discuss such an intimate subject with me. Rosabelle—'

Elizabeth gazed sharply about her. 'Where is Rosabelle?' she snapped. 'I understood her to be with you.'

'She left just before you arrived.' Angelina averted her face to hide the tell-tale blush rising beneath her skin. Lying did not come easily to the girl. 'I cannot say where she has got to,' she stammered.

'Cannot, or *will not*?' Expelling her breath in aggravation as the sound of several horses came to their ears, Elizabeth made swiftly for the door. 'The earl is meeting with the men of the district to discuss ways and means of catching the highway robber. It will not do for Rosabelle to make a display of herself. I want you to stay in your chamber until they've all departed. Do not show yourself at the window again.'

'No, Mama.' Angelina went back to her embroidery, knowing Rosabelle would blame her for the dressing down she would most surely get.

Half an hour later she was surprised, and a little dismayed, when her mother informed her her presence was required in the study. 'Your father intends to ask you questions about the highwayman.' Her mother fetched a silk shawl to drape around her shoulders. 'Do not speak unless directly spoken to, and keep a modest demeanour at all times.'

'You will come with me, Mama?' Her voice quavered at the thought of being questioned by several men whom she did not know.

'Of course I will.' Slanting her head to one side her mother regarded her with a smile. 'Do not look as though I'm about to throw you to the wolves. I'm sure it will not be the ordeal you imagine.'

Disinclined to believe her mother, Angelina clung to her arm when they entered the study. The room was thick with smoke. Glasses of port were being handed around by a manservant. The babble of male voices became a hush when the men were made aware of their presence. Although Angelina kept her eyes lowered, she sensed curious glances cast her way.

Then the earl was by her side, his voice gruff. 'My daughter, gentlemen.' There were murmured greetings and a general clearing of throats before the earl returned to his seat. 'I've acquainted the company of the unfortunate incident concerning the highwayman, my dear. As you're the only person who has seen him unmasked, the gentlemen wish to question you on his appearance.'

'Indeed, sir,' she said, stammering a little, 'I'm afraid I did not see much at all. It was nearly dark.'

'Can you remember what colour his eyes were, Lady Angelina?' This from a handsome middle-aged man who stood with his legs apart in front of the fireplace.

'Dark.'

'Dark blue, or dark brown?'

'Almost black.'

'Hair?'

'He wore a hat that came down over his face. It was black. The kerchief he wore as a mask was also black.'

'Coat?'

'Black . . . black boots . . . black breeches . . . black crop.'

And so it went on. She described a perfectly anonymous man dressed in black with no distinguishing marks, then described him all over again.

'Horse?'

'Black.' She smiled as a sense of the ridiculous took hold of her. 'The horse was black all over, shining black, as though the rider loved it well and took pride in its comfort. I hope I did not harm him when I brought the cane down upon its back.'

When Rafe chuckled, she dared to send him a smile.

'Was it a stallion or a gelding?' someone asked.

'My sister is not familiar with the gender of horses,' William said, as the room became embarrassingly quiet.

'My pardon, ladies.'

Aware of the difference between a stallion and gelding, Angelina coloured. She was grateful when William crossed to her side and gazed into her eyes. 'You mustn't worry, we have a good description from the Marquis of Northbridge.'

'Nice nag that,' the man at the fireplace said admiringly. 'Black as the devil's soul. I'd know it if I saw it again.'

William's eyes narrowed in on her. 'Think carefully. Can you remember anything at all about the highwayman's face?'

Something nibbled at the back of her mind, then slipped frustratingly away. Regretfully, she shook her head. 'As I mentioned before, he was young. It was nearly dark and it all happened so quickly.'

'Then you wouldn't recognize him if you saw him again?'

Why was he pressing her on this? 'It's possible, but I cannot be sure.' Forgetting she was not supposed to offer an opinion she gazed round the room. 'I suggest you seek the horse. Once you've found it, the rider will be within your grasp.'

'This is men's business,' her father said, his annoyance barely disguised. 'Your opinion was not solicited, nor is it welcome. I suggest you apologize before you depart.'

The shock of the earl's public censorship brought a hasty retort to her lips. Her mother's fingers tightened in warning on her arm and she practically bit her tongue. She gazed upon the earl's stern countenance with displeasure, encountering an equal measure in return. Her father did not approve of her any more than she approved of him at this moment.

She gave a tiny shrug as the appropriate words formulated and, lifting her chin, gazed into the darkness of his eyes. 'In the past I lacked your guidance and was encouraged to express an opinion freely. If my words caused you offence, I acknowledge your censorship and accede to your superior wisdom.'

Tension suddenly filled the room. Keeping her chin high, she bobbed a curtsy and saw colour mottle her father's cheeks as he gave a stiff, assenting nod. His eyes slid guiltily away from hers in dismissal.

The Marquis of Northbridge, sensing nothing untoward spoke from his position against the fireplace. 'Damned fine idea though, eh, Thomas? Look for the horse to find the rider. Why didn't I think of that? I'd know that nag anywhere. I wager young William here would too if he but saw it once. Damned fine judge of horseflesh, your William . . . damned fine. Black as the devil's throat that nag was. It must have been sixteen hands high.'

The marquis was still waxing lyrical about the horse when Angelina and Elizabeth left the room. She gave one last glance in Rafe's direction as the door closed. His gaze was fixed thoughtfully upon her, the faintly cynical curve of his grin applauding her courage.

She expected her mother to chastise her again. Instead, there was a quizzical look in her eyes. 'Damned fine nag, that,' she said, keeping her expression completely under control.

'Damned fine,' Angelina agreed, mimicking the marquis to perfection. Her eyes joined her mother's in complete understanding.

Elizabeth smiled. At first it was tentative, then a gurgle of laughter left her lips. 'If I hadn't enjoyed that so much I'd be tempted to punish you. Your father was at his most pompous and you took advantage of it.'

'He does not like me, I think.'

'As I told you, he's not a demonstrative man. You must reconcile yourself to that.'

'Forgive me for saying so, Mama, but I do not think I'll ever grow fond of the earl.'

'When we were first married I thought that too. There are worse husbands.'

'You did not love him when you married, then?'

'The marriage was arranged by my father just before he died.' She looked pensive. 'I grew to love and respect Thomas, as you will grow to love and respect your husband when you wed.'

'I do not intend to wed unless it's to a man I already love.'

'What nonsense is this?' A vexed frown creased Elizabeth's forehead. 'A daughter has very little say in whom she will marry.'

'James has promised not to force me into an arranged marriage against my wishes.'

'James is not your father.' She was the recipient of a rueful smile. 'I keep forgetting James is your guardian. And of course, he would understand your dreams perfectly.'

'He and Celine are so happy together,' she whispered. 'To love the person one marries must be wonderful.'

'But have you considered, Angelina? Your dowry will allow you to pick and choose a husband. Every invitation we sent out for the ball has been accepted since your eligibility has become known, even those we issued for appearances' sake. There are bound to be offers.'

'It's demeaning to be considered eligible because of one's wealth.'

'If money were the only consideration, Caroline Pallister would not still be a spinster.' Her mother's smile held satisfaction. 'You have beauty and intelligence, and will make a brilliant match.'

'I'd marry a peasant if I truly loved him,' Angelina said bluntly.

Elizabeth shuddered. 'It's just as easy to love a man of quality, my dear. You're fond of Rafe, are you not?'

'Of course I'm fond of him. He's my friend.' She blushed to the roots of her hair when the meaning of her mother's words sank in. Tentatively, she asked, 'Rafe has not made an offer for me, surely?'

'Indeed, he has not. Rafe's not the type to rush heedlessly into marriage. He's too sensitive about his circumstances.'

'Then Rosabelle—'

'Will be encouraged to wed the Marquis of Northbridge, who has already made an offer for her hand.'

'Rosabelle despises him.'

'He will make Rosabelle a fine husband.'

Angelina suddenly felt sorry for her sister. 'It must be awful to love one man and be forced to marry another. Rosabelle has set her heart on Rafe.'

Elizabeth turned her round to face her. 'Would you like Rosabelle to marry Rafe?'

'No,' she said truthfully. 'I do not think he is fond enough of Rosabelle to offer for her, even if he did have the means. But sometimes, he looks at her in a certain way that I cannot explain. . . .'

'As all men do. Rosabelle's appearance inspires men, but it is not spiritual, and many a man has been ensnared by his own desire.' She sounded bitter. 'When desire is spent there's nothing left unless friendship and respect exists between a couple. Sometimes, that's all a woman has, but it's better than nothing.'

'I do not understand, Mama.'

Tenderly, Elizabeth took her face between her hands and kissed her. 'I pray you never do understand,' she whispered. 'I pray you never do.'

CHAPTER ELEVEN

William and Rosabelle reined in their mounts at the top of the hill, and gazed down on Wrey House, set in the mathematical neatness of its grounds.

'That mealy-mouthed, whimpering snippet was responsible for me being locked in my room for most of the day.'

William laughed. 'She took Father to task. He didn't realize until it was all over. He's been in a foul mood ever since.'

'How did the prodigal daughter manage to do that?'

'By reminding him he hadn't raised her. She has a tendency to go for the jugular when cornered. You'd better be on your guard, Rosie.'

'I'm more than a match for her,' she boasted, tossing her head. 'Today, I spoiled her ball-gown.'

He fought off the rush of anger he felt. 'That was mean of you.'

Her shrug was indifferent. 'Why should you care?'

Odd, but he did care. Angelina intrigued him. Her vulnerable air made him feel protective towards her.

He suspected she intrigued Rafe, too, who seemed to harbour more than an ephemeral interest in her.

His glance went to Rosabelle, looking as smug as a cat because she'd ruined her sister's gown. For the first time in his life, he experienced dislike for her.

'Pettiness is never very pleasant. Your envy ill-becomes you, Rosie.'

Her face flamed red. 'She's won you to her side. How could you prefer her to me?'

'Stop being tedious,' he drawled, and knowing it wouldn't serve to make an enemy of her he kissed the pout from her lips. 'You're beyond compare.'

Nevertheless, he did compare. Her lush lips would droop with discontent in a few years, her magnificent bosom would sag with her first child. A redeeming feature was her sensuality. She'd keep a man's bed warm long after her charms had faded, and provide him with countless heirs. Whether she liked it or not, she would be a perfect mate for the marquis, who would service her with a dog-like devotion to his own bodily comfort.

Angelina's elegant delicacy was threaded with a tenacity that would make her bloom year after year. She'd endure against anything the elements threw at her.

Like her mother, he thought, surprising himself. Hadn't Elizabeth survived against the odds? Her roots were buried in Wrey House, and despite his father's infidelity she still flourished.

He experienced an unexpected sense of regard for his stepmother. There had been a change in her since Angelina had come into her life. She no longer accepted his father's dictates as law. There was a quiet determination about her these days, and it would bear watching.

He came out of his reverie when Rosie's hand slid across his thigh. He flicked it aside. 'You're disgustingly amoral, Rosie. I'll be glad when you're wed.'

'You won't forget your promise to help me compromise Rafe?'

He smiled. The little idiot, had she but known it she'd played right into his hands. 'As agreed, I'll pass a note to him at the ball.' He shrugged. 'I doubt if he'll fall for such a trick, he's not stupid.'

Rosabelle's eyes hardened. 'If he doesn't, I'll tell Papa exactly what has passed between us.'

'Nothing has passed between us, just the normal expression of affection of one sibling for another.' His fingers closed tightly about her wrist. 'Think on, you've got *much* more to lose than I. You'd be sent to a convent for the rest of your life.'

'You're an animal,' she whispered, jerking her wrist free.

'It's you who pursue me,' he reminded her, ashamed of his desire and feeling the need to rid his life of the temptation she presented.

He set his horse in motion, heading towards the forest deep in thought. His agreement with George to help consolidate his claim on Rosabelle would provide him with the means. Rosabelle's stupid plan to trap Rafe would be turned against her.

He began to whistle as his independent streak surfaced. He intended to leave England, and with the help of his French connections, establish the biggest horse stud in America. Neither the war, or Rosabelle, would be allowed to stand in his way.

He glanced back at her, following after with a dissatisfied look on her face. He grinned, he had Ellen to warm his bed; George was welcome to Rosabelle.

James brought Celine to Wrey House two days before the ball was due to take place. There was a great deal of excitement in the air as they entered the hall.

The house had undergone a thorough cleaning and was redolent of polish and lavender soap. Maids bustled about with arms full of linen to furnish the guest chambers, and gardeners were moving large tubs containing plants into the house.

The great chandelier in the hall was lowered almost to the floor. Gleaming with brilliance it was being refilled with thick, white candles. Once lit, they'd last throughout the night.

In the middle of the chaos stood Elizabeth and Angelina. Consulting plans, they directed the various workers about their business. They looked more like sisters than mother and daughter, James thought. Elizabeth's gown was a darker shade of green than Angelina's, her hair was drawn into a cap. Braided, Angelina's hair was secured by a green, satin ribbon.

'Those little trees go into the ballroom, Mr Curruthers,' Angelina said. 'How pretty they look with their tiny oranges. Were they very hard to grow?'

'They grew from pips in the hot house, My Lady.'

'You must show me how to plant them. They're most exquisite—' Her voice broke off when she glanced up, her face lit up in a smile. Her squeal of delight was spontaneous and unladylike, bringing heads swivelling her way. 'James! Celine!' For a moment she was poised and quivering like a deer ready for flight, then she ran across the room and nearly bowled him over with a fierce hug. 'You've no idea how much I've missed you, dearest James.'

Nobody had ever welcomed him quite so warmly to Wrey House before. He was quite touched by it. Swallowing the lump rising in his throat, he gazed down at her and discovered he couldn't stop smiling. His arms came around her and he kissed the top of her head. 'Angelina, my dear. You've been much in my thoughts. You are well?'

'Perfectly well.' Her glance shifted to Celine who was being greeted by

Elizabeth. She deserted him, transferring her hug to Celine. 'My dearest friend, there's no need to ask if James is looking after you. You're glowing with enough radiance to put the sun in the shade.'

Exchanging a glance with Celine, his lips curved in a loving smile when he saw a delicate blush rise under her skin. His wife was proving to be everything he'd hoped for, and he considered himself a lucky man. He tore his eyes away and embraced the smiling Elizabeth.

'Your usual chamber is prepared, James. Unfortunately, I cannot offer you the adjoining chamber, we will need every nook and cranny we can find.' She consulted one of the papers in her hand. 'Celine's maid can share with Angelina's just across the hall, and your servant will be accommodated in the upstairs nursery. We've turned it into a temporary valets' quarters. Is that satisfactory?'

'Quite.' He gave her another kiss. 'Is there anything I can do to help?'

'Thank you, but no. Angelina has turned out to be a treasure at this sort of thing. Between us, we have everything organized. Another's thoughts will only serve to confuse us.'

He glanced to where his sister and Celine were chatting animatedly. 'Has Angelina been accepted here?'

'Not entirely, James. She and your father are finding it difficult to come to terms with each other. I do not think the subject will arise yet, but I beg you to hold fast to your guardianship of her.'

'You have my promise.'

'As for Rosabelle, she did not welcome her sister at first, but of late she's been more civil. Angelina copes easily with the situation, but I doubt if she'll ever regard Wrey House as her home.'

'What did Will make of her?'

'Who can tell what he makes of anything?' Her smile was a trifle pensive. 'He gave her a most beautiful horse as a welcome gift and spent time teaching her to ride it. It was a lovely gesture. My impression is, he's not totally averse to the idea of having her for a sister.'

'Will has always been a law unto himself,' James smiled when he watched Angelina go arm in arm with Celine up the stairs. 'It looks as though you might be losing your little helper.'

'She will return when she's made Celine comfortable. She's enjoying helping with the preparations for the ball. However, you must be tired after the journey so I mustn't keep you talking.'

'I must greet my father before I rest.' He looked about him. 'Is he in his study?'

Elizabeth's voice reflected the insult offered to her self-esteem. 'If you recall, your father is always out at this time.'

He puzzled a moment on the sadness of her tone, then the full import penetrated his brain. His father had always been a man of habit. He took her hands. 'Forgive me, Elizabeth.'

'It's me who should be forgiven for reminding you.' She carried one of his hands to her face and gently caressed it against her cheek. 'This is a burden I must carry alone. I would not encourage you to think less of your father because of it.'

'I know that, Elizabeth.' She'd never hinted at her feelings regarding his father's affair before, and he couldn't help but ask. 'Have you considered discussing this with him?'

She looked horrified. 'I would not dream of subjecting Thomas to such humiliation.'

He kissed her cheek, marvelling at her loyalty. 'If I find the opportunity to broach the matter with him, I will.'

'Thank you,' she said quietly. 'He was a loving husband until the birth of our daughters. It seems as if fate took my husband and one of my children from me at the same time.'

Poor Elizabeth, no wonder she'd been unable to bring herself to love Rosabelle. The girl would have been a constant reminder to her of her husband's infidelity. *And she wasn't even her child!*

James wasn't usually given to irascibility, but his face darkened in the effort to keep his temper in check. Damn his father? Why hadn't he made the effort to keep his wife happy as well as his mistress? He could bring the whole lie crashing down around their ears, if he was not careful!

Frey Mellor was not in the best of moods. The clerkship had been awarded to another.

His mother was sorting through a bundle of clothes when he arrived home. His face darkened as he stirred the garments with his foot. 'My father was in one of his charitable moods, I see.'

Mary wore a defiant expression, but there was an air of repressed excitement about her. Perhaps the earl had parted with some gold again. 'There's some good stuff here. If you're too proud to wear them I can sell them at market. They'll fetch a copper or two.' She held up a voluminous black garment. 'Look at this coat. It just needs a stitch or two in the lining, and the sleeve seams sewing back where they've pulled apart at the back. Master William must have got too broad in the chest for it.'

Frey *was* looking. He'd never be able to afford such a fine topcoat. He shrugged, swallowing his resentment. 'Perhaps it will come in handy for next winter since I didn't get the clerkship.'

She stared at him in disbelief. 'But the earl promised he'd put a word in for you.'

'Damn you, Mother. Didn't I tell you not to ask him for favours?' He crossed to where she sat. 'The only favour I want from him is one he gives me because I'm his son, not one he's been asked to give.'

'He's done that all right.' Her face dimpled into a triumphant smile. 'He came here today with the finest gift a son could wish for his birthday. He was hoping you'd be here so he could give it to you himself. He had pressing business to attend to so he didn't even stay. . . .' She carefully pulled a line of thread through the eye of a needle and started sewing. 'Anyway, he come here special for your birthday.'

His heart leaped into his throat. 'What are you talking about?' he whispered, reckoning his mother had gone mad. 'Since when has he remembered my birthday?'

The reason for her excitement became clear. 'Since he came here leading the best horse I ever laid eyes on.' Rocking back on her heels, she laughed. 'He says it come from Master William's stud. Your brother chose it special when he knowed it was for you.'

'If William chose it for me there must be something wrong with it.' He strode to the door, then turned, his eyes wary. 'Did the earl bring its papers?'

'Aye.' She nodded complacently towards the dresser. 'It's all nice and legal like, he said, and what's more' – he waited impatiently whilst his mother bit through an end of cotton – 'what's more, it comes with a new saddle and bridle.'

When Mary looked up he was striding towards the door. Dropping her sewing needle, she picked up her skirts and hurried after him.

Frey couldn't believe his luck had turned. The day had started off badly, and now he owned a most magnificent horse, a black gelding with a white blaze on its nose and chest. It turned its head when he approached, stretched out its neck and blew gently through its nostrils. There was no fear in the horse. Its eyes were intelligent and inquisitive. It stood perfectly still when he mounted, then walked in a sure-footed circle to his guidance. The horse went through its paces perfectly.

'You look a proper gentleman on that,' Mary called out. 'You even talks like a gentleman now you've been educated. It's the Wrey blood coming out, I reckon. You ain't got my addled wits, that's for sure.'

'There's nothing wrong with your wits.' He smiled at her. 'If you'd had an education you'd be as good as anybody.' Dismounting, he tied the horse to a branch. His old mount would fetch his mother a shilling or two at the market.

'Ain't you going to ride it?' she said, her disappointment all too apparent. 'The earl said it hasn't been exercised much today.'

'Of course.' He threw an arm around her shoulders. 'I mean to write a note of thanks to the earl, then ride over and leave it with his gatekeeper.'

'Nobody can say my boy hasn't got nice manners.' Her face beamed with satisfaction when they walked back the house. 'Go through the village. That there horse will make the women's eyes pop out of their heads and keep their tongues wagging for a month of Sundays.'

He couldn't help but smile at her all too obvious pride in him. He just wished he could catch the same expression in his father's eyes.

He ignored her request, taking his usual short cut through the forest, marvelling all the while at his stroke of good fortune. The horse moved quietly, but swiftly, seeming to know its way through the trails without much guidance. He sat comfortably in the saddle, imagining he was a lord.

When he emerged on to the road Frey heard another horse coming up behind him. The rider had the look of the gentry despite his shabbiness. Frey stood aside to let him pass. Instead, the rider reined in beside him. 'Good day to you, fellow. If you're going my way I could do with some companionship.'

He doffed his hat in a show of deference. 'Sir.'

The man's eyes narrowed as he gazed at him. 'Forgive me if I'm mistaken, but would you be related to the Wrey family by any chance?'

'Only by chance,' Frey pointed out, his voice cool. 'My name is Frey Mellor.'

'Ah, that accounts for the likeness.' To Frey's amazement the man leaned forward, offering his hand. 'You may of heard of me. James is my brother-in-law, and good friend. Rafe Daventry, The Earl of Lynnbury at your service.'

'My Lord.' Grasping the offered hand, Frey found the handshake firm. The man's smile was wide. He returned it. 'I didn't know the viscount had married.'

'The marriage was recent.' Setting their mounts in motion they walked them leisurely along the road. After a while, Rafe said, 'James tells me you have a talent for figures and write a good hand.'

Frey was pleased to think that James, whom he hardly knew, would talk of him favourably with his friends.

'Aye. I've been schooled in such subjects.' This was no idle enquiry and he gave the man a shrewd glance. 'I'll go as far as to say I'm skilled at mathematics, am fluent in the French tongue and can also transcribe Latin text.'

'Can you, by God?' After a moment's hesitation, the earl enquired, 'Have you prospects?'

'I did have up until this morning.' Frey offered up a wry smile. 'I had expectations of employment on the estate of the Marquis of Northbridge. The position went to another.'

The earl gave a small nod and got to the point. 'Sir Edward Truscott has charged me with finding him a clerk. Although you're young, if you're interested I'd be willing to try you out. The permanency of the position would depend on Sir Edward when he returns a year hence, but if you prove capable I'll recommend he keep you on.'

Frey put the proper respect in his voice. He badly needed this position. 'I'm obliged to you, My Lord. I promise you'll not find me lacking in skills.'

'I hope not,' Rafe said ruefully. 'To be quite honest, I cannot make head nor tail of Sir Edward's ledgers. The letters and figures have a ruthlessly neat appearance, like soldiers standing to attention. I get the feeling they'll take aim and fire if I disturb their ranks with my untidy hand. I have been keeping tally of things on scraps of paper.'

Frey smiled a little as they came to a halt at the Wrey gatehouse, reckoning this blue-blooded stranger would be more welcome within the walls than himself. 'I'll present myself at Tewsbury Manor with my reference in the morning. Will that suit Your Lordship?'

'Admirably.' They shook hands on it, then when Frey turned towards the gatehouse, the earl said, 'You're not coming in?'

'I doubt such intrusion would be welcome. I came to leave a note with the gatekeeper.' He took it from his pocket 'Perhaps you'd oblige me by delivering it privately to the earl.'

'Of course.' He slid it under his waistcoat and smiled. 'Good day to you, Mr Mellor. I'll see you on the morrow.'

Mr Mellor? Frey watched the earl canter off down the carriageway with an unbelieving look in his eyes. The man was a rarity, and suddenly he was looking forward to the morrow with a great deal of eagerness.

Turning the horse back in the direction he'd come from he put the beast to a canter, feeling it surge forward in a smooth, fluid motion. Soon, they were galloping under the canopy of the forest. Exhilaration flowed though his body.

After he'd cooled and fed the horse, he loosed it into the adjacent meadow and went inside the house. His mother had gone to a special effort for his birthday. He tucked in to a meal of succulent rabbit and vegetables cooked in a crusty pie. It was followed by apple dumplings boiled in honey.

A bottle of red wine was opened for the occasion, and although it was cheap, to Frey it tasted like nectar. Holding up the glass, he gazed at her over the brim. 'To the future,' he said, unable to keep the smile from his face.

That same night the highwayman found good pickings at the other side of Lyndhurst.

The night was perfect for highway robbery. There was no breeze, the fine mist curled from the ground to hang amongst the trees. There, they drifted like wraiths to diffuse the brightness of the moon, yet allowed enough light for the business at hand.

Knowing the two inns in the area would be popular with the blades arriving for the Wrey ball, the highwayman, completely covered by a voluminous, cowled cloak, took up station a good furlong out of town.

A purse was snatched from one lone rider, an effeminate gentleman whose obvious terror made his teeth chatter. Sending the man's horse fleeing into the forest the highwayman pushed the gibbering idiot down with his foot, instructing him not to stir for an hour or so.

He was not about to take risks, a carriage with two fully armed outriders was allowed to pass unmolested.

Further along the road a man was relieving himself in the bushes. Startled, the man darted a swift glance at his saddle-bags for a second before saying with surprising belligerence, 'Damn you, fellow. Can't a man have a little privacy?'

The victim was more powerful and dangerous-looking than the highwayman liked. Leading his horse away proved the safest option. The saddle-bags contained a quantity of gold sovereigns.

Satisfied with the night's work, and not wishing to push luck too far, felon and horse backed into the forest and were swallowed up by the mist.

Angelina grew wealthier by the hour and all that interested her was the charity hospital her funds supported, James thought.

'It's settled then, James. You must try and persuade Rafe to accept the position on the board.' She came to stand in front of him. 'Your report that the board intends to draw a more generous salary is disturbing. I intend to remind the lawyer of the terms of the charter the hospital operates under, and instruct him to implement it to the letter. Aunt Alexandra would do so herself, in a most verbal manner, were she still alive.'

'She's not alive,' he pointed out. 'And I cannot guarantee Rafe will accept the responsibility.'

Angelina began to pace up and down the room. 'Damn their hypocritical souls,' she muttered. 'I have a mind to go to London and deal with them personally.'

Never in his wildest dreams had he imagined she could be so scathing in her condemnation, so adamant that her mentor's wishes be carried out to the letter. Seething with anger, her determination was made obvious by the set of her chin.

'Please stand still,' he said. 'My eyes grow tired from the exercise you put them to.'

She subsided into a chair, gazing at him with eyes of ice. 'If Rafe will not accept the commission and you cannot, I shall take responsibility upon my own shoulders. If you furnish me with the names of those board members who endeavour to better themselves at the hospital's expense, I will discharge their obligations. There is no room on the board for men lacking compassion or scruples.'

'You cannot be serious,' he reasoned, knowing full well she was *deadly* serious. 'You have no recourse to discharge anyone. Lady Alexandra was only just tolerated, and she had to concede the reins to Lord Sotheby for appearances' sake. A young, unmarried woman like you would turn them into a laughing stock. They'd resign *en masse* and the hospital would cease to function within a week.'

His advice had some effect, for she gave a thoughtful frown. He pressed for an advantage. 'I'll broach the subject with Rafe, but I warn you, he's proud. He won't like the idea of taking recompense from you.'

'Then you must make it perfectly clear the money does not come from me.' Temper forgotten, she was all smiles, as if the matter was already settled. 'Appeal to his good sense. If that fails, I'll appeal to his—' She gave a soft, mischievous laugh. 'No, I'll not presume to barter his pride for cash. I shall fall upon my knees in a most dramatic manner and implore him to come to the rescue of a poor defenceless female.'

James laughed. 'He will most likely threaten to throw you over his knee and give you a good beating for your trouble.'

'But his sense of gallantry is such he'll agree to take the position, afterwards. James, there is no one better. I'm sure a little persuasion will convince him of his suitability for the position.'

Her ability to read character so easily was unnerving, but he had to agree with her choice. With his honesty, compassion, and singular lack of avarice, Rafe was the perfect man to act as her representative on the board. He laughed. 'We shall see if the matter is as cut and dried as you imagine.'

As it turned out, it was easier than he thought to persuade Rafe. 'It will involve being in London for two days every second month,' he informed him the next day. 'Angelina needs someone she can trust to represent her.'

'Say no more,' Rafe murmured. 'I'm happy to place myself at her service. She's such a helpless little creature. The hospital must be a heavy burden for her to bear.'

Helpless? James had a sudden urge to guffaw. Flopping into a chair he shook his head, bemusedly. 'I believe you suffer from some degree of delusion about Angelina.'

'I believe I do.' Rafe looked just as amused as James felt. 'Do not be tedious and relieve me of it; she makes me feel quite noble at times.'

Gallant! she'd said. He grinned.

'I must tell you, a messenger delivered a letter from her regarding the matter in question this morning. A most heart-rending appeal. Her admirable turn of phrase nearly had me in tears.'

'I see,' he said faintly.

'I thought you would.' Rafe raised his glass. 'Let's drink to the fools who fall for the wiles of a pretty woman.'

'And all the fools who don't?' James suggested.

'Exactly.'

Clinking their glasses together, they dissolved into laughter.

CHAPTER TWELVE

The ballroom looked beautiful. The chandeliers sent out jewels of light as the sun touched upon them. At the far end, the minstrels' gallery was decorated with draped silk and garlands of leaves. Orange trees ranged down one side of the room; velvet-seated chairs gilded with gold had been carried down from the attics, dusted off and arranged in tasteful clusters.

The French doors framed a scene of magical loveliness, opening into the sheltered inner courtyard. There, the mosaic tiled pool had been scrubbed clean, and two stone dolphins sent forth spouts of glittering water. Candles in floating holders were lined up on the side, waiting to be sent journeying upon the water, coloured lanterns hung amongst the more exotic trees and ferns flourishing in the sheltered garden.

One of the two grottos had been decorated with silken hangings, a harpist hired to play soft music to those seeking respite from the dancing. The other had been curtained off. A gypsy skilled in the art of palmistry would occupy it to tell fortunes for a silver coin.

Angelina and her mother had come across the gypsy on the road. A small boy with dark, solemn eyes had clung to her skirt. A hungry expression rode his pixyish face, making Angelina wonder when he'd last eaten.

'Tell your fortune, ladies,' the gypsy said, her demeanour suggesting she expected a refusal.

'It would be a novelty to have a fortune-teller at the ball,' Angelina suggested to her mother. 'I'd love to know what the future holds for me.'

'I do not believe in such nonsense,' Elizabeth said, but she was plainly considering the idea. She suddenly smiled at the woman. 'If you're seeking to earn a little for yourself and your son, I can offer you the opportunity tonight.'

133

The woman gazed openly at Elizabeth then. She was young, her skin rough and weathered from exposure to the outdoors. Though ragged and dusty from the road, she had a proud look to her. Dark, penetrating eyes touched upon something in her mother.

'Lady, you are deeply troubled. You have a good heart, but you are deceived. Amber can give you answers to the questions which plague you.'

'I have no questions.' Her mother shivered and directed the woman to the kitchens for sustenance. Introspective for a while, she'd said nothing more about the gypsy and had soon returned to her former self.

They exchanged a smile of satisfaction when a servant finished placing the cushions on the stone benches of the courtyard. Angelina said, 'What if the orchestra doesn't arrive on time?'

'We'll dance without music.' Elizabeth smiled, took up a pose and began to hum the accompaniment to a minuet as she danced.

In the spirit of the occasion, Angelina made a small bow and held out her hand to her mother. 'My dance I think, Lady Elizabeth.'

They went through the motions of an exaggerated minuet, beginning to laugh when Angelina adopted the role of the dancing master she'd had in London.

'*Non, mademoiselle*, point the toe, thus. *Bon*! Zat is better. We will make a dancer of you yet. Hold up the head - up! *Non*, do not inspect the ceiling! *I am in despair*! You must be elegant - *elegant*.'

A cough sounded from behind them. Guiltily, they spun around, the laughter still lingering in their eyes. The earl had a bemused smile on his face, as if he couldn't believe what he'd just witnessed.

The carefree expression on her mother's face was replaced by a façade of calm dignity. 'There's something you wish to discuss with me, Thomas?'

He indicated the case he was holding. 'I wanted your opinion on whether this would be a suitable gift for our daughter, but as she's here, I shall seek hers instead.'

Angelina sucked in a surprised breath when he flipped open the lid. On a bed of faded green velvet lay a string of creamy pearls. An emerald set in gold filigree glowed in the middle.

'It's exquisite, more than I deserve.' She gazed at the earl with shy wonderment. 'Thank you, Papa.'

'I hope they bring you pleasure.' He cleared his throat. 'It belonged to my mother. I considered the emerald a suitable match for your eyes.'

'That was thoughtful of you, Thomas.' Elizabeth picked up the necklet and gazed at it approvingly. 'It's a fitting gift for her.' Clasping it around Angelina's neck, her glance went to her husband. Her smile was warm. 'You gave me the matching ring as betrothal gift. With your permission, I would pass it on to our daughter.'

A tender, faraway expression softened the earl's expression. 'I had not forgotten,' he said quietly. 'Your hands were so small it slipped from your finger and I had it altered to fit.'

Seeing her father thus, Angelina mused. His affection for Mama is truly written upon his face, so why is she beset by sadness in his presence?

He pressed a kiss in Elizabeth's palm. 'If it pleases you to gift the ring to Angelina, it's my pleasure also.'

The moment was lost when Rosabelle rushed impatiently into the ballroom. 'Mama, Ellen says she cannot arrange my hair in the style I want. The girl's a fool. I want her replaced.'

'She cannot be replaced at such short notice.' Elizabeth's eyes narrowed a fraction. 'If your maid is unsatisfactory, why haven't you complained sooner?'

Rosabelle took up position next to her father. 'She's always tired, and has become insolent. Why can't I have a maid from London, like Angelina?'

'Perhaps my maid will be willing to arrange your hair on this occasion,' Angelina offered. 'I'll ask her if you wish.'

'One does not ask a maid, one orders her.' Rosabelle's eyes focused on the pearls. They widened. 'Aren't those the pearls Grandmama Wrey wears in her portrait?'

Elizabeth's voice was almost a purr. 'It's your papa's gift to Angelina.'

'I'm not fond of pearls, they're reputed to bring tears.' Rosabelle feigned a yawn, but her eyes were sharp with annoyance when she slid her arm through her father's. 'The diamond set would suit me much better.'

'No doubt,' Thomas said drily when Elizabeth gasped. 'However, the diamonds are part of the Wrey inheritance. Traditionally, only the countess may wear them.' He gave Elizabeth a courtly bow. 'I hope you will please me by wearing them tonight.'

Rosabelle managed to smile, saying prettily, 'If Angelina is to be favoured with such a handsome gift, I cannot believe you plan to offer me something of lesser value.'

'The value of a gift is in the heart of the recipient, not in its cost, but I do not think you'll be disappointed, Rosabelle.' He took a box from his pocket and handed it to her. 'You are fond of rubies, I believe.'

The ring flashed fire when she slid it on to her finger. Three flawless rubies were interspaced with two diamonds. It was a pretty piece. She held out her hand, turning it this way and that. 'This is of the same design as the pendant I admired. They must have been a set; a pity to separate them.'

Her avarice had never been more obvious to those watching. The earl stiffened. 'The pendant had been purchased by another.'

Rosabelle's glance went to the pearl necklet then back to the ring, as if comparing the value. She removed her arm from her father's and smiled in an odd, secretive manner. 'Perhaps another will present me with the pendant. That emerald will look well with the green gown you intend to wear, Angelina.'

'Green gown?' Elizabeth gazed at her in astonishment, having inspected and approved of Angelina's gown just the day before.

'Did she forget to inform you?' Rosabelle flung over her shoulder as she flounced towards the door. 'The yellow one was roughly handled and became torn and dirtied. One cannot trust maids to do anything these days.'

Her mother turned, gazing at her in consternation. 'Why didn't you tell me?'

Angelina smiled a little. 'It was a day gown that was torn, and it was not due to Clara's carelessness, it was mine.'

Turning to her father, she smiled, thinking it time the air was cleared between them. 'Would it incur your displeasure if I spoke frankly, sir?'

'It might.' His smile was wry, as he attempted to put her at her ease. 'It depends upon what you have to say.'

'It grieves me that relations between us are strained.' She hesitated, giving him a nervous look. He made a humming sound in his throat, but his expression remained neutral. 'I do not expect you to feel as warm towards me as you do to Rosabelle. It brings no fault to either of us that we were strangers until quite recently.' When he winced slightly, she concluded hurriedly, 'I appreciate the thought behind the gift you gave me today, I'll treasure the pearls, always.'

'Thank you, Angelina.' He seemed to be about to say something else, for there was a struggle of emotions in his expression. He managed to compose himself, and giving her a formal little bow turned to Elizabeth. He pressed his lips to her hand, then strode away.

She turned to face her mother, who was staring at her pensively. 'Have I angered him?'

'If you had he'd have let you know it.' Elizabeth smiled, partly at Angelina's courage, and partly because Thomas had shown her affection.

She'd always thought she understood him better than he understood himself, yet his show of affection had been unexpected. He'd made her feel as soft and vulnerable as the girl she'd been when they first married.

Angelina had made a good impression on Thomas today, though he still struggled with his conscience over her. There had been a subtle change in him of late, and she could only wait and hope.

'Go and rest now,' she said to Angelina. 'A maid will bring you some broth. After you've eaten, you can sleep until it's time to ready yourself for the ball. I want you to look your best.'

'I shall be unable to eat or sleep,' she answered, her eyes sparkling. 'I'm much too excited.'

'Nevertheless, you'll try.' And taking her by the arm, Elizabeth led her away from the ballroom.

Later, when she checked on her daughter, she discovered her fast asleep. She stared down at her for a moment, then gently touched her cheek, marvelling at having this beloved child back with her.

A toss of her head banished the self-pitying tears that sprang to her eyes. She drew the curtains over the windows to shut out the sunlight and the noise of their house guests arriving. Once again, she gazed at the dear face of Angelina.

'Thank you, God, for restoring to me this most precious of gifts,' she said humbly.

'I'm sorry, My Lady.' Clara was near to tears as she picked up the hair-brush. 'I couldn't get here any sooner.'

Angelina stilled the strokes of the brush and reached out to touch a red mark on her maid's face. Her eyes darkened. 'Did my sister do this?'

Clara sniffed. 'She said she didn't like the style and made me do it all over again. It took ages to do all them curls again. Still, she wasn't satisfied.' Clara began to weep. 'She said I was making her look ugly on purpose so you'd outshine her at the ball. I told her nothing would make her better looking than you.'

'And she slapped you.' Handing her a handkerchief, Angelina smothered a grin. 'I'll make her apologize to you.'

Clara eyes widened in fright. 'Beggin' your pardon, My Lady, I shouldn't have spoken to her like that, and if I don't get you ready on time I'll be in more trouble.'

'You'd better arrange it in my usual style then, Clara, I doubt if there's time for the one we planned.'

'I can manage,' Clara muttered, her fingers deftly dividing her hair into sections. 'I'm not about to give that madam the advantage, not while I still live and breathe.'

There were two minutes to spare when Clara finished. Angelina gave her reflection an approving glance. Her hair had been curled, then drawn up into a circle of creamy silk-petalled flowers at the crown of her head. Small tendrils curled around her face, a longer one was arranged to spiral to her shoulder. Shaking her shimmering skirts into fullness she made her way to the door.

'Your birthday gift, My Lady.'

She planted a quick kiss on her servant's cheek as the necklet was clasped around her throat and the ring slid onto her finger. Then she was speeding through the corridor and down the stairs.

Her mother frowned when she hurried into the ballroom. She slowed to a sedate walk, grinning in triumph when her father slid his pocket watch out of sight with a smile. James beamed her an approving smile, a congratulatory grin came from Celine, and Will's lips twitched at the corner.

Her family looked splendid. The men cut handsome figures in their wigs and fine attire, her mother was elegant in blue silk with the diamonds at her throat flashing fire.

Angelina's face suddenly fell. 'I've forgotten my fan.'

'You'll have to survive without it,' Elizabeth said tartly.

Her father glanced around him in annoyance as the first guest was announced. 'Where's Rosabelle?'

'I'll go and find her,' William offered.

'No.' He exchanged a greeting with the guest and introduced Angelina. 'She can account for her lack of manners later. I'll not have Angelina's introductions spoiled by her tardiness.'

Angelina could have done without the introductions, which seemed to go on interminably. She doubted if she'd be able to remember a single name, except for those people she'd met previously in London.

Nicholas Snelling was embarrassingly voluble in his praise of her appearance. He recited a long and tedious poem which he'd composed especially for her birthday.

'Thank you, My Lord,' she managed to interpose, when he paused for breath. 'I'm honoured, and pleased you could come.'

Nicholas made no move to go, even though the line of guests waiting to be announced at the top of the marble staircase was growing longer. 'You're lucky to see me at all. I was set upon by a vicious rogue on my way here, and robbed.'

'The highwayman?' The earl's face lost its long-suffering expression. 'I trust you were not hurt.'

'I managed to fight him off,' Nicholas said with false modesty. 'The fellow did not get all I carried.' He tapped the side of his nose with the silver-topped cane. 'The bulk of my gold was secreted in a compartment in my saddle.'

'That was cunning of you.' The earl signalled the footman to announce the next guest. 'We'll talk about this later, My Lord. I must not keep the other guests waiting.'

'Of course.' Thrusting the poem into Angelina's fingers, Nicholas placed a hand over his heart, gave her a soulful look and passed into the ballroom.

'Sweet Jesus!' William whispered in her ear. 'Make sure I do not have a surfeit of wine. I might be tempted to ask the popinjay to dance.'

Angelina's quiet giggle earned an amused glance from the earl. 'You know the Earl of Lynnbury, of course, Angelina.'

Rafe looked wickedly handsome in dark blue brocade and ruffled lace. Her eyes widened when she stared at him and warmth filled her heart. 'How splendid you look, My Lord.'

Rafe gazed at her with pained amusement. 'Are you saying I usually resemble a vagabond?'

The regard in his eyes made her feel breathless and confused. 'Indeed not, I was merely complimenting you.'

'Then I forgive you.' He bore her gloved hand to his lips, murmuring with a grin, 'What a tiresome creature you are; it's *my* duty to compliment you, not the other way around.'

'Then pray do so,' she whispered. 'You are holding up the queue.'

'Alas, your appearance is so exquisitely beautiful I cannot find words poetic enough to do you justice.'

'Thank, God,' William muttered, thinking how pretty Angelina looked when she blushed. 'Nicholas Snelling has spouted enough poetry at her to last a lifetime.'

'Who am I to attempt to compete with such an accomplished bard?'

His green-flecked eyes caught and held hers for a few, delicious moments. 'Don't forget, Angel. I've booked at least ten dances, and *insist* on taking you in to supper.'

'You have only booked two,' she admonished.

'Then reserve me another eight.'

She tore her eyes away from his when her mother coughed delicately. 'Go away, Rafe. I always end up in trouble when you're around.'

'Until later.' Bestowing on Elizabeth his beautiful smile, and receiving a gently reproving shake of the head in reply, he passed on into the ball-room, leaving Angelina to be introduced to the Pallister family.

Just as the introduction was complete, a stir rustled through the guests. Turning towards the staircase, the breath hissed in Elizabeth's throat.

Poised dramatically at the top of the stairs was Rosabelle, her gown a froth of scarlet flounces edged with gold. Its *décolletage* was revealing, the filmy gold scarf draped around it designed to draw the eye rather than detract. Her hair was swept into a cluster of blood red roses and threaded through with gold ribbon and rosebuds. Gazing with haughty languor at the crowd, her lips parted in a smile as she swayed to where the family stood and said, 'I've arrived.'

'No one could doubt it,' William said, *sotto voce*.

The earl cleared his throat. 'You're late.'

Rosabelle shot her a triumphant glance as she took up station beside her sister. 'I was dissatisfied with my hair, and had to engage the services of Angelina's maid to arrange it a third time.'

'Where did you get that gown?' Elizabeth hissed. 'It's completely unsuitable for a girl your age. And you're wearing rouge!'

'Never mind that now,' the earl said testily. 'Let's get the guests in and start the dancing, or we shall be here all night.'

Angelina faded into invisibility with the flamboyant Rosabelle beside her. When the introductions were over, her sister was quickly surrounded by a crowd of admiring young blades and borne away.

William offered her his arm. 'Don't look so crestfallen. She's like a flame to the moths, the men she attracts are not of the type I'd have you acquainted with.'

Angelina stole a glance at Will's darkly handsome countenance. 'Such brotherly solicitude is a little misplaced, Will. You're the most enigmatic of men. I confess, I know you not at all.'

He returned her smile, but his eyes were emotionless.

She shivered. 'I can never read your mood, but sense your reticence where I'm concerned. I hope you do not decide to dislike me.'

'The truth is, sister, I'd rather have you for a friend than be your enemy.'

'So be it, Will.' Standing on tiptoe she gently kissed his cheek. 'You shall be as dear to my heart as James is.'

His expression became thoughtful as they continued the rest of the dance in silence. He gazed down at her when the music ended. 'I hope you're never forced to chose between brothers then. I'm very different to James.'

'That will never happen,' she said quietly. 'We're bonded by blood ties.'

A sardonic smile played around William's lips as he tried to squash the annoyingly warm feeling her words left in him. Obviously, she was unaware of the rancour existing between himself and Frey.

His glance played across the crowd as she began talking to a haughty-looking dowager. It lingered on George Northbridge, who was gazing at Rosabelle and hardly bothering to conceal his interest. His eyes narrowed. If all went as planned, the betrothal would be announced before the night was over.

Rafe was smiling politely at something Caroline Pallister was saying. The woman was as ugly as sin, he thought dispassionately, watching her thin mouth open and close. A man would have to be desperate to take her into his bed, despite her wealth. Would Rafe ever be that desperate?

When Rosabelle anxiously glanced his way, he smiled and patted the pocket where her note resided. After a while, he sauntered to where Rafe stood and drew him away from the braying Caroline.

'I have a missive for you from Rosabelle.' He slipped the note into Rafe's hand, warning, 'A tryst is not in your best interest.'

Rafe slipped the note back, his voice chilly. 'I'm surprised you'd imagine I'd indulge in a secret assignation with Rosabelle.'

'I'd supposed no such thing. I hope to prevent her petitioning you directly, thus making a bigger fool of herself than she already is.'

'I misjudged you then, William.' Rafe gave a small, relieved smile. 'My thanks for the warning, I'll be on my guard.'

Rafe was not booked to dance with Rosabelle until just before supper. There had been much comment about her dress and demeanour and he wasn't looking forward to the encounter.

Strolling to where Celine stood with James, Rafe offered her his arm. 'Would the most beautiful married lady in the room care to take a turn with her brother?'

'There are at least twenty unattached females in this room, just dying to dance with you,' Celine scolded.

'Only twenty?' He laughed as he drew Celine into the throng. 'I must be losing my appeal.'

'Or losing interest,' Celine said slyly. 'Can it be you're interested in dancing with only one?'

'But which one?' he grinned, refusing to satisfy her inquisitiveness. 'This year's crop are all as pretty as dragonflies.'

'And you are as elusive as a fox,' she grumbled, trying not to smile. 'Very well then, I shall not confide my news to you.'

Searching her face for a clue, Rafe saw only radiance in her eyes. A smile crept across his mouth. 'Let me guess.' His finger found her chin and tipped her face up. 'You're blushing, my dear; am I to become an uncle?'

'You most certainly are not.' This time Celine *did* blush. 'At least, I think you are wrong.' She bestowed a mock frown upon her brother when he laughed softly. 'My news is this: Mama has won a large fortune at cards, and Papa has taken her back.'

'*Good God!*' It was the last thing he'd expected to hear. 'No doubt the Marquis will throw Mercy out again once the money has been spent.'

'She's recovered the deeds to Monkscroft, and father has vowed to reform.'

This time his laugh was bitter and disbelieving.

'You must seek a reconciliation with him, Rafe.'

His voice was practically a whiplash. 'Never! His brutality drove my mother to her death.' He gazed at her stonily. 'I'm surprised you plead his case with me, Celine. Does James sanction this petition?'

She lowered her eyes. 'James doesn't know of it. Mama's letter begged me to keep the matter secret. Our father is ill from his excesses, Rafe. You *must* reconcile with him.'

'Celine, my dear.' He gazed at her with troubled eyes, unable to believe she would ask this of him. 'I know you act out of love for your mother, but you mustn't allow her to encourage you to deceive your husband. You must inform James of this contact with Mercy as soon as possible. If he considers it his duty to approach me on this, I promise to listen to what he has to say.'

'You're wrong, Rafe. I act only because of my love for you. Will you promise to take James's advice?'

'I promise only to consider it.' As he led her from the floor, he said, 'I won't tell him you've spoken of this with me.'

'Rafe?' Celine whispered, when he turned to go. 'There is more. Papa has reconciled himself to my marriage. He's now resolved to disown you legally and name any son I might bear as his heir. I *beg* you, seek a reconciliation with him.'

Sensing Mercy was behind such a move, his smile became slightly bitter. 'He seeks to divide us, Celine, but he won't succeed.' He kissed her cheek gently. 'My love for you will endure unto death, come what may.'

He left her, striding up the marble staircase, through the brilliantly lit hall and out into the darkness of the garden to be alone with his thoughts. Leaning against the trunk of a tree he waited for his anger to subside. Gradually, his breathing slowed, the red haze engulfing his mind less chaotic.

'Damn you, Mercy,' he said softly. 'How a conniving slut like you could have given birth to someone as sweet as Celine is beyond reasoning.'

At first he wondered at his anger, but as it ebbed he came to appreciate the reason behind it. For years he'd denied Monkscroft estate and the title meant anything, now he discovered he'd been lying to himself.

It was a matter of pride, of honour. If his father disinherited him, it would be the ultimate insult. He'd be publicly shamed, and for what reason? He scowled. He'd done nothing to deserve such treatment but stand up to his father's bullying. Whatever James advised, he would not seek reconciliation with his father, and if he was disowned...? He shrugged. It was not within his father's power to strip him of Ravenswood or his present title, which was inherited from his paternal grandfather.

The sounds of music reached his ears and he remembered he'd promised Rosabelle a dance before supper. Not that she lacked partners, he thought, reluctantly heading back the way he'd come, but not to dance with her would be a noticeable insult.

Both the Wrey girls had shocked him this night. Angelina was exquisite with her ivory shoulders emerging from a subtly tinted gown, and her hair decorated with flowers. Her innocence was infused with an air of self-consciousness, as if she'd suddenly discovered her beauty. She reminded him of a delicate butterfly.

Rosabelle's fiery beauty robbed him of breath. That her mother had sanctioned such a gown was questionable. The statement it made was both tempestuous and sensuous. She flaunted herself like a strumpet, he mused. The man who took her for his wife would have to beware.

The invitation to meet her in the pavilion had been indiscreet and he hoped William had disposed of the note. Attractive as she was, he had no intention of becoming involved with her, nor satisfying any romantic fantasy she had in her empty head about him.

James was waiting for him when he entered the hall, his lips carved into an apologetic smile. 'Celine has confessed all, my friend. Rest assured, I've promised not to beat her.'

Rafe smiled at the notion. James couldn't summon up enough aggression to beat a mad dog. 'I've been trying to figure this all out, James. One conclusion I've reached: I wouldn't stand in the way of a son of yours inheriting Monkscroft and the title.'

'Celine will not accept the inheritance,' James said quietly. 'If we are ever blessed with a son who inherits Monkscroft, it will be by God's will alone, not the will of your father and stepmother. We intend to inform your father of this decision as soon as we return to London.'

Rafe gave him a searching look. 'You're both agreed on this?'

'Our minds are as one.' James took his arm and steered him back towards the festivities. 'Celine merely wished to warn you of what was afoot.'

'James! You are depriving me of my dance partner. I insist you keep your business talk until tomorrow.'

Rosabelle attached herself possessively to Rafe's arm as soon as they descended the staircase. Her smile was over-animated, her voice assumed an archness that made him want to shake her. 'You've danced only with Celine tonight. I shall be the envy of every woman here.'

He assumed his amiable persona and pulled a practised smile to his lips. 'The men flock around you like bees to honey.'

'They are boys.' She slanted him a bold glance when she made a deep curtsy. 'There's only one man here, I admire.'

'Then he should consider himself a lucky man.' Rafe hoped the dance wouldn't last long. Her *décolletage* drew the eyes, and preventing his glance from lingering there was becoming a strain. He began to perspire a little.

'You've not complimented me on my gown,' she cooed, as if well aware of the effect she had on him. 'It's quite the latest fashion.'

'It is . . . sensational,' he murmured drily, and recalled Elizabeth's scandalized expression when she'd set eyes on it. 'Your mama was taken aback, I think.'

'It's not the gown Mama chose for me.' She fluttered her eyelashes at him as she dipped and swayed to the music. 'But you must be aware of that, Rafe.'

It was *definitely* not a gown Elizabeth would have approved for her daughter. 'I'm aware only that your mother's taste would not encompass such a gown,' he said carefully. 'It suits you.'

'I knew you'd like it.'

He smiled wryly at the enthusiasm in her voice. Her immaturity had never been more obvious. There was one last glimpse of her *decolletage* when she dipped into a curtsy. He brushed a kiss across her hand when the music ended, and only just avoided giving an audible sigh of relief.

'Until later,' she whispered in a husky voice when another, more eager partner hurried forward to claim her.

He relinquished her with a thankful smile, and could still smell her musky perfume clinging to him after she'd gone. Her last words alerted him to the fact she expected him to keep the assignation. She'd lose her bounce when he didn't turn up, and hopefully, her infatuation would fly along with it. He grimaced when he spotted Angelina, cornered by Nicholas Snelling.

Rescuing her, he partnered her in a minuet. Despite her late introduction to dancing, she was graceful and light on her feet. She had been partnered for every dance, and her complexion was beginning to glow.

'You look as though you need refreshment,' he said, when the dance ended. 'Lemonade is being served in the courtyard, and I wouldn't be averse to some myself.'

Her face dimpled into a relieved smile. 'Thank you, Rafe. My feet have been trodden on so many times you'll have to carry me off the dance floor if I stay here much longer.'

'That's a penalty beautiful young ladies have to endure when they're thrust into society.' He offered her his arm, guiding her to where Elizabeth stood. 'We're retiring to the courtyard for refreshment. Would you care to join us, Lady Elizabeth?'

Elizabeth graciously declined the offer. The courtyard was well lit, the fortune-teller attracting one guest after another. She saw no need to act as chaperon on this occasion. Angelina's behaviour had been exemplary all evening. It would not hurt her to have a little breathing space.

Between dances, her daughter had worked her way around the ballroom, exchanging pleasantries with each guest and making them feel welcome. Elizabeth had been complimented on her so many times she'd basked in her daughter's glory, until she suddenly remembered the girl had been raised by another. A grudging respect for Alexandra Chadwick came into her mind.

She was smiling when she watched the pair walk away. Rafe's eyes were full of amusement as he made an aside to Angelina from the corner of his mouth. She wrinkled her nose and laughed. They have a rare rapport, she thought in surprise. There is more to Rafe than meets the eye.

Although Elizabeth liked the impeccably mannered earl, she'd always thought his gallantry a little too practised. With Angelina he was spontaneous, as if her freshness penetrated the world-weary façade he wore.

He was protective of her, and it was obvious she liked and admired him. Rafe would make the perfect husband for her, Elizabeth mused.

Proposing marriage to anyone was the last thing on Rafe's mind as he found a vacant seat for them away from the gaggle of maidens and young blades waiting at the gypsy grotto. He signalled to a servant to bring them lemonade.

Angelina gave an ecstatic sigh and promptly relieved herself of her slippers. Hidden by her skirt she set her feet upon the cool, stone slabs of the courtyard.

Glancing sideways at her, he grinned. 'If I didn't know you to be the most circumspect person on earth, I'd imagine you'd just disposed of your slippers.'

A set of stockinged toes wriggled out from underneath her skirt. The throaty laugh she gave set the hairs on his arms upright. 'Circumspect or not, see how happy they are to be free of restriction.'

'Indeed, they're the happiest looking toes I've seen in a long time.'

The toes were discreetly withdrawn before they were observed by a pair of dowagers patrolling the paths around the courtyard. Both ladies simpered at him and bestowed approving smiles on Angelina.

He waited until they were safely out of earshot. 'You've conquered all tonight, even the dowagers. You'll be besieged with invitations, and the young lords will fight duels over you as they barter for your hand.'

'I refuse to be haggled over like an object on a market-stall.' She scowled fiercely at him. 'James and my mother are aware of this.'

'You think you'll be able to resist a male intent on conquest, little Angelina? They'll come courting in droves, flaunting their feathers like proud peacocks. Their fine manners and flattery will turn your head.'

'You are making the assumption my head is easily turned. Let them flaunt. I'll pluck their fine feathers and send them draggle-tailed back from where they came.' She turned her back on him, making her displeasure clear. 'You're an oaf if you imagine I'm susceptible to empty, male flattery, Rafe.'

'This oaf is worthy of your disdain.' He smiled a little as he slid his hand inside his jacket. 'Perhaps you'll forgive my teasing when I offer you a small token for your birthday.'

'You are a master at teasing me.' Her frown was a shadow of its former self when she turned back to him. He watched it replaced by a smile. Her laughter was gently self-mocking, sending a delicious tingle down his spine. 'I've decided to forgive you on this occasion, especially as you offer me a gift.'

'What a mercenary creature you are.' He withdrew his hand. 'I've half a mind not to present you with it now.'

Her eyes were sparkling with laughter as she cajoled, 'My curiosity is piqued, Rafe, do not keep me in suspense.'

'Very well.' His fingers closed round the tissue-wrapped package, withdrawing it a little. 'I warn you, it's but a poor token, not worthy of your splendour.'

As quick as a bird her fingers darted to the package and withdrew it. She laughed when he made to snatch it back, and quickly unwrapped it. Her gasp of pleasure was reward enough.

'It's the most beautiful gift I've ever received, Rafe.' Spreading the delicate ivory fan upon her knees she inspected its decoration, exclaiming in astonishment, 'This has Ravenswood painted upon it!'

'My grandmother's work. It was *her* fan.' Gently, he ran a finger over the surface, closing it. 'I thought you would like it.'

'I adore it.' Gracefully she fanned it open again, to gaze at him over the top. 'Thank you, Rafe. Because it must grieve you to part with it, I'll treasure this gift all the more.'

All he could see were her bright eyes slanting towards him. The same hue as the emerald she wore at her throat, they were soft, and luminous with unshed tears. Without even thinking, his fingers brushed the fan aside, he leaned forward and gently kissed her. For a moment she was unresponsive, then her mouth seemed to quiver a little and cling to his most sweetly.

Suddenly, she made a small sound in her throat and pushed him away, blushing scarlet. 'You should not have . . . I should not have allowed. . . .' Her eyes were mortified as she gazed at him. 'What must you think of me?'

'What must I think of you?' Rafe smiled a little at that. Taking a glass of lemonade from the footman who appeared, he waited until the man had gone before placing it in her hands. 'I think you're an innocent who has just experienced her first kiss, and was frightened by it. Rest assured, it was a kiss from a friend who holds you in high esteem. If I offended you, I most humbly apologize.'

'It was unexpected, that's all.' Her blush faded a little as she applied a cooling stream of air to her face. After a while her graceful movement slowed and she gave a cat-like grin. 'Did you enjoy kissing me, Rafe?'

He felt uncomfortable until he saw the mischief in her eyes. He shrugged slightly, appearing to consider the question. It would not do to admit his enjoyment of it was so unexpected, even to himself. 'As much as one enjoys kissing a frog.'

'A frog!' Indignation chased across her face, then she laughed and struck him lightly with the fan. 'You're an incorrigible rogue.'

'And you're going to get into trouble with your mama if you do not don your slippers,' he whispered.

Elizabeth had something more on her mind, and she didn't seem to notice Angelina scrambling into her slippers. 'Have you seen Rosabelle? I thought she might have come to visit the fortune-teller.'

'We've not seen her, Mama.'

'Perhaps she's in the garden, then. Thomas and William have gone to look for her.'

Remembering the note, Rafe grinned to himself. Thank God he'd not been tempted to keep the tryst. A dalliance in the pavilion with Rosabelle could have had dire consequences.

CHAPTER THIRTEEN

Rosabelle stroked the glittering diamond and ruby pendant the marquis placed around her neck. 'It's a most beautiful token, My Lord.'

'Call me George, my pretty one.'

She sprang away from the marquis when his lips brushed her shoulder. 'La, sir!' she exclaimed, her eyes sparkling. 'You must not presume to take liberties with me.'

At first, Rosabelle had been annoyed when she discovered he'd followed her to the pavilion, but his handsome gift had dispelled her bad humour.

'Ah, Rosabelle.' He placed his hands over his heart. 'I'd give all I possess for a kiss from those lips.'

'All?' Her eyes gleamed when she remembered his wealth. 'Be careful I do not hold you fast to those words.'

George was too seasoned a campaigner to let an advantage slip through his fingers. The girl was cocksure, and reckless with wine. Let her think she had the upper hand. Once she was his, she'd learn differently.

He smiled, stroking a finger over the plump red curve of her mouth. *Rouged! The girl sought to make the most of her attractions.* He moved his hand to the nape of her neck, drawing her towards him. The resistance he expected was not there. She gazed at him, excitement in her eyes.

'Perhaps I'll allow you one kiss, George. You'll not press me for more?'

One kiss was all it took, he discovered. He'd long suspected Rosabelle's pipkin was begging to be cracked, and set out to prove it to himself. His lips had barely touched hers when her mouth parted and her tongue moistly sought his. Her immodesty might have shocked another fellow, but it served to excite him. He had no patience with shrinking violets.

149

She swayed against him with a small sound of satisfaction when his arms came around her. Her breasts thrust against his chest and his response was swift. *Gad!* she made him feel like a young rake again.

He bore her down amongst the cushions and slipped his hand inside her bodice, thumbing her erect nubs. She arched against him. Wondering if he dare go any further, he explored the folds of her scarlet skirts, stroking the thigh beneath.

She stiffened for a moment, then giving a tiny gurgling giggle, relaxed. George frowned when his breeches grew tight. Either the girl was too tipsy to know what she was doing, or she was deliberately leading him on. If William hadn't extracted a promise from him not to violate the girl, he could have mounted her without one word of protest. Uttering an oath, he moved away from her.

Rosabelle's pout registered her displeasure. She enjoyed the power she had over the marquis, enjoyed his hands on her body, the unrestrained possession of his lips. She smiled as a hot glance raked her body. Light-headed from the wine she'd drunk, her body taunted her with the promise of reckless pleasure. She fluttered her eyelashes, inviting him to take liberties.

'You have the heart of a trollop,' George growled, his fingers unlacing her bodice. Released from their covering, her breasts sprang free. He touched his tongue to the fiery, rouged nipples.

'*La, sir*! you have me in spin,' she whispered, closing her eyes ecstatically.

Hardly able to believe his luck, George eased her skirt up, and was just about to explore what she was clearly offering when the door crashed open and a scandalized voice bellowed, 'Rosabelle, you'll go to your mother at once! And you, sir, will accompany me to my study without delay.'

'Papa!' Her eyes widened when she saw his outraged expression. Gathering her bodice together she gave a mortified sob. 'The marquis attacked me and I fainted.'

'Do not take me for a fool. I have eyes and ears.' Observing the triumphant expression in George's eyes the earl felt a twinge of sympathy for Rosabelle. 'Your behaviour makes it obvious you're not as averse to the attentions of the marquis as you indicated. To keep your reputation intact we shall announce your betrothal tonight. You agree, George?'

George inclined his head. 'By all means. I was encouraged to press my suit by Rosabelle's acceptance of the ball-gown and ruby pendant. You have always known my intentions towards her were honourable.'

So *he'd* been her secret admirer! Knowing she'd been well and truly out-smarted, Rosabelle gave the marquis a smouldering glance. 'You'll rue this night's work, sir, just see if you don't.'

'That's enough, Rosabelle!' her father barked. 'Go this instant. Tell your mother what is arranged. You have yourself to blame if this betrothal is not to your liking. Another man would consider such behaviour highly undesirable in a wife. Consider yourself lucky the marquis sees fit to overlook it, and is willing to shoulder the blame by offering you the protection of his name.'

Head held high, she gave the two men a cold look as she flounced away. George Northbridge had a shock coming to him if he thought she'd go willingly to his bed, she fumed, all the hate she felt for him coming back. She'd scratch his eyes out first and pickle them in brine.

When she'd gone, Thomas turned a stern glance on George. 'You've betrayed my trust, and that of an innocent girl.' The earl's voice was dry when he noticed the state the marquis was in. If he was truthful, Rosabelle's innocence in the matter was questionable now, but the rituals must be observed. He sighed. 'For God's sake, man, find some way to calm yourself. Come to my study in one hour. It will give James and myself time to prepare the settlement papers.'

'Innocent girl?' George muttered, when Thomas headed back to the house. 'She has morals of an alley cat and will need to be kept on a tight rein.' He was wondering if he had sufficient time to ride into town and visit his favourite whore when William emerged from the shrubbery, pushing a cloak-wrapped figure in front of him.

'This is Ellen,' he said without preamble. 'She's Rosabelle's maid and will do anything you ask. Let's say five guineas.'

'Five guineas?' the marquis hissed. 'I can buy twenty drabs for that price.'

William smiled a little as he drew the girl into the light of a lantern and removed her cloak. 'But do they look like this.'

The girl was clad only in a transparent chemise. Her skin was smooth and firm, her high, jutting breasts had been rouged. A jewel sparkled in the enclave of her navel. Her mound was as plump as a ripe plum, her furrow modestly covered by a wisp of downy beard. She was a tasty piece.

Absently, he scratched his cods. 'That's a fancy price you're charging me for wearing her muff.'

'She's lain with no one but myself.'

'Is he telling the truth, girl?' George walked around her, pinching her rear when she didn't answer.

'Yes.' She gazed sullenly at William, who smiled and said, 'She's reluctant to confer her favours elsewhere; she might need a little incentive.'

George's hand went to his pocket and came out with a purse. He was in too much need to quibble over price. Carefully, he counted five gold coins into William's palm then held one up to the girl. 'If you're willing, this will be yours. If you satisfy me there will be more to come.'

Ellen's eyes gleamed at the sight of the gold and she nodded. Taking it as an affirmative George pushed the girl into the pavilion and followed in after her.

William walked away, the coins jingling in his pocket.

Elizabeth was pleased. The ball had been a success, the announcement of Rosabelle's betrothal timely, especially when she learned of the origin of the gown. The marriage was to take place in three months' time and she was looking forward to arranging the event.

Another source of pleasure to her was the number of invitations Angelina received. The Dowager Duchess of Amberley had been especially pressing. Her grandson had been unable to keep his watery-blue eyes off Angelina.

The young duke was of pleasant disposition, if a little slow-minded. He was somewhat overweight, his chin receded and his nose was prominent. It wouldn't hurt to encourage him to call, Elizabeth thought.

She laughed when Angelina said with great seriousness, 'But the gypsy told me I'd marry my true love.'

Which was what she told every young girl who visited her. Elizabeth smiled to herself as she instructed her maid to brush out her hair. Chances of it happening were rare. Her glance fell on the charm the woman had given her in parting.

'Place it under your pillow and your dreams will give you answers,' she'd urged, gazing directly into Elizabeth's eyes. They were compelling eyes, their depths harbouring strange pin-points of light. Elizabeth's head swam as the woman continued in a low, murmuring voice, 'Amber advises you to do this.'

'The gypsy told me I must place this charm under my pillow,' she said, wondering at the absurdity of it. 'What do you think of that?'

'Gypsy charms are mighty powerful, My Lady.' The maid's expression was a comical mixture of awe and wonder that made her smile. 'Best to do what she says, else it might turn into a curse upon your person.'

Elizabeth sought to humour the maid. 'Very well. I have no wish for my *person* to be covered with warts when I wake. It would cause tongues to wag at the church service, and take the sinners' minds off the sermon.'

Despite the charm, Elizabeth's sleep proved to be dreamless. She forgot about it when she woke and readied herself for church.

The Wrey family filled the two front pews, whilst the remaining guests occupied seats normally used by the estate workers, obliging them to crowd together at the back.

The villagers turned out in force to see the spectacle of the gentry in their finery. Standing gave them a better view of the whole proceedings. Their ripe, earthy aroma filled the small church. Lavender-scented handkerchiefs were hastily applied to the more fastidious of noses.

The incumbent was delighted at having such a fine congregation and out-did himself with his oratory. Flinging his arms heavenward, he postured and ranted until a crusty old earl grumbled loudly to his neighbour; 'Confound the man, did you ever see such a bag of wind? If the bugger doesn't shut up soon, I'll run him through.'

Amid a gale of laughter the sermon was hastily brought to an end. There was a scuffle as villagers raced from the church to grab the best vantage points amongst the gravestones. There, they commented on the dress and manners of their betters. The crusty earl received a cheer when he emerged, leaning on his cane.

'Be off, you scurvy varmints,' the old man yelled, shaking the cane threateningly at them and nearly falling over in the process. 'Do you want me to set about you?'

Angelina exchanged a glance with James. The giggles she'd been holding on to during the sermon escaped in a gurgle of laughter. James grinned and crossed to her side. 'Behave yourself, Angelina. We're supposed to show a dignified countenance to the villagers.'

'Can't you imagine that old man waving his sword in the air, and the rector, with his frock held up over his knees running for his life over the fields with the earl after him?'

'I'd rather not.' He chuckled and moved in front of her to hide her wickedly gleeful expression from Elizabeth. 'Would you have me get into trouble, too?'

'You're too large and too old to get into trouble.' Sobering a little, she placed a hand on his sleeve. 'I'm glad you fell in love with Celine, dearest James. You look so happy together.'

'I've never been happier.'

'Then I beg you to talk to Mama on my behalf whilst you're here?' she blurted out. 'She seems intent on encouraging suitors.'

'A normal process for young ladies of your age, my dear.'

'But I do not wish to marry until I'm in love.' Her eyes became tragic. 'How can Mama be set on sending me away when we've only just found each other.'

'I'm sure that's not the case.' He put a comforting arm around her shoulder. 'If you refuse to meet marriageable men how will you ever fall in love? She will not force you to marry against your will, she told me so herself.'

'If that's true, why is Rosabelle being forced to wed the Marquis of Northbridge? And why is she confined to her room?'

He took a deep breath, wondering if she should be kept in ignorance of the reason. He couldn't imagine Angelina acting in such a manner, but the truth might serve to caution her against similar behaviour. 'Rosabelle is being punished. Her vanity led her into a compromising assignation with the marquis. There was no other choice for her after that.'

Her eyes rounded in astonishment, then narrowed as she said quietly, 'How can this be? She dislikes the marquis.'

He offered her his arm. 'Rosabelle is sometimes foolish. If George hadn't made good his offer of marriage, she would now be ruined.'

'Do you consider me jingle-brained, James?'

Taken aback by her tone, he could only stare at her.

'She would not deliberately place herself in a position of obligation to the marquis. He must have planned her downfall for his own nefarious ends.'

'We'll not pursue this matter any further.' Knowing she was right didn't lessen the severity of his voice. 'Let's return to the family, we're keeping them waiting.'

Tears stung her eyes as she said rebelliously, 'I didn't think you could be so hard-hearted, James. Rosabelle's affections lie elsewhere.'

'If you're referring to Rafe, he cannot be held responsible for the romantic notions of flighty young girls.' Seeing her flushed face, he sighed. 'I'm not unsympathetic to her plight, but she brought it upon her own head. If it's any consolation to you, Rafe has never encouraged her to harbour tender feelings towards him, nor had he intended offering for her hand.'

'I'm relieved.'

He smiled to himself when her lips curved upwards at the corners. 'This betrothal has made you unsettled about your own future. Rest assured, I'll never agree to a marriage of convenience for you, unless the situation warrants it.'

'The situation will never arise,' she said fervently. 'You may have absolute trust in me, James.'

No doubt she meant it, he thought wryly as he led her towards the carriage, but the men who would pursue her couldn't be trusted, especially with such a fortune at stake. There was only one man he'd trust her to. That man was impoverished and proud, and had shown no inclination to marry for fortune, thus far. But what if Rafe fell in love?

He tried to push the devious thought to the back of his mind, but it returned twofold when he saw the smile the two exchanged. James happened to glance at Elizabeth then, and she at him. Understanding passed between them and Elizabeth gently nodded. It seemed they were of one mind on this.

At that moment, Angelina saw Frey standing in the shadows of the church porch. Face wreathed in smiles, she hurried towards him before James could stop her, exclaiming, 'Frey. It's so nice to see you again!'

It seemed to Frey as if the earth took one long, quivering breath, and held it. 'Lady Angelina?' Cautiously, he gazed in the direction at the Wrey family. The earl had an ominous frown on his face. William was staring at him, malice in his eyes, a twisted half-smile on his face. James seemed rooted to the spot.

Angelina was unaware of the tension as she kissed his cheek. 'Do not be so correct with me, Frey. I'm your sister, and I insist you must address me as such.'

It was Rafe who took charge of the situation. Striding towards her he took her by the elbow, saying evenly, 'Your mother is waiting in the carriage, Lady Angelina.' He nodded. 'Good day to you, Mr Mellor.'

Bundled into the carriage, Angelina saw the embarrassed shock in her mother's eyes. Despite knowing she'd committed an unpardonable sin, she attempted to explain her action. 'It's not Frey's fault.'

'Be quiet, missy,' Elizabeth snapped. 'You've shamed me publicly.'

'It's not *your* shame,' she persisted. 'If it had not been for Frey I'd have perished when I was lost in the forest. He prevented me from riding into the bog and guided me safely back to Wrey House. I'll not forget that.'

Elizabeth stared stonily out of the window, her mind a turmoil. She was trying to pretend the scene she'd just witnessed had not occurred, and that Angelina had not added fuel to the fire with her words.

Celine placed a cautionary hand on Angelina's arm. 'Hush, Angelina. Your words grieve your mama.'

Nothing she did seemed to please her family, Angelina thought. 'If the saving of my life causes grief, then would my death have been easier to bear? Perhaps it would have been better if I'd never been restored to my family, for its heart seems carved in stone.'

When she turned, Elizabeth's eyes were blazing and her voice shook with the effort of controlling her fury. 'Perhaps you're right, Angelina. At this moment I wish I'd never set eyes on you.'

It seemed to Elizabeth that Angelina crumpled before her eyes. In a wounded voice, she whispered, 'If the sight of me offends you I shall return forthwith to my estate in Sussex.' Turning her face into the corner, she burst into tears.

Aghast at the callous way she'd crushed this most precious and vulnerable of her daughters, Elizabeth wavered between self-righteous indignation, anger, and guilt. Finally, she was forced to admit the truth in what Angelina had said: Frey's existence was not *her* shame. The boy had been given no choice in his parentage.

As for having a heart of stone? She'd been forced to learn to control her feelings over the years. Once, she'd been as passionate as Angelina, and now? Her lips twisted in an ironic smile. Unfortunately, the girl had unleashed something she thought she'd conquered years ago – her own fiery nature.

Ruefully, she listened to her gulping sobs, remembering a time when she'd also suffered such torment. There had been no mother to comfort her when she'd been given in marriage to Thomas Wrey. With a murmur of distress she indicated to Celine to change places, then gathered Angelina into her arms.

'Hush, my baby,' she whispered, rocking her back and forth. 'I spoke out of anger, not from the heart. I'd rather die than lose you.'

After a little while, Angelina's sobs quieted and she raised her head. 'I shouldn't have spoken so rudely. I'm sorry, Mama, I was so happy to see Frey again I did not stop to think how my action would affect others.'

'You spoke only the truth.' Elizabeth hesitated, deciding it wouldn't hurt her to be more charitable. 'If Frey truly saved your life I shall write and thank him for doing so.' Marvelling that she could finally bring herself to utter the boy's name after all this time, she surprised herself even further by requesting, 'Pray tell me what occurred.'

'It will not pain you to hear me praise him?'

'It might,' she said, 'but I have a feeling it may be good for my soul.'

Elizabeth heard herself moan. The pain shafting through her body was jagged, it knifed through her pelvis, gripping at her very entrails. The smell of blood was warm and sweet in her nostrils. It was her own blood, and it stained the apron of the woman who stood between her splayed thighs. She arched her back, straining against the pain as the woman took her leg against her shoulder.

'Push, My Lady.'

Elizabeth grunted, her head thrashing from side to side with the effort. Perspiration poured from her body, slicked her shaking thighs. She'd not realized childbirth was such a long and messy business. Her fatigued body was given no quarter by the agony of her pain.

'*Push*!'

The pain became so agonizing, Elizabeth screamed out loud. Then there was a hot, slithering gush between her legs and she fell into blackness.

Later, the child she'd delivered was quiet in her arms. The infant's hair was a wisp of gold, like sunlight. Elizabeth knew her eyes would be green. She experienced a surge of deep love and her senses whirled with indescribable happiness.

'Rosabelle,' she whispered, then became confused. 'No, she is called Angelina.' She gazed up at the woman and saw it was the gypsy. 'Amber, where's my other daughter?'

'You have only one true daughter,' the gypsy said. 'Your heart knows it.'

'You're wrong.' Afraid to admit to the truth she closed her eyes against the gypsy's power. 'Angelina has a twin sister, her name is Rosabelle.'

'You have only one true daughter,' the gypsy insisted as Elizabeth cuddled Angelina to her. 'Look at your child and tell me what you see.'

Afraid to look, somehow she found the courage. Her eyes filled with horror when she gazed at the infant cuddled in her arms. She shuddered with revulsion when she saw bold, black eyes staring back at her. 'The child is a changeling,' she cried out.

Turning her face from the infant she saw Thomas standing in the doorway. He was smiling oddly at her. 'Thomas, where is Angelina?' she screamed over and over again. 'What have you done with her?'

'Hush, Mama, I am here.'

Elizabeth jerked awake to find Angelina standing by her bed Behind her, the maid held a candle aloft. Her face was pale, her eyes frightened. 'You was screaming something awful, My Lady. I couldn't rouse you.'

'I was dreaming,' Elizabeth said vaguely. Gazing about her, she was relieved to discover she was safely in her own chamber. As the horror of the dream came back, she reached out to grip Angelina's wrist. 'They took you away from me, Angelina. They took my dear, sweet baby, and gave me another in your place.'

'It was a bad dream.' Angelina stroked her mother's brow to soothe her. 'I'll stay with you until you're less agitated and able to sleep.' Gently, she loosened her mother's grip, but kept hold of her hand. 'Close your eyes, Mama. I'll sing you a lullaby.'

'You're treating me like an infant,' she protested, smiling at her solicitude. Nevertheless, she did as she was bid, and soon Angelina's sweet voice filled her ears.

Thomas named this daughter of ours well, she mused as she began to relax. She sings like an angel.

The nightmare faded, replaced by another dream. She was dressed in her bridal gown, Thomas had an expression of great tenderness in his eyes as he gazed at her. He loved me then, she thought, her lips curving in a smile, so why did he stop loving me?

He loves you still! The voice was part of the wind that sighed in the chimney, and became part of the lullaby Angelina sang. *Thomas Wrey loves you still . . . he loves you.* Then the voice faded, becoming a joyous melody of sound.

Elizabeth opened her eyes to morning, saw in the branches of a tree outside her window a song-thrush warbling a refrain.

Angelina's hand was still clasped, warm and comforting, in hers. She was curled up next to her on top of the covers. Knees drawn up under her robe, her bare feet were peeping from beneath it. Her hair was spread in wild abandon, her face barely visible through the silken strands.

'My one true daughter,' she murmured, gently brushing the hair from Angelina's face. She regarded with sadness the child she'd held in her arms for one brief glorious moment and whispered, 'I did not have another.'

The bird finished his song and gazed at her, its head cocked to one side. 'So who is Rosabelle, and where did she come from?' she asked it.

The song-thrush had no answer. Fluffing up its feathers it gazed at her for moment longer, then with a swift, sharp movement, spread its wings and took flight.

CHAPTER FOURTEEN

'I suggest we search the area in pairs, gentlemen, then take up positions upon the road just before dusk.'

'You do not expect me to go,' Nicholas Snelling cried out in alarm. 'I'm exhausted, I spent the entire day wandering in the forest. The rascal came at me in broad daylight, wearing a great flapping coat, and fearsomely cowed. He chased me into the forest and robbed me a second time. He must have known the saddle concealed gold.'

'I'm not surprised,' William said caustically. 'You crowed about it like a scalded turkey cock last night.'

'That's enough, Will,' Thomas remonstrated.

Subsiding on to a chair, the agitated young man closed his eyes and executed a delicate shudder. 'The rogue was so strong.'

'You may stay and amuse the ladies; they'll enjoy having a London gentleman gracing the drawing-room,' Thomas said drily.

William and James exchanged a grin.

Nicholas inspected his jacket. 'I'll do my utmost to bring them up to date on the latest gossip and fashions, but first I must take advantage of your manservant, and perhaps partake of a little sustenance. I have no wish to insult the ladies by appearing in such disarray, nor faint from hunger in their presence.'

'*God's truth!*' Thomas muttered to himself as he jerked at a bell pull. '*Does this fop think the women of Wrey a spineless bunch who suffer the vapours at the sight of a little dust?*'

As soon as Nicholas had gone the men checked their weapons. They had a brace of loaded pistols apiece, as well as swords. One or two had stout cudgels as well. Quaffing a jug of mulled ale to fortify their spirits, they set off with spurs jingling, shouting instructions to one another.

'The highwayman will hear them coming from a mile away,' Angelina said irreverently, as she and Rosabelle watched the departure from the drawing-room window. Both pairs of eyes were on Rafe, tall and relaxed in the saddle as he rode side by side with James.

Rosabelle's sulky expression changed to one of sly amusement. 'I doubt if they'll catch him. The highwayman is too clever, and too brave.'

'A brave man would not have attacked our mother,' Angelina pointed out. 'Nor held the marquis at pistol point. That was the work of a knave.'

'A pity he didn't kill George,' Rosabelle said bitterly. 'If he had, I would now be betrothed to Rafe.'

Angelina smiled to herself. 'If Rafe had any intentions towards you he would have staked his claim before the ball.'

'Since you've only recently met, don't presume what his attentions were.' Rosabelle gave a superior smile. 'Rafe and I had arranged to meet in the pavilion, my dear sister. If the marquis had not seized the opportunity to follow me. . . ?'

'Your assignation was with Rafe!' The painful thump her heart gave, left her feeling hollow. 'That cannot be, Rafe is a gentleman.'

'Rafe is a man.' Rosabelle's smile was malicious. 'He's renowned in London circles for his affairs with married women. I daresay I'll become one of them when I'm wed.'

Angelina couldn't keep the anger from her voice. 'You're lying. Rafe is too honourable a man to pursue another man's wife.'

'Little innocent,' Rosabelle scoffed. 'Men need women for their baser needs, even unattached men. That's why Papa maintains Mary Mellor in the village; she's his mistress.'

Angelina gasped. 'Does Mama know?'

'How can she fail to know, when Frey is there to remind her?' She shrugged. 'If Mama cared, she'd have got rid of her. Her frigid blood prevents her from performing the duties of a wife. As you're like her, I daresay you'll suffer much the same affliction. Thank God my blood is warm. I shall enjoy many lovers once I'm married, and Rafe shall be the first.'

Shocked, Angelina wanted to slap the smirk from her sister's face. Instead, she accused with what she hoped was crushing finality, 'You have the mind of a gutter-snipe. I'm ashamed to call you sister.'

'Be that as it may,' Rosabelle taunted, enjoying Angelina's scandalized expression. 'When you are betrothed yourself, you may wish to come to me to be educated in the way men like to be satisfied.'

'If you're referring to the act of union between husband and wife, I'm well aware of what is involved. There were many medical text books in the Chevonleigh library. I read them all.'

'Did they tell you the pleasure a woman feels when a man touches her? I cannot wait until Rafe—'

'I refuse to endure your vulgar company a moment longer.' Rising, Angelina conveyed herself rapidly towards the door. She was about to pass through it when she collided with Celine and her mother, coming in the opposite direction. 'I'm sorry,' she gasped. 'I was just leaving.'

'So I notice from the direction in which you're heading,' Elizabeth said with a touch of asperity. 'Have you wings on your feet that you must rush about so?'

Celine laid a hand on her arm. 'We are to have Lord Snelling as company. If he's not to bore us completely, you must take a turn at the harpsichord between card games.'

Angelina's heart sank when she saw Nicholas mincing in their direction. She looked about her for means of escape, but was restrained by her mother's fingers gently closing around her wrist.

'It's *you* he's interested in, Angelina,' she teased. 'I do believe the boy intends to petition for your hand.'

'And he might get it,' she retorted. 'Only it will not be in marriage. He's an unmitigated bore.'

'You must learn to handle such people.' Elizabeth turned when Nicholas came up behind them, her face smiling and serene.

Angelina observed how easily her mother assumed the role of the 'countess. 'My dear Lord Snelling. I'm so sorry to learn of your encounter, you were not injured, I trust?'

Angelina adopted the same expression as she cooed in a tone exactly like Elizabeth's, 'We are *panting* to hear the account of your heroic encounter, you must tell us all about it, dear Lord Snelling.'

Celine's giggle turned into a discreet cough when Elizabeth's narrowed glance encountered Angelina's innocent, cherubic smile. 'Shall we go in?' she murmured, trying to keep the laughter from her voice. 'Rosabelle is waiting for us, I believe.'

'Ah, the fair Rosabelle!' Nicholas exclaimed, when he set eyes on her, and taking up a stance in the centre of the room, he placed his hands dramatically on his chest. 'How many hearts did she break last night?'

Rosabelle fluttered her eyelashes at him. 'I doubt if I broke your heart, My Lord.' Angelina was stung by a glance. 'It's my sister for whom you wrote that poem, I believe.'

'Ah yes!' Nicholas bowed towards Angelina. 'But I composed another whilst I wandered in the woods. *She was the queen of roses, alas I was but poor, I lingered in my passion, by her chamber door. She passed me – cruel cruel-hearted. Passed me by. Twas thus we met and parted, the thorned red rose and I.*'

'His Grace, the Duke of Amberley,' a footman announced, offering Elizabeth a card on a silver salver. 'He requests an audience.'

'Ask His Grace to join us, then bring some refreshment.'

Angelina exchanged a glance with Celine and rolled her eyes. Celine smiled in sympathy when the pale young duke was shown in.

He gazed around at the women, stammering painfully, 'I'd hoped for an audience with the earl.'

'I'm afraid he's out chasing the highwayman around the countryside, Your Grace.' Elizabeth smiled and invited, 'Will you stay and take supper with us? Lord Snelling has given us a recitation of his poetry, and my daughter, Angelina, will shortly entertain us on the harpsichord.'

The duke's watery eyes sought her out. 'I've heard you are singularly accomplished on the instrument, Lady Angelina. Would you allow me to turn the pages of the music?'

'I need no music for the piece I am about to play,' she murmured, rising to her feet. 'Pray be seated, Your Grace.'

'I cannot stay long, Mama is waiting for my return.' He turned again to Elizabeth. 'If I could prevail upon you to furnish me with quill and paper after Lady Angelina has finished her piece, I will leave a note and my card for the earl.' He spread his coat tails, setting his ample behind on a chair.

Angelina chose a piece which was short and easy to play. Nicholas draped himself decoratively against the harpsichord as if to stake his claim, gazing at her through soulful eyes. Every now and then he darted a fluttering sideways glance at the duke, whose second chin wobbled as he tapped his foot in time with the music.

'Charming,' the duke muttered, reddening a little as he kissed Elizabeth's hand and begged her leave to go. After a few painful attempts at conversation punctuated by awkward pauses, a servant was summoned to escort him to the earl's study to write his missive.

The evening was an ode to tedium. Nicholas bored them all, beat them at cards more times than was polite, and crowed all the while about his own cleverness. Her mother glanced at the clock on several occasions, but the hands seemed to creep around its face with irritating slowness.

Rosabelle gave up any pretence of making polite conversation and stared moodily out of the window. Celine smiled serenely, every inch the lady. She had a knack of being able to converse on any subject, and on more than one occasion, rescued the conversation from flagging.

Angelina wished she was more like her instead of seething with the impatience that bedevilled her. She wanted to kick this strutting little bantam in the seat of his breeches and send him about his business.

Finally, when she could take no more, she gazed appealingly at her mother, murmuring, 'You appear fatigued, Mama. Can I get you anything?'

Elizabeth stifled a yawn behind her fan. 'Perhaps Lord Snelling will excuse us if we retire a little earlier than usual.'

'I'd be desolate if I kept you from your beauty sleep,' he cried out. 'The earl has offered me the hospitality of his roof for the night. I'll wait for his return until I retire.' His glance fell on Angelina and his voice dropped to a more intimate level. 'There's something of the utmost importance I wish to discuss with him.'

What that something was, Angelina couldn't fail to know. With a noncommittal smile she rose to her feet when her mother did, then with Rosabelle and Celine in tow, thankfully escaped.

There was a collective sigh when the door closed. Rosabelle had a smirk on her face. 'I'd rather wed George than either of your suitors.'

'Good,' Elizabeth said crisply, 'because that's exactly what you are going to do.'

George had paired off with William. Dusk fell swiftly; the moon was a bright orb that sent fingers of light through the canopy of trees. They stood side by side in a listening attitude. The marquis' horse shifted nervously when an owl hooted nearby.

'Try and keep the beast still,' William whispered. 'I thought I heard something over towards the bog.'

A few seconds later they both heard the faint snicker of a horse.

'I think we've got the beggar,' George whispered.

'Not yet we haven't.' Shading the lantern they carried with his hat, William's eyes strained into the forest. He smiled when a shadow passed through a patch of moonlight. 'Try not to make a sound,' he warned. 'Whoever is abroad is taking this path.'

Pistols cocked, they waited as the sound of hoof-beats came to their ears. The fellow was making no attempt to conceal his movements and the marquis frowned. 'There seems to be two riders,' he muttered. 'Perhaps he has an accomplice?'

'We'll soon find out. Cover me, George, but don't shoot unless you have to; we want him alive.' Stepping into the path of the rider, William unshaded the lantern. 'Rein in your mounts and show your faces.'

The rider's horse came to a halt and stood quietly obedient, the other shied nervously until it was brought under control.

'That's him!' George shouted in excitement. 'I'd know that horse anywhere. Damned well-trained nag!'

'Not surprising,' William drawled. 'I trained him myself.' He kept his pistol pointed at his half-brother. 'Well, well, who would have believed Frey Mellor to be the highwayman. What have you got to say for yourself, Frey?'

'Just a minute, Will,' the marquis said uneasily. 'That nag has white on him. The horse I saw was black.'

'He's leading Snelling's horse,' William pointed out.

'I thought the pretty boy rode a chestnut.'

'The horse was trapped in the bog,' Frey said. 'I managed to free him, and was bringing him to Wrey House. He's distressed.'

Wheeling his mount forward William scooped a handful of black slimy mud from the chestnut and smeared it over the blaze of white on Frey's mount. He gazed at the marquis with a thoughtful look on his face. 'What think you now, George?'

'Clever,' the marquis mused, his glance coming up from the horse to Frey's set face. 'He's wearing the same type of coat. Yes, Will, I could almost swear this is the man who robbed me on the highway.'

'You are sure?'

'As sure as I can be. I warrant if we search his house we'll find my snuff box.'

'Then we'll do it.'

'Hold on, my boy,' George muttered. 'Let's not do anything rash. If he makes good the losses . . . damn it, the lad is your brother, after all.'

'Half-brother,' William reminded him.

'Let's wait to hear what your father has to say about this. Signal him whilst I keep guard.'

'I was given this horse only three days ago, long after the highwayman began operating in the district,' Frey said desperately, when the marquis held a loaded pistol to his head. 'It was a birthday present from the earl. You know that to be the truth, William. The horse was one he bought from you.'

'That horse was turned free each night in the meadow near my stables. Anyone could have taken it, I've often seen him muddied, and wondered at it.'

'But the coat is also one you cast out.' Frey stared at Will with a plea in his eyes. 'Would you see your own brother hang for crimes he didn't commit?'

'I outgrew that coat two years since,' William snarled. 'Are you trying to cast the blame for your scurrilous crimes on me, you bastard?' Lifting his crop he struck Frey across the face, sending him tumbling to the ground. Frey's face was bleeding when he got to his feet. He fell again when a second blow landed across his shoulders.

Leaping from his horse, William pressed his foot against Frey's spine to keep him there. 'Search the horses, George, we may find more evidence before we take him in.'

Nicholas Snelling's gold was still concealed in the saddle of the chestnut. From the hem of the coat, where it had slipped through a recently mended hole in the pocket, a silver snuff box and cameo brooch was discovered.

'I swear to you, I did not commit these crimes,' Frey said in desperation when William pulled him to his feet and bound his hands behind his back. 'You're making a mistake.'

It was no use. Roped to William's saddle, Frey was half-dragged through the undergrowth to the road. There, William placed his fingers to his lips and gave a piercing whistle. Within minutes, half-a-dozen men appeared in answer to the signal.

The earl gazed at Frey with sorrowful eyes when George told the tale of his capture. 'You've betrayed my trust,' he said heavily. 'What have you to say for yourself?'

Frey drew himself up, saying with as much dignity as he could muster, 'A mistake has been made, sir. All my life I've sought only to earn your respect and acknowledgement. I'm falsely accused of these crimes.'

'The evidence is overwhelming,' Thomas said quietly. 'Take him to Wrey House, gentlemen. Lock him in the cellar until I can arrange his transportation to the watch-house. I have the unenviable task of informing his mother.'

'Break it to her gently,' Frey shouted as he was roughly led away. He fell flat on his face when the rope jerked, and cried out in pain when his mouth made contact with a sharp stone.

Rafe snatched the rope from William's hand. 'There's no need for such rough handling. Fetch his horse,' he said, his voice ringing with such authority, William obeyed with alacrity.

Rafe unhooked the carcasses of a pair of rabbits from the saddle and threw them into the undergrowth. 'Can you mount unassisted, Mr Mellor?'

'Yes, My Lord,' Frey mumbled through his split lip. Scrambling on to the mount's back he gave Rafe a grateful look. 'My thanks.'

'We'll ride quietly together. If you promise not to attempt to escape I'll untie your hands.'

'You have it.' Frey winced when a knife sliced through the cord and the blood flowed back into his hands. The men ranged around him and, with William leading the way, they headed towards Wrey House.

Frey had often dreamed of being made welcome at Wrey House. When they cantered through the gates he considered it ironic that his first official visit should be his last.

He'd underestimated the animosity William held for him. Unless he was very much mistaken, his brother had plotted to bring about his downfall. The hangman would carry out William's dirty work, and his brother would walk free without a stain on his conscience.

William and George took him down to the cellar. Not for Frey the freedom of the larger space, led to a small, airless room he was pushed roughly inside. When the door slammed shut, he reached out in the darkness. Before his elbows straightened his hands touched wall on either side of him. When he stood, his head made contact with the roof.

The room was little more than a cavity. He sank to the cold stone floor and lifted his hands to his aching head. Not a chink of light pierced the blackness, not a sound penetrated from outside. Used to the outdoors, he felt as if he'd been entombed. He willed away the panic threatening to engulf him, and turning his mind to some Latin translation he'd been working on, in a little while, fell asleep.

'May I speak with you on a matter of some importance, James?'

Glancing up from the book he was studying, James gave a regretful smile. 'If it's about Frey, there's nothing I can do, Angelina. The evidence against him is too strong.'

She came to stand beside him, saying tremulously, 'Do the ties of blood mean nothing to you?'

Her face had a pinched look to it, as if she'd been crying. It was strange how much the family had come to mean to her. Much of his life had been spent away from Wrey House and he hardly knew his illegitimate half-brother.

Taking her hand in his, he smiled, sympathetic. 'Perhaps I could recommend a friend of mine to conduct his defence. The church rector has offered to give him a character reference, so has Rafe.'

He withheld a sigh when hope flared in her eyes. Neither would save Frey from the hangman's noose. Nicholas Snelling and George Northbridge had already signed statements, swearing he was the man who'd robbed them.

'Would you take me to see him?' she asked.

'Will's made himself responsible for Frey. You'll have to ask him.'

'They are enemies, and he refuses.' She placed her hand on his sleeve. 'If Frey is to die, I want him to know someone cares. It might bring him comfort to know I'll pray for him.'

James doubted if a prayer would be much comfort, but didn't have the heart to say so. 'I'll speak with Will.'

'He's gone about his business.' Anger flared in her eyes. 'You are the earl's heir, and also my guardian. Why should you consult Will? If you refuse to help me I'll go and make my request directly to my father.' Determination evident in her face, she turned and stalked towards the door.

He scrambled to his feet. 'You must not disturb him with this. He's sorely troubled, and has been sequestered in his study for two days.'

'But not as troubled as Frey must be,' she said tartly, and she turned to face him. 'Frey is facing death. He is your brother; how can you calmly read a book? And if the earl had any feelings he'd offer comfort and guidance to his son, not skulk in his study feeling sorry for himself.'

'Wait!' With an exasperated sigh, he joined her at the door. 'You have a knack of twisting things to your own advantage. Although there's truth in what you say, I cannot allow you to intrude on Father's grief.' Realizing she'd outwitted him with a simple bluff, he managed a rueful grin. 'I cannot think of one reason why you shouldn't see Frey.'

'Thank you, dearest James.' She threw her arms around him and kissed him soundly. 'I knew you wouldn't disappoint me.'

James enjoyed her unaffected display of affection as much as he'd enjoyed the skirmish. 'It's a pity you were not born a man, you'd have made an excellent attorney.'

Her face dimpled into a wicked smile. 'Sometimes it's better to appeal to the wisdom of men than argue with their logic.'

Delighted by her wit, he laughed and kissed her on the end of the nose. 'Then the man who wins your heart must be wise as well as logical, for you are fain to pit your wits against logic, and appeal only to wisdom when the situation warrants.'

'If this mythical man learns to read me as easily as you, then I'll be in serious trouble,' she said ruefully.

They linked hands as they walked towards the cellars. 'Not if he's a man of intelligence. He will treasure the unique qualities you possess and enjoy your companionship.' He stopped to light up a lantern before they proceeded down the cellar steps. 'Are you sure you want to see him, I don't want you to be upset.'

'I'm already upset over this affair.' Her eyes were troubled. 'I'm not convinced Frey is guilty. The glimpse I had of the highwayman. . . .' She shook her head at some elusive glimpse of memory. 'I'm plagued by the idea there's something I should remember, but I cannot bring it to mind.'

'If you recall it, let me know, however insignificant it seems.' Finding the cellar door ajar, he frowned. 'Shouldn't this door be kept locked?' he said, when a burly man sprang to his feet at the sight of them.

'There be no need, My Lord.' The servant jerked a thumb at a stout door set into the far wall. 'Master William said he must be kept in there.'

James's eyes darkened as he detected a distinctly foul smell. 'How long has Mr Mellor been in there?'

'Since he was brought in, My Lord.' The servant shifted awkwardly when James gave him a long, hard stare. 'Orders, My Lord. Master William said he must not be given sustenance or allowed out.'

Angelina gave an anguished gasp.

'And you obeyed those orders?'

The man had a defensive look in his eye when he mumbled, 'I wouldn't leave a dog that long without water, sir.'

James's lips twitched into a semblance of a smile. 'We wish to speak with him. After we're gone, he's not to be returned to the confinement of the store cupboard.'

The man's eyes flicked to Angelina. 'If you don't mind me mentioning it, like, Mr Mellor's present condition is likely to cause offence.'

James gave Angelina an apologetic shrug and indicated the steps. She was not to be deterred from her purpose. 'I'll return in one hour,' she said icily. 'I expect my brother to be made presentable, and fed.'

The servant gazed uncomfortably at James, who nodded in confirmation. 'What will I tell Master William if he returns, My Lord?'

'Refer him to me,' James said comfortably, before guiding Angelina back towards the door.

Frey was seated on a barrel when they returned. His face was pale and bruised, his lip swollen. Remains of some bread and cheese, and a pitcher of milk were set on another barrel.

He swayed to his feet when he saw them, distress darkening his face. Harshly, he said to James, 'Why did you bring her here?'

'Because I asked him to.' Angelina crossed to where he sat and gently touched his swollen lip. 'That needs salve if it's not to become infected. I've brought some with me.'

With a bitter laugh, he moved away from her. 'My executioner will not care whether it's infected or not; why should you?'

'Because you're my brother.' She guided him back to his seat and took a small jar from her pocket. 'Try not to lose faith,' she said, applying the ointment to his wounds. 'I caught a glimpse of the highwayman's face, and know it was not you. James has determined to find a competent advocate to defend you, and I'll appear as a witness, if necessary.'

'You can't!' James exclaimed, moving to her side. 'I absolutely forbid it. It will cause a scandal.'

'Would you leave our brother defenceless?'

He'd never felt such anger. 'This is neither the time or place to indulge in a battle of wits. I'm surprised you'd consider such a foolish notion when two peers of the realm have already sworn to his guilt. You're a woman, and your testimony, *which* I might add, is based on nothing but intuition, will cause derision to fall upon your head, and ... and ... embarrass the entire family.'

Her eyes flashed with scornful light. 'It's my head, and I do not give a tinker's cuss for anyone's embarrassment when Frey's life is at stake.'

'Listen to him, Angelina.' Frey's face was troubled. 'I'm humbled by your concern, and God knows, I need someone on my side, but you embark on a futile exercise. Such an action will alienate you from your family, and you'll gain notoriety, something that will haunt you throughout your life.'

'I do not care,' she said stubbornly.

'*I do!*' Pushing her hand aside he rose to his feet. 'You seem to imagine you and I are bound together. You're wrong. Neither you nor the rest of the Wrey family mean anything to me. I do not welcome, or *want*, your interference.'

'Frey,' she whispered, her voice so crushed and broken it brought a lump to James's throat. 'You cannot mean that, you saved my life.'

'The life of a rabbit would have deserved as much consideration,' he said stonily. 'Take her from my sight, My Lord, and do not bring her here again.'

'Frey. . . .'

'*Leave me in peace!*' he shouted, and James could see how hard he fought to keep from breaking down.

'I'll pray for you.' She glanced back at Frey, his shoulders slumped now, his face buried in his hands, calling out in desperation, 'Tell me you didn't mean what you just said.'

James answered for him. 'He couldn't have made it clearer. Go to Celine, I'll join you in a little while.' Understanding what Frey was going through, he made his voice unnecessarily harsh as he pushed her towards the door. He watched her stumble away before he turned back to the youth. The despair in Frey's face was terrible to behold.

'You understand,' he said miserably, 'I had no other choice. Later . . . after I'm gone, you'll tell her of my affection for her.'

James held out his hand. 'You're a brave man, Frey. If there's anything I can do, I will.'

'Just believe, as Angelina does, that I'm unjustly accused.'

Until then, James had not considered him other than guilty. Swiftly, he weighed up the evidence in his mind.

Neither of the witnesses had seen the highwayman unmasked, and Frey's account of the horse being rescued from the bog was plausible. Angelina's belief of Frey's innocence was emotionally based, but she'd said there was something she couldn't recall. He wondered if he'd misjudged him.

He shook his head. If it hadn't been for the snuff box and cameo brooch discovered in the lining of the coat, a coat Mary Mellor had sworn was amongst a bundle of discarded clothing from Wrey House, the evidence would be circumstantial.

Nicholas Snelling had said the highwayman was wearing a voluminous cloak that day! That tipped the scales slightly in Frey's favour, as far as James was concerned. No cloak, or other stolen items, had been found at the cottage. The small cache of coins concealed behind a loose brick were of insignificant value, and had been accounted for by Mary Mellor as her life savings. He'd thought it a small sum for her years of service, but knowing his father's leaning towards parsimony, he'd not been surprised.

He dismissed the servant and, seating himself on a stool opposite Frey, said, 'Tell me what you were doing in the forest that night.'

'Checking my rabbit snares.'

Memory provided him with a picture of Rafe throwing a brace of rabbits into the undergrowth. James smiled encouragingly at him. 'I'd like to hear your version of what occurred that night.'

Hope flared in Frey's eyes, then just as quickly died a painful death. 'What's the use? You'll side with the rest of them, whatever I say.'

'Don't presume to know what I'll do,' he said, sharply enough to jolt his bastard brother from self-pity. 'May I remind you, your life is at stake. If I think an injustice has been done, I'll do my utmost to right that wrong.'

'You'd oppose the will of the earl?' Frey gave him a sceptical look.

'Believe it or not, the earl is a fair and rational man. If he's convinced of your innocence he'll not stand by and watch you die.'

'And if he's not convinced, but you are?'

James gave a faint smile, and shrugged. 'No doubt I'll endear myself greatly to Angelina if I spit in the face of convention and take up your cause.' His eyes engaged Frey's, taking his measure. He liked the way the youth met his gaze squarely. 'You greatly resemble our father in appearance. I hope you do not prove to be as proud.'

'I've never been given reason to feel pride in my parentage.' Despite his heated tone, Frey gave a gentle self-deprecating chuckle. 'You're not like William, Brother James, nor do you favour the earl.'

'Now you've reached that conclusion, perhaps we can apply our minds to the business at hand,' James said drily. 'Now, tell me from the beginning. What were your movements on the evening you were apprehended?'

CHAPTER FIFTEEN

Elizabeth was pensive as the carriage conveyed her towards Mary Mellor's cottage. She'd intended to confront Thomas about Rosabelle's parentage, but he'd confined himself to his study, leaving strict orders he couldn't be disturbed by anyone except James.

The possibility of him admitting culpability was remote, unless she had proof. The only person who could provide her with it was Mary.

She'd also thought to approach James. Alexandra Chadwick had been party to the affair, and he would be fully aware of the situation. Deception would be distasteful to him, but given a choice, he would be bound by his duty to his father.

The thought of seeing her husband's mistress was upsetting, but Mary would be vulnerable now, and Elizabeth was counting on the fact she'd be angry about her son's treatment and would disclose the information she sought.

Since her dream, she'd seen Rosabelle through different eyes, and was certain she was not her daughter. They were nothing alike, and except for her dark eyes and hair she bore no resemblance to Thomas, either. Aware of possible ramifications, she harboured niggling doubts about the course of action she'd decided on, for, if word got out, there would be no marriage for Rosabelle. In addition, she and her husband would be branded cheats and liars. Elizabeth was prepared to pay heavily for Mary's silence.

She took a deep breath, steadying her nerves when the carriage drew to a halt in front of the cottage. Alighting from the carriage, she smoothed her skirt, then instructing her maid to wait, motioned to the driver to disperse the curious village women who'd followed after her carriage.

Mary's eyes were red from crying when she opened the door. She didn't seem surprised to see her. Standing to one side, she bobbed a curtsy and bade her enter.

The cottage was clean, if poorly furnished. Mary wore a patched and faded gown. Thomas might confer his favours on this woman, but she didn't live a life of ease. Elizabeth experienced an unexpected twinge of sympathy for her.

'If you've come to gloat,' Mary said, 'say your piece. I daresay you think I deserve it.'

Elizabeth seated herself on a wooden chair by the table. 'I find no room in my heart to gloat over your misfortune.' This was no place to indulge in social niceties, so she came to the point. 'I'm seeking information about the birth of Rosabelle. I think you're in possession of facts which may assist me.'

Mary's breath hissed in her throat and she took a few steps backwards. 'I don't know what you mean.'

'You know *exactly* what I mean. Rosabelle's not my child, is she?'

'I know nothing about it,' Mary whined, her eyes darting about the room as if seeking escape. 'If the earl found out I said anything. . . .'

'Do you think he'll remain in ignorance of this visit for long?' Elizabeth gave a light laugh. 'I intend to tell him once he's finished wrestling with his conscience over Frey.'

Throwing her apron over her face, Mary rocked back and forth. 'I'll be thrown out of the cottage,' she wailed. 'They be taking my boy to London in a day or two, I won't have any money to help him.'

The anguish in her voice touched Elizabeth. This, she could understand. Rising, she placed a hand on the woman's arm. 'I'll exchange a purse of gold coins for the truth. In return for your continuing silence, I'll make sure your son is helped. I have no quarrel with your son, and the viscount is interested in defending him.'

Throwing down her apron, Mary brought her hands to her hips. 'I brought Frey up to be honest, he ain't guilty of highway robbery. If you ask me, this lie is one of Master William's plots. That boy always hated Frey.'

Elizabeth refused to be diverted from her mission. 'Be that as it may, I'm not here to discuss Frey's plight, nor your past relationship with my husband. I'm here to learn the truth about Rosabelle's birth. I've made you a generous offer. Just bear in mind, once the earl hears of my visit, he'll have no choice but to throw you out.'

A sly smile crossed Mary's face. 'What's to stop me demanding more from the earl for my silence about Rosabelle?'

Elizabeth's eyes narrowed cruelly. Softly, she suggested, 'The earl might decide on a cheaper method of ensuring your silence.'

Mary blanched. 'Ain't you afeared of what you be doing, Lady Elizabeth? The earl has a mighty temper on him, at times.'

Elizabeth allowed herself a small smile at the thought of Thomas losing his temper with her. In nineteen years of marriage he'd never done so. But then, she mused, until now she had never given him reason. She discovered she didn't care. 'I have one to equal it, when the occasion demands.'

'The earl loves you true, so I daresay he treats you different to me.'

Surprise filled her. 'My husband told you that?'

'It's plain as the nose on my face when he whispers your name—' Abruptly, she stopped, red-faced. 'He loves you all right, I can vouch for it.'

Elizabeth's sensibilities were not quite as affronted as they should have been by this revelation from the mouth of her husband's whore, but she was not about to let Mary know it. She threw a purse on the table. 'Quickly now, have you made up your mind?'

The tip of pink tongue wet Mary's lips when she gazed at the purse. When her voice assumed a business-like tone, Elizabeth knew she'd won. 'I'll inspect the contents please, My Lady.'

Loosening the purse strings, Elizabeth sent a cascade of gold coins across the scarred surface of the table. Eyes gleaming, Mary reached out. Elizabeth stilled her wrist before she could pick up one of the coins.

'First, you'll agree to tell me the truth, Mary Mellor. After which, you'll gather your belongings together and my carriage will convey you to the coaching inn. The villagers are gathering outside. I cannot vouch for your safety if they think you no longer enjoy the protection of the earl.'

Respect grew in Mary's eyes. She nodded. 'Would you tell my boy I've gone to London, and will stand by him, come what may?'

'I'll make sure the message is conveyed to him.' She released Mary's wrist, allowing her to scoop the coins into the leather purse. When the purse was secured in the pocket of her skirt, Mary smiled with a new confidence.

'It was like this, My Lady. . . .'

Neither of them heard the back door of the cottage open a crack, or saw William, who stood with his ear pressed against the opening.

A few minutes later, he eased it shut and made his way across the back meadow to where his horse was tethered. Soon he was on his way, a disbelieving expression in his eyes.

It had only been by chance he'd seen the Wrey carriage; he usually by-passed the village. On his way back from selling his surplus horses at market in the neighbouring county, he'd resisted the urge to dispose of the black stallion, moving it instead to a secret location in the forest. It was too valuable an addition to the stud stock he intended to ship to America.

Had he stayed longer, he'd have witnessed his stepmother take a brand from the fire and throw it into the middle of the bed Mary Mellor had shared with his father, and the cheers of the village women as she emerged from the burning cottage.

Two hours later, when Elizabeth arrived back at Wrey House, there was nothing left of the cottage but smouldering ashes.

Elizabeth didn't waste any time. Thomas was still in his study, and although he'd left instructions not to be disturbed, she determined to risk his ire and charge him with what she'd learned. Slipping inside, she closed the door and stood with her back pressed against the oak panels. 'I wish to speak to you on a matter of great urgency, Thomas.'

Her husband turned and gazed at her. He looked haggard, and she briefly regretted the necessity to confront him when it was obvious Frey's plight weighed heavily on his mind. Yet she knew his anger would know no bounds if word reached him from another source.

'What is it, my dear?'

'I've been to see Mary Mellor.'

She held her breath when a startled look came into his eyes. Then his shoulders slumped and he said in a tired voice, 'I should have ended the affair years ago. I didn't intend to hurt you, Elizabeth.'

Encouraged by his words she crossed to his side. 'The reason I visited her was to confirm the suspicions I had regarding Rosabelle.'

'Then you know.' His voice was dull.

'I think I've always known.' Seating herself on the footstool she took her husband's hand in hers. 'Why did you do it, Thomas?'

His free hand brushed against her cheek. 'You wanted a child so badly, and I was convinced Angelina would die.' He gazed with sadness on her. 'I didn't want you to suffer the pain of losing your infant daughter after what you'd been through.'

'So you found me another child.' Tears came to her eyes and spilled unheeded down her cheeks. 'If Angelina had died we could have had another of our own.'

His voice strengthened as he said simply, 'I didn't want to risk losing you to childbirth, Elizabeth. I love you too much.'

'Oh, Thomas.' She laid her head against his knee. 'All these years I've longed to hear you say those words. So much time has been wasted.'

'And now it's too late.' He sighed. 'First I alienated you, then I sired a son who suffered because I couldn't acknowledge him. If Frey hangs it will be my fault. Now Rosabelle's life is to be ruined. Tell me, Elizabeth, what must I do to put things right?'

Surprised by her husband's defeated attitude, she lifted her head. 'To start with you must show some strength. James is not convinced of Frey's guilt. Go and talk to the lad, let him know you care. If you're convinced of his innocence you must fight to save his life.'

'You'd be prepared to suffer the scandal?'

Elizabeth's laugh had a bitter ring to it. 'I've lived with it for the past eighteen years. Frey isn't responsible for his parentage, and must not be made to suffer because of it.'

Rising, she shook the creases from her gown and delivered the rest of her message. 'Mary's on her way to London. I've paid her handsomely for her continuing silence. As for Rosabelle, she'll marry George, and need never know she's not of our blood.'

Relief in his eyes, Thomas got to his feet. 'I'll do anything you ask of me, Elizabeth.'

'Then we're agreed.' His unexpected declaration of love and loss of pride in her presence was discomforting. Nevertheless, while it lasted, Elizabeth intended to take advantage of it. 'There's a condition I would impose upon you, Thomas.'

His eyes darkened, a sure sign his arrogance was returning. 'What is it?'

'You'll remember I'm your wife.' Her voice faltered when his mouth curved into a smile. She coloured. 'It's unlikely I'll conceive another child, and you've not been a good husband to me in the past, Thomas.'

'It will be my pleasure to change that, my dearest Elizabeth.'

There was such a surge of emotion in his voice that Elizabeth stared at him for a few seconds. Then he closed the space between them and took her in his arms. 'Dear God,' he whispered hungrily. 'How I've longed for you all these years.'

'I have a confession to make first,' she whispered. 'I burnt down Mary Mellor's cottage today.'

He stared at her for a moment, then his eyes crinkled with amusement. Her heart missed a few beats as his lips tentatively touched hers, then he was kissing her with such tenderness and love she forgot all the hurt of the past. Sliding her arms around him, she pulled him close.

*

Rafe hadn't expected to see Angelina at Ravenswood. Clad in a black riding habit, her cream silk shirt was a perfect contrast for the gleaming rope of hair streaming down her back.

She'd discarded her jacket and hat and was kneeling, trowel in hand, digging weeds from around the rose bushes. One of the Ravenswood hounds flopped on the ground beside her. It gave a blissful sigh when she fondled its ear.

Rafe looked around for Elizabeth, but saw only Angelina's horse, munching at a patch of long grass.

Dismounting, he leaned against a tree-trunk and watched her for a while. She hummed a tune as she worked, and stopped now and again to brush away a troublesome insect or address a remark to the dog. Presently, she sat back on her heels and sighed with satisfaction.

'There you are, ladies,' she said to the roses. 'Those weeds who sought to confine you, are gone.' When she cupped a full blown rose in her hands and drew its scented beauty towards her, Rafe crept up quietly behind her.

'Would you have your nose stung by a bee, fair Angelina?' he whispered in her ear.

The rose sprang from her hand, scattering its petals. She gave a small yelp of surprise. The dog growled at him before recognizing him as master and looking sheepish.

A handful of ripe raspberries dropped from her skirt when she rounded on him, a hand pressed to her breast. '*La, sir!*' she scolded. 'How you startled me. Could you not have warned me of your visit?'

He laughed. 'Are you saying the master of Ravenswood must warn Angelina Wrey when he visits his own home?'

She took the hands he offered and, rising gracefully to her feet, gave him a teasing smile. 'I'd quite forgotten you were the master of Ravenswood. You have my permission to visit any time you wish.'

'And you have permission to steal my raspberries any time you wish.' He smiled at the smear of juice across her face, then gazed at her earth-soiled hands, holding them fast when she tried to pull them away. 'Your mama would not consider these the hands of a lady.'

'If you are going to bore me with a lecture I shall take my leave of you.' The glance she slanted his way was bright with merriment. 'It's quite tedious to be continually reminded of my faults. That's why I escaped from Wrey House today.'

Shock replaced the laughter in his eyes. 'You came here unaccompanied?'

'James is with me,' she assured him, and gazed around her. 'His horse has headed for your vegetable garden, I think.' Observing his relieved expression, she chuckled. 'What would you have done had I been unchaperoned?'

'Kept you captive.' He gently wiped the red smear from her face with his handkerchief, exposing the light gold dusting of freckles. 'There,' he said with a smile. 'That looks more like my angel. Where is your brother?'

'The last time I saw him he was in your library with his nose stuck firmly between the pages of a book about horse bloodlines.' She screwed up her face. 'Now I've told you, I suppose you'll join him.'

'There's not enough room in one book for the noses of both James and myself.' He raised her dirty hand to his lips. 'I shall enjoy your company instead. After I show you the rest of the garden, we'll flush James out and take some refreshment together.'

'What if he looks for me?'

'He deserves a fright for not guarding you carefully enough.'

'Oh, I daresay James would consider me safe enough with you.' Her slanted glance contained curiosity. 'But then, he knows you well, so perhaps he would not.'

He chuckled, but wouldn't be drawn as they took a path shaded with arches of sweet-smelling, rambling roses. 'Perhaps not,' he said agreeably. 'But then, James might not consider me safe with you.'

Her eyes rounded in astonishment. 'How do I present danger to anyone?'

He made her the recipient of an amused glance. 'Don't play the innocent with me, Angel. I've heard you've already broken the hearts of two men.'

'Oh them.' Laughter filled her voice. 'One has too much to say for himself, the other nothing at all.' Her voice took on the mischievous note he knew so well. 'Since it's you who has the reputation of heart-breaker, I'm sure you'll survive a few short minutes in my company and emerge unscathed.'

'The reputation is unjustified.' Leading her towards a walled garden he pushed open a door, standing aside to allow her to enter. 'I've made it a rule not to trifle with the affections of young ladies, nor lead them to have expectations I cannot fulfil.'

'Yet many at the ball sighed when you approached, and their mamas did likewise.'

He drew her on to a seat under the drooping branches of a willow tree and gazed at her. 'These things are part of the ritual. A good mama needs to find a husband for her daughter, and men need wives to bear them children.'

'Then why are you not married?'

Had anyone else asked him that, Rafe would have considered it impertinent, but her expression was so trusting and guileless, he forgave her. 'I'd like nothing more than to settle. Unfortunately, I have nothing to offer a woman except a house which is falling about my ears. I could not even guarantee to put food on the table.'

'But if you married Caroline Pallister. . . ?'

'You've been listening to gossip,' he chided, then gave her a rueful grin. 'I admit I've considered taking Lady Caroline to wife, but my fortunes seem to have improved a little of late.' He shrugged. 'I'm sure Lady Caroline would make an excellent wife, but. . . .'

'Not for the master of Ravenswood.' She slanted her head to one side, holding him in a steady regard. 'Perhaps I'll marry you, Rafe. You're not proud with me, and I have wealth enough to restore Ravenswood.'

'Are you proposing to me, Angelina?' Amusement surged like a river through his veins. He was about to throw back his head and laugh when he saw the gravity of her sweet face.

The laughter strangled in his throat, replaced by a lump when she said earnestly, 'Although Lady Caroline is a worthy person, I think you'd be unhappy wed to her.'

'And you wish to save me from unhappiness, my sweet?'

The enormity of her impulsive proposal began to dawn on her, for colour crept under her skin and she lowered her eyes to her lap. 'Your happiness means much to me, Rafe. I daresay you think me a foolish child, which of course I am.' Her hands covered her face and she whispered in anguish, 'If you laugh at me, I shall die a thousand deaths.'

He had an urge to reach out and comfort her, but restrained himself. He'd not noticed any behaviour that suggested she nurtured romantic feelings towards him, on the contrary. She seemed to be unaffected, affectionate, and unawakened. Her innocence and honesty endeared her to him. She was fair of face and figure, intelligent, accomplished, and wealthy. A stray thought lodged in his brain: she'd be a perfect wife for him.

A frown creased his brow. He'd be doing her an injustice if he wed her. He liked her too much to take advantage of her wealth.

Catching the gleam of her eyes through her fingers, he realized she was observing his reaction. 'It's highly unusual for a man to receive a marriage proposal. I'm at a loss.'

'You've already given me an answer.' Lowering her hands, she gazed at him, expression shamed. 'I deserve your derision. I've been much too forward, and presumptuous.'

'You deserve only my thanks.' Rising, he pulled her from the bench and tenderly stroked a finger the length of her soft cheek.

For a moment she closed her eyes and turned her face against his caress. He saw the woman in her then. His breath caught in his throat as his brain registered the delicate, sensual beauty of the face that rose from the creamy column of her throat. Her perfectly curved lips and the tendrils of gold hair grazing against her skin were exquisite, her eyes with their sweep of dark lashes, arrestingly lovely. For the first time, he saw her as a desirable woman. 'I'm unworthy of you,' he murmured.

'I know.' She gave him a cruel, cat-like smile. 'You need not patronize me, Rafe. I'm aware you have a preference for married women. Perhaps I should marry Nicholas Snelling and take you for a lover, as Rosabelle intends to do when she marries the marquis.'

Stunned, he dropped his hand and stared at her. Her eyes were wide, and cold with anger, yet her lips trembled as if she was about to weep. She turned, picked up the folds of her skirt and started to run.

'Wait.' He realized she'd lashed out at him from humiliation rather than anger. He was astounded she'd heard whispers of his private life – even more astounded that Rosabelle should make such an outrageous suggestion.

Catching her up in no more than half-a dozen strides he brought her to a halt. She didn't struggle when he turned her to face him, but her stillness spoke of a deeply felt hurt. His heart went out to her. 'I value your company and friendship beyond measure, Angelina.' Gazing at the dilapidated house, he shrugged. 'But I'd watch Ravenswood crumble to dust rather than lose your respect by marrying you for your fortune.'

'My fortune is but poor excuse, Rafe, since I did not earn it. Were we to wed it would simply pass to any children we might have.'

He searched her face. Despite her embarrassment, she held his gaze in a way that made him ashamed. His answer had hidden the real reason for his refusal, and she deserved only honesty.

'Pride forbids me from accepting a proposal from a woman. You've taken me aback, Angelina. Will you forgive me for being so clumsy?'

She attempted a laugh, but it had a forlorn sound to it. 'Only if you forgive my stupidity for putting you in such an awkward position.'

He grinned a little. 'Now you're wounding *my* feelings. I was flattered by your regard.'

She did not smile. 'You must allow me to apologize. I made unfair accusations – accusations I wish to withdraw.'

He was uncomfortably aware they'd bordered on the truth. 'We'll consider them withdrawn and forgotten.'

A glimmer of a smile touched her lips. 'Then we're friends again?'

'We've never been anything else.' He'd intended to kiss her cheek, but his lips slid round to her mouth. Its quivering fullness was sweet, tasting of the raspberries she'd eaten. Her lips parted a little and his hands scanned her small waist and pulled her against him.

She gave a tiny gasp as his tongue flickered into the dewy sweetness of her mouth. Well aware he'd not enjoyed a woman for some time, Rafe allowed the kiss to develop into a longer one.

Angelina's limbs seemed to melt. Her mind told her she should not be allowing this, but the sensations chasing through her body were entirely new, and unexpectedly pleasurable. One minute she seemed to be tingling and alive, the next she was without coherent will or thought.

She became aware of the silky material of her bodice, of its coolness against her skin when the breeze sent it against her body. The swell of her breasts seemed softer and fuller when pressed against the warm body of Rafe. They throbbed with an awareness of wild joy. She felt so alive to him, her body sweetly troubled, awakened to feelings she hadn't known existed.

The diagrams in the medical books she'd read suddenly took on a new meaning. All this knowledge from one kiss, she mused. Like Eve and the apple. *But that was the original sin?* Panicking a little, she slid her hands against his chest, pushing him away. For a moment they stared at each other, both a little surprised by what had occurred between them.

Rafe's eyes hooded over. 'I'd better take you back to your brother,' he said quietly. 'He'll be wondering where you are.' Without another word, he took her hand in his and led her back towards the house.

CHAPTER SIXTEEN

William was amused by the look on Rosabelle's face when Angelina announced her plan.

'Assist Frey to escape!' she gasped. '*Lucifer's oath*! Are you insane? They've sent a trained soldier to guard him because the watch-house is full. He has no claim to family name or estate, so why should we help him?'

'Because he's innocent of the charge against him.' Angelina sounded desperate. 'I saw the highwayman's face, Will, I swear it was not Frey.'

Rosabelle turned to stare out of the window. 'If you can identify the felon, why don't you?'

'It was only an impression I got, yet I know the highwayman wasn't Frey.'

'You expect us to risk our lives on a glimpse in the dark?' Rounding on her, Rosabelle gave a scornful laugh. 'Your brain is as addled as a stale egg if you expect us to endanger ourselves over him.'

'And yours is so swollen with vanity and self-importance there's no room in it for anyone but yourself,' Angelina hissed.

William laughed when they glared at each other. The insult had hit its mark, for Rosabelle looked as sullen as a thwarted child. Angelina resembled a feral cat, all spit and fury. Tempted to encourage them to trade insults, it would serve for nothing but his own amusement, but given the choice, he'd have placed his money on the sharper-minded Angelina.

Strangely, her foolhardy scheme touched him. Angelina had embraced the family with a loyalty he found hard to grasp. Someone prepared to risk life and reputation in such a futile cause, earned his admiration, if not his support.

The plan she proposed was simple. She would lure the soldier into the garden, then Rosabelle would unlock the cellar door and guide Frey to a horse William had saddled and waiting. Frey would be hidden at his stables until he could be put aboard a ship and sent to foreign parts.

She'd underestimated the intelligence of the soldier, and overestimated her power to execute such a plan. Even if she managed to lure the soldier away, she'd given no thought to the danger she'd placed herself in. William simply couldn't allow it.

'Squabbling amongst yourselves will serve Frey nothing,' he said. 'Your plan is unworkable. Do you imagine I'd allow you to place yourself in jeopardy with a rough soldier?'

His eyes brooded on her disappointed face. Why was she appealing to him for help when she knew he didn't care if Frey lived or died? 'If Frey's not the highwayman, chances are the man will strike again and prove his innocence beyond all doubt,' he pointed out.

Rosabelle clapped her hands and smiled, her altercation with Angelina forgotten. Her eyes sparkled with excitement as she gazed his way. 'How clever you are, Will. I'm sure the man will show up again in time to rescue Frey. What fun it will be, like a melodrama at the playhouse. Can you imagine the despair he'll be in when he walks to the gallows? Right at the last minute the highwayman will strike, and he'll be saved. It will serve him right for thinking himself as good as us all these years.'

'He'd better show up long before Frey goes on his last walk,' he remarked. 'The wagon is coming to take him to London before the week's out.' When Rosabelle dissolved into laughter, he grinned. What a bitch she was.

Angelina didn't see any humour in the situation. 'You disgust me,' she snapped. 'Our brother is facing death and all you can do is jest. If it was *your* neck destined for the noose, Will, it would not seem so funny.'

Uneasily, he loosened his stock with his finger. 'I daresay I'd find the experience most unnerving.' He shot a glance at Rosabelle. 'How about you, Rosie, do you relish the thought of dancing on air at Tyburn?'

Her smile faded; her face paled. 'I suppose we must think of some way to help him,' she muttered. Her face suddenly brightened. 'George is taking me to the horse sales today, perhaps I can persuade him to drop the charges.'

Angelina's relieved smile was dampened by the reluctance in her voice. 'Nicholas Snelling has taken up residence at the inn, and seems disinclined to leave. If I send him a letter beseeching him to withdraw his statement, he may find it in his heart to be agreeable.'

Rosabelle sent a sympathetic glance her way. 'The man's persistent. Beware, he may seem a fool, but he's capable of exacting a price. He's besotted with you, and I've heard he intends to stay until you agree to his proposal.'

'If that's the sacrifice I have to make for Frey's freedom, I will.' She gave a delicate shudder. 'Neither of us is in a position of making a choice, it seems.'

That they were pawns in the game of marriage temporarily united the two girls. William scowled. Be damned if he'd let her make such a sacrifice! And he intended to say as much to James. He'd run Snelling through before he let him ruin Angelina, and to hell with the consequences!

'Rosabelle?'

They all started when Elizabeth bustled into the room.

'You've kept the dressmaker waiting several minutes. Come and choose the design for your wedding gown before I run out of patience.'

The boredom in Rosabelle's voice was unmistakable. 'You can choose it, Mama. I care not what I wear.'

Elizabeth's eyes swept her from head to toe and her mouth curled in distaste. 'As I can see, that gown is dreadfully creased and the bodice soiled.'

Rosabelle's expression became sullen again. 'I told you my maid was incompetent.'

'I'll talk to the girl after we've seen the dressmaker together,' Elizabeth said firmly. 'If necessary, another will be hired.'

Rosabelle was all smiles now she was to get her own way. 'Let's go and choose a gown. If I'm to be sacrificed at the altar, I might as well do it in style.'

Elizabeth's eyes narrowed thoughtfully in on her. William wondered what she was thinking. His stepmother had always seemed a remote figure to him, not a person he could confide in or relate to. He'd been too young to remember his own mother. The studious James had been too engrossed by his studies to be companion to him, and he'd experienced a life of loneliness until Rosabelle had arrived.

He'd adored her right from the start and she'd loved him without reservation. He'd guarded her love possessively. Gradually, he'd undermined her feelings towards Elizabeth, paying his stepmother back for taking his father's love from him.

Now he recognized the strength in Elizabeth, and knew he'd been wrong all these years. He experienced an uncomfortable twinge of conscience for considering her an outsider. She was his father's wife, her loyalty to the Wrey name, unquestionable.

Moving towards the door he gazed at her. Her eyes had lost their wary expression and were alive and sparkling. 'There's something different about you today,' he said quietly. 'You look quite beautiful.'

Athough she appeared startled, a tiny smile etched her mouth and she reached up to tentatively caress his cheek.

He kissed her gently on the cheek, then moved into the hall, dismissing the lump in his throat as nothing more than a reaction to her perfume.

He had to get to Ellen before she did, and he didn't have much time.

'I can only imagine you've lost your senses. Under no circumstances will I allow you to become the wife of Nicholas Snelling.'

'But, James' – Angelina's chin tilted – 'if we're to save Frey's life—'

'You will not sacrifice yourself for Frey.' James was at his wits' end. Although he'd been primed by Will, and had prepared a perfectly rational refusal, he'd been obliged to argue the point for the last ten minutes and his temper was beginning to crack. 'You were wrong to correspond with him, and as far as I'm concerned, Snelling has demonstrated he's a man completely without honour.'

Her eyes filled with tears as she pleaded, 'Rosabelle has persuaded the marquis to retract his statement. Dearest James, let me do this for our brother.'

'*Definitely and unequivocally no!*' Her tears would not sway him this time. 'You will not wed that man, and I'll hear no more on the subject.' He stood, pointing his quill towards her as if it was a sword. 'I intend to inform Elizabeth of this rash action, and you must suffer the consequences of your folly.'

Without moving an inch, she gazed at him in wounded silence. A tear glistened as it slowly rolled down her cheek. Feeling like a bully, he sighed, adding lamely, 'I daresay she will only guide and comfort you.'

She moved closer to the desk. 'I didn't think you would be so intractable. As you pointed out, I'll have to marry eventually.'

He sighed. 'You once exacted a promise to allow you to marry only for love. I intend to honour that promise. No stretch of the imagination will lead me to believe you love Nicholas Snelling.'

'Perhaps I could learn to love him,' she responded artfully. 'As I learned to love you, dearest James.'

Her blatant attempt to appeal to his emotions made him smile. 'Love of family is different; we're united by blood.' Dropping the quill, he emerged from behind the desk and took her hands. A tiny gleam of triumph surfaced in her eyes and his smile became broader. You won't outsmart me this time, he thought, as he administered the *coup de grace*.

'I learned to love you too, Angelina. Because I love you, I cannot allow you to wed Nicholas Snelling. From now on, you will make no attempt to correspond with the man, and will accept no correspondence from him. Do you understand?'

James had an implacable expression in his eyes. For once, Angelina found herself unable to win him round. She experienced a tiny frisson of relief for herself, and a tremendous amount of respect for James.

Yet she was glad he'd not seen fit to extract a promise, in case circumstance forced her to break it. Keeping her face demure, she said, with a lilt of laughter in her voice, 'I'll trust you to find some other way of saving the life of Frey.'

He looked suspiciously at her. 'Then we're agreed?'

'Only on one issue.' Gently, she kissed him. 'Dearest ... *dearest* James, must I suffer one of Mama's discourses for such a tiny transgression? It's a lovely day and I promised Celine we would walk together in the garden. There is something she wishes to confide to me, I believe.'

James's smile broadened. When the happiness of his beloved Celine was involved, he would agree to anything. He'd hardly nodded his assent when she twirled about, her petticoats rustling provocatively about her. Her face was a portrait of seriousness. 'I've always thought I might make a suitable godmother for somebody's child. What do you think, James?'

Amusement bubbled up in him. She was incorrigible. 'I think you would probably drop the unfortunate infant in the font,' he muttered. He chuckled when she giggled. 'Be off with you, Angelina. I have work to do if Frey's name is to be cleared.'

When the door closed behind her, he started to laugh. It was a long time before he managed to stop and return to his task of tracing the offspring of a certain black stallion, which had once been owned by Rafe's grandfather.

The records he'd obtained from the blood-stock agent went back a long way, and covered many districts. It was painstaking work, with gaps where horses had been disposed of privately, or had died. He'd painstakingly worked his way through to the present day. Suddenly, a name jumped out at him.

'Godfrey Petersham,' he muttered, staring into space. His heart gave a sickening lurch when he remembered where he'd heard the name before.

Will had bought a couple of horses privately from Petersham when he'd started his horse stud.

'Angelina has a tendency to let her heart rule her head,' James stated.

Rafe glanced where she conversed with his sister, on a rug spread on the grassy river-bank. Their two heads were close as they laughed and whispered in the intimate way women did.

Angelina had avoided his eyes when they'd first arrived, but she'd gradually responded to his teasing. As always, she looked young and refreshing. Her lemon-tinted gown was decorated with a scattering of embroidered daisies, frivolous yellow ribbons secured her straw hat and streamed in the breeze. Two thin braids, threaded through with daisies, barely confined her curls. He could hardly tear his glance away from her.

He couldn't imagine the delicious Angelina married to Nicholas. She was a girl emerging into womanhood, who responded to love like rain to the morning sun. Her beauty shimmered and sparkled, was absorbed like happiness into the senses.

Someone a little older would be a perfect husband for her, someone who'd care for her, bringing her intellectually and sensitively into fruition. Someone like himself. Bemused, he shook his head. What the devil was he thinking of?

Just then, she turned and caught his eye. She'd been laughing at something Celine had said. The laughter died on her lips and her eyes grew wide and dark. For a second, Rafe saw the merest essence of sensuality emerge, and knew she was remembering the kiss they'd exchanged. A swift spark of desire made him suck in a breath.

She acknowledged his regard with a faint flirt of her eyelashes. In an instant, she spread her fan across her face and lowered her eyes.

James's glance was speculative. Rafe shrugged, knowing his friend had been talking, but unable to recall a single word.

Drily, James repeated, 'Snelling has vowed to stay here until Angelina accepts him, so I've delayed our departure. I'd prefer to have her under my close protection.'

Rafe's eyes narrowed. 'Say the word, I'll pay Snelling a visit on the morrow and encourage him to leave.'

Amused by his reaction, James chuckled. 'His prose grows ever more passionate, and ever more desperate. He gives the impression of a man deeply in love. Yesterday, he indicated he'd die of longing if he didn't receive an affirmative answer to his petitions.'

'Perhaps I could hasten the process with the point of my sword.' Rafe's wolfish grin was replaced by a worried frown. 'Does she appear susceptible to such empty flattery?'

The correspondence no longer reached her, but James didn't enlighten him of that. 'Will told me she dreamed up a wild scheme to rescue Frey. Angelina believes she owes Frey her life and indicated she'd sacrifice herself to save him. That's given Snelling a lever. Unfortunately, Lady Constance has arrived to back up his position. She has the scent of money in her nostrils.'

Rafe brought James to a halt. 'You must forbid communication between them. Constance is corrupt in many ways, she might persuade Nicholas to sign a retraction regarding Frey – for a price.'

James's spine stiffened. 'I'm surprised you'd suggest such a dishonest option.'

'Unbend a little, James. The retraction of George's statement weakened the charge against Frey considerably. If you cannot prove his innocence by other means, you may be forced to weigh one option against the other. If Angelina considers all is lost and becomes desperate. . . .' He gazed to where his angel sat. He couldn't bear the thought of her in the clutches of Constance Snelling.

Momentarily, he disregarded Angelina's relationship to James and spoke from the habit of a long association. 'If she was betrothed to me, the problem would no longer exist.'

James was suddenly enthused with delight. 'My dear, Rafe. I had no idea you were contemplating making an offer for Angelina.'

Neither had I, Rafe reflected, surprised his usual rationality had succumbed to impulsive action. He gave a wry grin, wondering if the bliss of James and Celine was infectious.

'It goes without saying you have my permission to pursue the matter,' James continued. 'Celine would be overjoyed if such a match took place.'

And you, my friend, have just overplayed your hand! 'Am I to understand you've discussed the possibility?' Rafe grinned when James shot a sideways glance at him. 'You're not usually such a clumsy manipulator.'

James didn't display one iota of embarrassment. He laughed, said agreeably, 'I'm not usually so desperate.'

'And you intended to push your problem on to me? That's not like you, James.'

'If I thought it anything but a good match for you both, I'd not do so. She is personable, accomplished and wealthy. What's more important, you appear to like each other. Admit it, Rafe, if you live to be ninety, you'll never find a woman more suitable.'

Rafe's earlier reluctance evaporated as his mind absorbed and accepted such a marriage. None of the eligible women he'd met so far could measure up to Angelina Wrey. It struck him as ironic that as Angelina had proposed to save him from Caroline Pallister, now he'd return the favour. A grin flitted across his lips. 'Her youth and innocence scares me; can you believe that, James?'

Two pairs of eyes glanced across at her. Skirts held at calf length, she was wading into the river shallows. Carefully, she launched two boats made from leaves curled around a twig, then waded after them when they went bobbing towards the mossy stone arches of the bridge.

James sighed. 'Her mother would be horrified by such unseemly behaviour.'

Rafe's smile was affectionately indulgent. 'Her free spirit is endearing. I'm delighted she feels she can relax at Ravenswood, especially if it's to be her future home.'

'You've decided then?'

Rafe closed his eyes for a moment, sucking in a deep breath. 'If she'll have me.' Without another word he strode off, his long legs covering the ground at a rapid pace.

Crossing to Celine, James gazed down at her with a smile on his face. 'Rafe's about to propose to Angelina.'

Celine nodded serenely. 'I hope she accepts him, they're well suited.'

'Of course she'll accept him.' Flopping on the grass beside her, James leaned against the trunk of the tree and gave her a complacent smile. 'Anyone can see they care deeply for each other.'

Celine tried to hide a yawn. 'You're right, of course, they do care for each other.' His arm came around her and she leaned her head into his shoulder. 'But it's too early to say whether that caring will turn into love. I'd hate to see her hurt. She's had enough to cope with over the past few months.'

'You're worrying unnecessarily.' He brushed the hair gently back from her forehead. 'Your brother would care for her as if she were his own child.'

'I know.' Turning her face up to his she kissed his cheek and said delicately, 'A woman needs more than fatherly affection from her husband.'

He smiled when her face turned a delicate shade of pink. 'You underestimate the male species, my dear.'

'So it seems,' she said. He watched her soft mouth curve into a smile. 'I thought you were quiet and safe and my life with you would be quite dull.'

'And now?'

'You are certainly quiet and safe.' Her eyes drifted shut and she laughed. 'I hope we have a son who is just like you.'

'Or a daughter as lovely as her mother.' Lovingly, he pulled her close and embraced her. Her mouth was warm and giving. Lost in the wonder of his love for her he quite forgot about Rafe and Angelina.

The water flowed like glass over the weir and frothed beneath it. Reaching out with a long twig, Angelina flicked at the leaf boat, which slowly revolved in an eddy. Caught by the current, it tumbled over the weir and was sucked into the turbulence. 'Devil take you,' she murmured. 'That' s both of you sunk.'

She gazed around her. She'd not seen this part of Ravenswood before; across the river was dense forest, behind her a bracken and rock-strewn slope, and she wondered what lay at the top. Hitching her gown above her knees she started to make her way to the top, pausing now and then for breath. A short way above her she could see a flat rock, but the nearer she got to the top the steeper the slope became. She began to slide backwards.

A hand closed firmly around her wrist. 'Give me your other hand.'

Instinctively, she did what Rafe asked. For a moment she swung in space, then was pulled on to the flat surface of the rock.

She blushed when a sweep of his eyes absorbed her dishevelled appearance. 'I cannot believe a lady would do something so undignified as to climb a mountain in her bare feet.'

'Neither can I,' she said candidly and, gazing down at her bruised and scratched feet, gave a rueful smile. 'If you hadn't been here, I'd have tumbled into the river.'

'It would have served you right.' His green-flecked eyes probed the depths of hers. 'Why on earth did you attempt such a climb?'

'I wanted to see the view from the top.' Recovered a little, she offered him a tremulous smile. 'I didn't know you were up here.'

'I was not up here,' he pointed out with a grin. 'You were down there. If you'd taken the track through the copse, as I expected, then you'd have reached this spot without effort. The river is deep below the weir, when it rains this stretch is particularly turbulent and dangerous.'

They stared at each other for a few seconds, then Rafe smiled, gesturing towards a stand of tall pines. 'This is the spot Ravenswood was named after. Legend says the wood is inhabited by goblins and witches.'

Her eyes grew round and wide. 'And is it?'

'Not that I recall.' His eyes roved over her lazily, noting the soft, womanly swell of her bosom, and a tiny waist his hands could probably span. She was exquisite, something to be treasured for her beauty alone.

Affairs had come easily, discarded without regret. He'd thought there was nothing of the predator in him; now, subtle bodily influences told him he'd enjoy making this girl his, body and soul.

'Rafe, you're not listening. If the house is called Ravenswood, where are the ravens?'

Cupping his hands around his mouth he gave a cry. A cloud of black birds rose squawking and protesting into the sky. She clapped her hands in delight when they circled the trees before settling back, grumbling and chiding each other, amongst the canopy of branches.

'The house is well named. It's such a wild and beautiful place. I love it here.'

'It can be yours.' His voice was gruff as he gazed at her, feeling like a love-struck youth. It was ironic, but his usual, urbane manner had deserted him. 'If you became my wife you could share it with me.'

Her eyes widened and she gave a light laugh. 'You jest of course, Rafe.'

This was not the reaction he'd expected. Miffed, he frowned at her. 'Not long ago, you raised the subject of marriage between us. I've reached the conclusion such an arrangement would be suitable.'

She drew herself up, gazed at him through eyes cool and remote. 'I spoke from impulse. Quite correctly, you took me to task. The fact that you choose to mock me about it now is . . . embarrassing.'

He sighed, managing to retrieve some shred of his former self. 'My proposal is sincere, I'd be honoured if you'd accept.'

'Why? You're under no obligation to offer me marriage.'

He hadn't expected to be questioned on his motives. Nettled, he spluttered, 'Because you need to be wed, and I need a wife with the means to restore Ravenswood and provide me with heirs. Why else do people wed?'

The expression in her eyes became a storm of furies. 'You could try asking James that, and who decided I need to be wed?'

'But, Angelina—'

'How dare you be so presumptuous to imagine I'd want to provide you with heirs and the wherewithal to restore Ravenswood? *Damn you. Rafe!*

Take your proposal to Caroline Pallister, she can provide you with exactly the things you desire.'

Faced with her lashing fury, Rafe found her a paradox. One minute she was childlike and innocent, the next a women magnificent in her anger. He deserved the tongue-lashing. He should have wooed her with sweet words and tenderness, now he was faced with a spitting she-cat who needed to be tamed. She excited him thus.

'You have the temper of a vixen,' he said, trying not to laugh when she stamped her bare foot upon the rock and winced.

The pain served to increase her anger. 'And you are an arrogant rake who thinks he only has to smile to have women drop at his feet.'

'Arrogant rake?' His hackles began to rise. 'I doubt if an innocent child like you knows the meaning of the word.'

The dark irises narrowed and her voice became silky soft. 'Choose your words with care, sir. I've heard more gossip about you than is good for you.' She took a step towards him. 'I've learned much about the ways of men since I left the confines of Aunt Alexandra's estate. Despite your unsavoury reputation, I cannot believe you're the type of man who would seek to wed someone you perceived as a child. You're too much the man for that.'

Her perfume drifted to his nostrils. Beneath its provocative fragrance was a deeper more sensual note, an essence of what lay beneath her surface. His mouth dried a little as his eyes were drawn to the depths of hers. The sparks of light in them mesmerized him, the surge of desire he experienced was unprecedented.

At that moment he wanted to take her sweet, innocent body and bend it to his will. He wanted to watch her eyes charge with excitement and desire, wanted her mouth swollen with his kisses, her breasts ripe and thrusting to his mouth, and her body quivering with both passion and acquiescence. His fingers circled the gleaming locks of hair lying against her creamy shoulders. Gently, he pulled her against him.

Her mouth quivered in outrage for a second, then parted under his. He felt her heart beat against his chest as he gently explored the soft curve of her mouth. She was giving and tender, and so damned trusting.

He couldn't bear to think of someone else kissing her like this. Angelina was his, had been from the moment he set eyes on her. Why hadn't he recognized the fact before?

His kiss became a passionate embrace as he pulled her hard against him. He ignored the hands pushing ineffectually against his chest, ignored the protest quivering in the confines of her throat. He was staking his claim, and wanted her to know it.

She stiffened a little, as if fighting what she was feeling, then became passive in his arms. *Damn, damn, damn!* he thought, and carefully withdrew from her. Tears trembled under her closed lids, and her lips were moistly sensuous.

'I deserve to be horsewhipped,' he muttered.

Her eyes fluttered open, overflowing with awareness of him, of herself. Her voice was almost a sigh. 'I provoked you.' She laid her head against his chest. 'I care for you more than I'm at liberty to say, Rafe, but I'll not wed you. I cannot.'

Though his heart leaped, her refusal was a crushing blow to his pride. When he realized why, his face darkened and his voice became menacingly soft. He pushed her to arm's length, held her gaze to his. 'I refuse to let Nicholas Snelling have you.'

For a few moments her eyes held despair, then they became strangely calm and remote. 'I intend to do whatever it takes to save Frey's life.'

'Snelling is a cretin, his mother a common—' Shame shafted through him when pain came into her eyes. So, he mused, someone has seen fit to inform her of my liaison with Constance. 'I was once acquainted with her,' he said honestly. 'She's not the type of person you should be related to. She rules her son with an iron hand and will make your life a misery. So will he.'

He wanted to shake the martyrdom from her mind when she said, 'Nothing matters but Frey's life. If I'm obliged to wed Nicholas to save him, so be it.'

'You don't know what you're saying.'

'I'm perfectly aware of what I'm saying.' His hands dropped to his side when she took a step back, her face strong with resolve. 'You must promise me you will not broach the subject of marriage again, unless. . . .' Colour rose to her cheeks and she stammered, 'I must go now, James will be wondering what has happened to me.'

He closed in on her again, his eyes blazing. 'Unless what? Unless Frey is found innocent by other means? Are you telling me I must take second place to another, wait for the outcome of the trial for an answer?'

'No . . . yes . . . I don't know.' She covered her face with her hands. 'You're confusing me.'

'Damn you, Angelina! Have you any idea what you're asking?'

'Nothing,' she cried out in distress. 'I'm asking nothing. Forgive me,

Rafe, I don't deserve you as a friend.'

Her gasping sob wrenched at the foundations of his heart. She was a stubborn, loyal, lovable little idiot who didn't deserve unhappiness – which was surely her future if she married the wrong man.

He drew her into his arms, experiencing the empathy flowing tenderly between them. He wanted to cry himself, and knew he'd wait for ever if she commanded it.

'It's all right, Angel,' he whispered into the fragrant silk of her hair. 'Stop crying, my dearest love. Whatever happens, I'll never desert you.'

After a while her sobs lessened, then stopped altogether. They sat quietly whilst she collected herself, then he led her back to where the others sat.

Rafe shook his head slightly when James and Celine gave him expectant smiles. Their expressions turned to disappointment. It was a subdued party which left the grounds of Ravenswood later on. Angelina managed a faint smile when he presented her with a parting gift of a wildflower posy, 'I will keep them for ever,' she whispered, but wouldn't meet his eyes.

Watching them go, Rafe's emotions were raw as he admitted to himself, he'd fallen in love. There was no question now of marriage to Caroline Pallister. If he couldn't have Angelina, he would never marry.

It was nearly dusk, the long shadows from the forest's edge clutched at the meadow with dark fingers. Concealing himself in the long grass, William smiled as he watched the two horses move amongst the shadows.

He didn't have long to wait. There was a soft whistle. A horse pricked its ears and gave an answering whinny, a muffled thud of hooves brought it walking towards the sound.

The person didn't bother checking the horse. It was the gelding purchased for Frey by the earl, its markings obliterated by a simple application of soot.

It stood quietly and was quickly saddled. Mounting from the top of the gate, the rider wheeled the horse about and cantered towards the hedge at the other side of meadow.

'Reckless fool,' William fumed, as horse and rider cleared the hedge.

Anger growing in him, he returned to his own mount and was soon following after the gelding. The rider in front knew the forest trails well, and William had no trouble guessing the direction in which he was being led. They'd emerge at the other side of the village, between the inn and the town of Lyndhurst.

Ten minutes later, he took up station in the shadows, keeping the other rider plainly in his view. As he heard the sound of single hoof-beats upon the dry packed earth of the road, he edged his horse forward.

A black scarf hid the other rider's face, the cowl of a cloak adjusted for concealment. The gelding stood perfectly still, perfectly quiet. It was an obedient horse, trained for an army officer who'd cheated at cards and been drummed from the service before he could take possession of it.

The rider took a pistol from the pocket of the coat as the hoof-beats got louder. There was a click as he cocked it. When the traveller was almost upon them he crossed the remaining few inches between them and brought his hand down hard upon the rider's arm. The pistol dropped to the ground and discharged harmlessly into the undergrowth.

The highwayman's cry of pain was lost in the drumming of the traveller's horse as it galloped swiftly past. The man seemed to be in a hell of a hurry, if his mount's laboured breathing was any indication. The horse was nigh on spent.

Grabbing the highwayman's reins with one hand, he stripped the concealing bandanna away from the rider's face. Staring into furious, black eyes, he chuckled. 'I thought it might be you.'

'You jackanapes. You could have killed me.'

'Well now,' he drawled, trying not to laugh, 'this puts me in a bit of a quandary. Shall it be Frey Mellor who dances at the end of a rope, or shall it be Rosabelle Wrey?'

CHAPTER SEVENTEEN

Rafe was enjoying a nightcap in the library when the hoof-beats approached the house.

It was not his first, and he was experiencing the warm buzz of mild intoxication, a state in which he didn't usually indulge. The rider seemed in a devil of a hurry and Rafe frowned as he noticed the lateness of the hour.

He'd been thinking about Angelina, remembering the way she held her head when she listened to him speak, the way she smiled and the light of mischief in her eyes.

Rafe couldn't remember what his life had been before she'd filled it with her brightness, nor could he imagine a future without her. Being in love had rendered him incapable of thinking of anything, but her.

He gave a faintly ironic smile. Love was a melancholy affair when it was not reciprocated. *If* it was not reciprocated, he amended. Angelina had admitted she cared for him. Hope flamed in his breast. *If Frey was proved innocent. . . .'*

'My Lord?' When a footman appeared at his elbow, Rafe jumped.

Thrusting thoughts of Angelina aside, he frowned at him. 'What is it?'

'A Mr Masterson has called.' The footman's face puckered disapprovingly. 'He said he's a former employee from Monkscroft Hall.'

'John Masterson?' Rafe straightened in his chair. John had been Monkscroft's steward before his father had dismissed him unfairly in a drunken rage. The man had taught him to ride. 'Show him in at once,' he said.

The servant hesitated. 'He's dusty from the road, My Lord.'

Made aware this was not his house, Rafe bit back the urge to snap at the servant. He was, after all, only protecting his master's furniture with his irritating efficiency. 'Send one of the housemaids in with a dust cover for the chair, then show him in.'

John was not kept waiting long. A few minutes later, the chair was protected, and he was hesitating in the doorway.

'Come in, man,' Rafe said, and was touched by a cold finger of dread when he observed the gravity of the man's face. 'You've made a long journey to seek me out, so your news must be of the utmost urgency.' He turned to the footman who was hovering anxiously nearby. 'Prepare refreshment and accommodation for Mr Masterson and tell the groom to attend to his horse. He will not be travelling on tonight.'

'My Lord,' John said, as soon as the footman departed, 'I'm the bearer of bad news. Monkscroft Hall has burned to the ground.'

'I see.' Rafe stared at him, failing to grasp the significance of it. 'I have sworn never to set foot on Monkscroft soil again so its loss causes me no pain.'

'There is worse news.' The man hesitated for a moment, then cleared his throat. 'Your father. . . .'

'Speak out man,' Rafe said sharply. 'What of the marquis?'

'He's dead, My Lord. He and the marchioness perished in the fire. The marquis was insane from the drink and they were quarrelling. Later, he went to her chamber, set a candle to the bed hangings and locked the door. He was raving, My Lord, the servants couldn't stop him.'

Rafe's face drained of colour. Crossing to the decanter, he poured himself a stiff brandy and drained it. As an afterthought, he poured another and offered one to John.

'My thanks,' John mumbled, accepting the brandy with a grateful look. 'You are now the Marquis of Gillingborn.'

To John's surprise, the new marquis slumped in a chair and began to laugh.

'My Lord?' he murmured, half-shocked and half-amused. He was well aware of Rafe's relationship with his father, but decorum should be maintained on such an occasion.

'I'm sorry if I've shocked you, John,' Rafe said, in a little while. 'Ten minutes ago I was an impoverished earl who'd been rejected by the woman he loves. Now I'm an impoverished marquis with the same problem. What do you think of that?'

John's face softened as he heard a slight slurring of Rafe's speech. He'd always liked Rafe as a lad, and had hated the father for his ill treatment of him.

Having taken it upon himself to inform the late marquis of that fact after Rafe had been subject to a particularly brutal beating, he'd been dismissed from his job. His dusty face creased into a smile. 'I think you should sleep on the problem, My Lord. We can talk again in the morning.'

'You're a wise man, John.' Rafe staggered a little as he got to his feet. 'The lady informed me I'm an arrogant rake,' he said in disbelief. 'And she just a little snip of a thing hardly out of the schoolroom.' He shook his head as he ambled towards the door. 'If she marries someone else, I'll pluck her from under his nose on the very steps of the altar. You see if I don't.'

'A good idea, My Lord,' John said, trying not to smile.

'It is, isn't it?' The young marquis frowned at him. 'Did you think of it, or did I?'

'You did, My Lord.'

He relaxed. 'That's good, I wouldn't want anyone else to know about my plan.'

John smiled when Rafe ambled away. Tomorrow would be as good a time as any to go through funeral arrangements with him. Draining his glass of brandy, John went in search of the manservant.

The impact of John's news didn't register on Rafe's mind until morning. He'd expected to feel joy at his father's demise, but instead, was beset by sadness. It was not the material loss of Monkscroft Hall he mourned, but rather the father and son relationship he'd never experienced.

Now, he had the unenviable task of informing Celine of the tragedy. He dreaded her reaction. She'd never been able to reconcile herself to the fact her mother was immoral, and lacked even a shred of maternal feeling. She'd always found excuses for their father's erratic behaviour, too.

Celine had been a plain and gentle child, her shyness a testimony to lonely hours spent in the nursery or schoolroom. She'd watched her mother from afar, worshipping her, her childish eyes seeing Mercy's tawdriness as glittering beauty. His sister had lived for a smile or a kind word from her mother. The smiles had been few, the kind words fewer.

'She will never be beautiful,' Mercy had often cried, parading Celine in front of her friends. 'She's a poor, mousy creature who takes after her grandmother.'

Anger licked at him when he remembered Celine sobbing her heart out after the encounters. Celine had always been beautiful to Rafe. Her impact was not immediate, but her fine bone structure had delicacy and her eyes were an appealing shade of blue. Married to James, well nourished and loved, she'd blossomed into a classic beauty; Rafe would be eternally thankful James had fallen in love with her.

The thought that Celine would not have to bear her grief alone, lifted his spirits. He was his usual urbane self when he sent word to John Masterson to take breakfast with him.

John handed him a satchel containing the Gillingborn seal and the deeds to Monkscroft. 'I hope you do not mind, My Lord. In the absence of a steward I took the liberty of removing them from your father's desk.'

Rafe nodded approvingly. 'Tell me what occurred, John.'

John related the whole affair to him again, concluding with, 'There's some furniture and books stored in the stables. There was very little of value left to salvage, what there is I've placed under lock and key.' He sniffed disapprovingly. 'Reverend Locke and his son were prowling around the property before the smoke cleared, acting as if they owned the place.'

'Were they, by God?'

'Don't worry, My Lord. They didn't get very far giving their orders. I'd already alerted the local garrison of the fire and they sent over a couple of soldiers to take charge and prevent looting.'

'Well, done,' he said warmly.

'The cellars remain untouched, but the way down is blocked by debris. I have reason to believe some Ravenswood chattels are stored there. They may be of value if they've not been damaged by smoke.

Rafe's ears pricked up. 'Ravenswood chattels? You're sure?'

John nodded. 'One of the servants told me they were conveyed there by the marchioness some years ago. I'll set some men to excavate the cellars once the heat has gone from the building. There are also one or two fine horses. I took the liberty of using your father's gelding to transport me here. The other is a mare in foal.'

'What of the servants? Were any of them injured?'

'There were only a few servants left in your father's employ. They're unharmed.' He hesitated. 'I understand they've not received wages for some time, My Lord. At the moment, they're residing in one of the empty cottages on the estate.'

'I see.' He gave John a wry smile. 'Would the sale of the furniture cover the wages?'

'More than enough, My Lord.'

'Then arrange its sale and make sure they get what they're owed up to the end of the year. I'll provide them with references. It's the best I can do for them at the moment. As for yourself, you may keep the gelding for the trouble you've been put to. I'm indebted to you, John.'

'They'll be most grateful, My Lord.' Once again, John hesitated. 'Would you like me to arrange a memorial service?'

'A simple funeral will be enough under the circumstances.'

'I'm afraid the bodies have not been recovered.' John spread his hands in a helpless gesture. 'No remains have been found, the fire was too fierce. It will have to be a service, or nothing.'

'Then a service will have to suffice. I will attend of course, and would be grateful if the servants could pay their respects.'

'I daresay they can be encouraged if they want their wages,' John murmured drily.

'And what of you, John? After my father's treatment of you, can you bring yourself to attend?'

'Oh, aye,' John said comfortably. 'I have no quarrel with the present Marquis of Gillingborn. I'll be happy to be of service to you in any capacity.'

'Thank you.' He gazed at John's shabby attire. 'How are you situated now?'

John shrugged. 'Tolerable enough. My good wife and I live with my married daughter and pick up some labouring work now and again. Beth does a bit of sewing for folks when she can get it. We're a mite crowded, but at least we have a roof over our heads and a meal in our bellies. It's been hard to find work in the district since Monkscroft started going downhill.'

'The owner of this estate is in need of a steward and has charged me with finding him one. The estate is small, but the owner has many business interests and spends much of his time abroad. He needs someone he can rely on in his absence. If you'd consider a move, there's a cottage that goes with the job.'

'That's kind of you, My Lord. Beth would be right pleased to have her own place again, I reckon. Them grandchildren of ours are lively little pups. With another on the way. . . .' His face creased into a smile. 'I could start right after the memorial service, if you're agreeable.'

'More than agreeable.' Breakfast finished, Rafe got to his feet. 'Now I must go and inform my sister of the tragedy. I'll notify the housekeeper of your appointment on my way out, and instruct her to send a servant to familiarize you with the cottage and grounds. We can go over the business side of it when I return.' Extending his hand, Rafe received a firm hand-shake in return before striding from the room.

With James by her side, Celine took the news more calmly than Rafe had expected. He spared her the more gruesome details, reporting only that there had been a fire in which their parents had perished, and there would be a memorial service at the local church. He explained he'd be travelling on to London afterwards to attend his first meeting of the hospital board.

'Under the circumstances, I'll understand if you do not wish to attend the service.'

'Of course I must attend, they were my parents. Indeed, it's my duty to do so.' A tear edged down Celine's cheek and she dabbed at it with a lace-edged handkerchief. 'I hope God will forgive them both their sins so they may rest in peace.'

'I'm sure He will,' Rafe murmured, doubting if God would be so charitable to such a pair.

'I will attend too,' James murmured. 'Celine will need the support of us both if she's to come face to face with Matthew Locke.' His hand covered hers in a comforting manner. 'Perhaps Angelina will allow us the hospitality of her estate for a day or two. It's not far from Monkscroft and Celine will need to rest before returning to Wrey House. I'll leave you together while I go and ask her.'

He was back in a short while with Angelina in tow. Crossing to Celine, Angelina drew her into her arms, saying fiercely, 'You shall not go unaccompanied. I'll be there to support you, even if I have to bully James into allowing me come.'

James was just about to point out that his wife had himself for support, when Celine burst into a torrent of tears. 'Dearest, dearest Angelina,' she sobbed. 'You're such a strength to me, I'll be so pleased to have your comforting presence.'

Closing his mouth, James glanced at Rafe, to find him gazing at Angelina with a hungry, brooding expression in his eyes. Good God! he thought in surprise. Rafe wears his heart on his sleeve for all to see.

His lips twitched at the corners, but he managed to keep his demeanour grave as he murmured, 'Of course you can come, if Rafe approves.'

He watched her glance flick towards Rafe, saw the colour bloom in her cheeks when their eyes met. Rafe's smile would have charmed the thorns off a rose.

Angelina's voice was a soft, husky whisper. 'Do you approve, Rafe?'

'Most definitely,' he drawled. Giving her a wounded look and a mocking little bow, he turned and strode rapidly from the room.

Angelina's smile crumpled, soon her tears matched those of Celine. Not for the same reason, James guessed as he did his best to comfort them both.

From the armoury window, William watched Ellen head towards the Northbridge estate and wondered how Rosabelle would react if she knew what she was up to.

He turned to his sister, who was sprawled inelegantly upon a chair, suggesting, with more mischief than intent, 'Why don't we visit George later?'

'What for?' she snapped. 'I'll be married to him soon, then I'll see him every day.'

Her answer was what he'd expected. He smiled at her predictability. 'What if you didn't *have* to marry him?'

Speculation filled her eyes. 'You have a plan?'

'I'm the possessor of certain knowledge which could prove useful.'

Avid inquisitiveness replaced the speculation. 'What knowledge could you have about George that would help?'

'I'll tell you when I think the time is right.' He crossed to where she sat, staring down at her with brooding eyes. 'I'm going to America soon, what if I asked you to come with me?'

Her eyes began to dance with excitement, then she sighed and her expression became morose. 'But the Americans are our enemies, Mama would stop me.'

'She wouldn't know until the ship had sailed with us aboard, and they'll become allies again before too long.' He smiled caustically when her face lit up again. 'Life there will not be easy. You'll have to learn to live without luxury, and there are savages to contend with. But the continent is young, and mostly unexplored.' Enthusiasm lifted the dark shadows of his face. 'Just think of it, Rosie. One day it will be a great nation. We could be part of that, if we worked hard enough.'

Rosabelle hesitated for a moment, then shrugged. 'I'll think on it, Will. George has promised me a house in London, and he said he'll take me to all the assemblies.'

His lips tightened. 'Perhaps I should remind you that you've placed your life in jeopardy taking to the highway. That gelding was sired by my black stallion, which is easily traceable. James is on the scent. If he discovers who owns it, the game is up. He's too honourable to let Frey hang for the crime of another, and be damned if I'm going to take the blame and dangle in his place.'

Rosabelle paled. 'If you'd allowed me to rob that traveller, Frey would be at liberty now. I'll not risk discovery again.'

William's mouth twisted in a smile. Casually, he asked, 'What did you do with the gold you took?'

'It's hidden under a flagstone in the cottage nearest to the meadow.' Her laugh had a hollow sound. 'I took to the highway only because I craved some excitement. You've no idea how boring being a woman can be, especially when stuck in the country.' Her eyes assumed a scornful light. 'Men are such cowards when faced with a loaded pistol. Except for George,' she amended, excitement flaring in her eyes. 'He would have disarmed me, given the chance.'

'And if he had?'

'I'd have thrown myself on his mercy.' Her expression became sultry. 'The man's in love with me, he'll do anything I ask of him.'

He gave an ominous frown. 'How did you manage to get him to drop the charges against Frey?'

Rosabelle's teeth worried at her bottom lip, then she giggled. 'Nothing too shocking. I allowed him certain liberties, then had a fit of the vapours. He was nearly frothing at the mouth.'

'Be careful of him, Rosie,' he warned. 'He has a strong appetite when it comes to women and is full of confidence now you're betrothed. Don't push him too far.'

'Pah!' she said. 'I can handle the old goat. I just wish I had the same power over Nicholas Snelling. Now Frey has been transported to London, Angelina will have to marry the wretch to clear his name. I bet she wishes she'd never heard of the Wrey family.'

'I wouldn't be at all surprised.' He moved to the window, and gazing down at the sunlit garden, murmured, 'She deserves better than him. She displays signs of being in love with Rafe, yet she's turned him down. She's got great strength of character and I believe she'll go through with her plan to wed Snelling. We must find a way of helping her out of her predicament.'

Jumping to her feet Rosabelle crossed to where he stood, staring at him in shocked surprise. 'Rafe's offered for her? That underhand little snit has been working behind my back, and you expect me to help her? Never in a thousand years! She can marry the devil himself, for all I care.'

He gave a pitying smile. 'You're not still harbouring hopes in that direction, are you? Forget Rafe. Haven't you noticed how he is around Angelina?' Sliding his arm around her he nuzzled her head with his chin. 'I'm the only one who loves you, Rosie. We're alike, you and I. We understand each other.'

She leaned into his body, sure of herself, teasing him into a reaction. 'I wish you were not my brother.'

'Do you, Rosie?' He smiled and turned her towards him, kissing her with more passion than was usual.

She pushed him away with a false show of shock, confirming his suspicion that it amused her to practise her feminine arts on a man she thought herself safe with. If she learned they were unrelated, what then? Would her feelings towards him be those of a lover?

If she agreed to go with him to America he'd inform her of her low birth on the ship, and they could be married by the captain.

In the meantime, he intended to retrieve the gold she'd stolen and cache it in a safer place. They would need it if she came with him, and once James found out about the horse, the village would be the first place to be searched.

He wasn't about to allow Rosabelle's stupidity to jeopardize his plan.

CHAPTER EIGHTEEN

The memorial service for the late Marquis and Marchioness of Gillingborn was a dismal affair. The church was almost empty, the locals who attended dour, as if they were there under sufferance.

The Reverend Matthew Locke and his family sat tight-lipped throughout the service. Their muttered condolences were barely civil. Matthew drew Rafe aside when the service ended, engaging him in a short, terse conversation.

It had rained on the journey from Hampshire, a light, but persistent drizzle which shrouded the day with gloom and dripped dismally from the overhanging canopy of trees. The carriage was splattered with mud. The men, who'd chosen to ride astride so the women could be more comfortable, were soaked to the skin.

They didn't linger after the service. Making a detour to where Monkscroft Hall had once stood, they gazed upon the gutted, blackened shell. The acrid odour of wet ashes came to their nostrils.

Rafe stared at the ruins for a long time without saying anything, then engaged Celine's eyes.

'Locke wants to offer for the land. His intention is to resurrect Monkscroft from the ashes. It was your home too, Celine. Would you mind if it was sold?'

Celine smiled as she gazed at James. 'I didn't know what a home was until I married James. But I beg you, Rafe, do not be too hasty in selling your birthright, especially to a man of Matthew Locke's ilk. You may have sons to inherit the land one day.'

Rafe's glance flicked to Angelina before he strode to where his horse was tethered; his smile was wistful. 'I'll call on the man and find out his terms before I follow you to Chevonleigh, then I'll consider his offer.'

Angelina caught her breath for a second. Rafe looked as though he carried the weight of the world on his shoulders. She watched him disappear from her sight, her heart riding with him.

Chevonleigh was a two-hour journey from Monkscroft Hall, and was a welcome sight. John Masterton had been sent ahead to warn the small household of their arrival and the staff were lined up in the hall, their faces wreathed in smiles of welcome.

There was a relaxed atmosphere about the house, James thought, watching Angelina greet her staff. She knew each one by name and enquired after their well-being with genuine interest and delight. She sought news of her old maid, Bessie. When the cook said a letter had arrived for her from Bessie's brother that very week, she sent someone scurrying in search of it, then read the poorly worded missive out loud to them all.

Afterwards came a scramble to take the baggage up, with the servants vying for the honour of carrying Angelina's.

James and Celine found themselves in a large, comfortable chamber with a fire burning merrily in the grate, a pot of hot chocolate to warm them, and a manservant laying out a dry set of clothing for James to change into.

Celine gave him an exhausted smile. 'It's been a long and trying day, James. Would anyone mind, do you think, if I didn't go down for dinner? I'm not in the least bit hungry.'

Instantly, he was by her side. 'You must rest now. I have a meeting to attend with Angelina and the steward. Afterwards, I'll have a tray sent up for us both. Promise me you'll try and eat. A little broth, perhaps? You would not seek to deprive our infant of sustenance, surely.'

She smiled at that. 'And what of Angelina and Rafe? Would you deprive them of your company?'

'I'm sure they can entertain each other without me, my dear.'

'Angelina will be embarrassed to dine with Rafe alone after turning down his proposal.'

He choked on a laugh. 'You underestimate her. Angelina is her mother's daughter in more ways than one. They are like chameleons, who change to fit in with their environment. She is very much the mistress here; she'll play the hostess to perfection and Rafe will be dazzled by her. Who knows what will come of throwing them together?'

Later, James saw another side of Angelina, and was surprised by her grasp of business matters relating to the estate. It reinforced his belief that females should be educated in their letters.

Her steward, Hugh Cotterill, was astute, and treated his mistress with the respect she deserved. He seemed a good and honest man and Chevonleigh was obviously in good hands. His sister was happy and relaxed at home, and he wondered if he'd done a wise thing by taking her away in the first place.

When Rafe arrived at Chevonleigh he was shivering, and soaked through from a heavy downpour. Angelina escorted him personally to the chamber she'd had prepared for him.

She indicated a pale youth standing nervously by the bed. 'This is Adam. He usually works in the kitchen and is not used to being a gentleman's servant. I hope you'll be patient with him as he's expressed a desire to learn.' She gave Adam a reassuring smile. 'Just obey the instructions of the Marquis of Gillingborn, Adam. I'm sure you will manage magnificently.'

Rafe could have done without a servant, but he wasn't about to tell her so in front of Adam, who was gazing at him with expectant eagerness.

'I've filled a tub, My Lord,' Adam said, in the voice of one out to impress his mistress. 'May I remove your wet garments and assist you into it?'

'I think we might wait until Lady Angelina has retired.' Rafe curled a grin at his hostess, who was beaming encouragement at Adam.

A delicious blush tinted her cheeks and she suddenly busied herself with a bowl of flowers on a small round table. 'If there's anything else you need, Rafe . . . a glass of brandy to warm you, perhaps?'

There was a jug of chocolate on the table and a bowl of fruit. He managed to smile as a trickle of cold water ran down his neck. 'The hot tub and chocolate will suffice, Angel. Thank you for your thoughtfulness.'

She turned and smiled then, shyly aware of him, of her responsibility to him as a guest. 'It's my pleasure, Rafe.' For a moment she stood there, not knowing quite what to do.

'I'll see you at dinner,' he prompted with a smile, knowing if he stood there much longer his dripping figure would dampen the Aubusson carpet.

'Goodness, yes.' She appeared slightly dismayed. 'I'd quite forgotten. Celine has overtired herself, she and James will be taking dinner on a tray. If you'd prefer to do the same I'll inform the cook.'

'And deprive myself of your company?' He raised an eyebrow. 'I was counting on you to lift my spirits whilst we were here.'

'Then I'll do my utmost to accommodate you.' A mischievous grin flirted at her lips. 'I intend to challenge you to a game of chess after dinner.'

'I'll probably beat you,' he warned.

'I would not count on it, My Lord.' Dropping him a mocking curtsy she was gone in a rustle of skirts, leaving a faint aroma of perfume in her wake.

Dinner was a delicious repast of trout baked in herbed butter sauce, served with delicately flavoured vegetables picked that day from the kitchen garden and several side dishes. To follow came syllabub and an apple pie sweetened with honey, and topped with cream. It was carried in personally by the stout cook, who grinned from one ear to the other as she set it on the table. 'Your favourite pudding, My Lady.'

Afterwards came a selection of cheese and slivers of thin golden pastry, served with coffee, which Angelina poured from a silver jug into tiny porcelain cups.

Later, when a manservant offered him brandy and a pipe to round off a perfect meal, Rafe declined out of deference to Angelina.

'You need not stick too rigidly to convention, Rafe, especially after such a tiring day. If it pleases you to have a glass of brandy and a pipe I will not mind. I find the smell of tobacco pleasant, and beg you to allow me to try it whilst James is absent. I've often wondered what it tastes like.'

Rafe chuckled when her eyes began to water after her experimental inhalation. Giving a strangled cough she handed the pipe back to him hastily, saying hoarsely, 'For once, I think James was right. Smoking is no pastime for a lady, and tobacco is more aromatic than pleasant tasting.'

'One needs to acquire the taste.' He grinned as she hastily took a sip from a glass of wine. 'Would you like to try again?'

Her smile turned into a gurgle of laughter. 'I'll content myself with watching you enjoy it.'

'After which, I'll beat you at chess.'

The glance she shot him was challenging, but all she said was, 'As you will.'

Used to James's defensive game, Rafe was hard pushed to keep up with Angelina's aggressive attack. He'd been prepared to indulge her a little, but soon realized she read the board brilliantly. Every risk she took was backed up by a manoeuvre that left him wondering how she'd managed it.

He gazed at her through narrowed eyes, watching her sharp, white teeth worry her bottom lip as she studied the board. Then she smiled slightly, and flicked him a glance before moving one of her remaining pawns. 'Check.'

Rafe gazed at his king, then at hers. She'd castled her king in the centre of the board. He took the pawn she'd checked him with, then watched in dismay as she pounced with a second pawn.

'Had you forgotten I'd queened that pawn?' she enquired sweetly.

He gave a rueful laugh and knocked his king face down on the board. 'Who taught you to play?'

'My music tutor.'

'He must have been an excellent player. You had me flummoxed.'

Her giggle was one of pure delight. 'He was a she, and she advised me that men have a tendency to underestimate a woman's power of observation. I have watched you play with James, and have studied your game. You're used to attacking, he defending.'

'So you reversed the procedure to throw me off.' Rising to his feet he gave her a lazy smile. 'You took quite a risk.'

'I fail to see why.' Her eyes were all at once winsome and appealing. 'There was no wager on the game.'

'If there had been, would you have been more cautious?'

She half-turned in her chair and watched him cross to the fireplace. 'It would depend what the wager was. Aunt Alexandra told me never to gamble unless I'm prepared to risk losing my stake.'

The portrait of the woman under discussion was hanging over the fireplace. Her eyes were bird-bright and seemed to be watching them. 'She was a lady of good sense,' he murmured. 'What would she say if she knew you were contemplating marrying Nicholas Snelling, I wonder?'

Angelina knew she'd have denounced him as a fortune-seeking coward, and forbidden such a marriage. Frey would have been condemned to an untimely death without remorse if her beloved Chevonleigh had been at stake, whether guilty or not.

For a moment Angelina felt unaccountably lonely. A lump rose in her throat, threatening to choke her. 'She would not have been happy about it.' Rising from her chair she crossed to where Rafe stood, gazing at him with troubled eyes. 'Perhaps James will find something to clear Frey's name.'

'And perhaps he'll find himself in the position of having to protect one family member at the expense of another,' Rafe murmured. 'Has he told you William possessed a horse such as the highwayman rode?'

'Will explained about the horse being taken from the paddock.'

'It's not that horse I'm referring to. William bought a black stallion a few years ago, sire to Frey's gelding. He didn't mention he once owned a black stallion when the horse was being discussed, or indeed, may still own it. Why, do you think?'

Uneasily, she shifted from one foot to the other. 'Perhaps he'd forgotten. I'm aware of the animosity Will bears for Frey, but I'd swear on the Bible that neither of them was the person I saw.'

Rafe's eyes sharpened. 'They're your brothers, Angelina. Perhaps your mind refuses to allow you to accept what you saw.'

'I've examined that theory already.' She smiled a little sadly. 'Why is my mind clear on that one point, yet it refused to release what my eyes actually saw, when my father asked it of me?'

'The circumstance of your interrogation may have been a little too intimidating,' he said. 'Perhaps if we talked it through now you're relaxed. . . .' He led her to the couch and poured her another glass of wine whilst she thought the matter over.

She was quiet for a while, her eyes gazing into the flames. With the rain had come an early dusk and the shadows flickered and danced upon the dark timber panelling.

Feeling a oneness with her, Rafe took the seat next to her and contented himself with admiring her delicate profile. The tender curve of her mouth and the long sweep of lashes that guarded the ever-changing jewels of her eyes seduced his senses. He feasted on her perfection whilst he was still in a position to do so.

Presently, a servant came to light the candles and draw the curtains across the windows. His presence brought Angelina from her pensive mood. She smiled at him. 'I believe your wife has presented you with a son in my absence.'

'Yes, My Lady.' The servant gave a pleased smile at being singled out for her attention. 'He's a strong lad.'

'You must be very proud of him. What's he called?'

'Luke, My Lady.'

'A manly name. I should like to see him before I leave. Perhaps your good wife would not mind if I called on her tomorrow?'

'She'd be right honoured, My Lady. I'll tell her to expect you.'

'We will not need you any more tonight, Jeffrey. Go home to your wife and son before darkness sets in. I'll ring for a maid should we need anything.'

'Thank you, My Lady.' Giving a bow, the man left as unobtrusively as he'd arrived.

'You treat your servants well,' he murmured. 'No wonder the house has a welcoming feel to it.'

'Servants are human. They work hard and earn little enough for their labours. A word of appreciation will never go amiss.'

'Sometimes you're wise beyond your years, Angel.'

'And sometimes, I'm not.' She gave him a rueful smile. 'I wish you hadn't told me about the stallion. Now my mind is filled with disquiet. James has indeed been placed in an unenviable position.'

'And so have you, which is why we should talk over the incident together. It may be enough to jolt your memory.'

'I'll do my best to remember.' She took a sip of her wine and turned her eyes up to his. The depths were troubled, like a turbulent sea. 'Where shall I begin?'

Rafe replaced the glass in her fingers, curling his hand around hers protectively. 'Lean back against the cushions and close your eyes. Go over the episode in your mind. When you're clear about the event, nod your head and I'll ask you some questions.'

At first, Angelina was self-conscious, but she allowed her mind to drift back to her first journey to Wrey House. Everything had happened so quickly. She pictured the forest, dark with shifting shadows, the carriage coming to a halt. The highwayman had been terrifying, a black, silent, menacing figure.

'How tall was he?' Rafe asked softly, when she nodded.

She saw an image of the man behind her closed lids. She'd thought the man to be large, but now she remembered the way James and Rafe rode, and saw that the felon's stirrups had been quite short in comparison. 'The horse was big,' she reflected, 'which made me think the man was also large. In truth, I believe he may have been quite short. He rode with his stirrups long and his knees straight. His feet were not quite level with his mount's belly.'

'Can you remember anything about his voice?'

'It was odd, high-pitched, and muffled, as though he was attempting to disguise it.' She gave a chuckle. 'He sounded like my old nurse, Bessie, when she suffered quinsy. When I brought the cane down upon his horse, he cursed, and he sounded almost like a woman.'

'What exactly did he say, Angel?' His mouth curved in a smile as her expression rearranged itself into a scowl.

'*Lucifer's oath!*' she hissed, throwing herself into the role with surprising enthusiasm. 'Then later, when I pulled the mask from his face, he said '*You will pay for that little lady.*'

Rafe's eyes narrowed. 'He sounded exactly like that?'

'Exactly.' She pictured the man raising the cane above his head. His wrist had been almost as slim as her own. There had been a glint of gold. 'I've just remembered something unusual,' she offered. 'He was wearing a gold chain around his wrist.'

Then she remembered something else, something that had lain at the back of her mind and could not be recalled, until now. When the man had lifted his arm above his head to strike, she'd clearly seen the swell of breasts under the cloth of his coat. His countenance came into her mind, the soft, youthful skin twisted into a scowl, the furious black eyes.

'*Lucifer's oath!*' she whispered. Her face suddenly paled and her eyes snapped open in shock. The voice, the figure, the chain worn around the wrist . . . twin hearts . . . Rosabelle wore such a bracelet. The highwayman had been her own sister!

'*Dear God!*' she moaned, her face completely draining of colour.

'What is it?' Rafe urged. 'What have you remembered?'

She swiftly veiled her eyes with her lashes, but couldn't disguise the nervous quaver which entered her voice. 'Nothing, I cannot remember anything else, Rafe. I'm tired, would you mind if I retired?'

Cupping her chin in his fingers, Rafe turned her face round to his and said gently, 'You know the identity of the highwayman, don't you?'

'*No!*' Her voice was edged with panic. 'I beg of you, do not ask me anything more.'

To her relief, Rafe didn't persist with his questioning, but his steady regard of her made her feel ashamed. Twisting away from him, she whispered in despair, 'I don't know what to do for the best.'

Rafe's heart went out to her. Drawing her gently against his shoulder, he said, 'I won't press you, but if you ever need anyone to confide in I'll always be here.'

She jerked away from him when the door opened and James strolled into the room.

If he observed anything amiss he didn't comment, but Rafe casually rose from the seat beside Angelina and took up position by the fireplace.

'Celine's asleep,' James said, his smile flickering from one to the other. 'The day has been exhausting for her.' His glance settled on Rafe. 'I was thinking of taking time to visit London. There's a colleague I'd like to consult about Frey's defence. You won't object to my company on the road when you leave for the hospital board meeting?'

Rafe inclined his head. 'You're not taking up his case yourself, then?'

James shrugged as he took a chair in front of the fire. 'The conflict of interests wouldn't work in Frey's favour. The man I intend to hire for his defence is quite brilliant.'

Angelina gazed at James with anxious eyes. For a moment, it seemed to Rafe as if she were about to say something. Then she bit down hard on her lower lip and rose to her feet. 'I feel quite fatigued. Is there anything you need before I retire? If not, I'll send the maid to her bed.'

'A fresh jug of coffee will suffice.'

Her smile was distracted as she bade them goodnight. James waited until it closed behind her, then turned to him, a query in his eyes.

'Something's playing on her mind,' Rafe said straightaway. 'I believe she knows who the highwayman is, and I'm very much afraid that person is a member of your household.'

'Will?' Pain came into James's eyes at the thought.

'She is adamant it was neither of your brothers.' Slumped into a chair now, Rafe gazed thoughtfully into the fire and related Angelina's description of her encounter with the highwayman. 'You know how well she mimics the voices of other people,' he said. 'I could have almost sworn it was Rosabelle speaking.'

James looked frankly disbelieving for a few seconds, then his eyes lit up with amusement. 'Rosabelle, the highwayman? My God, Rafe, she's either spun you a tale, or that brandy you're drinking is more potent than it looks.' He began to shake with laughter. 'I'll wager the clever little minx has been having fun at your expense.'

After his initial discomfiture at the thought, Rafe joined in the laughter. She'd been convincing, and he willing to be convinced. By now, she'd be safely in her chamber, and probably collapsed with merriment about the clever way she'd led him into her trap.

He shook his head, bemused by his own stupidity. The whole concept of Rosabelle being a highwayman was totally preposterous.

They returned to Wrey House later than planned.

No sooner had the men returned from London when the skies opened, sending down rain in a steady torrent. Obliged to wait until the mud dried a little so the carriage wouldn't get bogged, they were still forced to take lodgings at an inn because the river was so swollen, one of the bridges was awash.

The nearer they got to Wrey House the more damage they saw. There had obviously been a great storm. Branches were ripped from trees and leaf debris littered the ground. In one place, an oak tree had been split asunder by lightning. Half its blackened trunk leaned drunkenly to one side, the other half stood upright. The grass around it was burned black, yet surprisingly, its leaves were still green.

'I hope Ravenswood is still in one piece,' Rafe remarked, when they stopped to get a better look at the phenomenon. 'The storm seems to have been severe.'

'We can make a detour if it will put your mind at rest,' James offered. 'It will not take up much of our time.'

To Angelina's surprise, the shallow-bedded stream she'd previously paddled along had become a swiftly flowing river that had risen above its banks. The bridge was awash and piled high with debris, which had been carried down with the water.

From their vantage point, the house still seemed to be intact, except for a few missing slates. The figures of the mythical gods still kept vigil at the edges of the roof.

Rafe shrugged as he wheeled his horse about. 'It doesn't appear to have suffered severe damage. If we get no more rain the water will abate. I'll return to inspect the bridge and clear away the debris. The foundations may have been undermined.'

Angelina looked at the overcast sky and said a small, silent prayer. Rafe had suffered enough trauma of late, she reminded God, it would be unfair of Him to place another burden on his shoulders.

They parted ways with Rafe at the crossroads, and continuing on, were greeted by Elizabeth who came rushing from the front door as the carriage drew up, her face wreathed in smiles.

She looks younger, Angelina thought, when Elizabeth embraced her, and happier. The reason became obvious when the earl joined her. Linking hands like two young lovers they exchanged affectionate smiles. The intimacy between them spoke of love.

Angelina's breath caught in her throat. Unless she could persuade Rosabelle to confess to the crime of highway robbery, she was destined to marry Nicholas Snelling, and love like this would be forever denied her.

Although she kept a spark of hope alive in her breast, deep down, she knew that Rosabelle, having already ignored the opportunity to do so, would never confess to her crime.

Angelina would *never* reveal what she knew to save herself from a loveless marriage. She couldn't stand by and see either of her siblings put to death, not when she had the power to save them. But neither would Rosabelle emerge unscathed. She intended to tell her sister exactly what her foolish actions had brought about.

Rosabelle was in a temper when she went to confront her. Her maid, Ellen, was crouched in a corner, shaking with fright whilst Rosabelle shouted abuse at her. There was a welt across the maid's arm and tears in her eyes.

Angelina assisted Ellen to her feet, calmly instructing her to go and compose herself. She turned to her sister, who was staring at her incredulously.

'How dare you come into my chamber and dismiss my maid?' she snarled, her face flushed from her exertions. She was unattractive in her anger, Angelina thought, gazing at her in distaste.

'What I've come to say to you is best kept private.' Keeping her voice a discreet murmur, she informed her without preamble, 'When I was away, I remembered who the highwayman was: It was you.'

Rosabelle's complexion changed from red to a chalky white. Her eyes were enormous black holes in her face, her expression terrified. Angelina felt no pity for her when she began to tremble.

'Please do not tell anyone,' she begged. 'They'll hang me.'

Taking up position in front of her, Angelina stared at her. 'What about Frey? He doesn't deserve to die for crimes he didn't commit. How can you let such a thing happen, have you no sense of decency, no conscience?'

Rosabelle's tongue flicked over her lips. Angelina's hope that her words might have an effect faded when a sly expression appeared in her eyes. 'You couldn't prove it, you know. They'd say you made it up, that you were jealous of me and accused me unjustly.'

She smiled at that. 'I have no reason to be jealous of you. There's nothing about you I admire, nothing you have that I want.'

'Except Rafe.' Recovered from her shock, Rosabelle gazed at her with malicious amusement. 'I know he proposed marriage to you, but did he tell you he wants you only for your wealth? We were laughing about it together, just the other day.' Hand on hips, she swayed towards the mirror to preen herself before it. 'Rafe made love to me for the first time on my sixteenth birthday. I enjoyed it immensely.'

'I do not believe it.'

'No?' Rosabelle whirled towards her, 'I'll tell you exactly what your precious Rafe did to me.' Taking her arm in a firm grip, Rosabelle poured such vile words into her ears that she gasped.

'You're lying,' she stammered, tearing herself away and taking a step backwards. 'You're disgusting and vile, and you tarnish the very name you were born with. I'll not listen any more.'

'You stupid little infant,' Rosabelle scorned. 'Why don't you forget your romantic notions and grow up? Once you're married to Nicholas Snelling, Rafe will offer you the same favours he does to every married woman.' She smiled a little. 'We shall share him between us and compare notes.'

Face ashen, she backed away from Rosabelle, biting back a sob. 'You make me feel sick. I'm ashamed to call you sister.'

'Go away,' Rosabelle said, her face suddenly sullen. 'Go and marry that strutting little peacock if you want to save Frey from the noose. I'll dance at your wedding and smile upon your unhappiness. If I cannot have Rafe for a husband, then neither will you.'

'*Rosabelle!*' Face dark with anger, William strode into the room. Angelina quaked at the expression in his eyes. 'Get out,' he hissed at her. 'Say nothing about what has occurred. I'll deal with it, do you understand?'

'Yes,' she whispered, her shaking legs obeying him automatically. They carried her outside the door, where she was forced to lean against the wall to recover from the encounter.

She heard the unmistakable sound of a slap. Rosabelle gave a short, sharp cry of pain, then there was silence. Plucking up courage, she straightened up and moved back to the door. Her eyes widened at the sight of Rosabelle with her arms around William's neck, her mouth hungrily seeking his as if they were lovers. William kicked the door shut behind them.

Experiencing a sickening disgust, she realized she couldn't rely on Will to deal with anything. If Frey was to be saved, there was only one way to achieve it.

Picking up her skirts she fled back to her chamber. Safely inside, she took up a quill, and with shaking fingers drew a piece of parchment towards.

My Lord, she began. *With regard to your recent proposal of matrimony. . . .*

CHAPTER NINETEEN

Eyes scanning the note the messenger had brought him, Nicholas Snelling crowed with triumph.

'Angelina has played right into my hands.'

'*Our hands*, Nicholas,' Constance said and, snatching the note from his fingers, scowled as she perused the contents. 'I see we're not considered good enough for the Wrey family.'

One leg crossed over the other, Nicholas gazed at his mother in perplexity. His eyes were soft and anxious, reminding her of a spaniel she'd once had.

'She didn't say that, Mama.'

'Don't be a fool, Nicholas, she didn't have to.' She gave an exasperated sigh. 'Why does she suggest a secret marriage if you're acceptable as a suitor? Because her guardian has already said no.'

Nicholas thought about it for a moment, then he smiled. 'Angelina has a romantic nature. Her suggestion to elope is touching. Her initial reluctance was a ploy to gain my attention.'

His theory was so ludicrous, Constance gave an incredulous laugh. 'May I remind you this marriage is a business arrangement. The girl wants to save her bastard brother from the gallows.' Her eyes became as sharp as her voice. 'Surely you don't harbour romantic notions towards her, Nicholas?'

Nicholas flushed a dull red. 'I hold her in the greatest esteem. She has the elegance and purity of a Botticelli angel.' He gazed into an imaginary distance. 'Such colouring ... such eyes ... they're an inspiration to me! Angelina Wrey is to be set upon a pedestal and admired, no man shall ever defile her perfection.'

'I'm afraid someone will have to if she's to be got with child,' Constance suggested drily. 'You will need to beget an heir.'

Distaste took residence in Nicholas's expression. He shrugged, moving his glance away from her to murmur languidly, 'Must you be so vulgar?' He pulled a sheet of paper towards him and picked up a quill. 'I shall draft a retraction to the charges against her brother now she's agreed to my proposal. After all, I never saw the rogue unmasked so how could I swear it was him? It will prove I'm a man of honour.'

Her hands curled into fists and she itched to smack the smile from his stupid face. She'd already been bested in an encounter with the wretched girl, and didn't intend her control over Nicholas to be usurped because he harboured some idealistic notions about her. Snatching the pen from his hand she glared intimidatingly at him.

'Write it if you must, Nicholas, but she cannot have it until the vows have been exchanged. 'If you're not to become as impoverished as the Marquis of Gillingborn, we need control of her fortune.' Angrily, she dashed the quill down in front of him.

'I'd already reached that conclusion.' He picked up the quill, carefully examining the point for damage. His mother's background was an embarrassment to him, as were her many lovers. He didn't want Angelina to be tainted by her.

When he married, he'd move into Chadwick House. It was in a fine position, he mused. There, he would royally entertain the more intellectual of his companions. He would hold court with the beautiful Angelina at his side, and be admired for both his wit and good fortune.

Realizing his mother was bent over his shoulder, waiting to dictate every word, he gazed at her with genuine irritation in his eyes. 'A poet needs solitude to write. I'd be grateful if you'd retire from my presence.' Slyly, he suggested, 'Perhaps you should call on your old friend, Rafe, and renew your acquaintance.'

'He resides in the district?'

'At Tewsbury Manor, I believe. It's but twenty minutes' ride from the inn. It would be quite in order for you to visit the marquis to offer condolences on the death of his father.'

One hand fluttered up to cover her heart. 'Now the question of your marriage is settled, it will not harm for me to be seen abroad.'

Such pretty, artificial gestures, he thought disparagingly, after she'd gone. She could act the lady almost as well as she acted the whore. The finer sensibilities of love, those which grew from the heart and soul, had somehow escaped her greedy little clutches.

Dipping the quill into the ink pot, Nicholas drew two hearts entwined with ribbons and posies in the corner of the paper, then embarked on an answer to Angelina's acceptance note. He decided to write the retraction later. Her brother's life would be his gift on their wedding day.

When he finished, he summoned the Wrey servant who'd delivered the good news. He gave the man an arch smile. Nicholas had recognized at once that he was of a more sensitive nature than was usual for servants. As he'd earlier expressed a desire to work in London, Nicholas intended to offer him a place once he was married.

Gazing into his eyes, Nicholas murmured, 'You'll make sure this note gets to Lady Angelina direct. Let none intercept, it's of the utmost importance.'

'Yes, My Lord. Viscount Kirkley left with the Earl of Wrey for London this morning. They intend to stay there until after the bastard's trial. Only the missives sent with the messenger from the inn are intercepted.'

So that was why Angelina wished them to wed so soon? The dear soul truly loved him and had chosen a time when her guardian was absent. She would love him all the more when he saved her miserable brother's neck. She wouldn't be sorry she wed him, he vowed. He'd treat her like the precious creature she was. She was too delicate for the carnal, even had his inclinations towards her been thus.

His fingers curled around the servant's when he placed the letter in his hand. 'Such strong hands,' he murmured languidly. 'Do you know the art of body massage? My shoulders ache abominably and my servant is useless in the ministrations of such comforts. I will have to replace him one of these days.'

The man's eyes met his. 'I have some time to spare . . . if I can be of service. . . ?'

Forgetting about the urgency of his missive, Nicholas stood up.

The servant placed the letter on the dresser and moved towards Nicholas with a smile on his face. Carefully, he began to remove his lordship's garments.

Rafe was pleased John Masterson had not lost his stewardship skills. He and his wife had settled into the steward's cottage with a minimum of fuss, and now, barely two weeks later, it seemed to Rafe as if he'd always worked at Tewsbury.

Moreover, John was able to manage the clerk's position for the time being. Rafe was loath to take on another clerk until the outcome of Frey's trial was decided, and John relieved him of the monotony of doing a chore he hated.

He'd spent the past few days working in the library, today he was going to escape outside. He intended to inspect the Ravenswood bridge now the water was down to a decent level. If the bridge needed repair he'd have to employ a stone mason to carry out the work and make it safe, before it was damaged further.

About to call a servant to fetch his hat, he was forestalled by the sound of a single horse coming up the carriageway. A feminine voice drifted to his ears and he hastened towards the hall, a smile on his face.

'*You!*' he exclaimed, jolted out of his usual urbanity by the unlikely sight of Constance Snelling. 'I was not expecting you here.'

'Who were you expecting, Rafe?' She was outfitted in a fetching blue riding habit crowned with a high veiled hat. Giving a flirtatious laugh, she swayed past him into the drawing-room and looked around her.

Her eyes missed nothing. Within seconds, he had the feeling she'd inventoried every piece of furniture and fitting, and priced every ornament and painting. She turned to gaze at him, her expression both coquettish and calculating. 'No kiss for old times' sake, Rafe?'

Stonily, he said, 'The old times are over, Constance. Why are you here?'

She gave a small pout and smacked her riding crop against her skirt. 'It's not like you to be so brusque. Am I not to be offered refreshment after my ride?'

Rafe's good manners automatically reasserted themselves. 'You prefer black coffee with a dash of brandy, if I recall.'

'I think I'd prefer just the brandy. Why don't you join me, Rafe? Relax a little. I've been in that dreadful inn for over a week, listening to the furry-tongued dialect of the natives and the dreary love sonnets of my son. I've been deprived of civilized company.'

He gave a faint grin as he moved towards the decanter. He knew very well what she was hinting at. Her libido was such, she couldn't go a week without a man in her bed. He allowed his gaze to run deliberately down her figure and watched her eyes narrow. She compared badly with the fresh and piquant elegance of Angelina.

He wondered, had she come to the district to dissuade Nicholas in his quest to win Angelina's hand, or had she come to help?

The glass of brandy he poured for her was generous in proportion to his own. Constance seemed not to notice. Her hand trembled as she bore the glass to her mouth, and she drank it swiftly. His eyes narrowed at her haste, recognizing in her the signs of the craving that had afflicted his father.

He smiled as he poured her another. This time she sipped it slowly, all the while giving him sensuous little smiles. Finally, she patted the seat beside her, inviting archly, 'Come, sit beside me, Rafe.'

Disgust rose like bile to his throat. How had he ever considered her attractive? Refilling her glass again, he strolled to where she sat and, twisting sideways, fitted his hips in the small space beside her. It was too close for comfort.

Constance drained her glass with reckless abandon, then her tongue moistened the fullness of her mouth. 'You've no idea how much I've missed you, Rafe,' she whispered, picking up his hand and carrying it to her breast.

He resisted the urge to snatch it away, smiled at her. She was fast losing her looks. Her cosmetics had been applied to conceal rather than enhance, and made her look clownish.

'I'd not noticed you lacking in admirers,' he murmured carefully. 'Your assemblies are always very much in demand, if I remember.'

'They were until that episode with Angelina Wrey. That girl is a vixen, Rafe. She slandered me in public. Now, anyone who is anyone keeps a distance.'

Rafe's blood began to boil at the slur on his love's character. He took a steadying sip from his glass. 'I cannot believe it; Angelina struck me as being such a sweet child.'

Constance took the glass from his hand and drank from it. Her eyes had a glassy look, her voice slurred a little. 'You're sweet on her, Rafe. I thought so the first time I saw you together.'

Rafe managed to feign astonishment. Gently, he moved his hand from her breast to caress the hollow of her throat. She arched back her head, and a low satisfied murmur came from her throat. 'What would I want with a prissy little virgin when there are women who know how to please a man?'

'Money,' she whispered. 'The little bitch is drowning in it.'

'I've recently inherited enough to restore Ravenswood, and feel no need to tumble a maid straight out of the schoolroom,' he lied, for he felt every need. 'I'll leave her for the younger, less-experienced, fellows to play with.'

'Kiss me, Rafe,' she whispered, seeking his mouth with her own.

Complying with her demand was almost harder than he could bear.

Her breath was thick with brandy fumes, and he nearly gagged when she thrust her tongue into his mouth. Her eyes were drooping when the kiss ended, her mouth slack with the desire of her own wanting.

'Nicholas will not hear a word against the chit. Would you believe, the fool has proposed marriage?'

Rafe didn't bat so much as an eyelid. Feigning indifference, he slipped from her embrace and refilled her glass. 'She is a good catch, but I understood she'd refused the Duke of Amberley, as well as Nicholas. Has the situation changed, then?'

Her eyes were unfocused when he returned to her side, but still she reached for the glass. Slopping it a little, she bore it to her lips and mumbled, 'She's changed her mind about Nicholas. There will be a secret marriage.'

'Oh?' His eyes didn't betray his black thoughts. 'Why should it be a secret marriage, Constance?'

Owlishly, she gazed at him. 'Why do you think? Your high and mighty friend doesn't think my son man enough for his precious ward.' Her eyes filled with tears of self-pity. 'God knows, I have a suspicion he may be right, but what does it matter when her wealth is at stake? Nicholas adores her, and intends to worship her from afar. The Wrey girl doesn't look as though she has red blood in her veins, anyway. Still, if Nicholas wants her, he must have her.' Her voice became stronger, her face malicious. 'I intend to make her pay for stealing his affection from me.'

'How will you do that?' he said, his voice inviting her confidence.

Constance obliged. Laying her head on his shoulder she gazed up at him. 'The cunning little brat intends to trade her bastard brother's life for her hand in marriage. All this time she's pretended reluctance with Nicholas. She's out to usurp me in his affection. I'll not have it, Rafe. I will not allow a criminal who treated Nicholas so badly to escape his just reward.' Her eyes closed. 'I . . . will not . . . have it.'

His hand closed around her neck. Filled with loathing, he gently pushed her away, catching the empty glass as she slid sideways. Mindful of the fact he'd led her into this state, he said, with as much gentleness as he could muster, 'I'll call a servant to assist you to one of the bedrooms so you can rest before you return to the inn.'

'You . . . will . . . join me, Rafe?' Her voice was so thick and furred, Rafe could hardly hear it. When a snore came from her mouth, he heaved a sigh of relief.

'I think not, Constance,' he whispered. Crossing to the bell he summoned a servant. 'When the lady recovers, give her some coffee and see she's escorted back to the inn. If she's incapable of riding, use the carriage. I don't want her here when I return.'

He called for his hat, hurried out into the garden and took a long, deep breath of fresh air.

Basking in her new-found happiness, Elizabeth failed to notice Angelina had lost her aura of joy. Now she was back in favour with Thomas, everything else had faded into the background.

Rosabelle had reconciled herself to her forthcoming nuptials to George Northbridge, but Elizabeth didn't bother to ask herself why, just rejoiced that she'd seen sense. As a result, she'd become less critical of her, though she'd breathe easier when the girl was safely married and off her hands.

George had been a constant visitor of late. He brought Rosabelle expensive items of jewellery, and took her into the countryside. Rosabelle was no longer immune to his wooing of her, and Elizabeth was pleased with the brilliance of the match.

Today, Elizabeth and Angelina were engaged in the making of a layette for the forthcoming infant. Celine was resting. She'd begun to suffer from nausea in the mornings, and Elizabeth had insisted she should not stir from her bed until the unpleasant sensation had receded.

Angelina was working an intricate design on to a cambric gown. Her needle wove deftly in and out of the material, embroidering a border of tiny roses around the hem. Elizabeth admired her work for a few moments before returning to her own stitching. When she gazed at her again, the work was abandoned in her lap, and she was staring out of the window in a distracted manner.

'Is something the matter, my dear?'

When Angelina's eyes met hers, Elizabeth could have sworn there were tears in the corners. 'It's nothing, Mama, I have a headache, that's all. It's probably the overcast weather, I think there will be a storm tonight.'

'Put your embroidery aside for the day, close work will make it worse.' Setting her own aside, she rose to her feet. 'We shall go for a ride, the fresh air and exercise will help. We could visit Rafe.'

'I'd rather not visit him,' Angelina said listlessly. 'Besides, you have the dressmaker coming to fit your new gown for Rosabelle's wedding.'

'Goodness! I'd forgotten.' Elizabeth bustled towards the door, nearly colliding with Rosabelle who was about to come in. 'Rosabelle, my dear,' she exclaimed, 'Angelina is in need of fresh air and exercise. As William went out early, it falls on you to accompany her.'

Angelina gazed at Rosabelle with a reproachful expression, trying to encourage a twinge of conscience in her sister.

She turned away, muttering, 'If I must.'

Half an hour later, the two young women rode out. Angelina felt awkward and clumsy on a horse when she compared herself to her sister, who seemed part of the spirited chestnut she rode.

Moonlight was nervous, as if the sultry weather was upsetting her. She tried soothing talk, but the beast refused to settle. Her nervousness transferred itself to Angelina.

Rosabelle broke the silence with criticism. 'I hadn't realized Moonlight was quite so slow.' She cast an irritable eye over the horse as she came up beside her. 'Will was right, she'd not have suited me as a mount.' Her glance took in the tight grip Angelina on the reins. 'Relax your body and hands.'

Angelina tried to do what she suggested, but after a while her body tensed again. She brought Moonlight to a halt.

'Whatever's the matter with you?' Rosabelle said impatiently. 'Why have you stopped?'

They were at the edge of the forest, Angelina was remembering the time she'd been lost. She gazed with trepidation into its gloomy depths, some instinct warning her of danger. 'I don't want to go into the forest.'

'Stop being such a ninny,' Rosabelle scorned.

'That's all right for you to say,' she flared. 'The last time I entered the forest I would have lost my life if it hadn't been for Frey.'

'Are you saying Will abandoned you in the forest deliberately?'

Such an uncharitable thought had not entered her head. Now she stared at Rosabelle in dismay. 'Did he?'

Tossing her head, Rosabelle laughed. 'If Will had wanted to kill you he wouldn't have given you such a quiet horse, and if *I'd* wanted to kill you I would have shot you through the heart the first time we met.'

'I wish you had,' she answered listlessly. 'Then I wouldn't be obliged to wed Nicholas Snelling. Can you not bring yourself to confess to the earl?' she pleaded. 'I'm sure he wouldn't let you hang.'

'I'll think on it.' Rosabelle left her side and entered the forest trail.

Encouraged by her remark, Angelina followed in after her. There was an almost unnatural stillness about the forest, and the lack of sunlight made it a place of menacing shadows.

'Frey doesn't have much time left,' Angelina reminded her.

Rosabelle's eyes were sharp when she turned towards her. 'So that's why you're mooning about the place like a martyred saint; you've accepted the fop's proposal, haven't you?'

'What choice did I have?'

'None, I suppose.' Reaching out, she took Angelina's rein in her hand and brought Moonlight to a halt. 'Truthfully, Angelina, do you really intend to sacrifice yourself to protect Frey?'

'I can see no other way out if you refuse to help. As you pointed out, I cannot prove you were involved.' Her eyes became troubled. 'I would not seek to place trouble upon your shoulders, either.'

'Why should you care what happens to us? The Wrey family were strangers to you a few short weeks ago.'

'I felt so alone in the world at Chevonleigh. When James came to me and revealed my true identity, suddenly I had a family.' She shrugged. 'I know we lack the closeness of sisters, Rosabelle, and that distresses me, but I wouldn't do anything to cause you harm deliberately.'

Little fool! Rosabelle thought, satisfied she was telling the truth. A falsely sympathetic smile spread across her lips. 'I'm sorry, I cannot do what you want, Angelina. There's also Will to consider.'

'William's involved?'

'Of course he's involved.' Rosabelle's voice was creamy smooth when she added to the falsehood. 'Will and I have always done everything together. We meant no harm. It was something to relieve boredom. 'If I confess, then Will will also have to confess. Even if excuses were found for me, he wouldn't get away with it. He'd be bound to hang.'

Angelina's face paled. 'I did not consider . . . of course . . . you must not confess. The matter of my marriage is of little consequence when weighed against the lives of those dearest to me.'

'When is this marriage to take place? I'd be happy to attend you.'

'You'll not tell Mama?'

'It shall be a confidence between sisters.' She placed her hand on Angelina's wrist and hid her triumph. 'We'll both be married to men we do not care for; let that be a bond to bring us closer together.'

Angelina gave a wan smile. 'I should be pleased to have you attend me. The marriage will take place on Friday afternoon at the church in the next village. When that's done, and Nicholas has given me the signed retraction, I'll need William to convey it with all speed to James in London. You'll be able to give the retraction to William.'

'At least you'll be able to live a fine life in London instead of being buried in the country. That will compensate somewhat for your unfortunate husband.' Her laugh had a cruel edge to it. 'I think I'm better served than you: George is a real man. He may not be able to write prose, but he cannot keep his hands off me when we're alone.'

Angelina was shocked. 'It's not seemly to speak of such things.'

'I do not see why.' She released Moonlight's rein and set her horse into a walk with Angelina beside her. 'A man's touch upon the body is a pleasant experience, as is his kiss upon your mouth.' She was made recipient of a pitying glance. 'But then, I suppose you've not experienced such things.'

'Indeed I have,' she confided shyly. 'Rafe has kissed me twice upon the mouth.'

'Rafe kissed you on the mouth?' Rosabelle's eyes darkened and her lips curled. 'Did he touch your breasts, as well?'

Her face flamed. 'Certainly not, Rafe is a gentleman.'

Rosabelle felt sorry for Angelina. Married to Nicholas Snelling, she suspected she would live a celibate life. She wondered if her sister had it in her to take a lover.

'With a tiny amount of encouragement, Rafe could be persuaded to introduce you to the delights of lovemaking. You have no way of knowing how that can make you feel.'

Angelina had a very good idea. In the darkness of the night she relived the touch of Rafe's lips on hers, and experienced the strange, hungry awakening of her body. She had no wish to dwell on the thought that he may have initiated her sister into the art of lovemaking. Flicking her reins, she allowed Moonlight to take the lead and rode on without answering.

The path led them deep into the forest. A fitful wind had risen. Now and again the forest canopy shook with it. A more powerful gust sent a cloud of leaves twirling upwards. Moonlight gave a nervous whinny.

'We'd better go back,' Rosabelle shouted. 'There's going to be a storm.'

Angelina had difficulty turning her horse on the narrow track. Impatiently, Rosabelle took a hold on the rein and tugged Moonlight's head around.

Suddenly, a shaft of lighting lanced to the ground up ahead. The brilliant flash was accompanied by a clap of thunder that sent both mounts dancing nervously.

Rosabelle quickly got hers under control, then shouted over her shoulder as she set its head towards the direction from which they'd come, 'Come on, bring that nag's head round and follow after me. I know of a woodsman's cottage, where we can shelter.'

Moonlight had other ideas. Giving a squeal she began to sidestep. It took all of Angelina's strength to hold on to the reins.

Rosabelle lost all patience. 'For heaven's sake, you're the worst rider I've ever encountered. You're letting that stupid horse control you.' She brought her crop down sharply on Moonlight's flank several times, then kicked her own mount into motion.

All at once the heavens seemed to open. A torrent of wind-blown hail came in stinging shafts down through the trees. Rearing up on her hind legs, Moonlight turned away and bolted.

Angelina pulled with all her strength on the reins, but the horse wouldn't respond. All she could do was cling to the mare and hope she'd run out of wind before she was tossed to the ground. She held on desperately for what seemed to be an eternity. Then her way was blocked by a fallen tree trunk. It was not a large trunk and would have been easily stepped over had the horse not been galloping. When her mount soared over it Angelina parted company with the saddle. For a few short moments she flew through the air, then landed with a jarring crash upon the ground.

Winded, she doubled over and tried to get some breath back. Bruised leaves and stinging hailstones pelted down on her. She scrambled on all fours through the muddy slush to shelter amongst the foliage of a dense shrub. Huddling in fright against the trunk, she pressed her hands against her ears and whimpered in fear. She knew it was illogical to be afraid of storms, but somehow she just couldn't help it.

Angelina didn't know how long she stayed amongst the cacophony of sound, or how long it took to start thinking sensibly again. When she emerged from her hiding place the fury of the wind and thunder had abated. But the hail had become rain, a relentless, icy downpour that showed no sign of abating.

Shivering and shocked, she looked about her as the water soaked through her clothing. She'd lost her hat, her hair hung in dull, wet ropes. She had no idea in which direction to go, until she saw the indentation of a hoof in the slushy forest floor. She managed to smile. 'I hope you know your way home,' she whispered, her teeth chattering as she hugged her rapidly cooling body with her arms, 'because I refuse to stay here and die in the forest.'

It was almost dusk when she stumbled upon the bank of the river. She recognized the place at once. It was just above the weir, not far from Ravenswood. If she followed the bank to the bridge, at least she'd be able to find shelter there. She gave a thankful cry when she saw Moonlight standing dejectedly in the water, and called out her name.

Moonlight's ears pricked forward and she gave a plaintive neigh. A length of ivy had wrapped around her legs, effectively hobbling her. The water was running fast, but it was not deep above the weir. Ignoring the danger to herself, she waded into the water and gentled the horse with soothing words whilst she loosened the ivy.

Angelina was about to attempt to lead her to the bank when a keening gust of wind came pushing down the river. Moonlight tossed her head and squealed in panic at the eerie sound, then jerked her head free and headed towards the bank.

Goblins and witches came into Angelina's mind and her heart began to beat a little bit faster. *No, Rafe had said it was only superstition.* Automatically, she turned towards the source of the sound. Her eyes widened and her hair seemed to stand on end.

For a moment she gazed wildly about her, then, giving a scream of terror, she began to run.

CHAPTER TWENTY

Rafe had just noticed the gaping crack in the bridge, when the echo of a scream sent the ravens flying skyward. The satisfaction he felt at loosening the build-up of debris changed to foreboding.

Leaping on his horse he headed towards the sound. He was hampered by wet clothing, and knowing he couldn't beat the wall of water heading for the weir, he raced through the copse until he reached the rock overhanging the narrow part of the river. Throwing himself from the beast's back he gazed anxiously down at the water.

His heart began to pound when he saw a horse struggling to keep its head above the boiling maelstrom downstream. 'No!' he yelled in anguish, his eyes scanning the water for a sight of the rider. 'Not Angelina.'

'Rafe!' Her voice was a tiny quaver of misery below him. 'Thank God you're here. I can't free myself.'

Peering into the gloom, he spotted her pale, frightened face gazing at him. She clung to a thorny shrub, which was rooted tenuously to the slope, her hair tangled in its branches. Her lower half was in the water, her sodden skirt weighing her down. She would not have her perch for long.

'Hold tight,' he said unneccessarily, and grabbing a knife from his saddle-sag, he hacked a thick length of ivy from the trunk of one of the pine trees. He secured it round his waist, attaching the other end to the girth of his saddle. A murmur of fear reached his ears when the shrub gave a little under her weight.

Ignoring his own safety, he went hand over hand down the ivy and prayed his horse would have the wit to stand still and the ivy would be strong enough to take the combined weight of both of them.

'Give me your hand,' he said, stretching his own out towards her.

She gazed wildly around her. 'I'm too frightened to let go.'

If she refused to obey him, her strength would soon fail and she'd be lost. 'It's either me or the river,' he said harshly. 'Which would you prefer to trust your life to?'

Her sob nearly tore his heart from his chest. Tentatively, she stretched out one of her hands. Immediately, his own closed around it. 'Now the other.'

'I don't think I can reach, my hair is held fast.'

He inched downwards a fraction. She gave a panicky scream when the shrub tore from the bank, scrabbling desperately for his arm. His heart leapt to his throat when he took her weight and pitted his own against the shrub.

Angelina's eyes were desperate as her head was pulled backwards until Rafe thought her spine must be in danger of snapping. The ivy stretched, taking her almost under the water. Suddenly, the limb she was attached to snapped free.

It took all his strength to pull her up against him; he wouldn't be able to climb to the top, carrying her. Her heart beat rapidly against his. Quietly, he said, 'Angel, I need you to obey me without question.'

Her voice was a muffled sob against his chest. 'I'm sorry you have to risk your life in such a manner.'

Gently, he kissed her water-slicked scalp. 'I'd happily sacrifice my life if it saved yours.'

She raised her head and managed a small smile. 'What must I do?'

Blessing the indefinable substance of strength on which she was able to draw, he hoped she had an abundant supply. 'You must climb up my body. Once you stand on my shoulders you should be able to reach the top. Stand on my head if you have to.'

'I'll try not to hurt you.' The soft kiss she placed at the corner of his mouth was a treasure of immeasurable distraction.

'Once you reach the top, you must lead my horse forward. If the ivy breaks, go immediately to Ravenswood, wait there until someone comes for you.'

Fear trembled in her, but she said nothing, just gazed into his eyes for a deliciously meaningful moment. 'Go now,' he said tersely, 'my strength's waning.'

She scrambled over his body with surprising agility. There was a moment of fright when her foot slipped from his shoulder, but she quickly regained her courage.

She gave a grunt, and suddenly the strain in his shoulders was relieved.

He nearly lost his grip when the ivy suddenly tightened and he was jerked rapidly upwards. Scraped over the edge, he was dragged along the ground at a goodly pace. In her eagerness, Angelina was running as fast as her legs could carry her with his horse in tow. He experienced a moment of surprise that she had the energy left to run when he felt so drained.

'Stop!' he shouted, and laughed with relief when he came to an abrupt halt. 'You'll have me halfway to London if you are not careful.'

Dropping the rein, she ran towards him and hurled herself into his arms. 'The ivy was chafed almost through where it came over the edge. I thought it would break. Oh, Rafe.' She began to weep. 'I couldn't have borne it if you'd drowned.'

Covered in mud and leaf matter, her hair hung in bedraggled ropes, the thorny twig was a crown upon her head. He brought her against his chest and held her tight. They stayed like that for a long time, whilst unheeded, the rain washed over them in torrents and the river crashed through the gorge below. The sky grew dark, the wind rose to a keening pitch.

Rafe carefully unravelled the tangle of hair from the thorns. She didn't make a sound, even though her scalp bled where the thorns had dug in. When he finished she gave a tiny shiver. 'Poor Moonlight.'

'She might have made it to the bank,' he comforted, but not believing it for a moment. The cold seeped into his bones. He must get them to shelter before the storm worsened.

Stumbling to his feet, he placed Angelina on the saddle and mounted behind her. Her shoulders slumped with exhaustion as they slowly progressed towards Ravenswood. By the time they reached the house she was racked by shivers.

As he lifted her down she smiled dreamily. 'Mr Eastman is playing the harpsichord.'

The Eastmans were not there, they'd left Ravenswood to visit relatives and were not expected back for a week. For a moment, all Rafe could hear was the wail of the rising wind, then quite clearly, four clear notes rang out.

Pan's pipes, he thought, gazing in astonishment in the direction of the statue. All these years he'd owned Ravenswood, and this was the first time he'd heard them. He'd thought the tale to be a myth when he related it to Angelina.

Prickles raced up his spine as the notes rang true and clear above the storm once more. Then they fell silent. He stared down at her, a smile on his face. If the legend had any substance, she was destined to become mistress of Ravenswood.

Leading her inside the house, his eyes roved over her face. 'That was the wind blowing through Pan's pipes, Angel.'

Her eyes flew open. For a few, precious seconds joy flared, then the light in them died, as if she remembered something. Shivering violently she took a step back. 'I must return to Wrey House, my mother will be worried.'

'The bridge has been damaged, you must stay here until the water abates. I'll see if I can find you something dry to change into.'

She nodded, accepting his words without further question. Rafe applied a flint to the fire, then lit candles. He collected a neatly repaired gown and shawl from Mrs Eastman's chamber, and added a hairbrush as an afterthought. Pouring a measure of brandy into a tumbler, he handed it to her.

'Sip this, it will warm you. I'll go and stable my horse while you change, then we'll discuss what's to be done.'

She smiled. 'You're a good and true friend.'

His returning smile encompassed her bedraggled form. How could such a tiny, stubborn creature break his heart like this? She must know how he felt about her. 'I'm more than just a friend,' he murmured, making it clear to her. 'You know I'm in love with you.'

Her voice was a whisper and there were tears in the eyes that met his. 'How I wish it were not so.'

'Don't bother telling me my feelings are not reciprocated, I'll not believe you,' he said, before slipping through the door.

'I couldn't do that, 'Angelina whispered, staring into the crackling flames of the fire, 'for I love you with all of my heart, Rafe. I always will.'

William was chilled to the bone. He'd been out all night, searching the forest. All he had to show for it when he returned to Wrey House, was Angelina's horse and her hat. The mare had been wandering along the river-bank. Lamed, she bore the marks of a whip.

Angelina's whereabouts was causing him great concern, her footprints had been heading towards the river. He was coming to the conclusion she'd been stunned by a fall, and had wandered into the river and drowned.

The grief in his heart surprised him. He realized he'd grown to love her in a way he'd not thought possible. His protectiveness towards her had grown without conscious thought, and had only recently taken root. He liked the feeling of self-worth that came with it. His grief was increased by the anguish on Elizabeth's face when she watched him bring the horse in.

'Oh, Will.'

'There's still hope,' he said. With his father and brother in London, shouldering the responsibility of the estate was new to him. He felt awkward when she gazed at him with concern in her eyes.

'You're bone weary, Will. You must eat, then rest. I've sent a servant to alert George Northbridge, and another to Tewsbury Manor to inform Rafe. I'm sure they'll take over the search.'

Dismounting, he took Elizabeth's hand in his. 'I'll stay only long enough to eat and change into dry clothing. If Angelina's out there I'll bring her home to you. This, I must do.'

Elizabeth's glance touched his soul. Their eyes met in understanding, then she bore his hand upward and laid her cheek against it. 'Dearest, Will, I'm so proud of you.'

For a few, short moments he enjoyed the unexpected and intimate gesture, then a movement brought his eyes to Rosabelle. A sardonic expression twisted her face, her eyes were dark with jealousy. Her very presence seemed to belittle the emotion of the moment. Letting his hand fall to his side he stared hard at her, seeing her through different eyes.

She was what he'd made her, he thought sadly. He'd spoiled her, taken her innocence and twisted it to his own ends. Now she sickened him, as he sickened himself. 'You helped caused this,' he accused. 'God forgive you if she's harmed, and God help you: I'll make sure you never profit from it.'

Rosabelle took a fearful step backwards. 'You don't know what you're saying, Will.'

His eyes bored into hers. 'Do you deny you took a whip to Angelina's horse?'

Her lips curled. 'How was I to know it would bolt?'

'Because I told you it was whip-shy. If she's dead, I swear I'll never forgive you, Rosabelle. Do you understand me?'

'Yes,' she whispered, looking thoroughly frightened, now. 'I didn't do it on purpose.'

'I don't believe you.' With one last look of disgust, he strode into the house.

Elizabeth's eyes burned into hers. 'Is this true? Did you seek to harm Angelina on purpose?'

Her hands went to her hips. 'No,' she snarled, 'but if she hasn't survived the storm, I refuse to mourn.'

Elizabeth whispered in anguish. 'Why. . . ?'

Rosabelle swayed closer. 'You've given her the love you deprived me of. She has everything I have not. James adores her, Rafe loves her; even my father looks upon her with affection.'

'That's something she's had to earn.'

Rosabelle's face darkened. 'Now she's stolen Will's affections from me. Did you know he has plans to go to America, that he asked me to go with him? Now he hates me because of *her*. If she's dead, I hope she rots in hell.'

Elizabeth's face was ashen. The girl didn't know what she was saying? Britain was at war with America. How long had William harboured the intention to leave England? And why would he take his sister with him, when she was about to wed?

Although she dreaded the answer, she *had* to know. 'What's the nature of your relationship with William, Rosabelle?'

'Oh, don't worry, Will has more scruples than anyone gives him credit for. He wants me, but spurns all my advances. Does that shock you?'

Elizabeth's eyes swept over Rosabelle in disgust. The tension she'd been holding back for years, suddenly snapped. 'No, it doesn't shock me, I dare say you take after your mother. Thomas made a mistake when he tried to pass you off as my daughter.'

The girl's eyes widened, her mouth dropped open. Elizabeth patted her cheek. 'Don't worry, Rosabelle, you can still marry George Northbridge. Neither Thomas nor myself will tell him you're of peasant stock. And if you're a little soiled. . . ?' She shrugged. 'George will not mind, he's used to dealing with trollops; including your maid. He's growing very fond of Ellen, I believe.'

'Mama?' Rosabelle grabbed her sleeve, and stared at her in bewilderment. 'You must be raving, of course I'm your daughter.'

With a certain amount of distaste, Elizabeth shook off the hand. 'You were a foundling. Thomas took pity on you when he thought Angelina had died. I only have one daughter. If she's dead you'll leave this house and never return.'

'This cannot be true,' Rosabelle whispered, stunned to the very centre of her being. 'What if George gets wind of it? Where will I go, how will I manage?'

'However other girls of your age and station manage. Try the gutter, you display a certain inclination towards it,' Elizabeth said cruelly, and walked away from her.

Stumbling a little, Rosabelle fled to the safety of her chamber. The room was untidy, her bath water still unemptied. Ellen was asleep in a chair. Rosabelle stared down at her, knowing exactly how she'd manage.

'So, you stupid little bitch,' she murmured, 'you think you'll usurp me in George's affections, do you?'

Smiling cruelly, she reached out and took her maid by the hair. 'You have two choices, Ellen,' she hissed, and her hand lashed back and forth across the girl's face. 'You can leave the district by nightfall, or you can die!'

'Pan's pipes.' Angelina snuggled deeper into the warmth of Rafe's bed as the sweet, haunting sound rose above the howl of the wind for the second time that night.

Delighting in the fact her body lay where Rafe's had lain, she breathed in his scent and imagined what it would be like to live with him in this house, lie against his heart in this bed and bear his children. Before she drifted off to sleep, she prayed the storm would rage forever, then she could stay here, marooned with the man she loved.

But the morning broke calm, and the sun shone from the heavens with an unexpected brilliance. 'Dear God,' she prayed upon waking. 'if I must live a life of unhappiness to save Frey, I'll do so. I know it's not seemly to question Your wisdom, but why can't You think of another way to save him, when You *know* he's innocent?' As an afterthought, she whispered, 'If You decide to heed my prayer, please spare Rosabelle and William as well.'

The sound of a shot brought her from the bed. She rushed to the window, clad only in her chemise. The bridge was still awash. William waited on the other bank for a reply to his shot. Rafe appeared below her. He covered the ground with long, loping strides towards the river's edge, tucking his shirt into his breeches.

Angelina threw open her window and waved to her brother. He straightened in his saddle, his shout of relief was music to her ears.

The two men engaged in a short conversation, then with a wave of his hand, William wheeled his horse around and took off at a gallop.

Rafe came to stand beneath her window. His hair hung dark and wild about his shoulders; his eyes seemed to absorb the very sight of her. He was very much the man here at Ravenswood. The sight of him awoke some deeply rooted, primitive sense in her. She grinned with the pleasure of it.

'You'll be pleased to know your horse is safe.'

'That's wonderful.' Realizing she wore only a chemise and her hair was tumbled in disarray around her, she blushed, but made no effort to to cover herself. Her hair was sufficient. 'I'm sorry you're put to so much trouble.'

'The trouble's all in your mind.' His smile was relaxed and easy. 'I'll fetch you some hot water, then raid the hen house. We can have fresh eggs and cold ham for breakfast.' His smile became broader. 'We'll have to cater for ourselves. Can Lady Angelina cook?'

Her eyes began to sparkle. 'She can; she can also trap and skin a rabbit, catch trout with her bare hands and wring the neck of a chicken.'

'In that case, there will be chicken for dinner tonight.'

Consternation replaced her smile, and Rafe laughed. 'You appear somewhat disenchanted now.'

'I'd prefer not to hunt for my food.' Noting the mischief in his eyes, she giggled. 'Traditionally, man is the hunter: you provide the chicken, I'll cook it.'

'Then I have the easier task, there's one hung in the larder.'

They feasted like kings that night. There were turnips, basted with the dripping juices from the chicken, and tender young peas boiled in their pods. To follow were apples stuffed with crushed raspberries and honey. Baked in their skins, she garnished them with cheese curd.

Rafe leaned back in his chair with a satisfied look on his face. 'When Ravenswood is restored I shall employ you as my cook.'

'Then you'd be obliged to eat chicken and turnips every night,' she countered. 'Because I can cook nothing else.'

'I'd want for nothing else but to feast my eyes on you for the remainder of my life,' he informed her with a smile.

She gazed at the voluminous grey gown she wore, and giggled. 'Your eyes must be starving, half-blind, or both perhaps.'

'My words are sincere.' He slid his hand across the space between them and covered hers. 'I've declared myself, Angelina. If you wed another, you condemn me to a life of loneliness. None will ever replace you in my heart, and I vow to never take another for my wife.'

His words brought tears to her eyes and a poignant ache to her heart. More than anything, she wanted to accept his proposal, but she could not, nay, *would not* barter Frey's life for her own happiness.

She owed it to Rafe to tell him why. Perhaps Rosabelle had been right in one regard: if she spent one night in the arms of the man she loved, she'd have a precious memory to sustain her through the barren years of her life.

Tears glittering on her lashes, she met his gently probing glance. 'Our consciences would never allow us to sacrifice Frey to our own happiness.' She placed her finger gently over his lips to stop him interrupting. 'I'd rather our memories of one another were happy, Rafe.'

'What are you saying?' Eyes dark and turbulent, Rafe seemed to be having trouble with the simple truth she stated.

'I'm saying I love you, Rafe.' She lowered her eyes to the strong, slim hand covering hers, not sure how to continue, but knowing she must. 'I would become your wife this night in any way but in name, if it would please you.'

His hand tightened, until she gazed at him in protest. The protest died from the onslaught of his storm-flecked eyes and she flinched from the whiplash of his voice. 'It does not please me to have you cheapen yourself in such a manner.' He flung her hand away and rose. 'I'm no seducer of innocent young maids.'

Face flaming with bruised pride, Angelina responded in the only way she could think of. 'Rosabelle said you became her lover when she was sixteen.'

'*Damn Rosabelle!*'Rafe said coldly as he strode off towards the door. He turned to glower at her. '*And damn you for believing her lies.*'

'I didn't believe her,' she said mutinously. 'I struck out at you because I'm embarrassed, and you hurt my feelings. I'm perfectly aware you're a gentleman of honour.'

'You're aware of nothing when it comes to men.' Three strides brought him back to her again. His temper had subsided, but his eyes glinted as he reached for her. Jerked to her feet she was pulled against him. Rafe's smile had a strange pitying quality to it as he murmured, 'You're absurd if you imagine I'm not tormented by desire for you.'

This kiss was not like the others, it was a bruising force of possession. He invaded her mouth, forced it apart and used it for some devilish pleasure his tongue seemed to enjoy. The caress was an insult, and she struggled against him.

He merely pulled her closer. His mouth became a crushing implement designed to rob her of will. She couldn't respond, couldn't move, couldn't breathe. She panicked a little, a small, protesting sound strangling in her throat. Abruptly, he let her go. When she gazed at him wide-eyed, he smiled, his finger traced the outline of her mouth. His voice was a whisper of silk across her nerves. 'I've changed my mind; you may disrobe, my Angel.'

'I . . . I beg your pardon?'

'Remove your gown.' Slowly, his fingers reached out to loosen the laces at her breast. His smile was strangely seductive.

'What are you doing, Rafe?' she whispered, clutching the edges of the bodice together. 'Are you out of your mind?'

Hooded eyes flicked to hers. 'You offered me the use of your body, I believe.'

She clutched desperately at his hand as he moved to slip it inside the bodice. 'And you turned me down.'

'I've had a change of heart. I haven't deflowered a maiden for some time.' He followed her when she edged back against the table. 'I'm glad you come to me willingly, Angel.'

A sob tore from her throat, and her hand groped around on the table. It closed around a hard object. She waved it threateningly at him. 'Stand back, or I'll addle your brain.'

Amusement fill his eyes. 'With a loaf of stale bread?'

Her eyes narrowed and she wanted to howl with fury at the sardonic amusement in his eyes. 'I offered you something precious, Rafe, and you choose to mock and insult me. I'll never speak to you again.' Dropping the loaf to the table, she buried her head against his chest, and began to weep quietly.

'Yes you will, my Angel.' He tipped up her chin, and the kiss he placed on her mouth was an apology of softness. 'Tell me you love me again, so I can carry the words in my heart.'

'I love you,' she whispered. 'Forgive me for what I must do.'

He cuddled her close. 'I'll never forgive you for breaking my heart. You're mine, you were mine from the minute I saw you. I cannot bear the thought of life without you.'

'Yet you *must* live without me.' Her eyes came up to his, dull with despair. 'Perhaps Nicholas will release me if I appeal to him. He's not without sensibility. I'll tell him I love you.'

Rafe kissed her again, his long, slow, tender caress demonstrating exactly what love felt like. 'When will you tell him?'

'Early Friday morning before . . . before. . . .' She bit down on her tongue for a moment. 'Before Rosabelle and I go to see the rector about her wedding.'

She was a poor liar, he thought. The elopement coincided with Frey's trial date. If the lad was to be found innocent, a courier would have to take the retraction to London immediately after the wedding took place. That meant, Nicholas would have it on him when he went to the church. If he could be induced to part with it beforehand. . . ?

Rafe smiled. He'd need an accomplice, and James was still absent. William? He'd always been a dark horse, yet he seemed fond of Angelina. He smiled; he'd have a word with him and see what could be done.

The river dropped sufficiently for Angelina to be returned to Wrey House the next afternoon.

The water was belly deep and swift flowing as Rafe guided his horse across. As her skirt was already covered in mud, the soaking didn't bother Angelina.

Her sense of loss at leaving Ravenswood was acute. She'd enjoyed spending time alone with Rafe, and if she'd had freedom of choice, would have stayed there with him for ever.

Rafe seemed just as reluctant to take her home. Now and then she gazed up at him and he grinned. She was being made deliciously aware of the love between them. She reached out to it, drawing his spirit to hers in an empathetic contentment of soul.

Sometimes his breath stirred against her hair, sending a shiver of delight trickling down her spine. Leaning into his body, she experienced his movement against her back, the strength of his thighs against her hips and the living, breathing essence of him. Love swept through her like a warm, flowing river.

'I would like this journey to go on and on,' she whispered.

He placed a kiss against her ear. 'I'll make you my queen of the forest, build you a castle of clouds and place a circlet of stars about your brow. You will shine more brightly than the moonlight, and all will envy this man you made king, even though you intend to tear his heart asunder.'

The slight catch in his voice made Angelina gaze up at him. There was a tender smile playing about his lips and his eyes were filled with love.

Her body was charged with an elixir of longing. She revelled in it, in the wild female urge to take him for her mate. Convention seemed a mockery when faced with such loving spirit nature had endowed her with. The feeling between them was nothing to be ashamed of. She closed her eyes, refusing to think otherwise. 'Kiss me, Rafe,' she whispered.

His lips were like wild, sweet honey. Her own clung to them in confused delight, offering him the total gift of her love as she murmured his name over and over again.

How can I resist her? Rafe thought, as her magic wove a potent spell upon him. Why *should* I resist her when she owns my heart?

Not a word passed between them when he slipped from the saddle and led the horse into the forest. The quiet glade he brought her to was a palace of jade light, carpeted with soft, green moss. Spreading his cloak on the ground he drew her down beside him.

'Hush,' he whispered, when she opened her mouth to speak. He covered it with his own, sweetly, tenderly, and she melted against him in an agony of shivering anticipation.

Rafe knew he should resist the urge to take advantage of her innocence. In the normal course of events he'd have courted her in a most circumspect manner, keeping her intact until the night of their wedding.

Even as he caressed the sweet buds of her breasts and felt them respond against his fingertips, he knew she'd be changed, this day. Her eyes would hold the knowledge of him in their depths, of her power to take his love and make it her strength. As he kissed her mouth the chaste purity of it stole the sensuality from his own. She turned it against him, making him weak.

Dear God! Her flesh was like silk under his hands, and moulded over bones so fine he could have crushed them between his fingers had he not sensed the resilience of them. Her body was firm, but softly rounded in her femininity. Her pale slenderness was unblemished except for a tiny freckle at the curve of her waist. She shivered when he pressed his lips against it and he drew his cloak around them.

Her eyes were dewy soft when she gazed at him, her smile dreamy. She reached out tentatively to trace the contours of his face with her fingers. 'Do I disappoint you, Rafe?'

'*God, no!*' His smile contained a thread of shame. How could she think such a thing when his reaction was so apparent against her thigh? But in her innocence she would not know of man's baseness, he reminded himself. She'd be unaware of the inevitable incursion into her body that would change her from maid to woman. That would be his joy, and her downfall.

Tenderly, he took her lips within his own, caressing her mouth into trembling acquiescence. Slowly, gently, he gradually explored the secrets of her body – and how eagerly she learned them.

There was tension in her, but gradually her body opened to him like a flower to the morning dew. When he gazed upon her dear face he saw her eyes closed in rapture, and felt her moistness.

He could have taken her then. She would never have known what she felt was nothing to what lay ahead. Her consciousness of her sensuality was just below the surface, he wanted her submerged, unable to think, only to experience the sublime eroticism of the moment when he stole her maidenhood. Then she would remember it in the years to come as a loving exchange of gifts, not a ritual of pain.

Slowly, he tasted her perfection, his eyes alert for signs of distress. Only once did she display shyness, her hand covering herself in a fluttering movement.

She did not resist when he gently nuzzled under her hand. Her defeated fingers moved slowly and caressingly into his scalp, allowing him access in the most intimate of ways. It was not long before she uttered a long drawn out ecstatic, shuddering gasp.

Moving above her, he slid against her, felt her give to him and was enclosed within the sweet musky well of her, pulsing in the cradle of her sweetness. She pulled him closer, arched herself into him, accommodating his more muscular shape and making them one. Her eyes opened to gaze straight into his. They were luminous, and deep.

'I love you, Rafe,' she whispered, her voice seductive with her passion. 'I will always love you.'

He experienced the strong, hot urges of his body and moved inside her. A small sound came from her throat, a tiny ecstatic growl. She arched her head back, her hair spread like the shafts of silken sunlight. He took a strand of that hair and wound it about his fingers.

Blood pounded in his temple when he moved within her, slowly and carefully at first. Her calves slid sensuously around his waist, making him prisoner to her body. Such a sweet surrender. Her action was a catalyst, turning his control into a pulsing rapture of ecstasy. Abandoning his pretence of noble feelings in the primitive urge to conquer this woman, he drove deep into her, felt her body rise to accommodate his driving frenzy. There was a shuddering climax, as if the world had come to an end about them. They were one body, one heart, one mind.

After today, I may never experience such perfect union again, he thought, sadly, gazing on the one he loved.

A short time later, Angelina slowly opened her eyes to gaze with delighted wonder at Rafe. Her expression was a mixture of anxiety and shyness. 'Now I know what it is to love,' she murmured. 'I have never experienced such pleasure, and will cherish this moment between us forever.'

'Angelina, my dearest. If I hurt, you. . . .'

She placed a finger over his lips, making a tiny shushing noise as one would do with a child. 'There was no hurt, only joy. This is a gift we have given each other. None shall ever diminish it in my eyes.'

He drew her into his arms. 'I love you. God, how I love you.'

She felt like weeping at the blow fate had dealt her. She'd finally experienced the perfection of love, now it would be denied her. If only they could lie in each other's arms forever, die together in this spot. She felt no remorse at what she'd done, no shame. Only those who'd never experienced such a sublime union would regard it as a sin. If anything, she loved Rafe all the more for his weakness.

After a while her hand tangled in his hair and she brought his lips down to hers. The body lying against hers aroused most powerfully to the action, and she chuckled, delightfully aware of it.

Rafe gazed down at her, his eyes alight with laughter and love. 'You, witch,' he murmured. 'See what you have done to me.'

Her eyes rounded with innocence. 'I do not know what you mean, sir.'

'Like hell you don't,' he growled.

She couldn't stop her blush, and softly giggled. 'See how you make the colour rise to my cheeks, Master of Ravenswood.'

'It's too late to blush, my lady.' His mouth trailed over her bare shoulders, over the swell of her breast and teased the glowing buds of her nipples into life again. 'You've unleashed the beast in me and there's only one way to tame him.'

The beast was a delightful revelation to her, and when he was satiated, she felt extremely loved and well satisfied.

They came into the grounds of Wrey at dusk. William had been watching out for them. He gazed from one to the other, noting the loving glances they exchanged.

Angelina gave him a carefree smile as he lifted her down from the horse, but she couldn't quite meet his eyes. She enveloped him in a hug. 'Hello, dearest Will.'

The perfume of loving clung to her. Gently, he picked a leaf from her hair, saying drily, 'You'd best go and tidy yourself before you present yourself to your mama.'

A faint blush tinted her skin, but her eyes were clouded when she glanced at Rafe. 'Thank you, Rafe.'

'Angel.' Rafe's grin held a degree of intimacy as he blew her a kiss.

William could sense the thread of tension vibrating between them. They'd become lovers. He hadn't imagined Rafe would take advantage of the innocent sister of his friend, nor that Angelina was the type to give herself lightly.

Rafe's eyes filled with pain when he watched her walk away, as if he'd never see her again. The adoration in his eyes was plain to see, but what of Angelina? When she turned to give Rafe one long, lingering glance, William was shocked by the anguish in her eyes.

If these two are in love there's nothing to stop them marrying, he thought. *Except the question of Frey Mellor's innocence.* 'The situation between you is as plain as the nose on my face,' he growled. 'There had better be a good explanation.'

'Rest assured. If God permits, Angelina will become my wife. First, there's a small problem to overcome. In an attempt to save Frey from the noose, she intends to marry Nicholas Snelling secretly. I intend to stop her, but need your help.'

William nodded.

'Let there be no misunderstanding between us: I believe you know the identity of the highway robber, and I think Angelina knows who it is. If the worst comes to the worst, I'll not stand by and allow you sacrifice Angelina and Frey to protect another.'

William gave him a sharp look, wondering how much he knew. He shrugged, what did it matter now? 'I have no love for my bastard brother, but I've been thinking of late, it will do me no honour to let him die.'

'And you cannot let Rosabelle hang either, can you? James has already been put in an impossible position, this will add to his quandary.'

The fellow was astute. William gave a mirthless grin. 'James would choose me over Frey, however distasteful to him. As for Rosabelle, I'd willingly strangle her with my bare hands – but no, I can't let her hang on a public gallows for what was little more than a craving for excitement. She didn't kill anyone.'

'Then you'll help?'

'You have given me no choice. I had intended to flee the country and take Rosabelle with me. Events have progressed beyond that now, but I have another plan formulating in my head.' He began to walk towards the stable. 'First, I must take you to my stud. If anything should happen to me in the execution of the plan, some things need to be destroyed.'

When they reached the village, he led Rafe to the cottage he used as a

tack-room. Lifting a trapdoor, he lit a candle and started down a flight of
stairs.

Rafe whistled when they reached the cellar below and saw the goods
stacked to the ceiling. There were bolts of richly woven cloth, crates of the
finest French brandy, perfume and, in one corner, cases of duelling pistols
with intricate designs in silver.

'This village has always been used for smuggling,' William explained,
with a shrug. 'I decided to carry on with the tradition when I discovered
a tunnel leading down to a cave in the cove. A fishing vessel brings the
goods over from France. The trade has been lucrative, but I'm leaving for
America shortly and have brought it to an end.

'The remaining goods will be picked up a week hence. If anything
happens to me in the meantime, I would have it destroyed.' He indicated
a keg of gunpowder. 'Just lay a powder fuse down to the cave and put a
spark to it. The village will collapse on top of it. I would not have my
father know I trade with a country Britain is at odds with. Whilst he
enjoys the brandy, he wouldn't appreciate having a traitor for a son.'

Rafe resolved to act on the matter as soon as possible.

Picking up a bottle of brandy, Will surveyed the label with a certain
amount of satisfaction. His voice was ironic when he said, 'This is the
finest to come out of France, and the last of my own private stock. It
would be a shame to waste it. Will you share it with me while we plan the
rescue of my sister?'

Rafe smiled, wondering what James would make of this brother of his
if he knew of his deviousness. 'I'd be honoured. It will help ease the
conscience of our dishonesty.'

CHAPTER TWENTY-ONE

Nicholas was garbed in lavender brocade. A profusion of lace frothed at his wrists and flounced at his throat. In a black cloak lined with purple silk, he imagined he cut a fine figure.

They'd left the inn as soon as the look-out brought news that Angelina and her sister had left Wrey House together. The wheel marks of the Wrey carriage were plainly visible in the dust of the road.

Constance was peevish in the extreme. She was suffering from a headache, which the early hour and bright sunshine worsened. The malady was exacerbated by the cart they'd been forced to hire. It lacked any comfort whatsoever and jolted uncomfortably through every pothole on the road.

She cursed the fact that the horses in both the livery and at the inn, had all succumbed to stomach gripe overnight, which, according to the inkeeper, was brought on by a surfeit of molasses mysteriously added to their bran.

To add to her discomfort, she'd discovered the gown she intended to wear still contained creases from travelling. Not that it matters, she thought sourly, no one but herself and Rosabelle Wrey would witness the wedding, and she doubted if her future daughter-in-law would cut a bride-like figure.

She cast a derisive eye over Nicholas, smiling and nodding to himself. What a vain fool he was to imagine Angelina Wrey loved him. Had it not been for the retraction, safely concealed in the bag she carried, the chit wouldn't have given him a second thought.

Still, the money would sweeten the deal, and perhaps she could induce one of her more experienced friends in London to seduce her. A small amount of laudanum to keep her quiet ... she nodded maliciously. It would be amusing to watch her corruption.

Neither of them saw the highwayman until he laid a hand on the bridle and brought the cart to a halt. Nicholas's face turned the colour of clay at the sight of him, and Constance thought he might faint dead away.

'What's the meaning of this?' she said coldly. 'Only a coward would rob a defenceless woman and her son?'

The man edged his way towards the cart, his eyes a dark glitter as he aimed his pistol at Nicholas. 'Empty your pockets.'

Twittering in fright, Nicholas did as he was told. The felon inspected the displayed objects, then said curtly, 'Get down from the cart, disrobe to your breeches. Pass every piece of clothing to me, including your shoes and hose.'

Five minutes later Nicholas lay face down, naked and blushing. The highwayman's eyes flicked to Constance.

'You, madam. Get down from the cart.'

'You would force a lady to disrobe, sir?' Her eyes wandered to the man's thighs and her eyes narrowed a little. She stood so she was level with him, inviting softly, 'Perhaps you'd rather search my body with your hands. I have no weapons concealed about me.'

Derision flared in his eyes; the mouth beneath the mask stretched in a smile. 'You're old enough to be my mother, madam. Pray, do not make a fool of yourself. Get down from the cart.'

Constance's eyes narrowed at the slight, her face mottled red. Stepping to the ground she stared up at him, her face twisted and ugly in anger.

'Hand me your reticule.'

She clutched it tightly against her. It contained her jewellery and she had no intention of handing it over without a struggle. 'I refuse.'

The highwayman turned his pistol on Nicholas. 'I'll count to five, then I'll put a bullet in this skinny peacock. One . . . two. . . .'

Nicholas gave a terrified moan. 'For God's sake?' he cried out piteously. 'Do as he says.'

'Three . . . four. . . .'

Constance threw the reticule at him with considerable force. Her jewellery scattered on the road when he rifled through its contents. He plucked the piece of paper containing the retraction from the bag, quickly scanned it.

There was a shout from behind, and the sound of a horse. The highwayman cursed as his glance followed hers. She thought he'd slipped the retraction up his sleeve, but she was obviously mistaken, for he thrust it back into the reticule.

The oncoming rider was dressed in the uniform of the local regiment, and he drew his pistol as he came. Dropping the bag, the highwayman turned and headed for the forest. Constance heard him curse when a shot rang out. Then he bent low over his mount's neck and disappeared into the trees.

The officer was young, and had bold, dark eyes. Skidding to a halt, he leapt from his mount with the lithe grace of a cat. His eyes roved over her for few moments. 'You're unharmed I hope, madam?'

She forgot about Nicholas whimpering in the dirt. Pressing a hand to her chest, she swayed. 'I feel a faint.' Seconds later, she was supported by a strong pair of arms. Fluttering her eyelashes, she gazed up at an interestingly sensual mouth and her headache suddenly seemed to disappear.

'I declare, you are strong, sir,' she simpered. 'I would be indebted, should you escort us to the next village. And if you'd care to visit me at the inn before I return to London, it will be my pleasure to reward you in some small way.'

The soldier smiled back at her. She was older than he usually liked, but seemed to know what she was about. Perhaps he *would* visit her at the inn, then again, perhaps not.

There was a new girl installed in a house at Winchester, he was quite taken with, the fetching, sloe-eyed Ellen. The soldier compared Ellen's charms with the woman in front of him. It was no contest. Nevertheless, he smiled as he pressed her hand to his lips. One or two of the older fellows might appreciate giving her a gallop around the paddock.

William was reeling in the saddle as he reached the appointed spot. 'I have it, Rafe!' he shouted in jubilation, almost tumbling from his mount's back. 'I palmed the retraction from under their very noses. The painted old hen had it in her bag.'

Rafe tried not to laugh at his description of Constance Snelling. 'You're bleeding.'

'The damnedest luck, a soldier came along the road and fired on me. The ball passed through my shoulder, but you'll have to bind it.' Scrambling from the stallion he shrugged off his coat. 'Use my stock and bind it tight.'

Two minutes later, clad in brown breeches and with a fawn coat to replace the cloak, William mounted the gelding he'd picked out for Frey. He was grinning from ear to ear as he smacked the black stallion on the rump. 'A couple of my mares are in season, so he'll find his own way home. Go and rescue Angelina from the clutches of the perfumed bard. Well split another bottle when I get back from London, to celebrate.'

Leaning forward, he whispered in the gelding's ear. 'Come on, my beauty, let's see what you're made of. We go to rescue your master from the gallows.'

Within minutes, Rafe was galloping in the opposite direction. Fleetingly, he remembered the ugly wound in William's shoulder and hoped the bandage would be sufficient to stop the bleeding. But Rafe didn't worry about him for long, he had Angelina to rescue, and very little time left in which to do it.

Angelina and Rosabelle sat in the front pew of the church. They'd been waiting almost an hour and the rector was pacing up and down in impatience. A secret marriage was not to his liking, but the girl was probably in trouble, and the parents disapproving of the match.

She seemed a nice child, nonetheless. He darted her a glance, approving her neat gown of brown taffeta shot through with gold. The bodice was modestly filled in with cream lace at the top. Her only attempt at frivolity was a bonnet of straw with yellow daisies around the brim. She sat with her hands folded in her lap, an expression of serenity on her face. Her eyes told a different story.

Her companion was from a different mould. She had none of the bride's daintiness, but bold eyes, a full, sensuous mouth and an air of petulance. She gazed at the bride with barely disguised hostility and they seemed to have nothing to say to each another.

Rosabelle was not only hostile, she was racked with jealousy. Her saintly sister had spent two nights alone with Rafe, and had calmly told her they were in love. Only Angelina *wasn't* her sister, she reminded herself. Angelina was the true daughter of the house, she now the outsider.

How cold her mother had been. She shivered, knowing she'd deserved it. She'd seemed like a stranger.

Rosabelle sighed. She'd been forgiven when Angelina was discovered to be safe. But from now on, she'd have to do as she was told if she wanted to remain part of the Wrey family. Her position had suddenly become very tenuous.

Will had made it clear the offer to take her to America was withdrawn. It was either marry George, or end up back where she'd come from. That was the gutter by all accounts. She shuddered. Raised in luxury she took for granted, she couldn't imagine being impoverished.

George wasn't so bad, she mused, her eyes narrowing, and once she was mistress of his house she knew very well how to keep him interested. Now she'd given him a taste, she would keep him waiting until their wedding night, which suddenly couldn't come soon enough for her.

Glancing towards the door, she suppressed a smile when Nicholas and his mother appeared. In love or not, Angelina hadn't managed to catch Rafe.

The slimy Wrey footman who'd driven them to the church exchanged an intimate smile with Nicholas. She sniggered when she realized Angelina would have a rival for her husband's affections.

Angelina didn't smile when she caught sight of her groom. 'You've brought the retraction?' she asked, straight away.

Nicholas blinked, then took her hand and clasped it to his bosom. 'My mother has it safely in her reticule, my love.'

The hand was withdrawn. 'I would like to see it, please,' she said to Constance in a business-like manner.

Constance gave a thin-lipped smile. 'After the wedding, my dear, I'm not such a fool as Nicholas.'

'That' s a matter of opinion.' She calmly nodded to the rector. 'I'd like you to bear witness, this wedding is performed under duress, because my heart belongs to another. Should this woman not give me a signed statement testifying to the innocence of Frey Mellor, I intend to apply for an annulment.' She looked suddenly vulnerable as she appealed, 'Is that possible?'

The rector had met Frey, and considered him a fine young man. He felt a rush of sympathy for the girl. 'I cannot marry you under the circumstances.'

'You must,' she said desperately, 'else my brother will hang for something he had no part of.'

'I could call in the local regiment to sort the matter out.'

'There's no time.'

'Then I'll bear witness to the fact this marriage is made under duress. If called upon to do so, I'll give testimony.'

'Thank you, sir.' She took a deep, shuddering breath and glanced towards the door as if seeking help. 'I pray you then, let us delay this mockery of a marriage no longer.'

Nicholas glanced at her in confused consternation.

The rector was halfway through the first part of the marriage service when there was a commotion outside. It was a sound of a horse coming along the path.

To his annoyance the door swung open and the figure of a horse and rider was framed in the doorway. 'This is a house of God, sir,' the rector muttered, wondering what he'd done to deserve such intrusion into his peace this day.

Angelina smiled as the sound of a softly whistled tune filled her ears. It was the strange, haunting notes of Pan's pipes. Her heart became alive again. 'Rafe?' she whispered, her face alight with radiance when she turned towards the door. 'Rafe, my dearest love.'

Sound echoed in the empty church when Rafe picked his way down the aisle. He held out his hand to her. 'Come, Angelina, Frey is saved.'

Rosabelle's eyes widened as her glance swung from one to the other. Rafe had never looked at her like that, and Angelina had never appeared so beautiful and alive to her. A lump rose to her throat. Angelina had offered her the hand of friendship and she'd thrown it back in her face. Now it was jeopardized, she realized how much she loved the family she'd grown up in. She swore to redeem herself in their eyes if it took her the rest of her life.

About to comply with Rafe's request, Angelina's arm was grabbed by Constance Snelling. 'He's lying,' she snarled. 'I have the retraction.'

Angelina gazed from one to the other, uncertain when Rafe mocked, 'Are you sure of that?'

Springing from her seat, Rosabelle snatched up Constance's reticule and pushed the woman back into a pew. Pulling out a paper, she triumphantly waved it in the air. 'Take it, Rafe, and take Angelina.'

'Perhaps you'd care to read it to us,' he suggested with a pleasant smile.

Constance's face dropped when Rosabelle read its message. 'Compliments of the highwayman?' she spluttered, her eyes mean. She'd been out-smarted, and there was nothing she could do about it.

'I shall sacrifice my love for one greater,' Nicholas bleated, turning his defeat into triumph. His eyes shone with a strange light. '*What romance! What inspiration!* A knight on a white horse come to rescue the fair maiden.'

'You have no choice in the matter of sacrifice, for I'm taking her from you. As for my horse, it's a chestnut,' Rafe pointed out.

'No matter, I shall write an epic about this day. Go with your love, my chaste Aphrodite. I shall remember you for the rest of my life.'

Angelina giggled when Rafe winked at her.

'You fool,' Constance ranted and, snatching up her reticule, smacked her son about the head with it. 'She's worth a king's ransom.'

'Must you be so vulgar, Mama?' Nicholas drawled, when she finally controlled herself. He straightened the high dressed wig his mother had knocked askew. 'I was never interested in her fortune. She was my muse, my inspiration.'

'Thank you, Nicholas.' Giving him a hug, Angelina murmured, 'I'll keep a memory of you in my heart.'

And no doubt laugh at it, Rafe thought. Taking hold of his outstretched hand, she was pulled into his lap. He kissed her tenderly, announcing his feelings to anyone who cared to see.

'I knew you'd think of something heroic,' she whispered, her eyes shining with love. 'I was counting on you.'

'I know you were.' Without giving a backward glance, Rafe turned his horse about, and with his love cradled in his arms, rode out into the sunlit morning and set his horse towards Ravenswood.

He wouldn't enlighten her to the fact it was William who'd been the heroic one. At least – not yet. He wanted to bask in her admiration for just a little while longer.

They parted at the crossroads. Thomas, Earl of Winterbourne clasped his youngest son's hand and wished him well.

'You're sure you wish to stay in London with your mother, Frey?'

'Aye, sir. She intends to buy herself a pie shop. If I'm not there to keep the books she won't be able to manage it. I can pick up plenty of work in my profession.' The glance he gave James held gratitude. 'James has offered to recommend me to a few clients.'

James's farewell was shorter, but sincere. Frey appreciated the fact that the heir had believed in him, and knew his respect for him would last, always.

Frey glanced at William, who caught and held his gaze. The animosity was still there, flickering in the dark eyes. William had been responsible for saving his life, so he felt obliged to say stiffly, 'It seems I'm in your debt, William.'

William smiled a little mockingly, then held out his hand. 'I owed you something for the beating I gave you.'

'So you did,' Frey said, and taking William's hand in his, gently squeezed it, enjoying the pain momentarily clouding his eyes.

William's eyes narrowed when the squeeze became a relentless pressure. His shoulder was inflamed where the bullet had passed through it, and Frey knew it. Their eyes locked. He gritted his teeth when pain lanced down his arm, perspiration flooded from every pore in his body. Just when he thought he could bear it no more, Frey gave a wolf-like grin and released him. William's mouth curved in a grudging smile.

'Try that when it's healed and I'll knock your bastard head off!'

Frey returned the smile. 'There's nothing to stop you trying, but don't count on beating me a second time.' He drew a small, wooden carving of a bird from his pocket and handed it to James. Its wings were slightly lifted, as though poised to fly. 'Give this to Angelina, with my love. I carved it for her whilst I was imprisoned.'

There was something symbolic about the bird, and James knew she would appreciate the sentiment Frey had been expressing.

The three men came into the grounds of Wrey House at sunset.

James and Thomas supported William between them. Slumped in the saddle of a grey mare he'd purchased in London, his face was slicked with perspiration and scored with fatigue and pain.

The Wrey women were waiting for them on the steps. Elizabeth had a loving smile of welcome for Thomas, concern in her eyes for William. Her arms circled the waist of Rosabelle on one side, Angelina on the other. Celine stood a little to one side, her eyes seeking those of James, her fingers threaded through Angelina's.

There's a certain closeness women have when they share secrets, Thomas mused. A nurturing of each other when they were in need of support. They had that air about them now. He turned to James, remarking somewhat wryly, 'Mark my words, James, I think we are to receive some news later on.'

Thomas watched the women flutter about William, making soothing, cooing sounds, like doves. They were too exotic for doves in their fine plumage, yet Thomas felt strangely content that William's wellbeing was in their capable hands.

Thank God the boy would survive to achieve his dream of a new life in America, and although Thomas didn't approve, he wouldn't attempt to stop him.

They turned and gazed towards the village when a muffled explosion was heard.

William's head jerked up, he swore, and muttered something uncomplimentary about Rafe, and ill-gotten gains.

'Someone at the inn told me a French ship had been sighted off the coast,' James remarked. 'The navy must have found them.'

'Must be smugglers,' Thomas said. 'I hope they find the profiteering buggers who help them, and hang them.'

This time William laughed uproariously.

'I think he has a fever,' Elizabeth said, 'We'd best get him up to his chamber and call the doctor.'

The next morning, James and his father watched the Marquis of Gillingborn come towards the house. He cut a stately figure in his fine suit of clothes. Thomas smiled, murmuring, 'Your friend has the look of a suitor about him.'

And Angelina the look of a new bride, James thought, blinking when she hurtled down the steps with unseemly haste and threw herself into Rafe's arms. The smile the two exchanged was too intimate for comfort, and when Rafe casually kissed her upturned mouth, James was hard put not to gasp.

His father's face was set in an implacable mould, and he was very much the Earl of Wrey when he murmured, 'It seems you've been negligent in your guardianship of your sister; I intend to relieve you of it.'

'But, sir—'

'Enough! I have no intention of discussing the matter further.' The earl frowned as he strode towards the door. 'Send Angelina to her mother, and instruct the Marquis of Gillingborn to attend me in my study, at once.'

'As you request, sir.'

'And, James' – Thomas stared at him for a moment, a tiny smile edging across his mouth – 'would the marquis object if I suggested it might be judicious to arrange the wedding sooner, than later?'

2/5/02